LISA SUZANNE

THE BENEFITS OF BAD DECISIONS

Published in the United States of America by Books by LS, LLC.

ISBN: 9781090528247

Cover Designed by Najla Qamber Designs
Photographer: Wander Aguiar
Models: Colton and Elise
Content Editing by It's Your Story Content Editing
Proofreading by Proofreading by Katie

THE BENEFITS OF *BAD* DECISIONS

BOOKS BY LISA SUZANNE

Take My Heart

A Little Like Destiny
Only Ever You
Clean Break

The Power to Break
The Invisible Thread

It Started with a Lie
It Ended with the Truth

Clickbait
Stalemate
Outwait

Conflicted

Not Just Another Romance Novel

Vintage Volume One
Vintage Volume Two

Separation Anxiety
Side Effects
Second Opinion

How He Really Feels
What He Really Feels
Since He Really Feels

DEDICATION

To the boys who I'd want to tour the country with.

CHAPTER 1

ZOEY

I wring my hands nervously in front of me, and then I force myself to stop. I wipe them down the front of my dress that's purposely a little too short as I try in vain to eliminate the clamminess.

You can do this. You got this. Just go do it.

Be daring.

Be expressive.

Be bold.

I take a deep breath as I stare at the nameplate on the heavy wooden door. *Derek Jensen.*

He's a Hollywood heavyweight, the casting director for an entire network, and I'm here for my interview spot for the reality dating show *Single Life*. Twenty women vie for the attention of one hot single guy, and I want to be one of the twenty.

If nothing else, it'll get me a step closer to my real goal: a career on the silver screen. Plenty of successful actors got their start on a reality show. Jennifer Hudson, Emma Stone, Katharine McPhee...shit, even Jon Hamm failed on a dating show.

If they could do it, so can I.

I lift a shaking hand and knock on the door.

"Come in." The voice on the other side is deep and muffled by the weight of the door.

I turn the handle and let myself in. I spot an open chair in front of the executive desk, and I force one foot in front of the other to get to it. I pause in my pursuit and glance at the man behind the desk, and I find myself frozen for one hot beat.

He's a goddamn Greek god sitting there in a suit.

My first thought is that maybe it won't be so bad to do whatever it takes to get what I want.

I wonder what he's packing beneath his professional clothes. A six-pack of abs for sure. More than likely something long and thick beneath his belt. A broad chest that could hold me in the afterglow.

The door swings shut behind me as I study him. His lustrous and shiny dark hair is styled in a textured, slicked to the side way, and his dark eyes hold an edge of mystery as they pin me to my spot. I wonder for just a beat how old he is. Definitely older than forty...maybe older than fifty? It's hard to tell, but age is just an unimportant number. It wouldn't be so bad to do something illicit bent over his desk to get my spot on the show.

That's how Hollywood works, isn't it?

I tip my chin up with confidence. I refuse to be intimidated by a man even if he's a stunningly handsome one like this guy. "I'm Zoey Fuller."

He pushes to his feet and reaches his hand across his desk to shake mine. I place my clammy one in his and find his to be cool. Collected. Much like him.

"Derek Jensen. Have a seat."

I follow his orders, and one side of his mouth tips up in a smile.

He leans back comfortably in his chair while I sit forward with unease.

"Why do you want to appear on *Single Life*?" he asks.

I draw in a deep breath. "I've been looking for love my entire life, Mr. Jensen, and I haven't found it yet. Maybe I'm just looking in the wrong places."

"And this has nothing to do with the doors appearing on a television show might open for you? You're a gorgeous young woman, after all." He glances at the paper in front of him. "A background in dance," he says, and then he pauses as his eyes fall to my chest, my legs, and back up again, searing each part of my body as they trail along. "Lovely blonde hair, a pretty face that would work well on the screen. Big, blue eyes that scream innocence but a dancer's body that says otherwise. How many Instagram followers do you have? I can't tell you how many ladies who think they're Instagram famous come through my door."

A dancer's body that says otherwise. His words echo in my head as I basically ignore the other things he said.

Is he coming onto me, or is this just how these interviews work?

I'm not sure, but he did ask me a question. "This has nothing to do with doors opening, sir. I have connections of my own that I could use if that was my end goal." It's a lie, but I've practiced it so many times it feels like the truth. The lie is that this has nothing to do with doors opening. I want to go on television because I want to be discovered. And while my brother certainly has connections, I want to do this for myself.

He raises a brow and glances down at some papers on his desk. "I see that here." He nods. "Ethan Fuller, the drummer of Vail, is your brother?"

I was hoping to get through this interview without that coming up. I nod and lean forward a bit. I know exactly what I'm doing, and I watch as his eyes flick down to the cleavage spilling out the top of my dress before they trail back to mine.

"Hmm..." he muses. "How long have you been dancing?"

"My whole life. I started ballet before pre-school." I don't mention that it was also before my father was hauled off to prison. I leave out the fact that I missed a lot of lessons growing up because my mother was too busy with her man of the week to drive me to them. My aunt often helped out, and even today she's the mother I never had to my half-sisters. I was always quick to pick up what I missed, though. But dance isn't what I want out of life, either. "I danced all through high school, too. I taught a few private lessons during college to earn extra cash."

His eyes fall to my body again, and I feel their blazing heat everywhere they land. "Interesting indeed."

I take that as my cue. I've never been to one of these casting interviews before, but I'm sharp enough to understand why his door has no window on it. I stand and press my palms on his desk as I lean forward, allowing more cleavage to spill out. "I don't want to talk about my brother, Mr. Jensen."

He raises a brow at me. "What, exactly, do you want to talk about, Ms. Fuller?"

I look him square in the eye and use my most sensual voice to answer. "I'll do anything to get on the show, sir."

"Are you offering what I think you're offering?" His hands rest comfortably on the desk in front of him, and I spot an empty third finger on his left hand. My eyes fall to his lips. They're not too full, not too thin. They're firm, and they make me think he must be a really good kisser. I want to find out.

"I'm offering whatever it takes to get on the show."

His eyes dip to my cleavage again, and I can't help but think how *easy* men are to read. "I know what I want," he says. He flicks his head to indicate I should come behind his desk.

I step over to him, and he swivels in his chair to face me. He stands and kicks the chair out behind him with practiced ease. Clearly this isn't the first time he's allowed someone auditioning into the space behind his desk.

I gaze up from lowered lashes into those dark, mysterious eyes. I think for the briefest second that I'd like something more than a quick romp over a desk with this man. He's powerful. He's handsome. He's smart. He must be loaded.

That's all I'm looking for.

What I'm not looking for, however, is someone who would allow a girl like me to seduce him just for a spot on a television show.

So I'll do what needs to be done, and then I'll forget all about this Derek Jensen guy.

He sweeps my hair to the side before he runs a long fingertip along the curve of my neck. I whimper and allow myself to get lost in what's about to go down in this office. People on the other side are doing their jobs, earning a paycheck as they hustle and bustle around, with no idea of what's about to happen in here.

Or maybe they do know. Maybe this is something Derek does all the time.

But I'm in here now, and he's never done this with *me* before.

Not that I'll be the one to change him, to get him to stop his wild ways and commit to me. Not that I even *want* that. But for a split second, I get lost in the fantasy anyway.

He turns me quickly around so his front is to my back, and his lips replace his finger on my neck. I groan with lust at the feel of those lips on my body, and then he bends me over his desk so fast I don't even see it coming. I grunt as the edge of the desk knocks the wind out of me a little, but he doesn't stop, doesn't slow down. He runs those same fingertips along my spine, and then he reaches beneath my dress, not wasting a single moment. He probably doesn't have time to waste. Our interview was scheduled for fifteen minutes, and we already wasted the first five talking.

He pulls my panties to the side, not bothering with things like removing our clothes, and sinks a long finger into me. My eyes roll back and my abdomen presses harder into the desk as I fight the urge to come all over his hand. There's something so illicit, so hot, so *wrong* about what we're doing right now. I love it. I want it. I *crave* it.

"Shit, that's wet," he murmurs with appreciation.

I hear the zip of his pants followed by the tear of a wrapper, and seconds later he plunges into me. He's thick, so he slides in slowly to allow my body to adapt to his size. He pulls nearly all the way out before he thrusts back in, and once he's coated with my wetness, he drives in harder and harder. Each thrust forces a grunt out of me, and each time he rears back and pushes forward again, I find myself closer and closer to ecstasy.

It's only a few more thrusts before I lose control. I spiral down into the blackness of bliss, the pleasure spotting my vision as my hands clamp down on the edge of the desk to brace myself against the onslaught of an orgasm. My body pulses and I cry out with it, the soundtrack in this office our voices mingling in an orchestra of satisfaction. He grunts out his release after my body relaxes into his desk, and he pulls out nearly immediately after he finishes. He disappears into a private restroom connected to his office, and I smooth my dress back into place. I'm sitting back in the chair facing his desk when he returns.

He clears his throat. "My secretary will be in touch with whether you've earned your spot on the show early next week." His face gives nothing away, yet I can't believe what we just did didn't earn me a spot.

I grin. "Thank you, Mr. Jensen."

He doesn't smile back like I expect him to—like most men would after what we just did. "You can see yourself out, Ms. Fuller."

I nod and stand. I'm sort of at a loss for words. It's not like I expect that we'll do this again, but I did kind of expect to know by the time I left today whether I'd be one of the twenty women appearing on *Single Life*.

I don't say anything, though. I allow his words to be the last ones spoken in the office as I walk out the door with my head held high.

I did what I had to do, and it's not like I didn't *enjoy* doing it.

I completely ignore the dirty feeling that washes over me as I walk out of the building and toward my rental car.

CHAPTER 2

ZOEY

I reposition the bottles of lotion and open the blinds a little wider to give me some natural sunlight before I snap a few more photos. My job as the social media specialist for a small line of beauty products headquartered in Atlanta is both fun and occasionally exciting. My boss, Indigo, can be a little crazy sometimes, but that's what makes it fun. She finds her assistant, Ruthie, to be completely useless, and she's always complaining to me about her. Ruthie complains to me, too. I'm basically the girl on the computer in a small office posting content to Indigo Beauty's social media sites while I lend an ear to whoever might need it in the office.

That isn't what makes my job occasionally exciting, though. Sometimes Indigo runs beauty launch parties. She went to some school in Los Angeles that all the celebrities' kids went to, so some of her best friends are the people we see on television every day. Since my ultimate dream job is to end up in the movies, I never miss my chance to network.

Tomorrow night is one of those parties right here in the store.

"Not like that, Ruthie! God!" Indigo is on a tear today, and poor Ruthie has already cleaned every nook and cranny of the front room where the party will be held.

Indigo Beauty is a boutique, but the majority of Indigo's sales take place online. The shop is more for show plus a place to hold parties. It's decorated in pristine white and flashy golds with a peppering of peach accents. White leather couches with fuzzy peach and gold sequined pillows. A white coffee table with gilded accents. Tall champagne flutes filled with golden liquid tomorrow night will only complement the décor. It's bright and gorgeous out there, and a wall separates the boutique from the back offices where we work.

I've worked here for almost four years. Indigo was a colleague at a different company, and when she decided to start her own brand, I moved over with her. My salary is fine—nothing spectacular—but I never want for anything thanks to the bank account my brother funds for me. We only had each other growing up, so we're very close, and he's always taken good care of me. Now that he's married with a kid, it seems like family has become even more important to him. Ethan and I talk at least three times a week, and I Facetime with my sister-in-law and nephew often.

"Zoey!" Indigo's indignant voice interrupts my process of getting her newest line up on Instagram. Usually she keeps her crazy focused on Ruthie, but occasionally I'm the recipient. I've known her long enough to know it's not personal, though.

I glance up from my screen as I wait for the images from the camera to pop up in my phone's library. "Yes, Indie?" I say sweetly, using the nickname that she once told me makes her feel like a precious little girl. Despite my tone, inside I'm thinking I just want her to go away so I can focus on getting my job done and I can go home. My roommates and I have big plans tonight. It is, after all, Margarita Monday at our favorite bar.

"Ruthie can't do anything right, as usual. Can you show her how to line up the product on the shelves? You have an eye for it that clearly she does not possess."

"Of course," I say, silently gritting my teeth as she looks away. I set my phone on the desk to let the images finish loading, and I head out to the front room where I find Ruthie fighting back tears. "What's going on?" I ask.

She shrugs without answering, and I know if she speaks, she'll start to sob.

"Don't answer," I say. I take a vase out of her hands and set it on the table. I move a few products around—they were *almost* right, and they would've been fine if Indigo would've just given Ruthie a little more time. "Like this, Ruth," I say softly, and I glance over at her. She nods and stacks the next row perfectly. "Good," I say.

"Thanks," she whispers, swiping at her cheek.

"Don't let Indie get to you," I whisper. "She's just stressed about the party."

Ruthie nods. "I know. Thanks, Zoey."

I smile at her. "Any time. Kristen, Sawyer, and I are heading to Zombie's for margaritas if you wanna come." She nods, and I raise my voice a little. "Now get it right so I can do my job."

She giggles. It's sort of our thing. I go in, make her feel better, and yell at her a little at the end so Indie thinks I'm being a hard ass.

And then we go get margaritas.

When I get back to the office, my phone is ringing. I rush to grab it before it stops. I don't recognize the number on the screen, but the call is coming from Los Angeles.

"Hello?" I answer breathlessly.

"I'm calling for Zoey Fuller," the voice says.

It's male.

And familiar.

I distinctly recall being underneath that grunting voice less than a week ago.

My voice shakes when I speak. "This is Zoey," I say.

"Derek Jensen from Three M Entertainment."

I know, I almost say. I don't. I don't speak at all, actually, because my tongue is completely tied. Don't they usually come tell you in person if you got a spot? This must be the call to let me know I didn't make it on, though it's strange Derek Jensen would be calling me *himself* to tell me that.

"I'm calling today to let you know you've earned a spot on *Single Life*."

"Oh my God," I whisper.

I did it.

I actually did it.

"Production begins Monday, but we'll need you in Los Angeles no later than tomorrow night. An email will be sent to you from the production staff this afternoon with everything you need to know. This is where our contact ends, Miss Fuller. It was a pleasure meeting you."

My mind is totally blank. "Uh," I say stupidly. I don't even form a word. It's a sound. Not even a good one.

"Do you have any questions?"

I have about a million and one questions, but I shake my head before I realize he can't see me. I clear my throat and heave in a quick breath. "No, sir."

"Good luck to you." He ends the call, and that's it.

But I made it. I made the show, and this is going to be my big break. I can *feel* it.

Before I can even really process that, I'm on my feet. I grab my purse, toss my three personal items scattered on my desk into it, and glance around my little office.

Screw Indigo's photos and new product line. I love her, but I'm done here. I've got bigger things to move onto.

"Indie?" I yell from the back office as I sling my purse over my shoulder. My hands are shaking, and I still haven't really processed what's happening. "Indie!"

I find her standing in the front room, fingertip on her chin and brows furrowed as she observes the way Ruthie is arranging products.

"Indigo!" I yell at her to get her attention.

She looks up at me. "I'm right here, Zoey. There's no need to scream at me."

I clear my throat. "I, uh...I quit."

"You *what?*" she and Ruthie say at the same time.

"I quit. I just got a call and I need to be in Los Angeles tomorrow night for a television show."

"You're quitting and leaving me the day before a *launch party?*"

She didn't even ask me about the show. I never told her I was auditioning, but the selfishness of her answer just confirms I'm doing the right thing. I'm doing something for myself for once.

I nod. "Yep. That about sums it up. Love you girls." I wiggle my fingers on my way out the door in a breezy goodbye that's actually anything but breezy. I know Indigo, and I know she won't take me back after that stunt.

But I don't need her to.

I'm going to be a star.

CHAPTER 3

ZOEY

"Ladies, this is the final flower tonight."

I hold my breath at the host's words. There are two Zoeys here—me, otherwise known as Zoey F, and the other one, Zoey B.

There are four of us left without flowers, and I can't go home tonight. The last one *has* to come to me. How fucking embarrassing will it be if it doesn't? I have a famous brother, after all. I didn't mention it too much tonight—at least I don't think I did; all the tequila I had is making it a little hard to remember—but certainly it would've come up at some point anyway. So it's not like I'm here to get famous or something. I could do that on my own with Ethan's help.

I'm here for *love*. Isn't that why we're all here?

Jordan, the single guy and star of the show, is hot. He's a former pro football player and totally my type with big muscles and these arms that look like they'd hold and protect me. His dark eyes smolder when he looks at me and he has this scruff that isn't thick or bushy but gives him this mysterious edge. I just want to run my fingers through it.

But if he doesn't say "Zoey F" right now, I might not get that chance.

He will. I'm confident in that. I'm honestly shocked he didn't pick me a little sooner. I looked around at my competition, and I'm definitely in the top five hottest girls here. Definitely.

Jordan draws in a deep breath. He looks up at all the girls gathered, and it seems like he's only making eye contact with the ones who he's already given roses to. I'm sure the producers make him do that so he doesn't give anything away.

He finally opens his mouth, and as I hear him start my name, I smile widely. "Zoey..." I set my hand on the shoulder of the girl standing in front of me so I can move her aside to go collect my flower. "B," he finishes, and my heart drops.

Zoey B? He gave the final rose to Zoey-fucking-B?

I move my hand from the shoulder of what's-her-name and stand stock still, completely shocked.

He booted me.

On the first goddamn night.

The host reappears. "I'm sorry. If you didn't receive a flower, it's time for you to go."

Jenny's eyes meet mine, and she presses her lips together in one of those non-smiles. She got the boot, too, so she understands how I feel. I don't want to press my lips together in a fake smile, though. I want to yell. I want to kick and scream. I want to punch Jordan in his stupid perfect scruff.

I don't do any of that, though.

I wasn't here long enough to forge any relationships with the other women, and so I stalk out of the room without so much as a goodbye to anyone—including Jordan. That motherfucker.

One of the producers stops me just before I get to the limo waiting at the end of the driveway. "We need a quick exit interview."

I roll my eyes and fold my arms over my chest. "Fine." I follow the producer over toward a set of bright lights. The sun is just starting to peek out on the horizon. I'm tired after being kept awake all night, I'm honestly still a little drunk, and I just want to go home.

"Why do you think he didn't pick you?" a different producer asks.

"He saw something else in the other women, I guess," I say.

"How does that make you feel?"

I shrug. "If you think I'm going to cry because I'll never find a man to love me, you've got the wrong girl."

"Didn't you want to end up with him?" The voice oozes sympathy, and it's clear they're trying to draw out my emotions.

"I didn't even know him," I say. "Am I disappointed I got kicked off on the first night? Sure. Does it suck that I shelled out ten grand on a wardrobe I won't even get to wear on national television? Definitely. But will I pick myself up and dust myself off after this? Abso-fucking-lutely."

The producer sighs. "Fine. You're free to go."

Some guy opens a door to one of the limos, and I get in. My suitcase is already sitting on the seat along with my personal effects—my purse and my phone. They took our phones and said we weren't allowed to use them for the duration of our stay in the house. I wasn't even gone long enough for the battery to run out. I'm about to call my best friend, Kristen, when I remember I signed a hush agreement. I can't talk about it in public, but that won't stop me from sharing the news with my best friend in the world. We drive two blocks and the limo driver stops and pulls up to a curb. I figure he's picking someone else up or something, so I'm surprised when he opens the back door.

"This is it," he says.

I glance around. We're just at the entrance to the neighborhood where the filming house is located. "Excuse me?"

"This is your stop," he clarifies...but it doesn't actually clarify anything.

"There's nothing here."

"You have a phone," he counters, and I take a good look at his face. It's clear that he's been hired to do a job, and he's not gonna crack on this one. "Call for a ride."

"But you have a car that all my shit's in."

"Take your *shit*, then, and call for your own ride. The cameras only follow us to the front of this neighborhood."

The cameras. Of course. Once the cameras are off, no one cares anymore.

I heave my heavy suitcase out of the car, sling my purse over my shoulder, and stand on the sidewalk wondering what the fuck just happened.

CHAPTER 4

ZOEY

When I walk into my home less than a week after I left it, the first thing I do is collapse on the couch.

"She's home," Sawyer yells.

My two roommates and best friends rush to my side. Kristen kneels in front of me while Sawyer lifts my legs and pulls them onto his lap.

"They just ditched you?" Kristen asks, recapping the text I sent her last night when I was stranded in the middle of California before I called an Uber to get me to the airport.

I thought about calling my brother, but there were two reasons why I didn't. For one, I was mortified. For another, he's out of town for some private performance in New York with his band.

I nod. "It was awful. I need at least a week to recover."

"They can't just do that," Sawyer says defensively. He's falling right for my woe-is-me innocent act. He always has.

My blue eyes meet his brown ones. A lock of hair falls over his forehead, and he runs his hand through his hair to slick it back. We dated briefly—very briefly—and while everything was good (and by everything, I mean the sex), we both realized we just worked better as friends. Sometimes I miss him in my bed, though. And sometimes we fall into bed together just for old time's sake.

"It's just wrong," Kristen agrees, and I shake the thoughts of a naked Sawyer ready to comfort me right out of my head.

Sure he's hot, but he constantly has women coming and going from his bedroom.

It's part of why I went on that reality show to find love.

But there was another reason I went.

I have a famous brother, but just because he's famous doesn't mean I'm okay with using his powerful connections to find my way in the world. I want to do it on my own, and while my job with Indigo Beauty was good and fine, it wasn't what I really wanted out of life.

I want my big break opposite Zac Efron.

I know it's just a dream, yet a small corner of my heart believes it can really happen. My brother came from nothing and has gone on to have astronomical success as the drummer for the chart-topping, world-renowned band Vail. If he could do it, I can, too.

I took the first step. I quit my job, stepped out of my comfort zone, left my two best friends, and flew to Hollywood for a chance at love on a television show. I'll debut on the small screen in a month—once the show's editors have enough time to get to know the women and can put a stereotype to each one. I wonder how I'll be portrayed, but it doesn't matter. The fact is that *I made it on television.* I have my shot at getting discovered now, and I didn't even have to use my brother's name to get me there.

So what if I slept with some producer to get there? It was still by my own merit, and I don't have any regrets. In fact, I'd do it all over again if I had to.

Except maybe I wouldn't have spent the *entire* ten grand Ethan gave me on clothes. Maybe it would've been smart to put some of that money to the side as a just-in-case scenario. But I've never lived by the just-in-case scenarios, so why start now?

I've always been more of a live in the moment, make impulsive decisions, and deal with the consequences later type of person.

"What did you wear on the first night?" Kristen asks. "Please tell me it wasn't the red dress." She pushes her palms together in prayer, and I giggle.

"It wasn't the red dress, but what do you have against it?"

She shakes her head. "Too flashy for the first night."

I narrow my eyes. "I went with the gold sequin one instead."

"Much more sedate," Sawyer nods, and Kristen and I both giggle.

At least I can laugh about it.

"So what's next?" Sawyer asks.

I lift a shoulder. "I don't know. I was only gone a week. Maybe Indie will take me back?"

"Is that what you *want*, though?" Kristen asks.

I lift a shoulder. "I never *really* get what I want, do I?" I think first, of course, of Mark Ashton, my brother's best friend and the lead singer of their band. I wanted him since I was fifteen, and while I had him—more than once—I never landed him the way I *really* wanted to. No, that honor went to someone else, someone he married then impregnated...twice.

I can wish and hope all I want, but in the end, they're just wishes and hopes. He didn't choose me, and this is me moving on with my life. That has taken on many shapes over the years, but getting myself on a television show was a new low...or, at least the way I got on it was.

"It doesn't matter what I want," I finally say on a heavy sigh. "I've dried up my brother's well of cash for the moment. I can't ask for another loan a week after I just milked ten grand out of him."

"Can you return any of the clothes?" Sawyer asks.

Kristen and I just look at him, both of us with our mouths hanging slightly open. "You're kidding, right?" Kristen asks. "Did you even *see* the gorgeous fabrics and rich colors she brought home? I forbid returning any of it. Out of the question." I giggle, but I'm happy knowing I have someone on my side who just gets me. "Call Indie and see if she'll take you back."

"She won't," I say, but I pick up my phone anyway. "But I'll give it a shot."

I push her number and the phone starts ringing. It rings six times and I'm about to give up when her familiar and breathless voice answers. "It's the big Hollywood starlet who left me in the lurch."

She sounds angry.

This isn't going to go well.

"I'm so sorry for what I did to you, Indie." I use the nickname to soften her up a little. "Please take me back. I'm begging."

"Beg and plead all you want, sister, but you left me the night before a launch party. Ruthie has proven her worth since you've been gone and I don't need you anymore."

Ruthie has proven her worth? What the hell does that even mean? It would've taken a small miracle for Indie to have said that to me before I left. "I'll do whatever you need me to do. Bring you coffee, paint your toenails..." I trail off, looking wildly at my roommates for more examples. They're staring at me with wide eyes and closed mouths. "Donuts!" I exclaim. "I'll bring you fresh donuts every morning."

"No, Zoey. I love you and treasure your friendship, but our professional relationship has to be over. I can't take someone back I can't depend on, and you leaving the way you did, when you did...it all just adds up to someone I can't trust."

I sigh. "I understand. I'm sorry, Indie."

"Call Ruthie and get on my calendar for tea next week, yes?" Her voice is a few octaves brighter than necessary.

"Sure," I mumble, but we both know I ain't calling to set up tea.

CHAPTER 5

ZOEY

A little over four weeks later, Kristen sits with a tub of popcorn on my left, Sawyer sits with an open bottle of Fireball ready to pour at my right, and I sit in the middle. I'm wearing the flashy red dress Kristen forbade me from returning, and I'm already tipsy enough to consider screwing around with Sawyer when the night comes to an end.

A large group of friends has gathered here tonight for the viewing party. Even though I was kicked off on the first night, a fact that most of the people in this room don't know yet because of the hush agreement I signed, I still can't wait to see myself on screen. It'll be my first insight into how I look on camera, and I'm hoping I'll find some footage to use for future audition tapes.

The show begins with a spotlight on the star of the show, retired football star with scruff of a god Jordan. We see footage of him in his uniform running into the endzone on a scoring drive, of him tousling a golden retriever's fur, of him bringing his mom a bouquet of flowers. They're certainly painting him as the all-American hero, a mama's boy with a soft spot for animals and chiseled facial features.

And then the women are introduced. They're in random order, and just like Jordan was introduced, each woman gets a short intro package. Some have videos showcasing their lives and others don't. After each personal introduction, the first meeting between Jordan and each woman is shown.

I'm trying to remember what that was like, but the whole night is sort of a blur. It all happened so fast.

At least that's what I keep telling myself.

I feel the anticipation building as I wait for my own spot to shine. After the third commercial break, it's my turn.

I come up somewhere in the middle, after seven or eight girls have been introduced. "Zoey Fuller, best known for being the sister of multi-platinum band Vail's drummer, hails from Atlanta, Georgia."

Best known for being the sister?

I shake my head and draw in a breath. Kristen squeezes my hand and Sawyer's hand finds a spot on my thigh. My friends apparently are already anticipating what this is going to look like after that first sentence.

Being Ethan's sister isn't what I ever wanted to be *best known* for. That was the whole point of even doing this stupid show—to find something that could just be *mine.*

The screen lights up with my face. "I'm thirty-three, and I'm in social media marketing." Some of my Instagram posts from Indigo's product line show up on the screen. "I'm passionate about men with a strong ab game, dirty jokes, and tequila." I'm shown holding my margarita glass in the air with a wide smile and semi-glassy eyes. Just as Sawyer's fingers flex on my thigh, a memory from that night slips through.

Shit.

I don't think it was the fact that it all happened so fast that made the night such a blur to my memories. It *might* have been the margaritas.

I sip my Fireball as I try to calm the emotions warring inside me. Half of me is still hung up on the "best known for being Ethan's sister" comment, while the other half of me sort of wants to skip out on watching the show and just take Sawyer upstairs to help me forget I was ever even on it.

I can't, though.

I have to watch the train wreck unfold.

The rest of the girls are introduced and Sawyer tips more liquid into my cup. The more I sip, the more I want him and the less I care about how I'm about to be portrayed.

The first night was all about Jordan getting to know the women, and the next time I'm on the screen is when he sits down with me on a couch out on the patio near the pool. "So, Zoey F.," he starts as we all watch the screen. A few people cheer when they see me appear again, but my eyes are laser focused ahead of me. "Tell me all about you."

"I love camels," I blurt. I watch myself take a bolstering sip of margarita, but clearly it isn't my first. My eyes seem a little glassier than before.

"Camels?"

I nod. "Yep, camels. When I was a teenager, someone told me dreaming about camels symbolizes the hard work it takes to reach your goals. I've loved the animal ever since."

A beat of awkward silence follows, so I fill it with, "Wanna hear a camel joke?"

I watch in complete mortification as I know exactly what's coming next. Jordan's brows furrow and he looks like he's about to say no when I launch into the joke. "What did the camel say when the elephant asked why he had boobs on his back?"

He closes his eyes and shakes his head. "I don't know. What?"

"At least I don't have a d—k on my face."

Laughter explodes around me in the room. The word the show's editors cut out is still clear enough to understand that I just told a dick joke to the star of the show.

To be fair, it's a pretty funny joke...just not for the night you're trying to make a good impression not only on the hot guy starring in the show but also on the general viewing audience—and the potential producers and casting directors watching from other areas of the entertainment world.

Jordan laughs uncomfortably on the television screen, and I can't watch anymore. I hold my hand over my eyes in embarrassment as Sawyer's fingers inch further up my thigh, comforting me the way he knows how, and Kristen squeezes my hand again, trying to give me some silent support in the way she knows how.

None of it makes me feel any better, though.

That's about it for my big television debut. The elimination ceremony comes not too long after that, and I'm shown with a cocky look on my face as he says my first name. We all watch as my face drops from cocky to angry when he gives someone else's last initial.

I'm angry in my exit interview, and then the show is over.

I made a damn fool of myself on national television. I returned half the clothes I bought on my brother's dime, so at least I have a little money to support myself for now...but I still don't have a job. I don't even have any *prospects* of a job. I was so sure this was going to be my big break. I had some great moments with the other ladies, and the rest of my conversation with Jordan hadn't been as hellishly awkward as telling the dick joke had been. But the producers didn't show that. Instead, they made me look like a drunken idiot who tells dirty jokes.

So much for my big break.

Tomorrow, the job hunt begins again—if I can even find anyone who would want to hire a reality show castoff.

But tonight? Tonight's agenda includes more Fireball and a little tango beneath the sheets with my roommate. It may not be the smartest agenda, but it's certainly the one that'll get me through to tomorrow with a smile on my face.

I don't even wait to clear the place out. I'm drunk enough to send the vibe to Sawyer, and by *vibe* I mean I grab his hand and pull him toward the stairs. He knows what's coming next. This isn't our first friends with benefits roll in the hay.

"No kissing," I remind him once my bedroom door has slammed shut behind us and we face off in front of my bed.

I have a strict no kissing rule when it comes to Sawyer. Kissing tells me everything about a man, and I don't want to know everything about Sawyer. I don't want feelings beyond the physical for him.

We know each other well enough at this point to know that we'd never be able to make things work long-term. He's too much of a dog for someone like me, and besides, I need someone who can hold my hand in support through my poor choices. Someone who can handle my special brand of crazy that spawns from growing up with two absentee parents and a brother who was always getting himself into some kind of trouble or another.

That's not Sawyer.

He's not insensitive, exactly—he's just not sensitive. He's pretty to look at, he has biceps that are porn-worthy, and he's fun to drink with, but even I know that's not enough to sustain something longer than a few fun nights.

He nods, that lock of hair falling over his forehead again. He brushes it away. "No kissing," he agrees, and then he shoots me a sly smile. "Not on the mouth, at least."

I chuckle as I purse my lips and shake my head. He always finds a loophole. "I don't need foreplay tonight. Now take off your clothes," I demand.

"You first," he says, and before he even hits the hard *t* stop on the end of his second word, my dress is fluttering into a pool on the floor beside me. He tears his shirt over his head while I unhook my bra, and he unbuttons his jeans. That's as far as he needs to go, because he turns me around and crudely pushes me so I'm bent over the foot of my bed.

He fumbles around for a few beats, and then his fingers push inside me. I'm ready for him, my body aching as I try to forget this night and focus on the feel of his fingers pulsing in and out of me. I pinch my own nipples, pushing myself closer to the edge of ecstasy, and then his fingers are gone. I slide mine down inside to keep myself warm while he does whatever he has to do, and then a few seconds later he bats my hand out of the way and slides his hot cock inside.

I moan at the familiar feel of him. God, he knows how to move his hips to hit me right where I need it. His jeans are still on, like he only shifted his clothes enough to get his cock out and grab a condom, and the denim is rough against my skin as he slaps into me.

My moans turn into high-pitched grunts as he thrusts roughly into me over and over, gliding faster and faster as I push my hips back to meet his. He picks up speed even more as we both near the finish line, and I pinch my nipples still harder. The pleasure lined with pain always gets me, and just as I squeeze so tightly it hurts, he reaches his fingers around to brush my clit. The full feeling of him inside combined with the tight clamp I have on my tits and the stroke on my bundle of nerves pushes me into an explosion of pleasure. Little black dots line my vision as my body pulses out wave after wave of pure, unadulterated bliss.

He shoves that cock harder and harder into me, and it isn't long before he pulls out, rips off the condom, and spurts right onto my backside.

No one ever said sex with Sawyer was romantic.

But after I clean up and slide into bed by myself, I can't help but think the mess is worth it.

CHAPTER 6

BRODY

"Fuck, dude. Are you serious?" I look at my best friend, my brother from some other mother, the lead singer of my band, as I wait for him to tell me this is some kind of joke. We're sitting in the house the five members of MFB live in, five phones piled high in a stack in the center of the table for our weekly band meeting at the house we all share in San Diego.

This is the first tour my band is headlining as we come off a successful tour opening for the multi-platinum band Vail, and it seems like everything that can go wrong so far has. Our tour kicks off in Los Angeles in ten days, and now we're short one back-up dancer.

Dax shakes his head. "No joke. Beth is *pregnant* and said she can't do the tour."

"Dammit. I knew it was a mistake to add to our set. Fucking Kylie and her goddamn ideas," I say, naming our manager and the woman my best friend and former wingman is currently banging. I know she'll be here any minute, so I take the cheap shot at her while I can.

Dax shoots me a look of warning for talking shit about his woman, but I ignore him.

"So what the hell are we supposed to do?" I ask.

He shrugs. "We don't *need* the dancers."

"Maybe not, but the whole thing is planned out already. It'll look weird with two instead of three based on the choreography. One stage left, one in the middle, and no one on stage right?"

"Look at you using big words like *choreography*." He grins at me, and I roll my eyes and punch him in the arm. "I'll check with Mark and see if he can think of anyone on short notice."

"Speaking of Mark," Kane, our bassist, interjects, "is everything set for *Rock on the Road*?"

He nods. "We have two cameramen who will be on our crew bus for the duration of the tour. We have a few extras scheduled for the bigger venues to get a cleaner backstage look. Most importantly, the five of us will have final approval of every episode before it airs."

"This is so fucking cool," Rascal, who plays keyboards for our band, says.

Dax teamed up with Vail's lead singer, Mark Ashton, to create a new reality show that follows bands from the start of a record through the tour promoting it. *Rock on the Road* will premiere a few weeks after our tour, and MFB will be the featured band the first season. Our album just dropped a couple weeks ago, and so far the response has been more than any of us could've imagined. Our tour is short—only eight weeks—but almost all the dates are sold out, something none of us ever expected.

We're at the precipice of stardom. It's something the five of us dreamed of each in our own ways, but it's something that always seemed just out of reach. It was Kylie who managed to secure our spot as openers for Vail, and despite the shit I give Dax about her, I know how much we're all in her debt for everything she's done for us.

I bounce my knee under the table, a habit I can't seem to break as the beat of some song plays in my head. I've had bouncy knee syndrome since I was a kid. Drumming was always inside me, I guess, but when I'm really thinking hard about something, sometimes my fingers get in on the action, too. I drum a beat on the edge of the table.

"What are you thinking?" Dax asks, his eyes shifting to me as he observes my habit with the judgmental eyes of a best friend.

"I'm thinking you need to get your phone out of that pile and call Ashton to get this dancer thing solved."

Dax heaves out a sigh as he rolls his eyes. "You're just looking for your next babe to bag."

"Maybe we need a No Bang Oath for the dancers," Kane says, and everyone laughs—except me. We instated a No Bang Oath when we hired Kylie, but Dax went and banged her anyway. And fuck that noise—if I want to bang a dancer, I'll bang a dancer.

"Fuck off," I mutter petulantly. Then I lift my palms up in confusion. "Beth's already out if she's knocked up, so at least give me a shot at one of them."

Everyone laughs again, but I'm not actually joking. No one ever takes me seriously.

Dax pulls his phone from the pile and puts it on speaker after dialing Mark's number. "What's the word, Hunter?" he answers after a few rings.

"One of our back-up dancers is a no go," Dax tells him as the rest of us listen in.

"Ten days before launch?" he asks. He lets out a curse.

"You know anyone who'd be able to fill in on short notice?"

Mark laughs. "I know many who would do anything to get up on that stage, but one old friend comes immediately to mind. Hang on." His voice muffles a little as he moves the phone away from his mouth, but we can all hear his conversation. "Ethan!"

He's yelling to the drummer of his band, and we hear a muffled, "What?" back.

"You think your sister is looking for something to do after that epic mess she made last night?"

We all hear a laugh, and then we hear Ethan's voice as he obviously moves a little closer to Mark for their conversation. "For what?"

"MFB needs a dancer for their tour."

"She doesn't want to dance professionally. She wants TV time," Ethan mutters.

"Right," Mark says. "And the cameras will be following MFB for *Rock on the Road*."

"Okay, but I'm not involved," he protests.

"We'll do what we can to minimize it, but eventually she's gonna figure out we had a hand in it," Mark points out.

They both mumble a few other things, and then Mark's voice gets louder. "Ethan's sister has a dance background. She's, uh, currently unemployed and might be interested."

"What happened last night?" Dax asks, voicing the question we all have.

"She got the boot on episode one of *Single Life*."

"Is she ugly?" Rascal asks from Dax's right. Dax punches him in the arm and gives him a sharp look that clearly says he needs to shut the hell up.

Mark laughs. "No, she's not. She's beautiful. She can just be a little crude, and I don't think that's what the dude on the show was looking for."

"Crude?" I whisper. Dax's dirty look darts to me, but fuck—she sounds like the perfect addition to our tour. Crude and hot? Yes please.

"Well, if it means anything, she did grow up with Ethan as her big brother," Mark says. "She can hang with the guys and dance with the girls. She's familiar with life on the road and might be the perfect fit if she agrees to it. "

"So how do we get her to agree?" Dax asks.

"I'll have someone get in touch with her so it comes from a talent agent and not from the Vail guys. She's always been adamant about making it on her own, but a little push to help out never hurt anyone, right?"

"Right," Dax says. "Thanks, Mark. You're a lifesaver."

"Just another day as a rock star."

We all laugh as Dax cuts the call, but he isn't wrong.

CHAPTER 7

ZOEY

"What the hell?" I mutter as I rub the sleep from my eyes and try to focus on the email I'm attempting to read on my phone.

Zoey,

I'm Wesley Bruno, a talent agent with DVT Productions. I saw you on the premiere of Single Life *last night and would like to discuss a dancing opportunity with you. I was given this email address after asking producers of* Single Life *where to direct business inquiries. If you're interested, please reply to this email or call me at the number listed below my name. I look forward to hearing from you.*

Best,

Wesley

I read it over again. Surely I'm just confused. The Fireball hangover is muddying my brain. This can't be legit. A random email from some supposed talent agent? Yeah, right.

Yet something pokes at my thoughts.

What if it *is* legitimate? What if he can put me on television? What if this is just my life working out the way it always seems to for me despite the poor life choices I make?

I pop his name into the search engine on my phone and his LinkedIn profile immediately pops up. He's been a television talent agent for twenty years with the same company. I search the company next, and sure enough, that's legitimate, too.

But why would they want me? They didn't even see me dance, yet this guy is hitting me up for a dancing opportunity? I don't *want* to dance—at least not for a long-term career. There isn't much longevity in dancing, and I'm already in my thirties. What I really want to do is *act.*

But sometimes we do the things we *have* to do so we can do the things we *want* to do.

Maybe this is one of those things I have to do to get to where I want to be. I'm not sure, but a Hollywood talent agent contacted me the morning after I made a fool of myself on national television. That has to mean something, doesn't it?

I think I may need an energy drink before I can really process what that email said, so I force myself out of bed and down to the kitchen. The house is kind of a mess. Plastic cups litter the tables, and it's clear a party happened here last night but life kept all of us from actually cleaning up after the guests went home.

Kristen and Sawyer are both at work, and as I reach into the fridge for my drink, I can't help but recall what Sawyer and I did last night. It was a really good time, but I feel a little cheap this morning. He's always just such an easy person to turn to whenever I need to forget, but it doesn't change the fact that what's between us will never be more than a roll between the sheets.

I take a few sips and feel the sugar and caffeine start to wake me up. I pick up the kitchen and the family room, and then I read Wesley's email again.

I glance around the house where I live. Atlanta isn't where I ever really wanted to be. I grew up in Chicago and came here for college. Kristen was my roommate in college, and we just kept living together after we graduated. I've lived with her for nearly fifteen years now, and it'll be hard to leave her.

Yet I can't help but think about how if I want something to change, I have to make it change. This opportunity from Wesley might be my ticket in.

Maybe it's another bad decision, or maybe it's the first *good* decision I've made in a long time.

Only time will tell.

So, with a racing heart and shaking fingers that both come from either the energy drink or the thought of what I'm actually doing, I email Wesley back.

Wesley,
I'm interested in hearing more. My contact information is below.
Thanks,
Zoey Fuller

I list my phone number below my name before I hit send, and my phone rings less than a minute later.

I recognize the area code—213, the same as my brother's, which tells me the call is coming from the Los Angeles area.

I accept the call and answer with a shaky voice. "Hello?"

"I'm calling for Zoey Fuller."

"This is Zoey."

"Zoey, hi. Wesley Bruno from DVT Productions."

I clear my throat, but my mouth is suddenly too dry to swallow. "Hi Mr. Bruno."

"Call me Wes. My agency saw you on *Single Life* last night and several of us agree you have the perfect look for what we need. If you're serious about dance and you can prove you're a real dancer, I have a potential opportunity for you."

I'm not serious about dance, not anymore—but I don't let that slip. Instead, I grab onto this chance with everything I have. I have nothing left to lose except maybe this break if I don't take it. "I'm serious," I say softly.

"We have a band who had a back-up dancer back out of a gig last minute. It's an eight-week headlining tour with thirty performance dates. They launch in ten days. I have two questions. Are you available for those dates and can you audition tomorrow afternoon?"

My brain goes blank. I try to think if I have anything going on tomorrow, and I realize with some combination of sadness and regret that I don't have anything going on at all for the next...ever. "Yes, I'm available," I manage to say. *Why me?* That little nugget nudges at my brain, but I refuse to let insecurities lose me this shot. He saw something in me and is giving me a chance that millions of women would take in a heartbeat. I'm not about to let that go, because even though I don't want dance to define my future, this is only two months. I have no idea how big this band is, but I do know that it could open the same doors I thought were shut forever after I told a dick joke on national television.

"Great. I will have my secretary send a follow-up email with the details for the audition. You're based in Atlanta?"

"Y-yes," I stutter. I draw in a breath to try to gain control of myself again.

"We have a local agent so you won't need to fly to LA unless you're chosen. Are you also available today?"

"Yes. I can make it today." I'm proud of myself for forming a complete sentence.

"I'll mark that in my notes. Look for an email from Bailey Crane, my secretary, with all the details. She'll text you the audition information as well."

"Bailey Crane. Got it." I fidget then add, "Thank you for this opportunity, Wes."

"Nothing is final until the audition, but we all liked what we saw in you."

"I appreciate that."

He ends the call, and I stare at my phone for a few beats. *Nothing is final until the audition.* Way to scare the crap out of me.

I take a shower then spend some time at the ballet barre I had installed in my bedroom when I moved in. It sits in front of a mirror and I use it all the time as I dance in my bedroom...and I don't always just use it for dancing. Today, though, I'm watching as I practice the smooth ballet routine I've used for auditions in the past. Wes didn't give me too much to go on, but I assume the email I get from the secretary will tell me more.

I'm wrong.

When the email comes through with the subsequent text message telling me that my audition is in four hours in downtown Atlanta, I skim it to find out what type of dancing they're expecting. When I don't find anything, I stand in front of the mirror and practice the hip hop dance I've used in other auditions just in case. Surely they won't be expecting a ballet routine for a band needing back-up dancers.

And then I'm pulling on a leotard and leggings, smoothing my hair back into a neat ponytail, and punching the address of the studio into my GPS.

Be daring.

Be expressive.

Be bold.

I repeat my mantra in my head on my way toward the studio, and by the time I've arrived, I'm brimming with confidence.

I give my name to the receptionist in front, and she dials into someone and announces my arrival. "Take a seat," the receptionist says, nodding toward the four rows of hard, plastic chairs.

The room is about half-full with people waiting, and I wonder how many are here to audition for the same role I am.

I wonder how many are here in support of other people auditioning for other roles. I wonder if anyone famous has walked these hallowed halls.

I think for a second how weird it is that I'm here and no one even knows. Not Kristen or Sawyer. They're both still at work. Not Ethan, the guy I tell everything to.

This is just for me. If it's an epic failure like last night was, no one ever has to know about it but me.

I spot two women who look like they could be dancers, but there's no way of knowing. I sit in an empty seat two away from one of them, and just when I'm about to strike up conversation to ask if she's here for the same gig I am, a woman with auburn hair pulled into a tight bun appears from around the corner. "Zoey Fuller?"

I stand, and I feel eyes around the room fall onto me. Jealousy, maybe, that I'm being taken right back while others have been waiting longer than me.

It's not the first time people have eyed me with jealousy. I felt it when I dated my brother's best friend, Mark Ashton, on and off for a couple years. We were never serious—we never had the chance to be. He was too busy building a successful band to commit to something serious with me...or, that's what I tell myself. He made the time when the right woman came along for him.

"Right this way," the woman says, and I follow her. We stop outside a room, and when she opens the door, I find a small area set up for dancing. One wall is mirrored, another has a ballet barre similar to the one in my bedroom, and chairs and a table sit on the opposite wall. She takes a seat there, where a man also sits, and nods at me to sit in the chair opposite them, so I slide in.

"Welcome, Zoey," the woman says. "I'm Madeline Carver, and this is Andrew Abraham. We have a few interview questions for you first, and then we'll ask you to dance for us. First, tell us a bit about yourself."

"I've always loved dance," I begin. "I started ballet when I was three and took that all the way through middle school. I was on the pom team in high school. I've studied everything from ballet to jazz to modern to hip hop. In my college years, I taught a few dance classes as a way to earn some extra money. I majored in business and thought about opening my own studio, but ultimately I decided I didn't want the pressure of running my own business. A friend started a beauty line, and I took on a job to help with her social media since my background is in business."

"Are you still working with her?" Andrew asks.

I shake my head. "I was recently on a reality television show which required me to clear my schedule for a month. My boss chose not to hire me back upon my return." It's a diplomatic way of saying I quit.

Madeline and Andrew glance at each other, and I wish I knew what they were thinking.

"What's your end game?" Andrew asks, narrowing his eyes at me.

"I'm sorry," I say. "I don't understand."

"What's your career goal? Is it dance?"

I feel a little flustered, like he can see right through me, but I hold onto my cool. I shake my head. "No, it's not. My end game is acting, and I'm willing to work hard to find my break. I'm hoping that whatever opportunity this is might be it. Can I ask you a question?"

They both nod, but Andrew says, "You can ask, but we may not answer."

"What band is this for?"

"It's confidential," Madeline says. Damn, she was the one who I thought was more on my side.

"And now we'd like to see what you can do," Andrew says. "Part of what you'll do is already choreographed, but a lot of it will be freestyle on the fly. We'll play a mash-up of a few songs of varying speed and range. Do what comes naturally to you as you hear each section. We'll also be video-recording you so we can watch you back later and send your audition to our folks in Los Angeles. Any questions?"

I stand and push my chair in. "What songs will I be dancing to?" I ask.

"Watching you on the fly is part of the audition," Madeline says.

"Okay," I say, and then I take my position at the barre while I wait for the music to begin.

When it does, I recognize the first song as one by David Guetta, and I kill it with a hip hop routine. I smile my way through the entire song, making eye contact with the two people watching me and exuding confidence. I realize midway through the next song, one by Pink, that I've missed dancing. I've missed performing in front of an audience that watches me move my body the way it was meant to be moved. A classic Whitney Houston number comes on last, and as she sings about wanting to dance with somebody who loves her, I lose myself to the song. It's something I want, too. I want to smile through life with a partner who will let go with me.

The music stops, but the dance still moves within me.

Both Madeline and Andrew clap, and that's when I finally slow to a stop. "Don't let us stop you," Madeline says with a laugh.

I grin, my chest heaving with exertion. "I just haven't felt this free in a long time."

"That freedom was really clear in your dance," she says.

I'm about to respond when Andrew cuts in. "That's all we need from you. We'll get your audition tape to Wesley and he'll be in touch with whether you've made the cut."

I nod and tamp down the brimming confidence in order to appear humble. "Thank you for allowing me to audition."

They don't say anything else as I see myself out, and despite their impassive faces, I have a good feeling about this.

CHAPTER 8

ZOEY

I haven't even pulled onto my street yet on my way home from the audition when a text comes through from Wesley. I force myself not to read it until I'm safely parked in the driveway. Kristen is already in the garage and Sawyer's truck is on the street.

Wesley: *They loved you, I watched the tape and I love you, you're in. We need you in Los Angeles to meet the band and practice with the ladies ASAP. When can you be here?*

When can I be there? Shit, I can hop on the next flight!

I push down my excitement for a beat.

I still need to tell Kristen and Sawyer. They'll want one last night with margaritas and memories. It's only for a little over two months, but it could also lead to something permanent.

This is all happening so fast that my head is spinning.

I run a quick search on flights and see that I have plenty of options.

Me: *I'll be there by tomorrow afternoon.*

That gives me a little time to pack, a little breathing room to make arrangements, plus one last night with my friends.

His response is immediate.

Wesley: *Excellent. I'll schedule a dinner meeting for tomorrow night. Bailey will send confirmation details and she'll need your measurements to place an order for your outfits.*

Before I get out of the car, I text my brother.

Me: *Long story but I got a job as a dancer on tour. We leave in ten days from LA. Can I stay with you starting tomorrow?*

Ethan: *Congrats and sure. Fair warning, Eli is teething.*

I honestly don't know what that means, but I don't care. I have a place to stay, I have a job, and I have excitement running through me once again.

When I walk into the kitchen, Sawyer is grabbing a beer from the fridge and Kristen is studying takeout menus like the food might leap off the page if she stares hard enough.

"I have news," I announce. I drop my purse on the kitchen counter dramatically.

Sawyer slams the fridge and cracks the tab of the can, and Kristen looks up at me and squints like she didn't even hear me come in.

"Big news," I say, trying to get some reaction out of them. Anything.

"What is it?" Sawyer finally asks after he guzzles down half the can.

"I got a job." I squeal a little at the end of my sentence.

"That's great, babe," Kristen says. Her eyes return to the menus as Sawyer grunts a little then tips his can back to his lips.

"What the fuck is up with you two?" I finally ask.

They both look at me again.

"Huh?" Kristen asks. Sawyer just stares blankly at me.

"I. Got. A. Job. Did you hear me? Why are you both ignoring me?"

Kristen shakes her head. "Sorry. I'm just really hungry. Borderline hangry."

"Fine. It's the hanger talking. What's his excuse?" I ask, jabbing my thumb in Sawyer's direction.

"Shitty day at work," he grunts.

"Well I had a great day, and I was really excited to celebrate with my two best friends, but you're both knocking the wind out of my sails and making me feel like it's not really such a big deal that I'm going to be moving to Los Angeles."

Both of them stop what they're doing as their heads whip in my direction. "What?" they say in unison.

Sawyer's brows furrow. "You're moving to Los Angeles?"

"For a little while, yes. It all happened so fast. A talent agent contacted me and they had me audition for a back-up dance spot on tour with some band! It's eight weeks and they need me in LA tomorrow to meet the other dancers."

"Oh my God!" Kristen squeals at the same time Sawyer asks, "What band?"

I shrug. "I don't know the details yet. They'll tell me once I get to LA."

"Do you think it's a good idea to accept a position you know nothing about?" he presses, further deflating my sails.

"I think it's better than any prospects I have here," I say, purposely glaring at him as I imply *he* is part of those prospects.

He sighs, and then he walks out of the room with his beer can. Just walks right the fuck out in the middle of our conversation. It's shit like this that clearly defines for me why we're never meant to be anything more than fuck buddies.

"Is this legit?" Kristen asks me once it's just the two of us.

I plop into a chair at the table. "I looked up the talent agent, and yes, it's legit."

She joins me at the table. "What if other opportunities pop up after you were on *Single Life*?"

I shrug. "What if they don't? I don't know, Kristen. I think if I pass this up, I'll regret it."

She reaches across the table and squeezes my hand. "Then trust your gut. It's gotten you this far in life."

I force a smile that doesn't really reach my eyes as her words percolate in my head. *Trust your gut. It's gotten you this far.*

To where, exactly? I'm thirty-three-years-old. I live in a small house with two roommates, one who I occasionally screw, and I don't have a job. I don't have money of my own in the bank. I'm living off someone else's success, and I have been for far too long. *That* is where my gut has gotten me.

"What's wrong?" she asks.

"I don't know if my gut has gotten me anywhere, really. But if I don't take this leap, I'll never know if it could pan out to something bigger and better."

She fingers the takeout menu she's holding but not really reading anymore. "You're right. So congratulations, babe. I'll miss you like crazy, but you're gonna rock the shit out of this thing."

"Thanks, Kris. I might even be back once the tour's over. Who knows?"

She shakes her head a little sadly as her eyes turn glassy. "No, you won't. This is it, Zo. Your big break."

"You think?"

She nods. "I do. I want this for you even though the selfish part of me wants you to stay right here with me. But you need this. You've always needed something bigger than Atlanta, and I want you to chase your dreams and get everything you deserve."

I stand and pull her up with me. I hug my best friend. Life's sure going to be strange without her by my side, but it's time to let go of the past and forge a new road.

"I need to talk to Sawyer, but will you help me pack later?" I ask.

She nods and returns her attention to the takeout menus. "As soon as I eat, I'm yours for the rest of the night."

I giggle, and she sits at the table to order some food while I head into the family room to find Sawyer. He's not there, so I climb the stairs to his bedroom. I knock on the closed door, and when I hear a muffled, "What?" I open the door. He's sprawled on his bed with his beer in one hand and his phone in the other.

"What's up your ass?" I ask.

He heaves out a sigh then sets the phone on his nightstand and sits up a little. "LA, huh?"

I shrug and perch on the edge of his bed. "It's not television, but it's got the potential to get me closer."

"Is that really what you want, Zo?" he asks the question softly.

"It's what I've always wanted."

"It's not just the money. Do you realize the pressure that comes with fame and stardom?" he asks.

I roll my eyes. "You do know I have a famous brother, right? Of course I know what that life's like."

"And that's what you want?" He studies his can of beer rather than meeting my eyes.

"Taking pictures of someone else's beauty products was never my dream job when I was a little girl thinking of her future." I pick absently at his comforter.

When he speaks, his voice is low and filled with vulnerability. "I suppose those dreams always had a Prince Charming, too."

"Of course they did. Riding in on a white horse, obviously."

"Not drinking a can of beer in the next bedroom?" He sighs softly.

My eyes whip up to his at his implication and my brows draw down in confusion. "What?"

He shrugs and continues to avoid eye contact. "I just figured you and me...Never mind."

"No, Sawyer. Not never mind." I reach over and touch his leg to get his attention. "Say it. Say whatever it is, because I'm leaving in the morning and I can't leave with shit between us."

"I thought maybe somewhere down the line we'd end up together."

My eyes nearly pop out of my head when he actually says the words. I'm at a complete loss. I never saw this one coming. "You...you *what*?"

"It's stupid. We just always have such a good time together, and it's always so easy with you."

I nod, not sure how to say this gently. I don't want to hurt him. I love Sawyer, but his vision of what our future together might look like and mine are vastly different. "I think that's what makes us all wrong for each other. Neither of us puts in any effort. What kind of life would that be?"

I think about what a future with Sawyer would hold. Lots of drunken nights together, great sex, and a barrel of laughs. But that would be about it. No deep, meaningful chats so late into the night that we fall asleep mid-sentence because neither of us can keep our eyes open any longer. No feeling like I'm one half of a team and can't function without my other half. No dependence on each other, no searching for the other in a roomful of people, no feeling like I found the other half of my heart.

No emotional connection other than friendship.

"It would be exactly like what we have now, except we'd wake up together instead of going our separate ways after sex." The vulnerability is still in his voice, but my personality just isn't docile enough to handle this one with grace.

So I give it to him straight. "That's not what I want, Sawyer. I love you and I love our friendship, but I don't want a future that's exactly like what we have now. I want excitement and passion. I don't want to slide by because it's easy. I want to face challenges together as a team, to appreciate the good because we overcame the bad."

He nods and reaches across the bed to grab my hand in his larger one. I gaze at our hands where they're connected for a few seconds, those long, strong fingers that know what the hell they're doing as they graze over my most sensitive parts, those hands that would hold mine in support and friendship forever if I'd let them. He's offering *himself* to me in his own roundabout way, and I'm rejecting him. We both know that's what this is.

Our eyes finally meet, and while there's hurt in his, there's also understanding. This isn't a break-up because we were never together. This is simply one friend telling the other that the benefits are over.

"That's what I want for you," he says. "The passion, the excitement, the challenges—and anything else you ask for. You deserve it, Zo."

"I want that for you, too. And I know you'll find it if you just get off your lazy ass and look."

He laughs, and it's a real, genuine sound that I'll hold onto when there's lonely or dark times ahead. We always tease each other, so why should it be any different in the middle of a serious talk about our future apart?

"Love you, Sawyer." I squeeze his hand, and he squeezes mine back.

"I love you, too."

I sigh. "I need to go pack."

"Call me when you get to the panty drawer."

I stand and smack him in the arm, and I leave his room surprised at his revelation but feeling better that we had this chat. I feel like all my loose ends here are tied up and I'm ready to face whatever the future might hold for me.

CHAPTER 9

BRODY

"I fucking knew this would happen." I shake my head with disdain at Dax and Kylie. They're snuggled on the couch watching a movie on a Thursday night. A fucking movie. On a goddamn Thursday night—the first official night of the weekend.

What the fuck happened to my friend?

Love.

That's what the fuck happened.

Before he even snagged a spot on a reality show to find love, we had a talk about this very thing. I knew as soon as he signed up that he was ready to find someone, and even though that someone didn't end up being a contestant on the show, the outcome is the same: he'd rather hold some chick's hand on the couch while they watch a rom com than case the bar for a new piece of ass with his favorite wingman.

Adam and Kane are both in serious relationships, so that leaves Rascal as my bar-casing partner. Man, I need to find some new single friends and *fast.*

The problem, which isn't really a *problem*, is that ever since MFB opened for Vail, we've become sort of *known*. Dax attracts the most attention as our front man, but I don't do too bad for myself. Rascal isn't really the wingman type, though. He's more of a get drunk, puke, and fuck everything up type of bar friend, so he's typically not my first choice when it comes to these things.

But I miss my natural habitat, Emerson's—the bar we played for years and years before we caught our break. I miss hanging with my best friend as we search for hot babes fresh off San Diego State University's campus out for a good time. We're bigger than local celebrities now, which comes with its perks...but now that I'm twenty-seven and have started to see some measure of success, I wonder if bagging an eighteen-year-old who got into a local bar on a fake ID is just a short cry from Creepytown.

"You knew what would happen?" Dax asks from the depths of his cuddle.

"You'd be too goddamn lame to go out with me once you found a woman." I roll my eyes. "Tonight's our last night in San Diego, and I wanted to hit Emerson's one last time before...you know." I trail off as I'm not quite sure how to finish that sentence. It's all so surreal still—we're headlining our own tour.

I still haven't been able to actually say the words for fear that someone will look at me like I'm crazy, that it was all just a dream.

I don't know how we got so goddamn lucky, but we did.

Kylie glances at Dax, who nods. "We'll go out with you," she says.

"Thanks, but I don't need a pity party. I guess I'll see what Rascal's up to."

Kylie laughs. "That's a serious pity party if I've ever heard one." She flips the blanket off to reveal that they're both actually wearing clothes and shoes. "Surprise!" she says as she stands. "Wing-woman for one at your service." She holds up her pointer finger.

I raise a brow. "Wing-*woman*?"

She nods. "Let's do this."

I narrow my eyes at both of them. Dax is just grinning like a lovesick idiot. "You're serious?"

"Brody, think about it. What's better than a girl talking you up?"

"I don't really *need* the help," I say. "I do okay on my own. It's just more fun to go with a buddy."

"Then think about how much *more* fun it'll be to go with two buddies!" She's borderline gleeful and it's sort of grossing me out.

I heave out a breath. I don't really like this idea...but I'm out of options. "Fine," I mutter. "Let's go."

"Hold on!" Kane's voice yells from upstairs.

Kane and Sierra walk down the stairs. "Four buddies," Kane says as he links his fingers through Sierra's.

"Make it five," Rascal yells as he bounds down the stairs behind them.

The front door opens, and Adam stands there with Bree. "Might as well make it seven," Adam says.

I grin at my friends as a chuckle huffs out of my chest. "Is this for real?"

"It's our last fucking night in San Diego, man," Dax says, giving me a bro-slap on the shoulder. "Of course we're all spending it together."

"And Kylie promised she'd find you a girl to fuck," Rascal says.

"I can probably handle that on my own, thanks," I say, narrowing my eyes at Kylie again. She shoots me an innocent look, and I just laugh. "Let's go."

The eight of us walk to Emerson's. When Dax bought the house where we all live, he chose something close to the bar where we played several times a week. It has been our hangout for years, and I'll miss it. I picture a future where we stop by for a random performance. I don't ever want to get so big that

I forget my roots, and we owe a lot to the owner, Emerson Graff.

When we walk in, seven of the eight of us are surprised at what we're met with, while the eighth—Kylie—has a smug grin on her face.

A loud wave of "Congratulations" hits us as we enter, and I glance around and see banners hanging everywhere. *Goodbye and Good Luck! Thanks for the memories. MFB will always be My Favorite Band!* Television screens broadcast footage of us playing in this very bar, and one of our most popular songs pipes through the speakers.

It's a going away party for the five of us, and I feel an unfamiliar sting behind my eyes. I'm not an emotional guy, but I wasn't expecting this tonight. I figured we'd come to the bar, we'd get drunk, and I'd take a random girl home—business as usual.

I'm excited for the prospects ahead. We had a fucking blast as the openers for Vail, and in a way that was far more pressure than this tour because we had to prove ourselves. We did—we were good enough for the frontman to sign us to his record label. We were good enough to earn our own spot outright as headliners for our own tour. We were good enough for one of our songs to hit the radio, and it took off from there. I can't wait for our tour...and yet I didn't think I'd be forced into saying goodbye tonight to the friends and fans I've made here—people who have become like a second family to me.

Tonight isn't going to end with me bagging a random babe. Tonight's for memories. It's for me and the guys and their women who are as much a part of this band as the rest of us. It's for being grateful and for showing that gratitude to the people who deserve it.

Besides, there will be plenty of babes to bag on our upcoming tour. I glance at Dax with a slight edge of regret for what this tour could've been if he wasn't in a serious relationship. He's kissing Kylie's cheek, a thank you for organizing this party, and a dart of jealousy in my chest surprises me.

To be clear, I'm not jealous of Kylie getting the kiss. I'm not even really jealous that Dax is kissing her.

It more has to do with the fact that they *get* each other. They *have* each other.

Adam has Bree.

Kane has Sierra.

Dax has Kylie.

And I have...Rascal?

Fuck that noise.

Dinah, the bar manager, presses a bottle of beer into my palm and a matching one for Dax. The rest of the guys are given their usual orders as well, and then the party starts.

The booth we almost always sit in is empty—reserved for us—and it features a brand-new tabletop. Photos of the five of us playing and partying here night after night litter the entire thing. Our band logo is in the center, and the entire table is covered with some sort of epoxy coating to preserve the photos in there forever.

Dax points to one of the photos. "Holy shit, we were fucking babies in this picture!"

We all look at it, and it's a photo from one of the first nights we played this bar. We *were* babies back then. I was just twenty, not even legal to drink in the bar we were playing. My dad knew Emerson and got him to let us play. "Remember how we had to leave right after our set since we weren't twenty-one?"

Kane laughs. "It was our first official gig as a band once Rascal and I joined the three of you."

"And we killed it," Adam says.

We all nod in agreement. Our first show was pretty solid for a bunch of twenty-year-olds who had no idea what the hell they were doing.

Dax's eyes edge over to the stage we've played hundreds of times, and mine follow his. My drums used to be set up there all the time—convenient since they're a pain in the ass to put up and take down, something I no longer have to worry about.

God, that's just another surreal tidbit to add to the list. I don't have to set up my drums anymore. Someone will do it for me.

I can tell he has it in his head he wants to play this place one last time, but our equipment is currently on a truck headed toward Los Angeles a day ahead of us. We'll be practicing for the tour in a practice venue near the offices of Ashmark, our record label. It's some old building Mark Ashton bought and renovated for smaller shows, but the sound system is state of the art, and being close to our label means we'll have the men from Vail close enough to help us finalize all our tour plans. They're the ones funding this tour, and I often take pause to process that fact.

None of us get drunk, but we have a great time laughing at all the times Rascal has puked into the bushes in the back alley, the *I Can Drink You Under the Table* challenges, the good shows and the not so good ones.

It's the perfect way to say goodbye to our past as we all take a giant leap together toward our future.

CHAPTER 10

ZOEY

I stare out the tiny airplane window with a small measure of regret.

I didn't want to kiss him because it's just Sawyer, but part of me feels like one final kiss would've sealed our goodbye. Instead, I think about what I'm leaving behind as the flight attendant talks about oxygen masks and water evacuations.

I zone out as I watch the plane back up onto the runway. I gaze at the city that's been home for the last decade and a half. I do love it here—so much that I've even grown accustomed to the hot, humid summers. The only other place I've ever lived is Chicago, which has its own share of humidity.

I realize this isn't a forever type of goodbye. My plan at the moment is to be gone for a couple months.

Yet as the plane starts moving faster on the ground and then we lift off, it feels pretty permanent.

I don't know what the next two months will hold, but I just have this premonition that my course won't be steering me back to Atlanta unless it's to visit the friends I'm leaving behind.

It's surreal to do this for *me*. Even though I've lived my whole life selfishly, this feels different. I'm making this decision for my own future. I'm leaving behind the comfort zone I've built with my two best friends. Like I told Sawyer just last night, I'm creating my own challenges to overcome, and part of me wonders whether this journey will lead me to someone who wants to hold my hand as we jump those hurdles together.

Sitting in the middle seat next to me is a little girl. Her mom sits on the other side of her, and her dad and brother are across the aisle. The little girl must be four or five. She has about a thousand stuffed animals on her seat, a fact I first noticed when the monkey's long hair tickled my elbow. The flight is about five hours, but this kid has at least twenty hours of entertainment on her—not to mention the backpack full of snacks her mother has stowed under the seat in front of her.

When I was around her age, my dad was released from jail. He'd been caught selling drugs before I was even born, and after serving a few years, he was released. He didn't learn his lesson, though. The second time he went to prison, the crime was armed robbery and possession, but in the time he was out, he and my mother spent all their time screaming at each other.

I distinctly remember nights where I crawled into a six-year-old Ethan's bed and we cried in fear together while we listened to our parents fight.

And now he's gone.

They are memories better left in the past, but they're also the reason I'm in my thirties and have a fucked up view of love. I thought it was love when I seduced Mark and we dated on and off for a few years, but really that was me trying to please him—trying to be whatever it was I thought he wanted because the *real* me would never be good enough for someone like him.

Rejecting Sawyer last night marked the very first time I've ever acted for *myself*. I've always taken on whatever persona I thought someone wanted me to be, but maybe I just need to be me. I realize this as I'm sitting on a plane taking me on a one-way route toward my future. I never really wanted to just be someone's fuck buddy like I was with Sawyer. I'm worth more than that, but it's what worked for us at the time, so I pretended like it was what I wanted because I was too scared to work for something more than that.

Maybe Jordan didn't like my dick joke and that's what got me kicked off *Single Life*, but someone out there will find it funny. Someone out there is my exact match, and my future won't be like it was for my own mom and dad.

I glance at the little girl beside me and hope she has a better upbringing than I did. When I catch a gaze between her parents, I know immediately that she does. Her dad loves her mom—I can see it from where I sit. They don't scream at each other. Her dad doesn't throw tumblers filled with whiskey at her mom, and this little girl and her older brother don't have to mop up the floor and pick up the shards of glass when the fight is over and the light of morning dawns.

No, this girl has a very different life than I ever had, but my brother is living proof that we can escape our past.

Now it's my turn.

* * *

I hug Ethan for about a full minute longer than is totally comfortable once the driver drops me at his front door. I didn't realize how much fear had bubbled up inside me about this transition until I walked into Ethan and Maci's Hollywood Hills home.

He gently pushes back from me and takes my oversized handbag. He sets it next to my suitcase. "Hey, you okay?"

I take a deep breath and nod. "Yeah. I'm good. Where's my nephew?"

"Napping," Maci says, stepping into the foyer and coming in for a hug of her own. Even though my brother is an international star and I watched them get married almost a year ago, it's still surreal that one of my favorite singers in the world is now my sister-in-law. I cling to her a little longer than I should, too. It feels good to be with family. "Welcome to California." She squeezes me and lets go.

"Thanks," I say.

Maci turns and motions for us to follow her. "So what's this job?"

I leave my bags by the front door and follow her into the house. "I'll be back-up dancing for some band on tour."

"What band?"

I follow Maci into the family room with my brother close behind me. "I'm not sure. I guess I'll find out tonight."

"What's tonight?" Ethan asks.

"There's a dinner scheduled at some place." I pull out my phone and find the email I got from Bailey with all the details. "Polo at nine."

"Polo?" Ethan repeats, his tone laced with skepticism as we all flop down on the creamy leather couch.

"Yeah. Why?" I ask.

"Polo is the hottest new restaurant in LA," he says, crossing his feet on the glass table in front of him. He looks relaxed and comfortable, but it only lasts a few seconds. He stands and picks up a toy in the middle of the floor and tosses it into a basket I hadn't even noticed in the corner. "Whoever your agent is must be legit."

I shrug. "I checked him out. Seemed legit enough. Can I borrow a car?"

"I'll do you one better, little sister. I'm staying in with the wife tonight, so Chuck's free to take you," he says, naming his security guard. He picks up a cup on the edge of the table.

"You don't have to go to all that trouble."

He shakes his head. "Do you even know who the hell I am?"

I giggle and shake my head as I watch him pick up a bowl filled with cereal. "Not anymore."

He laughs and carries the cup and bowl to the kitchen, and Maci and I stay where we are. She's become a friend to me over the past year, so we catch up on all the details of our lives.

"Sawyer told me last night he saw a future with me."

Her eyes widen. "Is that something you want?"

I shake my head. "It's not something I ever wanted with him. We had sex the night my episode of *Single Life* aired and I knew the next morning it would never be more than just sex."

Ethan walks back in the room just as I'm announcing the dirty details of my sex life. He makes a face. "Do I need to leave?"

"If you don't want to hear about your sister's sex life, then probably," Maci says.

I hold up both hands. "I won't talk about my sex life."

Maci narrows her eyes at me and jabs her thumb toward her husband. "Just because he doesn't want the details doesn't mean I don't."

I laugh. "I should probably get ready for my dinner anyway."

"You have something to wear?" Maci asks.

"Ethan subsidized my entire wardrobe for *Single Life*, so I think I can dig out something." I turn to my brother as I stand. "Thanks for that, by the way."

He nods and settles in next to his wife—something I really never thought was in his future—and I see the picture of pure contentment in the two of them as I slink off to get ready for my night.

I walk down the hallway toward the bedroom that's mine until further notice. I've visited plenty of times before, but this hallway always amazes me.

The walls are lined on one side with Maci's accomplishments. Framed platinum records, images from her album covers, pictures of her on stage, even a guitar signed by her entire band for some tour they played together. On the other side are Ethan's accomplishments. A pair of drumsticks from his first tour, pictures of the Vail men, graphics from advertisements of some of Vail's biggest shows, and even drumheads shouting the band's name all hang on the wall to showcase everything this husband and wife have accomplished in their careers.

I want a wall of accolades. I want something to be proud of, something besides a failed appearance on a reality show, a job I quit as a social media marketer, and a bank account my brother feeds for me.

Maybe this tour is just the start I'm looking for.

CHAPTER 11

BRODY

"This is fucking bizarre," I say as I slide into the backseat next to Dax. Kylie is on his other side, and Rascal, Kane, and Adam sit across from us, riding backwards.

"What is?" Kane asks.

I shrug as I pull the door shut. "Getting chauffeured around Los Angeles like we're somebody important."

"We *are* somebody important, dude," Rascal chimes in. "Didn't you get the memo? We're the fucking *headliners*."

I settle my gaze out the window. The night sky is dark, but the streets are lit with action. The hotel we're staying at is in downtown Los Angeles, close to the Staples Center where we played when we opened for Vail. On this tour, we'll be playing a slightly smaller theater, but I have aspirations to run our headlining tour through Staples one day. It's where the Lakers play, where every major name in recent music history has set up a stage...it's a goal that always felt like a pipe dream until we checked into the Sheraton across the street.

This is really happening, and I feel it changing who I am already. I never gave a shit about much of anything, but now I want to see the success we all envision, and not just for myself. I want this for my brothers of MFB. Some of these guys have been my best friends as far back as I can remember. Through thick or thin and for better or worse, we find ourselves about to embark on the most important tour of our career.

Mark Ashton sat us down on the last tour and told us the story about the tour that launched Vail's career. That tour with them opened doors for us, but this is where we strike out on our own. This is where we make it or break it. This is where we really prove what we're made of, that we're not just some one hit wonder but we've got talent and longevity.

And it all starts with this dinner meeting tonight. MFB and Kylie will be breaking bread our tour manager, Mitch. In addition, the three dancers, two of whom we've already met, the choreographer, and Wes, the talent agent Dax found through Mark who was in charge of filling their spots, will be there.

When we arrive, we're brought to a private table in a side room of the restaurant, which is unexpected. I'm not used to getting recognized quite yet—this is all so new to us, but it does happen on occasion. Since we have business to attend to tonight, it's probably better this way.

I slide into a chair between Dax and Adam. While I'm close with everyone in the band, I'd call Dax my best friend and Adam is probably his back-up. The three of us formed our own band in middle school and added Kane and Rascal later, and we've been jamming for more than half our lives together.

Mitch is the only other one already there, something Kylie planned on so we could talk a little business before the dancers and Wes arrive. We order our first round of drinks, and I wonder if my standard Miller Lite is a little boring considering this is our first dinner that we can officially expense. And then I realize I don't really give a fuck if it's boring. I have nobody to impress. If the fact that I'm headlining a tour at the age of twenty-seven isn't impressive enough, I don't think my choice of beverage would change someone's mind.

Mitch is one of Vail's old roadies. He's been in the business a long time and came highly recommended from Mark, so we hired him. We're still in the getting-to-know-you stage to some degree, but Kylie has spent a lot of phone time with him as they arranged venues and dates for the tour. I don't really know what Mitch's responsibilities are versus Kylie's—all I know is it's my job to show up when Kylie tells me to and play the fuck out of my drums. There's other shit, of course, like meet and greets and interviews and photo opps, but it's all part of this dream I'm suddenly living.

We sit around shooting the shit, but once our drinks arrive, Mitch answers the question in my head. "Let's get started since the others will be arriving any minute. My role is basically anything to do with your performances on this tour. I handle accommodations, getting you to and from the venue and any additional travel arrangements, set-up and take-down, roadies, all that shit."

"And my role is anything to do with the five of you personally," Kylie says. "If you need anything while we're on the road, whether it's..." she pauses as she thinks up an example off the cuff, "a set of drumsticks or a new pair of shoes or whatever, come to me and I'll handle it."

"Even pussy?" Rascal asks.

Dax shoots him a look that tells him to shut the fuck up.

Kylie glares at him, too. "You're on your own with that, though clearly you'll need the help."

A round of childish *oh burns* and *oooos* ensue, and then Kylie continues. "I've arranged all the press interviews during this tour, and every night I'll text out a schedule that has everything you need to know about the next day. I am here to be your biggest cheerleader. With that said, I'm also here to be the biggest bitch you've ever seen if you need me to be." She glares at Rascal on that last sentence, and I have to be honest: I'm glad it's not me she's looking at with all that murder in her eyes. "Any questions?"

"No, ma'am," Rascal says obediently with his eyes downcast toward the table, and the rest of us shake our heads. We all know she can turn up the bitch when she needs to. She may be the most intimidating woman I've ever met, but somehow Dax has gotten her to soften on us over the six or so months they've been together.

Mitch and Kylie fill us in on some more details, and then the door opens and Wes walks in followed by the two dancers I've already met. I reach for my drink as I debate which of those two will end up in my bed first, and when I glance up at the doorway, a woman I've only seen once before fills my vision.

She was stunning on television—of course we had to pull up the clip of her on the reality show the second we heard Ethan's sister was one of the castoffs. We had to make sure she had the right look to fill the shoes of a back-up dancer on our tour.

Okay, if I'm being totally honest, we had to make sure she was hot.

And she was hot on the show...but in person.

Holy fucking smokes.

She's got a dancer's body for sure—she's long and lean with two globes on her chest that appear to be the perfect handful. But it's not just her body that's causing my dick to beg for escape from my pants.

Her long, blonde hair falls in loose waves around her shoulders, and her blue eyes move assuredly around the room. She exudes confidence even though she's walking into a den where she knows literally no one. She might not even know that it's MFB she'll be dancing with for the next couple months, yet she walks in like she owns the damn place.

And something about that is *insanely* hot.

This woman might be even more intimidating than Kylie, and I have to remind myself for a moment that she works for *me*, not the other way around. But something tells me we might be working *together* at some point in the near future.

Naked.

I'll have to turn up the old Brody charm. It works every time.

Kane's words about a potential No Bang Oath flash briefly through my mind, but we never officially made one—which means I'm in the clear to bang whoever I want.

And I want Ethan Fuller's sister.

Bad.

I watch as Wes introduces himself to her. She shakes his hand with her chin tilted up and a slight flick of her neck—enough to make her hair shimmer around her shoulders. I suddenly wish I wasn't sandwiched between two guys. The seat on Adam's other side is empty, which means it has the potential to be filled by her.

She looks around the room when Wes's attention moves to one of the other dancers, and our eyes meet for the first time. She holds my gaze a beat longer than she should, and I allow her to shift her eyes first.

I can't stop looking at her. I can't stop thanking God for putting women who look like that in my direct path. I can't stop thinking about what that dancer's body looks like without a black dress covering all my favorite parts.

Her eyes land on Dax next, and there's a hint of recognition there. It makes sense that she'd know who we are since we opened for Vail on their last tour, but I have no idea how close she is to her brother.

I don't want her eyes on him. I want them back on me. I push back from my chair and throw caution to the wind as I walk right up to her.

"Are you our new dancer?" I ask.

She nods. "Zoey Fuller." She sticks out her hand to mine, and I slide my palm against hers. Her hands are smaller than mine and cold as ice, yet something pulls inside my stomach and tightens in my chest at the same time.

What the fuck is that? I must just be hungry, yet the connection of her cold skin against mine manages to have the effect of warming me from the inside out as an achy need pulses in my balls.

She glances down at where our hands are connected for a beat, and then she looks back up at me.

"I'm Brody. I'm the drummer."

She wrinkles her nose as she drops my hand like I have the plague. "Drums? That's unfortunate."

I laugh. "Why's that?"

Just as she opens her mouth to answer, Dax interrupts loudly from where he sits beside Kylie. "Since everyone's here, why don't we all take a seat and get the introductions going?"

"We'll finish this conversation later," I say. I throw in a cheesy wink for good measure. I'm not sure why, but it always works on women.

Not this one, apparently.

"We'll see," she says, shooting me her own wink back.

I laugh and wonder where the hell this woman came from.

CHAPTER 12

ZOEY

Dammit.

Brody certainly had potential until he told me he's a drummer.

He has the tall, dark, and handsome thing nailed down to a T. Dark eyes with a hint of cockiness behind them, lustrous dark hair that's the perfect length for grabbing onto during sex, and those hands...good God, those hands.

I should've guessed either guitar or drums just from his hands. Sexy and strong, long fingers that look like they can get the job done.

But he's a drummer, which immediately and firmly plants him right into the friend zone. I know way too much about drummers.

Every single one I've ever met—and I've met a few courtesy of my brother, a drummer himself—has been known for banging more than just the drums. They talk about their conquests like it's water cooler chatter, and I refuse to be one of those girls...especially not on a tour this important, when this could be my stepping stone to the place I really want to end up. My job here is to keep my eyes on the prize, not to get involved with some drummer who'll only hurt me in the end.

The guy who looks familiar interrupts Brody's intense gaze as I'm about to tell him I don't involve myself with drummers. Only a few seats are open, and just as I'm about to grab one far, far away from Brody, he motions for me to follow him. He tells another guy to move over, and then he sits and nods toward the open chair beside him.

Getting special treatment from one of the members of the band feels like the wrong foot to get off on, but being too standoffish seems like a bad idea, too.

So I sit next to Brody and await the introductions.

"I'll start," the familiar looking guy says. He's got the bad boy thing going on, too, but the way he's looking at the woman next to him with his arm tossed casually around her shoulders tells me he's probably off the market.

Brody has already made it apparent he's fair game, though. Just the way he's been eyeing me since I walked into the room tells me he's interested. And if he wasn't sex on a goddamn stick, rejecting his advances might come much easier.

"I'm Dax Hunter, MFB's lead singer." As soon as he says the words, everything clicks in my head.

MFB? As in the band that opened for my brother's band on their last tour?

You have got to be kidding me.

I'm such a stupid, naïve idiot for thinking some talent agent called me out of the blue for a dancing gig after seeing me on television.

How did I miss this? How did I not see it coming?

I'm seething. I can't believe it. Obviously Ethan is behind this, and all I ever wanted was to find my own way and make my own breaks.

I didn't want him to get involved.

I glance over at Brody and narrow my eyes at him. "MFB, huh?" I ask. The others are introducing themselves and I'm sure I'm being rude, but anger has pushed me past the point of caring.

"Ever hear of us?"

I nod. "You opened for Vail." I say the words flatly.

"We did, and we signed with Ashmark shortly after." He grins widely, clearly proud of his accomplishments, and I let out an annoyed breath.

Of fucking course he did. Dammit, Ethan.

I'm about to stand and get the hell out of here when Brody's hand on my arm followed by his deep voice stops me. "Are you okay?"

"No," I say, shaking my head. "I thought my appearance on television and subsequent audition got me this gig." I grit my teeth. "My own merits. I didn't know the fact that my brother is in Vail got it for me."

"That's not how it went down." His eyes soften as he takes in my fury.

I know my expression will give me early onset wrinkles, but I'm too angry to smooth out my forehead and relax the glare in my eyes. "Oh? It's not?" Sarcasm drips from my voice as my volume starts to increase through no control of my own. "Then tell me, how does Ethan Fuller's sister just so happen to end up as the last-minute back-up dancer for the band who opened for Vail's last tour?"

Brody glances at the group gathered beside us. My eyes follow his, and I notice that they've fallen silent as they take in my outburst.

Clearly this is not the impression I want to make, but it doesn't matter. I'm not staying.

I grab my purse and move to stand. "I'm sorry, but I have to leave. I can't do this."

I storm out of the little private room and through the restaurant. It isn't until I've reached the sidewalk that someone grabs my arm. I whip around and find Brody's dark eyes full of concern.

It hits me with such force that I'm momentarily frozen to my place.

I don't know if *anyone* has *ever* looked at me with such compassion in my entire life.

I want to drink it in. I want to swim in the pools of darkness hidden under his lashes. I want to luxuriate in the burden of apprehension I see there before I smooth it over and turn it from anxiety to serenity.

I shake my head.

I don't even know this guy. Surely the concern I see written in his eyes is purely selfish—because *all* men are selfish. It's the one fact I'm certain of in this everchanging world.

He doesn't want me to go because nine days—almost eight—isn't enough time to find a suitable replacement.

"Don't go." His voice is the play button that moves me from frozen into action.

"Why should I stay?" I spit out. I rip my arm out of his grip.

"Because we need you."

I sigh as I start to soften. There's no use being upset with this guy. It's not *his* fault my brother got involved in my life when I specifically asked him not to. "Any one of a hundred other women could easily take my place."

"If you think that's true, you're sorely mistaken," he mutters.

"Why's that?"

He gazes at me for a long time before he answers. "Never mind. Look, we don't have time to book another dancer. Besides, we want *you*. Please just stay."

"Why do you care?"

He looks around wildly for a few seconds before his eyes land back on me. "I'm not sure. But since you were on that other show, I assume you want a spot on TV. We'll be filming Dax and Mark Ashton's new show *Rock on the Road* this tour. I'll make sure you get a feature in the episode where we have to hire a new dancer."

I narrow my eyes. Sure, his blazing brown eyes pin me to my spot on the sidewalk and just looking at him makes me want to rip off all his clothes. Or all my clothes. Maybe both. He's stupid hot, but that doesn't mean I trust him or his intentions.

Even so, the thought of TV time is appealing.

I'm not in love with the fact that my brother somehow had his hand in this since I want to hold my head high and proud when I catch my big break, but what's done is done. I still want to know a few things, though. "Why are you bothering? Because Ethan's my brother?"

He shrugs then heaves out a breath like he's about to make a confession. "If that's what you want to think, then sure. That's why. It has nothing to do with the fact that I haven't been so attracted to a woman I know nothing about in a long time. It has nothing to do with wanting to get to know you, with wanting to see you dance in the space between my drums and where the rest of my band stands during a performance. It has nothing to do with maybe wanting a private dance lesson of my own. It's obviously just because I want to impress your brother." His final sentence drips of sarcasm.

My jaw seems to drop dumbly open with each new confession he makes, and I don't know why...but I believe him. It might be the earnestness in those dark brown eyes or the sincerity in his pleading tone or the fact that I feel this connection between us even though I know nothing about him. I'm not sure, but his argument is convincing enough in this moment.

Besides, he came out here.

For me.

I've never had a man chase me down like that, and just that fact alone has me wondering what kind of person he is on the inside.

Better than the men I'm used to hanging around, anyway.

I follow him back inside. Once we're seated again, I feel all eyes on me. I address the obvious elephant in the room. "I'm Zoey Fuller, your new dancer. I'd like to offer my sincerest apology for walking out. I was just a little blindsided when I realized how this opportunity presented itself, but you have my word it won't happen again."

"Thanks, Zoey," Dax says. "I'd like to apologize to you as well. We never meant to blindside you. I simply called up Mark because I knew he'd only offer the very best of the best."

"Mark?" I ask, genuinely surprised at this turn of events.

He shrugs. "We've gotten pretty close over the past few months. We're co-producing a reality show together, and I knew as soon as Beth backed out, he'd know someone who could fill her spot."

"I figured it was my brother."

Dax shakes his head. "It was Mark's idea."

"Oh." It's all I can think of to say.

Kylie must sense my total discomfort, because she jumps in. "Speaking of co-producing a reality show with Mark, let's talk a little about *Rock on the Road*." She launches into the details we need to know, but I'm only partially listening because I'm stunned and appreciative that it was Mark and not Ethan who orchestrated this opportunity for me.

I glance over at Brody and our eyes lock for a beat. His lips quirk up in a half-smile, and I wish he wasn't the damn drummer of this band, because I think we could have a lot of fun together if I didn't hold a grudge against guys like him.

CHAPTER 13

BRODY

"What was that?" Dax asks me once we're back at the hotel. We—or rather, our record label—sprung for a suite, so the five of us plus Kylie are all staying together. Dax and I are sprawled on the luxurious couches in the living area after our dinner meeting. Kylie's working in one of the other rooms, Rascal is playing video games, and Kane and Adam disappeared to call their women.

"What was what?" I ask as I scroll mindlessly on my phone.

"You running after Zoey."

I shrug. "I didn't want her to pass up this opportunity because of some misunderstanding."

"What misunderstanding?"

I click my phone off and toss it on the table in front of me. "She thought it was her brother who set her up with this gig."

He sits up a little and grabs his beer from the table. "So what if it was?"

"Don't you remember Ethan saying something about not wanting her to know he was involved?"

He shrugs. "I don't think I was paying close enough attention. But you were. Why?"

"She's hot."

"You didn't know that when we called Mark to see if he knew anyone." He's prying, but I'm not sure what he's prying for.

I lie on my back and stare up at the ceiling. I haven't been able to get her blue eyes out of my head since they burned into mine on that sidewalk out in front of the restaurant tonight when I begged her to stay. I still don't know where that came from, but something deep within me told me to go out there. It felt like I'd be making a huge mistake to let her walk. "I don't know, all right? I just remember him saying that."

"Be careful, man." His voice is full of caution, but I'm not sure why. He's never cared who I screwed around with in the past.

"About what?"

"Getting involved with her could be bad for business," he warns. "I don't want you to do what you do with women and create bad blood between us and Ethan."

"To *do what I do* with women? You mean the same shit you pulled less than a year ago before you found yourself wrapped around Kylie's pinkie?" I taunt.

"Exactly where I like him," Kylie says from around the corner. She walks into the room and plops down next to Dax. "What are we talking about?"

"Brody chasing Zoey tonight after she bailed," Dax says.

"Oh yeah, what was that about? You like her?" Kylie asks.

I roll my eyes. "Is this fourth fucking grade?"

"Far from it. As your manager, it's sort of my job to talk you out of bad decisions."

"But you and Dax sleeping together doesn't count?" I ask. I realize I'm being a snide little prick, but the double standard here is pissing me off.

She shakes her head. "It doesn't because it's totally different. Dax and I had real feelings that we'd both been hiding for months. You just met this girl and think she's some hot piece of ass or whatever you want to call it."

"What if it's more than that for me, too?" I ask. I do my best to hide the unfamiliar vulnerability that darts through my chest. "What if I have feelings?"

Kylie purses her lips and Dax laughs, both serving to ignite my anger.

I sit up. "What the fuck? I'm not allowed to *feel* something?"

"Dude, calm your tits," Dax says. He eyes me for a second and then turns to Kylie. "Can you give us a couple minutes, sweets?" he asks her.

She kisses Dax, gives me a lethal look, and leaves the room.

"What's going on with you?" Dax asks me. "Is your tampon in crooked?"

"Fuck you," I mutter at his lame attempt to insinuate I have PMS.

"I've known you a long time, man, and I know your game here. Think about the opportunities we've gotten because of Vail before you fuck one of the member's sisters."

"So I'm just supposed to kiss all their asses?"

Dax shrugs. "Basically, yeah. We owe the launch of our career to them, and screwing around with someone in one of their families just isn't a good idea. Not when I know what your intentions are."

I blow out a breath. "You know what you just did, don't you?"

He wrinkles his eyebrows. "What?"

"You made her forbidden and now I want her even more."

Dax laughs, but I'm not joking. He dismisses our conversation like it's over, but for me...it's really just beginning.

I don't know what it is about this girl, but as soon as she walked in, it was like a spotlight shone down on her and followed her as she moved around the room. She's something different than the girls I'm used to. Maybe it's Mark's assessment of her being crude, or maybe it was the dick joke she told on national television. These are the little pieces of her I got to know before I even met her, and now that I've seen the girl in the flesh?

I'm interested.

I'm about to open my mouth to try to articulate all that to my best friend when Adam walks back in and takes a seat on the couch.

"How's Bree?" Dax asks.

"Fine," he says absently.

Dax glances over at him. "You okay?"

He shrugs. "She's not handling this well." He shakes his head as he waves a hand in the air. "She wanted to come on tour with us."

"You told her no?" I ask.

"I didn't tell her no, exactly," he says. "I just told her it wouldn't be smart to quit her job to go on the road when it's not like it'll be some vacation where we get unlimited amounts of time together."

"You didn't want her to come?" Dax presses.

"Of course I did, but I just didn't think it was the right move." He draws in a deep breath. "I need to focus on playing guitar, you know? Not on sightseeing and making sure she's comfortable on a tour bus and that she gets a shower or whatever."

"Fair enough," Dax says.

"She just kept bringing up the fact that Kylie is coming along, and I had to explain to her that it's not because she's dating you but because she's our manager and we need her. Then she got all butthurt that we don't need *her* that way, and it just turned into an argument."

"Women are exhausting," I say.

"Not all of them," Dax murmurs, and I glance over at him. God, he's a lovesick idiot.

I've never been in love. I've never felt what he feels for Kylie. I've never *wanted* that, either. I've always done just fine going to the bar and picking up a woman—or sometimes two—to keep me company for the night and then moving on to someone new in the morning. I'm about having fun and being free, not about being tied down and miserable.

It's my dad who set that example for me—even though I don't want to be like him, that's still the truth.

I pick up my phone and pretend to scroll as I find myself lost in thought.

From the outside, we look like the perfect family. A mom and dad who hold hands in public and are still in love after thirty years of marriage. One older boy aged twenty-seven—me—and twin girls, my sisters Abigail and Allison, who turn twenty-three soon. The perfect upbringing with picturesque Thanksgiving dinners and portraits in front of the Christmas tree.

But we all know my dad runs around on my mom. He spends the weekdays working such long hours in Los Angeles that he actually has his own place in the city. He spends the weekends in San Diego with his family. It's been that way as long as I can remember. My mom never wanted to move to Los Angeles, and it's the price she decided she could live with.

I see what it does to her, though. I know how hard it is to know her husband is fucking around on her, but it's been a part of my life so long that we all just sweep it under the rug. We don't talk about it. We continue to live our fake plastic life while Dad goes into the city and stays in his sex den for the week before returning home and playing the role of doting husband for two days before the cycle starts over again.

I don't want a fake plastic life, and I certainly don't want to follow in dear old Dad's footsteps. I don't want to get bored with my wife at home after I made promises to her and had children with her. I don't want to find pussy in the city when I have a family back home.

In fact, I don't want any of that shit. Commitment, serious relationships, kids...those are better left to people who don't carry the genes my father gave me.

I want something different for my life.

It might be why everyone looks at me like I'm the rebel of the family.

The boy who wanted a career in music, the wild child who doesn't have any inclination to settle down.

The one who doesn't want a woman arguing with me because I didn't take her on my first headlining tour and the one who doesn't want something serious pulling me down and making me someone different than who I've always been.

The one who wants to go on this tour and fuck my way through a different woman or two in every city.

The one who doesn't want what my parents have, which is why I wrote off relationships a long time ago. I sometimes wonder if my father realizes just how much his cheating hurts everyone in the family—not just Mom, but his kids, too. We may be grown adults who are moving forward with our lives, but that doesn't mean we don't feel the lasting effects from the choices he's made our whole lives.

I glance at Adam and see his misery over his fight with his woman, and the devil on my shoulder confirms this is the way it's supposed to be for me.

But then I look at Dax. A thump sounds from the room Kylie disappeared into. She's taking off her shoes, maybe, or let the lid of her hard cover suitcase fall down too hard. The way his eyes soften as he looks in the direction of the room where we all know she stands is something I've never felt. She's not even in the goddamn room and his expression makes it clear: he's waiting for her to come back. He'd rather sit snuggled with her than shoot the shit with Adam and me.

The angel on my other shoulder pokes at my curiosity. What's that like?

It's been Dax and me as far back as I can remember.

Brody and Dax.

Jensen and Hunter.

B-Jen and D-Hunt.

Chode-y and D-Cunt.

But it's not anymore. He changed things when he decided to commit to one woman. My wingman is gone, replaced by this guy I don't even know anymore, but I'm still the same old guy out for a good time.

Except when Zoey stepped foot into that restaurant, my first thought when my eyes landed on her was whether it might be okay for me to change, too.

A new tour and a new Brody.

I don't want to change. It's like the dope who finds a girlfriend his first day on a college campus when he has the whole world ahead of him to explore his options. I want that. It's what I've always wanted.

A flash of her blue eyes plays in my mind again.

Maybe it isn't what I've always wanted. What if it's just what I've always told myself?

I don't want to be thinking of her again, yet I can't seem to stop myself.

I don't even *know* her.

But I want to.

She's already confusing the fuck out of me and I've known her about four seconds. What would that be like if I gave it a little more time?

Adam and Dax are talking about something, but I've totally zoned them out as my mind details the curves of her tight little body one more time.

"Brody."

"Brody?"

"BRODY!"

I finally register that someone is calling my name. I snap back to attention and realize Adam isn't in the room any longer. "What?"

"Did you smoke some bad weed or something?" Dax asks.

I shake my head. "I haven't smoked since we all got high in Denver on the Vail tour. You know that. Why?"

"What's going on with you? I just called your name three times and you were somewhere in space."

I shrug.

"Don't gimme that shit. I know you better and I have never seen you like this."

"I don't want to be like my dad," I finally blurt. "And I think I already am."

His brows furrow. "Your dad? Is this coming out because you had lunch with him today?"

"We all know what he does during the week when he's here in LA, and then there's me. I've never committed to anyone except MFB."

"That doesn't mean you're the same," he says gently. Sometimes I forget how in tune with people Dax really is. "Actually, I think the fact that you recognize it tells me you're already not like him."

I shake my head. "I don't know what's bringing this out in me tonight. I'm sorry. Let's get wasted and find me someone to fuck."

He stands and stretches on a laugh. "I'm beat, man. I'm going to bed."

I shake my head. "We all know what you're off to do. You've already found your someone to fuck."

"Can you blame me?" He holds both hands up innocently. "Have you seen her legs?"

"Have fun," I say impassively. I can't muster up enthusiasm for my friend who's getting ass on the reg when I'm over here fighting these strange emotions I've never had before.

This is crazy.

I met the girl *tonight*. I don't know her from any other girl in the bar downstairs.

That's my solution.

The bar downstairs.

I'll find someone down there to help me get back to myself, someone who I can lose myself in for a few hours (okay, minutes) of pleasure and leave behind in the morning.

That'll surely solve everything.

CHAPTER 14

ZOEY

"You made me look like an idiot in front of all those people," I yell at my stupid brother when I walk in his kitchen and find him cleaning out the dishwasher—another sight I don't think I've ever seen in my life.

"What the hell are you talking about?"

The anger built in me as I rode in the back of Ethan's car chauffeured by his security guard. Anger and lust over that damn drummer that I've already written off are warring in me, but anger is taking the edge.

Maybe Chuck should've followed me inside, because I'm about to throw down with my brother and he could probably use his security guard right now.

"Throwing my name in the ring for this dancing gig, acting like you didn't know anything." I walk right up to him and slug him in the arm. "Fuck you, Ethan. Fuck you!"

"Jesus Christ, Zoey!" he yells, rubbing the spot of my offense. "What the hell is wrong with you?"

I lunge for him again, but I'm held off by a woman who is apparently much stronger than me as my arms are pinned to my sides from behind. I wrestle out of her grip but back off Ethan.

"Whoa, whoa, whoa," Maci says, clearly ready to play peacekeeper. "For one thing, we've got a sleeping baby and I'd really appreciate if he wasn't woken up by yelling curse words. And for another thing, what the hell is going on?"

"I'm sorry. I wasn't thinking about Eli. I was too pissed at your stupid husband."

She rolls her eyes. "Been there. What did he do now?"

"He lied to me about this gig. I thought I got it on my own merits, but he jumped in to play fucking Superman." I cover my mouth in apology for the swear.

Ethan holds up both hands. "I didn't do anything. I said I didn't want to be involved from the start. I knew you wouldn't take it if you knew I was anywhere in the vicinity, so I didn't touch it."

"So you did know, then," I say flatly.

Maci clears her throat. "We both knew, honey. But listen. It's not how it looks. Dax called Mark desperate for someone to replace their dancer. Mark named the first person who came to mind. We all knew you quit your job for *Single Life*, babe. He was just looking out for you, trying to get you something to fill the time and maybe nudge you toward the career we all know you'll excel in."

"I don't need anyone's nudges, but I do need to get the hell out of here." I stalk toward the door, not sure where I'm going or how I'm getting there.

"Where are you going?" Ethan asks.

"Wherever Chuck takes me." I go to my bedroom first and get my suitcase and purse, and then I stalk back outside without even saying goodbye to my brother or his wife.

I'm being a little brat, and I know it. But I told Ethan a million times not to get involved. He could've easily told Mark no, but he didn't.

Now everyone on this tour knows how I got the gig. It has nothing to do with my ability to dance or my own hard work. It has everything to do with who I'm related to. And that's a really embarrassing nugget to have to live with.

I get in the car that's still waiting in the driveway, and Chuck takes off before I even have to say a word...which tells me that Ethan stuck his hand in my business once again.

"Where'd he tell you to take me?" I ask.

"The Sheraton downtown. Ashmark has an unoccupied room reserved for the evening that you're welcome to stay in until you cool down."

"Thanks, Chuck," I say. I stare out the window as I realize my anger has much more to do with being embarrassed than actually being angry.

I stay in the car while Chuck checks me in and delivers my bag to the attendant on duty, and he returns a few minutes later with my key. "You're in room twenty-four eleven," he says. "Ethan said to text him when you're ready to check out and stay with them. He also said to tell you he's sorry."

I blow out a breath. "Thank you, Chuck."

I get out of the car and head into the hotel lobby. I'm not really paying attention to my surroundings, but I suddenly feel awful for making such a big deal out of this. I start and stop ten different texts to my brother before I settle on the one I send.

Me: *Sorry I was such a bitch. Thank you for taking care of me and setting me up here. I shouldn't have stormed out. It's just mortifying that everyone knows how I got here. I'll be back tomorrow after rehearsals to see my nephew. Maybe he can spare five minutes awake to visit with his aunt?*

His reply is fast.

Ethan: *I'll always take care of you, Zo. You earned that spot. Have fun with it and I'll be sure to wake Eli up to say hi.*

I'm smiling at my phone when someone bumps into my elbow. "Oh, excuse me," I say absently as I look up.

The smile freezes on my face and disbelief takes over. "What are you doing here?" I ask as my eyes lock onto the dark brown ones of the *drummer.*

He chuckles. "It's either a drink or fate. Take your pick."

"Maybe a little of each?"

"More importantly, what are *you* doing here? Looking for me?" He gives me a boyish grin that sends a little tingle through my tummy.

"I wish I could say yes just to stroke that big—" I glance down at his pants before I finish my sentence, "—ego of yours, but I stormed out of my brother's house and his driver brought me here for the night."

"On Ashmark's dime?" he asks.

I nod.

"Same here. They must have a Groupon or something."

I giggle. "I'm sure Mark Ashton uses Groupon regularly."

"Don't we all?" He lifts a shoulder. "I just got one for skydiving lessons and another for a pottery class."

"Ooh, I've always wanted to try pottery," I say, playing along with his joke.

"It's a date. We're making pottery sometime in the next two months."

I raise a brow. "Challenge accepted."

He laughs. "Can I buy you a drink?"

I point at his chest. "You can buy me two, little drummer boy."

He laughs and leads the way toward the bar. Here in Los Angeles, we're just two people—albeit two *attractive* people. It doesn't matter that he's in a band about to take off toward stardom and it doesn't matter that I'll be dancing across the stage during his tour. It's a little after midnight on a Friday night, and the bar is crowded. Brody manages to squeeze us both into an open spot so we can order. The lady occupying the stool next to me is obviously tipsy, and she's using her arms wildly to punctuate her story. I shift over just a smidge, which causes me to bump right into Brody's front side.

Oh my dear God. It's hard *everywhere.* I suddenly have the image of solid cuts of muscle moving above me just before he sinks that other hard part right into my soft part.

I clear my throat, a little breathless. "Sorry," I mutter. *He's a drummer*, I remind myself.

He grins and I feel his hand move to my hip to steady me. His fingers dig into the flesh around my hipbone, pushing a needy ache down low in my stomach. "Don't be."

"What can I get you?" the bartender asks.

I glance up. "Mexican mule." I need tequila for this night, that's for damn sure.

Brody's brows furrow as he looks at me. "What's that?"

"Tequila and ginger beer."

He wrinkles his nose in disgust, and it strikes me as incredibly cute. I don't know if I've ever been so attracted sexually to someone who I also find *cute.*

"Make it two," he says.

I glance up at him and find his eyes smoldering down hotly at me. I have to look away. Sirens are blasting in my head.

Danger!

Danger!

Danger!

Getting dirty with this guy would be a bad decision. I know this. I'm sure he knows this.

Despite that, and despite my promise to just be myself from now on, something tells me this is inevitable.

But I need to fight it, and not just because he's the drummer—something I guess I might be able to get past eventually. Surely nothing more than one hot night will come from it, and then we have to work together for the next two months. If anything, we should wait until the end of the tour. Then if shit gets awkward, at least we won't have to see each other day in and day out for much longer.

That doesn't mean we can't flirt a little, though.

A table opens, and I motion to Brody that I'll grab it while he waits for our drinks. I settle in and cross one leg over the other, and then he saunters over with our drinks a minute later. He's got this swagger to his stride, this confidence that's insanely hot, and he strikes me as the type of guy who could have any woman in this place.

Yet he's buying *me* a drink and sharing a table with *me*.

Not that blonde over there with her eyes on his ass, and not that brunette over there with her eyes on his dick.

Me.

A little pride blooms in my chest at that thought.

He sets my glass on the table in front of me and holds his up in a toast. "To ass," he says.

"Uh, excuse me?"

"Mexican mules," he clarifies.

"Oh, of course." I clink my glass against his, and he takes a sip.

He makes a face. "That's fucking gross. And you could've interpreted my toast however you wanted. You are, after all, the girl who got kicked off a reality show for telling a dick joke."

"Oh my God," I say, covering my eyes in mortification. "You saw that?"

"I thought it was hilarious." His eyes twinkle as he teases me. "I would've given you my first flower for that."

"I have a ton of dirty jokes if that's what you're into." I take a bolstering sip of my Mexican mule, which, for the record, is *not* gross.

He holds both palms up. "Go for it, but make them about camels since you love camels."

I laugh. He really *was* paying attention to my short segment on the show. "How do you have sex with a camel?"

He shrugs. "Probably pretty much how I have sex with any other animal."

I may have met my match in this one. I giggle. "The correct answer is one hump at a time."

He lets out a bellow of laughter as he slams his palm on the table. The noise garners a few heads turned in our direction. "Gimme another one."

"How much sex does a horny camel need?"

He shakes his head like he has no idea where I'm going with this.

"Just one hump and she's good for a month."

He laughs loudly again, and I love how he literally gives zero fucks that he's turning heads in this rather swanky hotel bar. "You're funny, Zoey. I have a camel line for you. Ready?"

"Show me what you got."

He takes another sip of the mule before he gives me his line. "Want me to chop your camel toe with my morning wood?"

My brows shoot up. "Um, you chop wood. You don't chop *with* wood. But was that an invitation or just a line?"

He shrugs, and then he leans in a little closer to me and lowers his voice. "It's whatever you want it to be."

The husky timber in his tone sends shivers down my spine.

God, I want him.

Why does he have to be so damn hot?

I clear my throat as I pretend goosebumps haven't broken out along my flesh just from the sound of his sexy voice. "Why don't we get to know one another a little better before we decide the answer to that?" I ask in an effort to remain true to what I promised myself.

"I'm Brody. My parents are still married, though not happily. I have twin sisters, Abby and Ally. They're five years younger than me."

"How old are you?" I ask as I play with the tiny straw in my drink. I stir the liquid around the ice cubes.

"I turn twenty-eight next month."

Oh God. I'm robbing the damn cradle here.

"You?" he asks.

"Thirty-three."

His eyes widen. "Damn girl, you're fine for being in your thirties."

I close my eyes and shake my head. "Did you seriously just say that to me?"

He laughs. "Age is just a number, babe. It's never meant anything more than that to me."

"To me, too," I lie. I've never been with anyone younger than me, but I wouldn't have guessed Brody was six years younger than me. I mean, when I was a senior in high school, he was in sixth grade.

Gross.

But he's certainly not in sixth grade now, and I definitely want to cut off a piece of that deliciousness and savor the flavor.

I sigh as I try to shake that thought out of my head. We both finish our first drinks and he heads up to get us each another, though he returns with a Miller Lite for himself.

"No on the mule?" I ask.

"Had to try it, but I'll stick with Old Faithful." He holds up his bottle.

"Fair enough." We clink glasses again, but this time with no words exchanged.

"I have a donkey joke," he announces after he chugs half the bottle.

"Back to jokes?" I ask.

"The dirtier, the better."

"That's my motto, too. But not for jokes." I flash a smile and wink, and he laughs.

"God, I really like you, Zoey."

I lift a modest shoulder. "On with the joke."

"I have a rooster and you have a donkey. What do we have if your donkey eats my rooster's feet?"

"What?" I ask.

"Two feet of my cock in your ass."

I let out a bellow of laughter almost as loud as his was earlier. "Oh my God! A dick joke!" I clap my hands together. "I love it."

He shoots me this wicked smile that's so sinful it nearly ignites my panties. Instead it just ignites a fiery ache inside me.

I take a sip of my mule to cool the fire just as he says, "I'd like to hear you say that naked."

I choke on my mule. I think some liquid might spray out of my mouth and onto his black shirt as I cough to try to clear my throat.

"Jesus, I'm sorry," he says. "You okay?"

I nod and take another sip, which seems to help solve all my problems.

Once I stop coughing, he asks, "So I told you a little about me. Tell me a little about you."

I lift a shoulder. "Not much to tell. My claim to fame is being related to one of the biggest rock stars in the world. I have two half-sisters who my aunt raises. My mom died when I was in my twenties and my dad died last year."

"I'm sorry," he says.

"It's okay. My dad was in prison basically my whole life. My mom was sort of just a tragic figure. Everyone said she was happier once she was dead, and I sort of believed them."

"How'd they die?" he asks, completely shocking me. Normally when I tell people my parents are both dead, they make some awkward move to change the subject. Not Brody, though. He sits staring at me with those blazing eyes. Just seconds ago he told me the two feet of cock in my ass joke, and we switched gears to a totally different type of conversation so fast that my head's spinning.

"We never really talk about what happened with my mom," I muse. I hold my glass in both my palms, letting the ice freeze my skin until it's uncomfortable. I stare into my glass as I talk. "But she took some sleeping pills and just never woke up from them. To this day I don't really know whether it was intentional or not. She took four, twice the recommended dosage, and she'd been drinking. She was with her man of the week and he couldn't wake her up."

"God, that's awful. What about your dad?"

"He was in prison when he died from a brain tumor. It was aggressive and quick and I didn't get the chance to say goodbye." I realize as I talk that this is the most I've ever spoken to anyone about either of my parents. I'm not sure what he's doing to get me to open up, but it's clear that this is different with him. "Ethan and I were never close to him, but at least I tried a little toward the end. It was too late, though." I fight back the heat behind my eyes. I'm not a crier. I didn't cry at my mom's funeral, and I only shed a few tears for my father.

But maybe that's all they deserved. They never gave me anything, either.

He reaches across the table and takes one of my hands in his. His hands are big and strong drummer hands, the kind of skilled hands that grip sticks and tap out a beat, and I stare down at our connection for a few seconds. He squeezes my hand gently, mine ice cold from palming my glass and his warm—maybe a little like our personalities. From what I've learned of him so far, I see him as someone warm and kind, where I can be kind of a cold bitch.

It's only at that revelation that I lift my eyes from our hands. Those brown orbs are gazing across the table with so much tenderness that I almost feel like I could give into whatever this feeling is between us.

Almost.

Despite my habit of bad decisions, common sense wins out. I haven't even gone to a rehearsal for this tour yet. I had one dinner with the band and the dancers and I don't really even remember anyone's name because I was so overcome with fury.

But Brody's eyes blazing into mine make me think this might be something worth pursuing...just at a little slower pace. Something tells me it's smarter to let this one build, because if I jump into bed with him the way I've historically done with men, I have this distinct feeling that I'll live to regret it.

"Sorry for being a downer," I say, breaking the connection of our hands as I reach for my glass and take another sip. It's going down fast, and he only promised me two drinks.

Besides, I need to get to bed. Rehearsals start at seven in the morning, and it's probably close to one by now.

"It's your *life*," he says. "And you've clearly dealt with a lot in your thirty-three years. It's not a downer, Zo. It's you, and I'm honored that you let me in even just a little bit. Life isn't all dick jokes, you know?"

"But what a wonderful world it'd be if it was."

His lips lift in a smile, and I force my gaze away. I have to, because I don't know if I can control what I'll do next if I let myself get lost there.

CHAPTER 15
BRODY

"I need to get going. Early morning and all." She drains the final sip of her mule in a way that's both sexy and unrefined at the same time. She just really doesn't give any fucks, and it makes me feel like she's being herself with me.

I can't remember the last time I was with a woman who wasn't some plastic mold of what she thought I wanted.

And that was always fine by me. The only part of their inside I cared about was the part my dick saw.

But Zoey is different. I just can't put my finger on what it is that's so different.

She's got these cherry lips I can't seem to take my eyes off of. The bottom one is slightly fuller than the top. She doesn't wear any lipstick, yet they're this gorgeous beam of color across her face.

She tells dick jokes unapologetically. She drinks tequila and I get the distinct feeling she could drink me under the table. She could hang with me like she's one of the guys, yet she's got a body that's definitely all woman.

She's lived through tragedy, and I wonder what else she's gone through. It's hard to imagine why someone like her—someone funny and crude, gorgeous and smart—would still be single at thirty-three.

Women typically fall at my feet. It's just one of those departments I've never had any trouble in. But that's another area where she's just different. She's not falling at my feet.

She's hot and cold, interested then standoffish. She looks at me like she wants to tear my clothes off, but her words and actions seem to tell a different story.

She's a challenge.

That's all this is. I'm interested because I can't have her on top of the fact that Dax made her forbidden fruit. Plus she's older than me. Does thirty-three count as a cougar? Does six years even make the radar of an official age gap?

I don't care. I just know that every second I spend with her, I want her in my bed a little more.

She slams her glass on the table. I still have half a beer left in my bottle, but I've never been one to ditch a half a beer. I take the bottle and stand before offering my hand to help her off her own stool. She grazes her tits on my elbow, and their softness immediately has a contrasting effect on my dick.

Jesus, I want her.

My eyes fall to her chest for a beat, and then I shake it off. "What time do you need to be at the studio?"

"Seven."

"How are you getting there?"

She pauses like she hadn't really thought about it. "I guess I'll grab a cab or Uber it."

Not if I have anything to say about it. "You're part of our family now, so I'll make sure there's someone out front for you by six-thirty."

"You don't have to do that," she says softly.

"I know I don't." I say it gently, matching her volume and making sure she knows I'm taking care of her because I *want* to, not because I *have* to. "Let me walk you to your room."

"Thanks, Brody, but I can manage." She flashes me a smirk.

"I promise I have no plans to invite myself in," I lie. "I'm just trying to be a gentleman."

She narrows her eyes at me. "I'm not sure it suits you, but I don't know you well enough yet to make a final decision on that."

I laugh. "It doesn't suit me. You're absolutely right." I lean in closer to her, lowering my voice to a gritty husk that has always worked in the past for me. "If you were any other woman, I'd have you naked and begging for your second orgasm by now."

She doesn't back down the way I expect her to. Instead, she clears her throat and leans in a little closer to me, lowering her voice as well. "If you were any other man, you'd already be passed out from coming so hard on my tits."

I ignore the painful ache in my balls as I try to come up with something witty to say. I fail, so instead I say, "Let's pretend for the night that you're a different woman and I'm some other man, then."

She laughs. "Let's not."

Ouch. That's a clear rejection if I've ever heard one, but somehow it just makes me even more determined.

"Okay, Brody, this is really embarrassing and I wasn't going to say anything because I sort of figured you would've left by now, but since you haven't..." She trails off and leans in closer to me, and I think for a split second how this is it. She's giving in. She wants me as much as I want her.

And then she shatters that hope with her next words. "I totally forgot my room number, so I need to go to the front desk."

I can't help my laugh. "Then let me walk you there, at least," I say. I take my bottle off the table, grab her hand, and weave through the people in the bar toward the reception desk.

Zoey gives her identification to the clerk and asks for her room number. "Georgia?" I ask as I glance at the state on her license.

She nods. "I attended Georgia State and just stayed there with my best friend after graduation."

"You like it there?" I ask.

She shrugs. "As much as anywhere, I guess. I grew up in Chicago and I miss it there. Where are you from?"

"San Diego, born and raised."

"You like it there?" she tosses my own question back at me.

"It's my favorite place on Earth."

The clerk hands her an envelope with her keys and the numbers *2411* printed in black marker. "Here you go, ma'am," he says.

I memorize the numbers. I know she's only staying here one night, but you just never know.

"I'm on twenty-four, too," I say. I set my hand on the small of her back to guide her toward the elevators. A girl I slept with once told me that all women love being touched there, so it's become a habit. I let my fingertips graze a little lower on her back than I need to. I fight with everything inside not to reach down and squeeze that gorgeous ass.

I move my hand once we're near the elevators because it would be weird to stand here with my hand halfway between her back and her ass as we wait for the doors to open. When we step on, I hit the button for our floor and then the doors close, sealing us in alone together.

We're in a confined space for the next twenty-four floors, and I'm at war with myself once again. Dax is on one shoulder, telling me this is a bad idea.

But my dick is louder than him tonight, and he's fighting with every thick, solid inch to escape his confines and curl up into her for a few hours.

Just as I'm about to move in and trap her between the wall and my body before I slam my mouth over hers, she glances at me in the mirrored doors. "I've got one more dirty joke."

"Let's hear it."

"What's the difference between being hungry and being horny?"

I lift a shoulder, and the elevator doors glide open as she delivers the punchline.

She raises a brow, a habit I noticed earlier when she makes a joke. "Where you put the cucumber."

I laugh, but it dies quickly in the quiet hallway as I think about a horny Zoey with a cucumber. It's food for thought, anyway. Literally.

Her room is to the left and mine's to the right. We both pause under the sign directing us to our rooms.

"I had fun tonight," she says.

My eyes flick to her lips just as her tongue peeks out to wet the bottom one. She snags it between her teeth for a beat before she lets it go. "I did, too," I murmur.

"Well, goodnight. I'll see you tomorrow."

I nod once and force my eyes back to hers. "See you tomorrow."

She smiles and gives me an awkward little goodbye wave, and then she turns to head down the hallway toward her room. As I watch her walk away from me, I know I can't let her go without feeling those cherry lips moving beneath mine.

"Wait," I call. I amble toward her without really thinking this through. When I catch up to her, I grab her arm. "Zoey?"

When she turns toward me, her eyes are filled with the same thing I've been staring at all night.

Lust.

Passion.

Curiosity.

Hope.

Need.

Desire.

"Yeah?" she asks, her voice low and sultry.

"I just..." I don't know what to say. My mind goes blank as those blue pools full of emotion stare up at me. "Just one more thing."

Her brows furrow a little as she waits for me to spit it out. "What?"

"This." I can't waste this moment with a slow build or with a question. If I do, I run the risk of her stopping me. So I go for it.

My hand moves from her arm to her neck and I pull her in as my lips move down to hers.

I start it the way I always start a kiss. I brush my lips across her bottom lip first, that one that's been taunting me all night, before I tilt my head and move to her top lip. She's immediately responsive, which tells me this was the right decision. I kiss her bottom lip a little harder than a brush. When she kisses back, I feel her tongue at the seam of my lips, and I'm momentarily floored that she opened her mouth first.

She wants this, too.

I open my mouth, and our tongues meet somewhere in the middle. I wrap my arm around her waist and guide us toward the wall. Her ass hits it first with a soft thump, and then I press her into the wall the way I wanted to back in that elevator. It's just her full length against mine, and she gives in as she rests her palms on my shoulders, kissing me back like she needs this kiss to make it through the night. I refrain from thrusting my hips against her as I fight every instinct inside me. This is just a kiss. That's it. I had to kiss her before we parted ways tonight.

But even though I don't thrust, we're close enough that I know she feels how hard she's making me.

I give her some of my best tongue moves—the kind of moves that prove I know what I'm doing, the kind that will leave her begging for more and wanting my mouth on other parts of her body.

She plays along step for step, and it's hard to tell who's leading this kiss. It doesn't matter. We're in it together, and where I've almost always found myself the leader, I find this to be so much hotter. We're partners here, a team of kissers, and this whole kiss isn't satisfying some need I had like I thought it would. Instead, it's pushing me into the type of arousal that will leave me feeling a little blue, if you catch my drift.

This kiss isn't scratching the itch. It's heightening the itch into a burning rash.

Okay, so that's maybe not the best imagery when it comes to sex, but as I kiss her, I simply know that it isn't going to be enough to satisfy the sudden hunger I have for her.

She starts to slow the kiss, and we end with a few gentle brushes, coming full circle like how we started.

She looks up at me with those big, blue eyes, and I get this weird notion like we know each other on some deeper plane than we should after one night. She feels it, too. I see it all there in her eyes.

"I should, uh..." she says. Neither of us moves as our eyes burn into each other's.

I nod. "I know. I should, too."

"Okay," she says. She nods and breaks our eye contact, and then she moves her hands to my chest and pats me there, eyes widening for a beat before she backs up out of my orbit. "Goodnight, little drummer boy," she says.

My lips lift in a half smile. "Goodnight, back-up dancer girl."

CHAPTER 16

ZOEY

I touch my lips for the tenth time since I shut the door behind me less than five minutes ago.

My golden rule has always been that kissing tells me everything about a man, and that rule has never proven more true than kissing Brody. That single kiss told me more than our conversation over two drinks did.

He gave it one hundred percent, and from past experience that tells me that he's into me. He wasn't half-assing a kiss as a way to get me into bed. He sees more than one night with me, but I could also sense his confusion in that. He's not just a good kisser.

He's fucking incredible.

The way his tongue moved against mine and the erotic, slow sensuality of it told me he knows what the hell he's doing with his tongue.

As I stand here with my back against the door, silently cheering to myself after he chased me down to kiss me the way he did, I can't help but wonder what that magical tongue would feel like rubbing against my nipples or lapping at my clit.

I fan my face as heat creeps up my neck and into my hairline at the thought. I'm suddenly sweaty, like I need a cold shower.

God, that was hot.

He is hot.

Ridiculously hot.

Like I've never been kissed that way kind of hot. I have to remind myself that it was just one kiss after one night.

Yet it held the promise of way more than that.

I take that quick cold shower and slide into bed with thoughts of Brody pervading my mind.

It's doesn't stop when the light of morning dawns.

In fact, it didn't stop all night. I spent the entire night tossing and turning as I wished it was Brody beside me instead of the pillow I set beside me as a makeshift Brody. I could've had him here with me, but for some reason, I stopped it.

I'm not sure if that was smart or if it's just another in my string of bad decisions.

As promised, a car is waiting out front for me. The driver stands by his trunk with a little sign that says *Zoey Fuller* on it. I smile in spite of myself and hop in.

The first order of business is getting to know the other dancers and starting to learn the choreography. When I arrive at the studio, the driver hands me his card and tells me to let him know when I'm ready to head home. Apparently Brody took care of everything.

I find the two dancers I met just last night are already at the studio. I take a quick glance at the clock hanging on the wall as a rush of unease passes through me that they're here and waiting, but I'm actually four minutes early.

"Zoey!" one of them exclaims with way too much chipper glee for seven in the morning after I had two tequila drinks too late last night.

"Good morning," I say.

"Denise," the chipper one says as she reaches out for a hug. "Just in case you forgot."

I laugh but wait for the other one to say her name, too.

"Lauren," she says, hugging me as well.

"Of course I remember your names," I lie as I repeat *Denise and Lauren, Denise and Lauren* over and over in my head. They both have dark hair, though Denise has brown eyes and Lauren has blue.

"Jessa's just confirming our schedule for the rest of the week with the studio," Denise says, and I gather that Jessa must be the choreographer whose name I forgot the second she said it last night. "She'll be right back. We're so excited to have you with us on this tour!"

I wonder for a minute when we'll be practicing with the band—something I might have learned last night if I'd been paying attention. Instead of paying attention, though, I was fighting the temptation of Brody and simultaneously trying to fight off the anger at my brother.

My brother.

Of course.

He must be the reason Denise is kissing my ass so hard already. He's the reason women who've never met me before *always* kiss my ass.

"I'm happy to be here," I say, and I realize for the first time since this whole whirlwind began that I actually *am* happy to be here.

I'm doing something with a talent I've had since I was a little girl. I'm gainfully employed again. I'm going to be on television, which is my ultimate goal. Maybe I'll even get a chance to redeem myself for the dick joke, though it appears that *some* people actually enjoy crude humor.

His dark eyes flash through my mind, but I push them out as soon as I see them. I need to focus, and thinking of Brody when I'm supposed to be learning choreography for a two hour performance seems counterproductive.

"Great, she's here. Let's get started," Jessa says, rushing into the room and clapping her hands together as her blonde hair flies around her shoulders like it can't quite keep up with her quick pace. She's all business, unlike the other two, but I can't really see myself becoming close with any of these three. It's unfortunate that I'm already judging them and placing a wall between us, but the only girl who gets me is back in Atlanta.

I suddenly miss Kristen and home and even Sawyer with a deep ache. It hasn't even been twenty-four hours since I left, but so much is already different. I'm bouncing between Ethan's house and a hotel. I'm about to live on the road for two months in a tour bus I'll share with these three ladies, so I suppose it's time to suck it up and make some friends. It might be the only way I'll get through the next two months with any sanity.

But if they knew I kissed the drummer last night, how would they react?

Jessa focuses on directing me while Denise and Lauren practice what they already know like the back of their hands. It doesn't take me long to pick up the routines. A lot of it is instinctual when I hear the music, and some of it is just moving in a way to pump up the audience.

Our first break comes a little after ten, and I've already got the opening sequence and the first four songs down. The set is a total of eighteen songs, so we have a long way to go, but I feel good about what we've accomplished in a short time. It's largely freestyle, but the choreographed parts combine an easy mix of hip hop with contemporary and a little bit of pole dancing thrown in. For someone who's been dancing her entire life, it's second nature.

I check my phone, and I have a few new texts. One's from Kristen asking how things are going. Another is from Ethan letting me know he's at the Ashmark office today if I need anything. And the final one is from a number I don't recognize. It was just sent a few minutes ago.

Unknown Number: *What's the difference between eggs and me?*

I smile as I *think* I know who it is, but I play it safe just in case I'm wrong.

Me: *What?*

Unknown Number: *Eggs get laid.*

I laugh out loud, garnering a curious glance from Denise. "Sorry," I murmur. I cover my mouth.

Me: *Who is this?*

Unknown Number: *The guy who kissed you in a hallway last night.*

Me: *Steve?*

Unknown Number: *Ha. Funny.*

Me: *Joe?*

Unknown Number: *I'm rolling my eyes.*

Me: *Oh right, Joe got laid.*

Unknown Number: *You're hilarious, back-up dancer girl.*

Me: *Thanks, little drummer boy.*

Unknown Number: *I have to get to practice but wanted to say good morning and let you know I procured your phone number.*

Me: *I can see that. How'd you manage that?*

Unknown Number: *In the most illegalest of ways.*

Me: *I don't think illegalest is a word.*

Unknown Number: *Is now, and to answer your question, I got it from the tour book.*

Me: *Wow, brains like those and a mouth that can kiss like yours can? Lethal combination.*

Unknown Number: *I can't wait to show you just how lethal, babe.*

I giggle at my phone, and when I glance up, I find six eyes trained on me. "What?"

"Just an FYI, new boyfriends aren't great for the road," Jessa says as if she's speaking from experience.

"What do you mean?" I ask.

"I just mean the only time I've ever seen someone all moony-eyed like you are was at the start of a relationship. It's hard to leave for two months when you're just starting something up with someone, especially at the last-minute like you joined us," she says.

"It's not a new boyfriend," I say.

"Sure," she says, her voice laden with sarcasm. I notice that the other two girls are quiet during this exchange, and I can't help but wonder whether they're the doormats Jessa likes to stomp all over. I realize I'm judging Jessa after I judged the other two, and I get that it's her job to take charge...but her little condescending speech about a new boyfriend set me on edge a little. She doesn't know me apart from the fact that I'm Ethan Fuller's sister.

And quite frankly, I'm not really used to women talking to me like that.

People tend to treat me like royalty because they think they can get some benefits out of me—whether it's a slice of my brother's money, front row tickets, or some small claim to fame of their own that they know the sister of someone who's part of such a worldwide phenomenon.

The truth of the matter is that I distanced myself from my brother's fame a long time ago. The only time I ever experience it is when we're together. Otherwise I just live a normal life in Atlanta with the occasional extra luxury or deposit into my bank account from my big brother. But those are things he offers to me, things I'd never dream of taking advantage of, let alone of offering to someone else.

Part of me admires Jessa's directness, but the other part of me hypocritically sort of enjoys the fawning I typically get because of Ethan.

"It doesn't matter," I say. "I'm here to dance."

"Are you sure?" she asks. "Because you sort of seemed unsure last night, and I've spent the last three hours determining that you can, in fact, do this, and I don't want to lose you to something silly like a boy who's making you giggle over text messages."

"I'm here to dance," I repeat through gritted teeth this time, though her warning doesn't go unnoticed.

Jessa nods once. "Then let's get back to it."

We have a quick lunch break before we hop right back in. I don't make the mistake of checking my phone in front of these women again, though I'm burning with curiosity as to when I might get the chance to see him again.

We work until a little after five—a ten-hour day in all—and I've mastered about half the setlist by the end of the day plus watched Denise and Lauren go over the second half a few times. I text the driver from this morning then make a playlist with all the songs we'll be dancing to so I can practice when I get back to Ethan's—or the hotel...I still haven't decided where I should stay tonight, but I feel great about my progress. One more day like today and I'm sure I'll easily pick up the rest.

"I'll see you ladies tonight at the bar at the hotel," Jessa says. "I have a few things to finish here, but you're free to go."

I glance up with a furrowed brow. I must've missed the memo. I clear my throat. "What?" I ask

Jessa rolls her eyes. "Didn't you read the email Kylie sent last night?" she asks.

"I'm sorry," I say as I shake my head. "I didn't. But I promise it won't happen again." I use the most genuine tone I can possibly muster.

She raises a brow. "It better not, Zoey. We've got a standing seven o'clock happy hour meeting each night with MFB's managers in the private room beside the bar at the Sheraton starting tonight. It's informal and will give us a chance to check in and make sure everything is on track."

In the whirlwind of storming out of my brother's place last night, learning dance all day, and fighting off all thoughts of a certain sexy drummer who really knows how to kiss a woman, I guess I missed the email.

But my heart races a little at the thought of meeting with MFB's managers tonight. That means there's a chance I'll see Brody. I shake off the thought. I don't like how he keeps creeping into my brain. "I will be there."

Jessa raises a brow but doesn't say anything, and I get the distinct impression that she doesn't like me.

The feeling's most definitely mutual.

My driver is waiting out front, and I slide into the backseat. I sort of wonder if I'm supposed to ride with Denise and Lauren back to the hotel. Maybe I should have asked how they were getting back. It might give me the opportunity to sort of feel them out about Jessa.

But we have two whole months for that.

I text my brother on the way back to the hotel after reading the email Kylie sent with the agenda.

Me: *I'm sorry again I was a bitch last night. I had a great session today learning the routine and I'm excited for this. Nothing personal, but is it okay if I stay at the Sheraton? The other dancers will be there and it'll give me a chance to get to know them.*

His reply comes as we're stuck in some traffic on the way to the hotel.

Ethan: *That's fine. No hard feelings. You know I love you and I never meant to upset you.*

Me: *I know. You're the one person I can always count on.*

Ethan: *Always, Zo. Enjoy getting to know the dancers. Let's make sure you get to see your nephew before bus call.*

Me: *Deal. I've got practice every day from seven to five and then a meeting at seven, but I should be able to come to your place for a late dinner one night.*

Ethan: *Let me know what night. I've got a few things scheduled this week but would love to see you.*

I feel a twinge of guilt that I'm not staying with him, but he's not the reason I'm here.

If I'm being totally honest, though, the other dancers aren't the reason I want to stay at the hotel.

I refuse to admit the real reason, though. Not even to myself.

CHAPTER 17

BRODY

"I need to head down for the dancer meeting," Kylie says from her spot tangled in Dax's arms on the couch.

I'm standing by the window staring out, lost in thought about a hundred different things after a quick shower. I'm exhausted from drumming for the better part of eight hours today in between adjustments and reworking shit for the show, but my ears perk up at the mention of the dancers.

"We just got here," Dax whines.

I roll my eyes. Whining is not becoming on him.

"Come with me, then," Kylie says. "We're just doing a quick happy hour check-in with the ladies and Mitch. One drink, a little business, and then we can go grab dinner."

"Let's all go," I suggest.

Kylie narrows her eyes at me. "So you can spend more time flirting with Zoey?"

"It's not *flirting*."

She raises a brow. "Then what is it?"

I shrug. "Seducing," I mutter.

"Oh, that's so much better." She rolls her eyes, and Dax remains quiet. I confided in him during a practice break today that I kissed her. He obviously hasn't told Kylie, a fact I'm exceedingly grateful for, but he did give me a stern talking-to of his own at my confession. "Hands off the dancers, Brody."

"I don't need my hands for what I want to do to her."

Dax laughs, Kylie smacks him in the arm, and I'm a little surprised I actually voiced that thought aloud.

"In all seriousness, Kylie, the dancers will be on the stage right in front of me. It's important for us to be informed of what's going on," I say, coming up with a feeble excuse. "Besides, then we can all go to dinner."

"Now *that* is a good point," Dax says, rubbing his stomach. "I could really go for some pancakes."

I roll my eyes. This guy and his pancakes.

"Fine," Kylie says. She points at me and glares. "But no funny business."

"Nothing funny about what I want to do to her," I mutter, and just like seconds earlier, Dax laughs and Kylie smacks him in the arm. I'm not as surprised about my comment this time, though.

We gather Rascal, Adam, and Kane, and the six of us head down to the hotel bar. Kylie leads us into the private room beside the bar. The choreographer and the two dancers who aren't Zoey are already there, and I'm surprised at the level of disappointment I feel that she isn't here yet. It's a stronger feeling than I expect, and it hits me down low in my guts.

The choreographer steps over toward me. "I'm so glad you made it," she says. Her voice is all low and sultry and I feel bad that I don't remember her name.

Blondes are typically my type, and the choreographer would normally meet all the prerequisites for landing in my bed...but she doesn't hold a candle to Zoey.

"Glad to be here," I say, trying to give off the vibe that I'm not interested. I'm already working on bedding one of the dancers—going for two and creating strife where there doesn't need to be any before the tour has even started just seems like a bad idea.

A waitress takes our orders, and she seems slightly overwhelmed that there are so many of us here when she was expecting six people. "I'd love a glass of chardonnay," the choreographer says to the waitress. Chardonnay seems like an ordinary drink choice from someone unwilling to step out of her comfort zone. There's nothing exciting about chardonnay—in contrast to, let's say, a Mexican mule.

Just as I finish saying the words, "Miller Lite," Zoey walks into the room.

It's like a goddamn breath of fresh air.

My breath catches in my throat when our eyes meet.

How could it really be just yesterday that I met her when I feel like I've known her my whole life?

The choreographer says something beside me, but I don't bother to comprehend what it is. I don't even excuse myself as I beeline toward the girl I haven't stopped thinking about since I first spotted her less than twenty-four hours ago. Our eyes never leave each other's, and I can't help but wonder whether the attraction between the two of us is as palpable to everyone else in the room as it feels like it is to me.

"Hey," I say in what is most definitely not the smoothest moment of my life.

I can't help it. She somehow short-circuits my brain.

This is fucking ridiculous. This isn't me, this guy who can't stop thinking about a woman he hasn't even banged yet. I don't like how just seeing her walk into the room makes my chest tighten. I don't like how I can't seem to tune her out the way I do everything else.

I want my life to go back how it was before—when I would've bedded the choreographer without a second thought and bid her goodbye in the morning without worrying about it.

I don't want this and I didn't ask for it.

"Hi," she says, ducking her head with a small smile.

"How was practice?" I ask.

Her eyes light up as she starts talking about a topic she's clearly passionate about. "Really great. I caught on fast, and with another day or two like today, I think I'll be ready to take the stage."

I raise both brows, impressed with her talent. "That's amazing, Zo."

She lifts a shoulder like it's no big deal when it is. I didn't peg her as the modest type. "The routines are really simple." She pauses and eyes the choreographer as she sidles up next to me. I hadn't noticed. "Hey, Jessa."

Jessa. Now that I hear her name again, I remember it.

"Really simple?" she repeats Zoey's words. "They had to be since our dancer bailed and we didn't know what we'd be getting with *you.*"

Her voice is snide, and I immediately jump to Zoey's defense. I wrinkle my brows at Jessa. "Don't simplify for her," I say, nodding at Zoey. "She's a pro and can handle whatever you throw at her."

My words shut Jessa up. She spins on her heel and makes her way toward Kylie, but not before she saves a really special glare for Zoey.

"You didn't have to jump in like that," Zoey says quietly.

"I know I didn't." We're both quiet for an awkward beat. To break the tension, I ask, "Why is bunny sex so quiet?"

She fights a smile as she lifts a shoulder.

I lean in, catch a whiff of her citrus scent, and whisper, "Because they have cotton balls."

She giggles, and then the waitress stops by, interrupting our moment to take Zoey's drink order. Kylie calls for all our attention, and the *meeting* portion of this meeting begins.

We all settle into seats around a large conference table big enough to accommodate the eleven of us and then some. I'm between Dax and Adam again, which is a real shame. I'd like to breathe in Zoey's citrus a little longer. The bonus, though, is that she's seated directly across the table from me.

I focus on Kylie, who checks in with Jessa first. As Jessa recaps the day of rehearsals, I do my best to avoid looking at Zoey. The last thing I want to do is draw attention to the fact that all I can think about is sliding my dick into her. She knows I'm interested, and I get the distinct feeling that it's mutual.

Mitch talks a little about the stage set up and the practice schedule for the rest of the week. The dancers will have one more day in their studio to practice before they join us at our practice facility.

And I can't wait to watch Zoey move her ass right in front of me.

I glance over at her and find her eyes zeroed in on me. I don't lift my lips in a smile, and neither does she. It's just a single beat of an unadulterated, lust-filled lock of our eyes.

I break the gaze first.

I have to, but it doesn't mean I have to like it.

As Kylie wraps up the meeting, I realize that if we're going to do this, we need to keep it quiet. It wouldn't be right for the other dancers to think she's getting special treatment—especially not if she's already insecure that she got the gig because of her brother.

I won't even tell Dax since he's already made it clear he disapproves. I haven't worked out the logistics of that quite yet considering we'll be traveling in close quarters together, but I'll figure it out. Shit, *figuring it out* and keeping this secret might be exactly the sort of excitement I crave.

I need to get her alone. I need to talk to her, to see if she's just flirty by nature or if there could be something more there.

But that kiss last night...that told me there could be something more there.

I'm sandwiched between two of my best friends who will see if I try to shoot her a text. I fake an incoming text by grabbing my phone off the table. I excuse myself to the hallway, where I draft a quick text to her.

Me: *Go to dinner with me. I need to talk to you.*

I head back into the room and watch as she glances down at her phone. She looks up at me and shakes her head a little. I raise both brows. I'm not sure if she's declining or if she's inwardly laughing at my bold move.

The meeting ends, and she pulls her phone out.

"There's a little café around the corner. That sound good to everyone?" Dax asks the rest of MFB. We all look over at him. Shit. I forgot I said I'd do dinner with the guys.

They all nod their consent and start to head toward the door, but I hang back a second. Somewhere in the time it took for me to look at Dax and try to come up with some reason as to why I can't go to dinner with the rest of my band, she slipped out of the room.

My phone buzzes, and I glance at the screen.

Zoey: *I don't think it's a good idea. I'm sorry.*

I stare at her words on my screen. It's not a good idea? Why the fuck not?

"You coming, dude?" Rascal yells at me from the doorway as I stand frozen by a text message.

I shove my phone in my pocket along with my feelings on the whole thing then follow my friends out to dinner.

My quick temper takes over.

Fuck these stupid ass feelings. Fuck this idea that I can change because of some chick.

After dinner, I'm getting laid.

CHAPTER 18

ZOEY

As I listen to Denise and Lauren dish about their torrid love lives over salad, I can't help but think I just made a really big mistake.

But as I sat in that meeting tonight, I realized how essential it is to ignore my feelings going forward. I like Brody. He's hot. But there's too many strikes against him.

And, maybe most importantly, Jessa couldn't have made it more clear that she's interested in him.

She's sort of like my boss on this tour, and the last thing I need is the choreographer pissed at me because I hooked up with the drummer before she did. When he ditched her to talk to me, the look on her face was absolutely priceless.

But as much as I allowed myself to enjoy it for a split second, it was just one more sign that giving in to the lust I'm feeling for him is a bad idea.

Besides, Denise asked me if I wanted to do dinner with her and Lauren so we could get to know each other a little better, and I'd already accepted her invitation. It makes sense to befriend the girls I'll be working closely with on this tour. We'll move better together on stage if we understand one another, and so I'm half-listening to Lauren talk about her ex-boyfriend who apparently had a hot brother that she just couldn't resist taking a bite of for herself.

"Speaking of brothers, I need all the dirt on yours," Denise says just as I take the last bite of my salad.

"He's happily married with an adorable baby boy," I say, gushing over my brother's happiness in part because I'm thrilled for him and in part to hold these chicks at bay. "What else do you want to know?"

"I don't know," Denise says. "What's he *like*?"

I shrug. "Do you have a brother?" I ask.

She nods. "Yeah. Two, actually, and both younger than me."

"Are they annoying and gross boys?" I pick up my water glass as I prepare to deliver the punchline.

"Yep. They burp the alphabet *still* at nineteen and twenty-one, they leave a mess in the bathroom—especially in the sink when they shave and there's these little hairs everywhere. They tell disgusting jokes about poop." She rolls her eyes. "Typical boys."

I raise a brow. "Kinda like that."

Denise's jaw drops and Lauren laughs.

"Did you really not see where I was going with that?" I ask Denise.

She shakes her head. "I figured someone like him was...I don't know. More refined?"

I bark out a loud laugh. "Hardly. He's probably grosser than your brothers."

"No..." Denise says, shaking her head. "No way. He's the gorgeous drummer of an amazing band."

I nod. "And he still burps the alphabet."

Lauren giggles. "Hey, speaking of gorgeous drummers, what do y'all think of Brody?"

My hackles immediately rise, but I force the defensiveness I feel away. I have no hold over him—and probably even less so now that I wrote that rejection text.

"So damn hot," Denise says.

"Super hot," I agree. "Did you guys see how Jessa was all over him? I think she might be into him."

Both their faces fall, which just tells me I made the right decision. "She is?" Denise asks.

I shrug. "She seemed like it."

"Damn. I don't want to do anything to piss her off," Lauren says.

I shake my head more to throw them off the scent than anything else, but all I can think is that it's not like either of these two had a shot with him for more than a night anyway.

I don't know about Jessa. He did brush her off when he spotted me, but that doesn't mean he wouldn't toss a shot at her if she presented the opportunity. I don't like how that makes me feel, but I'm sticking by my decision.

"Do you wanna hit a club tonight?" Denise asks.

Dancing at a club after dancing all day sort of makes me think of how chefs probably don't want to cook when they get home and gynecologists probably don't want to stick their faces in more vaginas. I spent the better part of ten hours dancing today, and dancing more at a club tonight when we have to be back for practice early in the morning just feels like a bad idea.

But in an effort to avoid drawing additional attention to myself, I wait for Lauren to answer first. I'll force myself to be on board if she is.

"Yes!" she exclaims with glee, clapping her hands together like a child.

I guess my fate is decided.

Denise is from Los Angeles, so she knows the hot spots. "West Hollywood is where it's at," she tells us, and the three of us grab an Uber toward Tango.

I'm midway through my first Mexican mule and moving my hips to the beat absentmindedly while Denise and Lauren dance with me when a group of guys saunters toward us. They've got this swagger in their step that tells me they've been drinking, and my first thought is that none of them even come close to Brody in the looks department.

I shake him out of my head.

I wonder how old these three guys are. Are they twenty-seven going on twenty-eight like Brody? Are they closer to my age?

Does it matter?

I'm not going home with them in the exact same way I'm not going home with Brody.

Home. The word percolates in my mind like the slow drip of a coffee maker. *Home.*

I don't even really have a *home* right now. My bedroom in Atlanta that I rented from Sawyer? I guess that's home, but I already wrote returning to that place off when I accepted this job. Ethan's house? Maybe. The hotel where I'm currently crashing a room on Ashmark's dime? It's not home, but it's working for now.

And it's closer to Brody.

"I'm Julian," one of the guys says to me.

"Is that your pick-up line?" I ask. My voice is maybe a tad snider than it should be.

He shakes his head. "Should I start with a line instead of my name?"

"The proper way to start is by offering to buy me a drink." I hold up my glass. "This is still my first, and if you've got *any* shot, you need to get me drunker than one drink."

He raises both brows and huffs out a surprised laugh. "You're mean."

"No," I say sweetly. "I'm Zoey, and I drink Mexican mules." I refrain from adding *now skedaddle along to the bar* to the end of my proclamation.

"I'm Julian, and I prefer a dry scotch."

"My grandfather did, too." I'm really being bitchy here, but I can't seem to stop myself. I don't want to fight off Julian. I just want to go home.

"How old are you, Julian?" I ask.

"Twenty-six."

I nod. He's just a kid.

A kid that's only a year younger than the man I can't stop thinking about.

"You should probably run along and find someone closer to your age, sweetie pie."

He shoots me a glare but doesn't bother to reply before he jets off to find his next victim. Denise and Lauren are both giving Julian's friends their attention, so now I'm just the woman standing by herself in the middle of the dance floor.

I stalk over to the bar, where I fend off the attention of yet another guy who isn't nearly as hot as Brody.

And another, and another.

By the time I've finished my second drink, I'm ready to leave. Denise and Lauren are cozy with their new friends as they grind to the latest Bruno Mars hit. I let Denise know I'm out, and then I grab my own Uber and head back to the hotel.

My head pounds and my ears buzz a little on the ride back from the club. The music was too loud and I didn't have enough to drink to tune it out.

The closer we get to the Sheraton, the more I wonder what Brody ended up doing tonight. It looked like the guys in MFB were headed to dinner, and a little part of me twinges with anxiety that my rejection might've sent him into someone else's arms.

It doesn't matter if it did.

That's the way it should be, and I shouldn't care.

So why do I?

I open my phone and start to type out a text message.

I'm sorry I was rude earlier.

Backspace, backspace, backspace.

I didn't mean to...

Backspace, backspace, backspace.

I like you and I want you to kiss me again.

I stare at the words for a long time before I force myself to click the backspace button.

I click my phone off and stare out the window as I try to shake off the night I just had. A week ago, I might've given in to one of the men who hit on me tonight. At the very least, I might've danced with him or gotten drunk with him or allowed a kiss and first base on the dance floor.

So why didn't I tonight?

I can act like the answer to that isn't *Brody*, but he's still there, pervading my thoughts and confusing my heart.

Different sources of light illuminate the dark night, and I put my focus on that instead. Billboards and streetlights and buildings glow against palm trees in a way that's unique to this city.

There's something magical about Los Angeles. I can't put my finger on what it is, exactly, but there's something in the atmosphere that has always made me feel like anything and everything is possible. It's inspiring to drive down the same streets where so many of the actors and actresses I love and admire have also traveled. I'm following in their footsteps—literally—and I feel like it can happen for me, too. Success is just one lucky break away, and as we pull into the hotel, my heart holds all the hope that this tour is my lucky break.

I step out of the car and toward the elevator. I press the button for twenty-four and stare motionless at my reflection in the mirror on the way up. I'm tired and kind of emotionally drained. I want to go to bed and shut off my traitorous thoughts a while.

When I turn off the elevator, I can't help my glance in the other direction. I know Brody's staying on this floor, too, but I don't know which room. I just know he's to the right and I'm to the left.

I wonder if he's here. If he's alone. If he's thinking of me.

When I turn to the left, I see someone down the hall sitting on the floor and leaning against a door.

My heart beats wildly because even though I can't make out who it is from this distance, my gut tells me who it is.

One foot moves in front of the other until I get close enough to confirm my theory.

It's Brody.

And he's leaning against my door.

CHAPTER 19

BRODY

"What are you doing here?" she asks. Her voice has a calming effect on the thunderstorm inside my chest.

"I don't really know." I don't move from my spot against her door.

"Are you drunk?"

I lift one shoulder. "Maybe a little."

She turns to lean against her door then slides down until she's sitting beside me, the two of us leaning on the door and talking in a hallway.

"Aren't you going to invite me in?" I ask.

"I don't think it's a very good idea, Brody."

As the single word I'm known by rolls off her tongue, I can't help but imagine her saying it again—but this time, breathless and naked.

"Why are you so convinced of that, *Zoey*?" I ask, enunciating her name.

She stares straight ahead as I sneak a peek at her. She's as confused about whatever feelings seem to cross between the two of us as I am.

"I think Jessa's into you." She pauses like she wants to add something else, but then she shakes her head a little and says, "Plus, you're a *drummer*. I know what drummers do."

I want to laugh at that, but I sense the true vulnerability in her tone. This isn't about me being a drummer and it isn't about Jessa.

It's about being scared to get into something with someone you shouldn't.

I know the feeling well.

I lean a little closer to her, close enough that I can smell her citrus scent even through the haze of tequila.

Yeah, I drank tequila tonight. Something came over me when I ordered my drink at dinner, and the words "Mexican mule" spilled out of my mouth before I could stop them.

The first one's gross, the second one is all right, the third one is pretty good, and the tequila has burned all taste buds by the fourth.

For a guy who sticks to Miller Lite, four tequila drinks in under two hours was enough to make me a little drunk—not sloppy, certainly not disgusting, but enough to realize there was no one in the lobby bar tonight that I wanted as much as I want Zoey.

If I hadn't been a little drunk, I wouldn't be sitting outside her door.

If I hadn't had tequila and settled on my standard beer, I'd have done what I always do. I'd have found a woman to bring back to my room only to kick her out in the morning.

That was my plan.

But the second my mouth formed the words *Mexican mule*, it was over.

I keep fighting myself on this, and I'm starting to wonder *why*. Sure, I have those deep-rooted daddy issues—is it still called daddy issues for a guy? Father issues. I have father issues. I don't want to commit to a woman only to find myself bored of her. I don't want to cure that boredom by being unfaithful. I realize we're not the same person, but I have this fear that he gave me that gene anyway.

I push those thoughts away and brush my lips against her neck. Her skin is warm and sweet, and it's like the first hit of some drug I know I'll never get enough of. "Let me show you just how much I'm not like all the other drummers."

She freezes for a beat, but then she turns toward me. Her eyes are a little glassy, like maybe she had a Mexican mule or two of her own tonight. I lift my face toward hers and brush her lips with mine.

She gives in for a few beautiful seconds of lip on lip, and then she pulls away. She leans her head back on the door with a small thud and blows out a deep breath, and then she stands. She pulls her key out of her purse and goes to open the door.

I'm still leaning on it, and I fall backward into her room when she opens it.

She giggles. "Just *a little* drunk?" she asks.

I recover nicely as I stand. "I did it on purpose. Figured it was the only way you'd let me in."

"You could've just asked to come in," she says. The door clicks shut behind me.

"And have you reject me again?" I shake my head.

"How do you know I would've said no?" She narrows her eyes at me.

The answer to that is pretty simple. "You have yet to say yes to me."

She tilts her head, conceding as she studies me. "So now what? You made your way in. I haven't kicked you out...yet."

I laugh. "Yet."

She lifts a shoulder. "You wanted to talk, right? So talk."

This girl causes a whirlwind of conflicting emotions in my chest, and I both love and hate it. I hate how she puts me on the spot and calls me out, but at the same time...I love it. In my experience, women never do that. They're pliable, they do what I say without asking questions, and then they leave. Maybe they're a little starstruck because they watched me up on that stage hammering out the beat to MFB's tracks, or maybe it's the practiced way my eyes fall onto them that shuts them the fuck up and leaves them begging for my cock every time.

Whatever the case, my charms don't work on Zoey.

She isn't starstruck because for the last decade, her brother and his best friends have skyrocketed to the top of this profession. I'm not even close to their radar, and if that's what she's used to, I probably don't deserve for her to even give me a second glance.

And it's clear that a single gaze in her direction with my lust-filled eyes isn't going to work. It hasn't worked so far and I've been shooting her some of my best work.

I wander over toward her window and look out at the buildings surrounding us. Her view looks out at an office building with a bank's name lighting up the marquee at the top. It's mostly dark, but a few lights are on here and there. On one floor, a cleaning crew walks around with backpack vacuums. On another, someone's emptying the trash bins. On another, someone's working late into the night to try to get ahead or prove himself or avoid going home to his wife.

And here I stand, looking over at them as I try to gather the storm of emotions pouring through me into something I can articulate to her. It was easier when I thought we'd have dinner as our excuse. We could chat about food, get to know one another better, and maybe I could kiss her again.

But this is different. Here, the focus is solely on conversation and why I'm here—what I needed to talk to her about.

Before I have a chance to really think through what I want to say, the question that's been on my mind since we were at the dancer's meeting by the bar earlier ejaculates right out of my mouth. "Is there something between us or am I just really fucking crazy?"

She's quiet a long time. I keep my gaze focused out the window, surprised at how vulnerable I feel as I wait for her to speak. I watch her reflection in the glass as she moves across the room toward me, and then she's standing beside me. She looks out at the same building I've been studying.

"Maybe a little of both," she finally says.

I look over at her and laugh, but when she turns toward me, I see how gravely serious she is. I open my mouth to say something, but she speaks first.

"But both apply to me, too."

Her admission is so momentarily surprising that I take a step back like she gut punched me. She sort of did by admitting that there's something between us and we're both a little crazy.

"Then why do you keep pushing me away?" I ask, suddenly grateful for the tequila that's giving me the courage to ask the questions I need the answers to.

"I just got this job, Brody. I want to prove that I'm here because I can dance, not because of my brother and not because I hooked up with the drummer before we even hit the road." Her eyes tell me she's letting her guard down and that she's terrified of it. That single look hits me square in the chest.

"So what are we supposed to do, then?" I ask.

She shrugs. "I don't know. Take it slow? Get on the road and get to know one another? Become friends and see what happens from there?"

I take a step toward her to close the gap separating us, and then I reach for her hip. I pull her a little closer to me, and she allows it. I lean down and nuzzle her neck for a second, and I'm rewarded with a tiny moan out of her. I move my lips closer to her ear and whisper, "I can't be your friend when all I can think about is kissing you again."

"Then kiss me," she says, her voice a soft but needy groan.

I chuckle with my lips against her neck. "What happened to all that *take it slow* talk?"

She doesn't answer. Instead, she takes my face between her palms, petting my scruff softly as her eyes burn into mine for a beat. She's crazed with lust, and I am, too, but her words make me think maybe she's right.

She's different.

She's not like the women who I bed for one night and ditch the next morning.

Dax told me once he met Kylie, it was over for him. No other woman could compare despite his best efforts to try to get her out of his head.

Part of me wants to skip the burden of fighting what's between us just to get to the good part...but the other part of me wants to cherish every aching moment so the reward is all the more gratifying in the end.

Something tells me she'll be worth it.

She closes her eyes and presses her lips softly to mine. Her warm hands on my face and her sweet lips against mine are heaven on Earth, and my mind goes immediately to sex. If this small ounce of intimacy with her has this sort of effect on me, what would sex be like?

And what would it be like further down the road after we've both developed real feelings for each other, not just an instant attraction?

It's something I want to know.

I bring my other hand to her other hip and grip her tightly for a beat. I kiss her back, but neither of us opens our mouths. We don't deepen this one, we just stand holding one another, and somehow it's more erotic than when a woman shoves her tongue down my throat or chokes when my cock hits the gag reflex at the back of her throat.

That's not what this kiss is about.

This one's about connecting with another person. It's about exploring feelings that might turn into something real. It's about anxiety and fear for the future that we can share and face together.

Together. I repeat the word in my mind.

Like a teammate.

I stop the kiss first.

Me.

I'm as shocked as she is when I pull away.

"I should go," I say, my dick fighting for escape from my pants and my balls aching for her.

She masks her disappointment, but not before I see a quick flash of it cross her face. Her hands drop from my face, and the sense of loss I feel is overwhelming.

"Why?" she whispers.

"Because you're right. We need to take this slow. I need to prove to you that I'm worth it, and if I stand here and kiss you another second, I'll have you naked and on your back so fast you won't know what hit you. That's not what I want for us, Zo. I want this to be different."

Understanding followed by anxiety flashes through her eyes. "So what does that mean?"

"It means I'm not going down to the bar to find some random girl to bring to my bed. It means I'll go to my room alone and fall asleep thinking of your lips against mine. I'm not sure what else it means, but I know that much."

She turns from me to look out the window again. She fidgets for a beat before she asks, "Can we keep whatever we're starting just between the two of us for now?"

I nod, grateful she brought it up first. "I think that's probably a good idea. Dax already warned me off you."

She looks surprised. "He did? Why?"

I shrug and go for honesty. "He doesn't want to cause any bad blood between us and Vail."

"Oh," she says. "Well, just for the record, what happens between us is between *us*. It has nothing to do with my brother or his band." Her voice is a little colder than it was a minute ago, and I'm not sure how to get back the ground we broke through tonight.

I work hard to keep the desperation out of my voice. "Dax is just worried I'll hurt you. My track record with women hasn't exactly proven I won't." Her eyes whip up to meet mine, and I worry for a minute I've scared her off. I reach for her again and pull her close by her hips like we were just a minute ago. My eyes burn down into hers as I try to show her all the sincerity I feel in my words. "I won't hurt you, Zoey. I promise."

"You can't promise something like that when you don't even know me."

I nod. "Okay. Fair enough. How about this, then? I promise to get to know you. I promise to tell you dirty jokes. I promise to fall asleep tonight thinking about your palm on my cheek. I promise this won't be a one-night stand."

"I can live with that." Her hand finds my scruff again at my promise, and I rest my hand over hers.

"What did the dirty frog say?" I ask.

Her lips tip up in a small smile. "What?"

"Rubbit."

She giggles, and then she drops her hand from my face. I don't let go, though, and I twist my hand around and lace my fingers through hers. I walk toward the door with her beside me.

"Good chat," I say once I reach the door.

She nods. "Really good."

I lean in and press one more soft kiss to her lips, and then I open the door. "Goodnight, Zoey."

"Night, Brody," she says.

I stare at her door for a second after it latches shut, lost in thought about my first good, adult decision maybe ever when it comes to a woman. I'm allowing something real to start with her, and I feel this unfamiliar sense of peace about what lies ahead.

I finally turn to walk down the hallway back toward my room. As soon as I turn, though, I'm met with a familiar face.

It's the choreographer.

She's standing a few feet down the hall, looking back and forth between me and the door. The look on her face tells me she thinks she knows something, and that sense of peace that just washed over me slips from my grasp as quickly as it came.

CHAPTER 20

ZOEY

"No, no, no," Jessa says, shaking her head. "Dammit, Zoey. Like this." She models as she barks at me. "Circle the hips, shoulders up, and glide."

That's what I fucking did, but we're six hours into today's practice and this bitch is riding me *hard* today. I'm just trying to figure out *why* she's being so unbearable today after she was fairly decent yesterday.

I have a sneaking suspicion I know why.

I think it *may* have something to do with a certain dark-haired, dark-eyed man who has this unbelievable scruff lining his jaw and full lips that know how to work a kiss.

Just thinking about him and that kiss and those promises last night makes my heart race and my stomach flip

I circle my hips, raise my shoulders, and glide like she just showed me. "Better," she mutters. "Let's take a break."

I'm silently grateful for the break. I head over to check my phone.

Brody: *Hope your practice is going better than mine today. I'm distracted as fuck because I can't stop thinking about a secret kiss in a hotel room.*

He sent the message over two hours ago, but I haven't had the chance to look since I've been working my ass off today. I've got the basics down for the entire show, so now it's a matter of fine-tuning, muscle memory, and lots of practice.

Me: *I must be distracted AF too, because Jessa isn't pleased with my performance.*

I run to the restroom, and as I'm walking back into the room, I get a reply.

Brody: *I'll talk to her.*

I'm about to reply a big, fat negative to that when Jessa starts yelling at me. "We don't have all day, Zoey. Put the phone down and let's get back to it."

By the time practice is over and I'm heading back to the hotel—this time in the same car as Denise and Lauren—I'm fucking exhausted. I want to crawl into bed and stay there until it all starts over again—but this time as I share the stage with Brody and the rest of MFB.

I'm nervous at the thought of that. I'm a pro, and I can dance in my sleep...but I'm not used to the guy I'm hot for sitting behind me watching my every move. I suppose he'll be caught up doing his own thing, but I'll still feel his eyes on my ass with every move I make.

We have our nightly check-in with Kylie at seven, and my plan is to head back to my room, order room service, eat in bed, and call it a night.

I take a shower since I'm a mess from dancing for the last ten hours, and I realize I may see Brody at tonight's meeting again. Even though I'm lazy as fuck right now, I still force myself to put on some make-up just in case. I dry my hair and toss in a few wavy curls, throw on a pair of jeans and a simple vintage Nirvana shirt, and head down to the meeting. When I walk in, my eyes immediately find Brody's. He raises his brows but doesn't otherwise make any indication that there's anything going on between us. The seat to his right is open with Dax on his left, but it just seems like a bad idea to slide into it. Instead, I sit on Kylie's other side since she's the one heading up this meeting. It puts me on the same side of the table as Brody, which means fewer *secret* looks that others might pick up on.

What I didn't account for, though, was the fact that Jessa would plop down beside Brody.

I totally forgot that he said he was going to talk to her earlier, and a bolt of fear lances through my chest at what he might say.

It'll be way too obvious to lean forward and look over at him to assess the situation, so I'm forced to sit back and allow whatever this is to go down.

Kylie talks, but my brain talks louder.

Is he bending his head close to hers? Is he breathing in her scent? Does he feel a spark with her the way he claims to with me?

I'm not sure, but unease fills my bones as I wait for this meeting to end.

Tonight's meeting is short—more of a check-in, really, but that doesn't make me feel any better.

Denise stops me on my way across the room as I beeline for the door. "You wanna go to dinner again?"

I shake my head. "I'm exhausted after today. You two go. I'm just gonna head up to my room and order some room service." I say it loud enough for Brody to hear, but I can't tell if he's listening and I don't want to draw attention to the fact that I'm wondering if he is.

"You sure?" Denise presses.

I nod. "Yeah, I'm sure." I can't help when my eyes dart over to Brody, and what I see has me gritting my teeth.

His head is bent close to Jessa's, and they're both laughing. She looks up at him with stars in her eyes, and that's all I can take.

I thought he was going to talk to her and defend me, but it looks like I was wrong. I don't want to jump to conclusions here because maybe he's just ignoring me and playing nice with her to throw everyone else off the scent of our connection.

But maybe that's not what it is at all and I'm a total fool for believing his promises last night.

I'm too tired to sort through it now, and I'm crabby after a hard day with the bitch who's currently making the guy I'm interested in laugh.

I turn away in disgust, and as I walk over to the elevator, I can't help but feel a twinge of homesickness. Maybe what Sawyer and I had was imperfect and it was me playing a part I thought he wanted me to play, but at least it didn't leave me with this bitter, sad, jealous feeling when the light of morning dawned.

I half expect Brody to stop the doors and magically slide onto the elevator with me before they seal the two of us in together, but it doesn't happen. Instead, I ride up to the twenty-fourth floor by myself. When I get back to my room, I grab the room service menu off the little desk and flip through it mindlessly, not really caring what I eat but knowing for sure I need a drink. I call for my order, and they inform me that it'll arrive within thirty minutes.

I change out of my jeans and into the shorts I wear to sleep in and I wrestle my bra off from under my shirt, all the while wondering what Brody is up to and whether I'll get to see him tonight.

When I hear a knock at my door, my heart leaps thinking it's him.

It's not.

It's the salad I ordered with my sad little bottle of wine that I'll be drinking all by myself tonight.

I get to it, wishing I had something more exciting than salad for dinner, but I have to maintain my weight to fit into the clothes that have been custom-ordered to fit me. I haven't seen them yet, but Jessa mentioned something about how tomorrow will be our first practice with MFB playing live and the next day will be our first dress rehearsal with them.

When my salad is gone, half the wine bottle is empty, and I've already watched three episodes of *Friends* on Netflix, I'm ready for bed. I slide under the covers, close my eyes, feel the hazy wave of sleep washing over me, and make a wish that somehow Brody will show up at my door again tonight.

Not every wish we make comes true, though, and this is one of those times it doesn't.

CHAPTER 21

ZOEY

When my alarm wakes me in the morning, I'm disappointed that I don't even have a text from him...but then realization dawns. I have no ownership over him and I have no right to assume he was even thinking about me last night. Sure, we said some things and shared a few kisses, but in the grand scheme of life, it's not really that big a deal.

As I get dressed for today's practice session, I can't help but think of his head bent down toward Jessa's as the two of them smiled about something. Maybe he took her to bed last night. Maybe he's already tired of the challenges the two of us are trying to overcome. She's more in his league, anyway. She's closer to his age. She doesn't have a brother whose career is a little too close for comfort.

But, much like me, she'll be traveling in close quarters with him for the next two months. As a professional, she should know better than to risk that relationship, but the choreographer doesn't spend as much time on stage unless one of the dancers isn't in a position to perform.

The whole reason the choreographer travels with the band is to study and observe the dancers, to take care of them and ensure their needs are met. We'll have ear pieces to tune out the audience so we can hear only the music the band plays along with her voice directing us from her seat in the crowd. If I roll an ankle, it's her job to get me ice and tape. If Denise drinks too much at dinner, it's her job to hold her hair back.

It's not like that on every tour, but since there are only three of us and this is MFB's first time using dancers, it's what they hired her to do.

When I head downstairs to meet Denise and Lauren so we can travel together to the practice studio, I'm surprised to find Jessa with them. She smiles smugly at me, like she won the prize, and I want to strangle her.

Was she with him last night?

I won't let her get to me. I stick my hands in the muff of my sweatshirt, lacing my fingers together to keep warm in the sixty-two degrees of a June morning in Los Angeles. Our car pulls up, and the four of us get in. Denise and Lauren look like they had a bit of a rough night last night.

"The band will arrive at noon," Jessa says. "Our goal this morning is to try on everything and make sure it all fits. We'll also tour the stage and run through everything aside from freestyle at least once. Any questions?"

None of us answer, which to me signifies that none of us have questions.

"Any questions?" Jessa repeats a little louder like the bitch she is.

"Nope," I say snidely. Denise and Lauren both shake their heads.

"What is *wrong* with everybody this morning?" she asks.

"Tired," I say absently. She overworked me yesterday, but I'll never admit that to her. I need a day to allow my body to recover. I haven't danced for ten hours straight in a while—probably since before I took the job working for Indigo Beauty. At least we'll get a short break as we try on our outfits this morning.

She turns to Denise and Lauren. "And you two?"

"Hungover," Lauren admits.

Jessa shakes her head. "We don't have time for shit like that. You know better."

Denise just sighs as she leans back into the seat and closes her eyes, and Lauren mumbles an apology. I don't point out to Jessa that things might go a little smoother if she could just be a little nicer to us. She may be the choreographer, but she isn't signing my paycheck. I don't *need* this job, and I certainly don't need her.

I might feel differently if I didn't have that image of her and Brody laughing together constantly flashing through my brain like some sort of vicious attack.

The studio is a block behind the Ashmark offices, and as we drive by the building with the record label's title lighting the top, I can't help but think of Mark Ashton. I still think of him often even though what we had ended a long time ago. He has long moved on, and I've made peace with that. He was my first crush, but the adult me can finally say it's time to move forward. He's happily married with a kid and another on the way, and all I ever really wanted was his happiness. I wished for a long time it could be me who gave him those things, the classic tale of the older brother's best friend, but that wasn't our fate.

We tumble out of the car and into the studio. Jessa navigates the place like she has been here before, and we follow like good little dancers toward the dressing rooms, where we find four racks of clothes. We each have one—including Jessa, just in case she has to step in as an understudy one night. We have four outfit changes, two of which need to be quick changes.

The first order of business is to try everything on and check each other to be sure everything fits and looks exactly as it should. Lauren's leotard is a little big, and Denise's shoes are a little small. One of my corsets has a frayed strap, and Jessa's is missing a small row of sequins. Thankfully, they're all easy fixes.

We practice our quick changes a few times, and by the time we're done, we're ready for lunch and my body is grateful I haven't had to dance at all yet today. We visit what's called the craft table, where we find a spread of sandwiches, fruits, and vegetables, and my heart pounds with each passing moment that brings me closer to Brody.

I haven't heard a word from him since yesterday's text, and I can't help but wonder what that means or where it leaves us. He'll be here soon, but that doesn't mean I'll have answers to my questions.

Jessa dumps half a plate of food in the garbage can and practically runs away from the craft table the second we spot Kylie leading the pack. I'm trying not to roll my eyes as I hear her say with way too much enthusiasm as she claps her hands, "We are so excited to practice with the band!"

I've got a ham and cheese sandwich shoved halfway into my mouth just as Brody walks in. His eyes immediately connect with mine.

In the spirit of just being myself, I bite down on the sandwich and chew it slowly. Fuck it. I'm too old to play the *I don't eat anything* game. My eyes flick down to those kissable lips that I can see even from across the room. They're tipped up in a small smile as he watches me, and then Jessa sidles up beside him. I can't hear what she says to him, but he breaks our eye contact to look down at her.

"I'm so jealous of Jessa," Lauren whispers to my left.

"Why?"

"Look at them," she says, nodding toward Jessa and Brody.

I glance over and wish I didn't. My heart drops. His arm is around her shoulder, and it might mean nothing at all...but it might mean everything.

"So?" I finally mutter.

"They just seem like they're so into each other and he's so fucking hot. I wish I was the one who snagged his attention first." Lauren sighs with heavy disappointment.

I dump the rest of my plate in the trash. I suddenly lost my appetite.

"Let's go stretch and get ready to dance," I say, completely changing the subject as I sidestep that landmine.

Kylie gathers most of us backstage a few minutes later. Dax and Kane are here, and Mitch, the tour manager, is listening in. The dance crew is all accounted for, and a couple roadies stand with us. The *Rock on the Road* cameramen are here. One is filming, and the other is ready to listen to Kylie. Adam and Rascal are toward the back of the group, present but not paying attention. Noticeably missing from this gathering is Brody.

And Jessa is the first to point that out. "Where's Brody?" she asks.

"Fixing his drum kit," Kylie says absently. "We're going to get started. We'll practice the opening number a handful of times to make sure the transition is smooth, and then we'll run through the full set at least twice. The guys have their little routines they do, their talking intercessions, et cetera. Dax tends to move around the stage a lot, so today is more about getting everyone comfortable with *where* they need to be and when. If we bump into one another today, it's part of the learning process. If we bump into one another tomorrow, it's a mistake. Does everyone understand where to go for the opening number?" she asks.

The guys will take the stage first, and midway through the first song, the lights will flash a bunch of times before it goes dark during a quick pause in the song. The three of us dancers will appear in our spots on the stage when the lights come back up.

I don't get a chance to talk to Brody or even make eye contact with him before we start practice.

Jessa sits in a seat out in the audience, her voice in our ears. "In three, two, one...GO!" she says once the room goes dark.

The lights come back up, Brody smacks his drums, and Adam joins in on guitar as Dax's voice fills the large practice arena.

Kylie waves her hands at the front of the stage. "Again," she says.

I hear Jessa in my ear. "Lauren, you need to get into position faster."

Everyone resets, and we do it again.

I haven't even turned around yet to make eye contact with Brody, but I feel his presence behind me. I can't tell if I feel his eyes on my ass or if I *want* to feel his eyes on my ass.

"Again," Kylie says, waving her hands again.

"Zoey, clean it up," Jessa says in my ear. "And Denise, that step was left-left-right-left, not left-right-right-left."

Fuck her for implying my dancing is sloppy. For one thing, this is practice. She never said we were going full out, but I will now.

We reset and do it again, and this time I give it my all. Kylie doesn't wave for us to stop, so we finish the opening number.

When the song ends and the room quiets, the sound of a single person clapping greets our ears.

When I place my focus out into the audience rather than on my dance, I see a familiar person standing there. My heart warms at seeing him, but not in the way it used to. Now it's like seeing an old friend. A ridiculously hot old friend, but nothing more.

"That was sick," Mark Ashton says from the fourth row. "If this is what you're doing the full two hours, we made the right choice with MFB."

"Thanks, man," Dax says into the microphone.

"Let's run through the opening song one more time for today, and then we can move on to the rest of the set," Kylie suggests.

This time when I turn around, I glance up at Brody. His eyes are on me, but he makes no motion to indicate it's anything more than taking an interest in the dancers on his stage. Either he's an excellent bluffer or he's already lost interest.

I'm forced to run off the stage and break our eye contact so we can reset for the opening number again, much to my disappointment.

We run through the opening song again but roll right into the second song. Mark sits in the audience, observing and taking notes. Kylie told us that the entire set runs just under two hours, and I'm frankly sort of shocked that Mark hasn't moved yet and we're on the sixth song. He's a busy man, but he also obviously cares about the bands he signs to his label. It's such a personal touch for him to be here when he has other things to do.

I want to say hi to him—and maybe even thank him for thinking of me to fill this position—but for the first time since my crush started at the age of fifteen, I feel a stronger tug pulling me toward someone else.

Nearly every time I've turned and had the chance to look at Brody, his eyes have been trained on me. I listen as he pounds out the beat, the raw talent he possesses that I hadn't even really thought about before. I've listened to his music a lot over the last couple days and knew some of MFB's songs before I came on this tour, but hearing it in person as I stand ten feet away from him is another matter entirely.

He's not just good at drumming.

He's phenomenal.

I could be here all day dancing for him. It's fun, even—not like in that tiny studio with Jessa the Bitch riding my ass. This is different. Her voice is still in my ear telling me I'm doing it all wrong, but it just *feels* right to be up here moving across the stage in front of him.

There's a break for us dancers during the eighth song. It's a ballad with a single guitar played by Adam harmonizing with Dax's voice, and it's one of the places where we'll have a costume change, so normally I'd be running to the dressing area. Today, though, I get the luxury of being able to run to the restroom, a private single stall affair on the opposite side of the building down a long hallway.

When I emerge from the restroom, a lone figure waits, his back against the wall and a knee bent with his foot resting flat on the wall. My heart races as my mind catches up that Brody and I are finally getting a moment of privacy.

He's every inch the bad boy standing there. I move to walk past him, but he takes a menacing step toward me. I freeze, and then he takes another step. I step backward, but the hallway is small and my ass bumps against the wall. He takes one more step, pinning me to the wall with his hips. His eyes blaze into mine for a beat before he leans in and runs his nose along my neck.

"You think you can just shake your ass for two hours in front of me like that and expect me to *take it slow*?" he asks, thrusting his hips toward me on his last three words. His breath tickles my ear and the hardness pressing into my lower belly sends a shiver down my spine. He grabs both my hands in one of his and pins them above my head against the wall, his other hand gripping my hip as he pushes toward me again.

He's making it hard for me to think straight, but I still manage to get a response in.

"You think you can drum ten feet away from me with all that talent and sexuality?" I ask, and I push back with my hips. Our eyes meet for an erotic beat, and then I clearly enunciate each word as I say, "Fuck taking it slow."

His mouth crashes down to mine, my words the invitation he needed. His tongue pushes into my mouth and thrashes around as all the pent up need the two of us have for one another finally bursts forth to the surface.

Suddenly Jessa is the last thing on my mind with Mark and everything else a close second. All I can focus on is the feel of his lips on mine, his tongue exploring my mouth, his hand pulling my hip closer into him, so close that I can practically feel the length of his dick as it presses harder and harder into me. A little moan escapes me, and then we both hear someone clearing a throat and Brody jumps back so fast he nearly crashes into the wall on the other side of the hallway.

I giggle a little, and the throat-clearer lets out a loud laugh.

"Looks like you two are getting to know one another," Mark says.

I glance over at Brody, whose poker face is completely shot.

"It's so good to see you," I gush to Mark, walking over to him for a hug. When he hugs me back, my heart doesn't race the way it used to.

"You too, Zo," he says softly. "How have you been?"

"Really good." I smile. "Thank you for hooking me up with MFB."

He raises a brow. "To be clear," he says, motioning between Brody and me, "I didn't *hook you up*. I simply recommended you for a position I thought you'd excel in."

I giggle nervously and glance at Brody. He looks a little scared that Mark knows he was just kissing me, and I remember him telling me why Dax thought the two of us hooking up was a bad idea.

"Can we, uh, keep this between the three of us?" Brody finally asks Mark. "It's just...we don't know what this is and we aren't ready for anybody to know about it."

Mark nods. "Of course." He leans in toward Brody and claps him on the shoulder. "But fair warning, man. She's my best friend's little sister. Don't fuck her over."

Brody nods and holds up both hands in surrender. "You have my word." He glances at me. "And she does, too."

Mark looks at me. "And you," he says, pointing at me as he narrows his eyes. "I've known you a long time, and I know what you're capable of. Be careful with this guy. Don't fuck up his first headlining tour."

"I won't," I say softly. I know he's just trying to protect both of us. With me, it's personal, and with Brody, it's business—but the end result is the same. He wants this tour to go off without a hitch, and it's a fair warning for both of us.

But we're grown adults, and we're going to do what we please despite the warning.

CHAPTER 22

BRODY

"Happy birthday Abby and Ally," I sing a few days later. I glance around at my family. My parents look like the picture of happiness, my mom smiling over at her two daughters, my dad standing next to my mom, his arm casually flung around her shoulders like they're still in love after thirty years of marriage.

I don't buy it.

Or maybe their secret to happiness is unfaithfulness.

The thought leaves a bitter taste in my mouth. I want to be enjoying this moment where I spend the last bit of time with my family unit before I leave to headline my first tour. Life may change for me, or it may stay exactly the same. Whatever the case, this feels like a *last time* of sorts, and I'm not sure why. We're actually coming through San Diego on tour next month, so I may be standing in this exact place again soon.

Abby blows out the large number two on the cake, and Ally takes the three. My mom brings the cake to the counter to cut it while my dad brings the stack of presents on the counter over to the table.

"Start with mine," I say.

"Wait for me!" Mom exclaims from the other side of the room as she slices then pulls out the piece of cake to set it on a plate. I stand to help, bringing the plates with cake over to the table.

Once everyone has a piece, we all sit at our kitchen table to watch the girls open their gifts. I got them each a card, and when they open it, their present falls out.

"A backstage pass!?" Abby exclaims at the same time Ally yells, "Oh my God!"

"There's one for each of you, too," I say to my parents. "We're coming through San Diego next month and I want you all to be there."

I don't really mean it. I'm not totally convinced I want my father there, but since I grabbed tickets for everyone else, it seemed like the right thing to do. I don't even know if he'll make it. He's probably got some whore in the city who he'll need to entertain that night.

"This is great, Brody," my dad says. "We'll all be there."

I breathe out a quick sigh of relief. I don't know why I'm a little unsure around my dad. I guess it's the secrets my family keeps pressing down on me, but I can't say he hasn't been supportive. He's worked hard to help MFB find ways to break out, and if not for the strings he has pulled, I'm not entirely sure we'd be where we are today.

Sometimes Dax and I talk about our fathers. Dax's dad never supported his decision to make music. They cut ties years ago. My dad is supportive as can be, yet there are times I wish I could cut ties with him, too. I hate the fake life we live. I hate how we all pretend. Yet when Dax comes over, all he can talk about is what a great family I have. The family he always wanted. His dad cheated on his mom, too—and it produced a child who was dropped on their doorstep, outing the affair. That hasn't happened with my dad, at least not that I know of, but I can't help wondering whether I have other half-siblings out there.

I shake off the thought and try to focus on the sisters I do know about. They've always had a special relationship, and while I'm their big brother, I'll never be able to touch the bond they share. *It's a twin thing*, they always tell me—which is fine, but it also puts distance in our relationship.

Dax always says the band is his family, and while I do love and appreciate most of my blood relatives sitting in this room, the older I get, the more I understand what he means.

After the girls unwrap their gifts from my parents, my dad heads upstairs to make a call and I catch my mom in the kitchen alone.

"You doing okay, Mom?" I ask.

She nods as she tosses the cake dishes in the sink and fills it up with hot water to wash them. "Just dandy," she says.

I perch on the counter next to the sink to study her for a second. She looks tired, or maybe it's stress.

"You sure?" I ask.

She keeps washing the dishes absentmindedly, wiping the mess off one and setting it in the other side of the sink to go into the dishwasher. She pauses and looks up at me. When our eyes meet, I know she's really not okay, and maybe she never has been, but it's the sort of discussion she can't have with her child—even though he's a grown adult now.

She seems to shake it off. "Yeah, Brody. I'm sure. Where's this coming from?"

I shrug. "I don't know. I just want to make sure you're okay before I leave for two months."

"Are you excited for the tour?" she asks, changing the subject.

"Of course. Excited, a little nervous."

"You behave yourself," she threatens, narrowing her eyes at me.

I chuckle as I think of Zoey. Behaving myself isn't exactly on my To Do List. Zoey's on it, though.

"There's a dancer," I blurt before I can stop myself.

She raises both brows. "I assume there's more than one dancer, but is there something special about one of them?"

I chuckle. "Yeah. There's something special." Her sweet ass is pretty special. The way her blue eyes blaze into me like she's looking through me. That tight body moving across my stage like she fucking owns it.

She shuts off the water and wipes her hands on a towel even though the dishes aren't finished yet. She stands in front of me with her hands on my knee. "You're a big boy now, Brody," she says. She sighs. "I want the best for you. I want you to find someone who will make you happy and who will treat you right. You deserve that."

"I think she will," I say softly. "I don't know." I shake my head. "I think I want you to meet her."

"You've never brought a girl home," she muses.

"I've never had one I wanted to bring home." I lift a shoulder.

"So why do you want to bring *her* home?"

I set my hands over my mom's. "Because I barely know her, yet I find myself thinking about her all the time. I want to know her. I want to know everything, and I want to share all of me with her."

She nods a little and studies my face for a beat. "Yep, that's what I thought." She moves away from me and back to the dishes in the sink.

"What is?"

She chuckles. "She might be the one for you."

"I don't even know her, Mom."

"Is she going on this tour with you?" she asks.

"Yeah."

"Then I think you'll have plenty of time to get to know her." She finishes the last dish then opens the dishwasher to load it. I hop down from my perch on the counter to help.

"I think you're right," I say.

My dad comes back into the room, and I'm grateful I had a quiet moment with my mom. "Your mother is always right," he says.

She glances over at him and smiles the fake plastic smile. She let that moment of vulnerability slip through when I asked her if she was okay not five minutes ago, but as soon as my dad stepped back in, the mask moved firmly back into place.

That's certainly not what I want for my future.

I want my mom to be happy, too. I want her husband to treat her right, just like she wants me to find someone who will do the same for me.

I just know I never want to end up like them.

CHAPTER 23

ZOEY

"This is delicious," I say, slurping down another bite of Maci's spaghetti and meatballs. I'm only allowing myself a small bowl to celebrate dinner with family. Eli grabs a noodle and tries to slurp it the same way I just did, and we all giggle at him.

"Thanks," Maci says. "It was my mother's recipe." Eli throws the noodle on the floor, and Maci immediately goes to pick it up.

"Leave it, babe. There's just gonna be twenty more by the time we're done," Ethan says.

We're leaving for our first stop in Denver tomorrow morning. This is the first meal I've had with my brother and his family since I arrived in Los Angeles, but since we've been practicing every day, I haven't had much chance to escape to have a home-cooked meal.

I also haven't had a chance to kiss Brody again since that secret kiss in a bathroom hallway nearly an entire week ago.

We've only seen each other at practice, though the texts he's sent me since then at least make me feel like he hasn't lost interest. His schedule has picked up significantly as the band closes in on the final days before we leave for the tour. He had to head back home to San Diego for a night to celebrate his twin sisters' birthday. I wondered briefly if he'd invite me, but I wasn't offended when he didn't.

Not really, anyway. I mean we're not even really a *thing* yet, even though we both have indicated we want to be.

And nothing drives that point home more than seeing my brother interacting with his wife and baby. They're the last couple in the world I could've ever imagined would be in this position. My brother's tattoos snake up and down his arms as he proves in a very visual way something about who he is. Maci's skin looks the same, and it's not just the tattoos. Both came from broken families but have found a way to mend in each other.

I want to find a way to mend with Brody.

I look at Eli, this little boy who has his daddy's eyes and his mommy's nose, a perfect composite of his parents, and I spot the love in the eyes as those parents look upon the life they created.

I never really wanted kids. It was just never something on my radar, not really with the way I grew up. I didn't want a child to have a life like my mom gave us, but I never knew anything different.

And now I sit here and see my brother with his son, and I realize that I won't make the decisions my mom made. Ethan hasn't. He's created this beautiful portrait of love. If he can do it, certainly I can figure out my way, too. Right?

I wonder if I'd be having these same thoughts and feelings if I hadn't met Brody.

I wonder what he'd be like with kids and whether he'd make a good dad. I don't know him well enough to say yes to that question, but I certainly never wondered that about Sawyer or any other guy I've ever dated in the past.

Dated. Are we even really *dating*?

I'm not sure, but I do know I can't wait for this tour to get underway. Once all the prep work is out of the way and we're on the road, there will have to be pockets of time we can spend together.

"So what am I in for on this tour?" I ask.

Ethan shrugs. "You'll be logging lots of hours on the road. It can be boring and lonely, but doing it with my best friends always makes it worth the ride. Have you gotten close with the other dancers?"

I lift a shoulder, and I notice as Maci's eyes seem to narrow in my direction.

"Or someone else?" she asks like she can sniff out a scandal.

"I, uh..." I pause, positive I shouldn't bring this up to Ethan but still desperate to know whether I'll have time with Brody on the road. "One of the guys in the band has sort of shown an interest in me." I refrain from mentioning that it's the drummer.

Ethan glares and Maci smiles.

"One of the guys?" she prods as she sets more noodles on Eli's high chair tray.

"It's new and I'm not sure about anything yet," I say softly, staring down into my plate of pasta as my face turns a bright shade of red.

"But you want to know if you'll have time to be alone with him," she says, finishing my thought for me.

"Mace, that's disgusting," Ethan says as he pulls a face.

"It's not disgusting," Maci says, shaking her head at her husband. "It's how you and I got started," she reminds him.

"Yeah, but she's my *sister*," he says. "I don't need these kinds of details."

"Heard enough of them when I slept with your best friend?" I tease him, and he rolls his eyes as he makes a gagging face. Maci laughs, which causes the baby to let out a little baby giggle, which in turn causes Ethan to laugh.

Three smiling faces where two years ago permanent scowls resided. It's funny how quickly life can be completely flipped upside down, and this picture-perfect moment of a happy family will stick in my mind for a long time to come.

Even after the smiles fade and everyone resumes eating, that feeling of joy is still in the air.

"You want the dirty details?" Maci asks, pointing the tines of her fork in my direction.

I nod.

"From sound check until bus call, he'll be busy. I don't know their schedules, but if it's anything like the tours I've done, there's a lot of free time before and after that." Maci winks at me.

"But it has to be secret," I say.

"Nothing makes tours more fun than keeping secrets from the rest of the band," Ethan mutters sarcastically, obviously speaking from experience.

Maci laughs, and Eli mimics her again. "Just remember, bathrooms are gross. Every girl deserves better."

It's my turn to giggle. "Noted. Any other tips?"

"Hotels are your best bet, especially if you two can swing your own room," she says. "Fake an illness and meet up if you have to. Just don't try to sneak sex in a bus bunk. Everyone knows when the bus is a-rocking—"

"Don't come a-knocking?" I guess, cutting her off.

Maci shakes her head. "No. Somebody's a-focking." She whispers the last part so Eli doesn't hear her almost-swear word, and I can't help another laugh.

Man, I missed seeing these two. I need to come to California to spend time with my big brother and his adorable little family more often.

* * *

Despite the fact that it's a mid-June morning in California, I still shiver as I wait outside to board the bus I'll call home for the next two months.

We're assembling in the parking lot for a quick meeting before we board. Because this is MFB's first headlining tour, Ashmark only paid for two buses—which doesn't come cheap at nearly two grand per day. Each bus has an office set up in the back and nine bunks. Kylie is going to give us our bus assignments, and I can't wait for everyone to get here so I can get out of the freezing ass morning cold.

Everyone except Brody, Rascal, and Jessa are here, and if it wasn't for Rascal being part of that equation, I'd be a nervous mess right now. Brody and Rascal emerge from a car a minute after I have that thought, and Jessa rolls in with sunglasses perched on her stupid perfect nose and a Starbucks cup clutched between her stupid petite fingers.

"All right," Kylie says. "That's everybody. We've got two buses here and for the most part we'll have the band on one bus and the crew on the other. We have to split somewhere since we have an uneven number, so if you have any problems with your assignment, this is your time to speak up." She glances at the clipboard she's holding. "Bus one will have myself, Dax, Kane, Brody, Adam, and Rascal." She pauses and looks around. "We'll also be traveling with Denise and Zoey, and the final bunk is for the driver."

I breathe out a huge sigh of relief that I won't be in tight quarters with Jessa the Bitch. "Bus two will have Mitch, Jessa, Lauren, our road crew, Wyatt, Steve, and Spike, and our two cameramen for *Rock on the Road*, Gary and Abe. Bunk nine is for bus two's driver."

"I'd like to be with Lauren," Denise immediately says. She looks apologetically at me, and I can't decide if it's because she thinks Kylie will switch out me for Lauren and they'll get to ride with the band together or because it means she's throwing me to the wolves with Jessa.

Kylie huffs with annoyance but doesn't otherwise appear fazed. "Fine. Denise and Jessa will trade places. Jessa, you'll be on bus one, and Denise, you'll be on bus two."

Denise looks sorely disappointed at that turn of events, and I feel that same sense of disappointment that Jessa will be on the same bus as me, going after the same guy I am, for the next two months.

My eyes automatically find Brody, whose gaze is turned down toward the ground. I'm curious as to what he's thinking knowing both Jessa and I will be in his space as we tour the country.

"First stop is Denver, Colorado," she says. "There are tour bibles on each bus. You'll find a clipboard pinned just outside each of your bunks. Mitch and I will update those with the daily itinerary. Even on days off, we'll often still have work to do. We're both here for any questions or concerns along this ride. Oh! And I almost forgot. The forward cabins on each bus are set up with cameras to film for *Rock on the Road.* Just be aware that they'll catch anything that happens in the forward cabin and in general, the cameras are almost always watching. Private conversations need to happen in the back office. Are we ready to rock?"

"Ready to roll!" Brody, Dax, Adam, Rascal, and Kane all yell together.

Rock and roll. It's cute, but I'm still annoyed about this whole Jessa thing and I'm not sure how I'm possibly going to keep my feelings for Brody a secret when we're sharing a bus.

"Okay, everybody to your buses and we will see you in about eight hours in Beaver, Utah," Kylie says.

Brody, Dax, and Rascal start laughing. "Beaver," they all say at the same time, and I'm torn between rolling my eyes and laughing along with them.

Seriously? This is the guy I have this rush of feelings for? A twenty-something who giggles at the word *beaver*?

To be fair, though, it always makes my brother laugh, too, and he's now in what I like to call his *late* thirties.

The guys board the bus first, as they should. It's their tour, and I don't really care which bunk I get. I've been on my brother's bus enough times to know that it doesn't *really* matter. Vail's number one bus rule is don't be a dick, and I wonder if MFB has a similar rule.

I'm on the top step just about to turn the corner to look into my home for the next two months when I hear Dax's voice. "Once everyone picks a bunk and gets settled, let's have a quick bus meeting to go over expectations."

A round of agreement follows, and then I look up at the driver. He's old enough to be my grandfather and while his face is gruff, he has the kind of eyes that tell me he's seen it all, but underneath his tough exterior he's really a nice guy.

"Hi, I'm Zoey," I say as I remember Ethan telling me once that you always want to stay on the driver's good side.

"Harvey," he grunts.

"You take good care of us," I say.

He doesn't smile, but he shoots me a wink. "You got it, kid."

It's pretty standard as far as tour buses go. Couches up front, a couple chairs that recline, television screens on both sides, a table with four chairs around it, a sink, counter, and a few small appliances. A curtain is pulled aside that leads to the bunks, and I can see from behind Rascal that everyone's picking out their bed and setting their bags down.

I wait patiently for my turn, and once I get past the curtain, I find one spot left. It's on the bottom closest to the curtain. It'll be the loudest in terms of hearing noise from the front of the bus, and it's the furthest away from the bathroom and quieter office in the back of the bus, but it's what's left. I set my bag down and get in, reminding myself that there's a clearance issue so I don't hit my head on the bed above mine.

I look around to see who settled where. I'm disappointed to find Jessa right across from me, and I'm suddenly grateful for the small privacy curtain hanging over my bunk. Kylie is in the one behind hers, and Dax is in the one behind mine. The rest of the guys in the band chose the top row, probably because they're guys in their twenties who still think it's cool to sleep in a top bunk. Whatever the case, I appreciate having the bottom.

I spot Kane and Adam across from me, which means Brody is either right above me or Rascal is. When I glance over at Jessa after settling into my bed for a second and see the way she's staring with lust-glazed eyes at the bed above mine, I can guess who's above me.

So Brody will literally be sleeping on top of me, five feet away and just out of my grasp, for the entire length of this tour.

I glance away before Jessa can see my look of disgust, and then I hear Dax say, "Everyone in the forward cabin in five minutes!"

I set myself up in my little cubby, plugging in my phone charger to one of the outlets dedicated to me. I put my earbuds on the little shelf hanging by the foot of my bed, and I click the remote for my little private television to be sure it works. It's a pretty sweet deal, actually. When I want to escape the world around me, I have my own little place of privacy.

I head out to the forward cabin, and I'm only the third one there behind Kane and Adam. They're sprawled on the couches, and I want to stay out of the way as much as possible, so I slide into a chair at the table. Kylie comes out next and sits next to me with a binder and a clipboard, and then Rascal, who is perpetually bounding, comes bounding in. Dax is next, and he claims one of the recliners.

That means Brody and Jessa are back in the bunks by themselves. I want to turn around to see if anything's going on, but I force myself not to. I can't draw attention to my attraction to him ten minutes after we boarded the bus. We haven't even pulled out of the parking lot yet. The roadies are still loading our luggage carts into the storage compartments beneath the bus.

Brody steps out first, and my eyes fall to his ass as he walks toward the couch. I shake the lusty thoughts off, but the truth of the matter is that we're going to be in this confined space and *I want him.*

Bad.

And so does the bitch who plops down next to him on the couch. It's a tight squeeze between him and Kane, but Jessa manages to jam herself in.

I let out an annoyed breath. I only have so much self-control, and I've already let her get under my skin.

I feel Kylie's gaze on me, but I shift my eyes off Brody and down to the table. I have no idea what he's confessed to Dax or what rumors have made it to Kylie's ears.

"Okay, now that everyone's here, let's get started," Kylie says, calling Dax's meeting to order.

"There are three rules on this bus," Dax says. "Rule one: clean up after yourself. We all have to live together for the next two months in this tiny space, and no one wants to move anyone's dirty socks to his bunk for him. I'm looking at you, Rascal."

Rascal shoots him the finger.

"Rule two: bunks are sacred space. Stay out unless you're invited in." He winks at Kylie on that one, and everyone laughs.

"Rule three: don't be a dick."

I chuckle. Jessa's already breaking that one.

"That's it. The only three rules to live by." Dax nods proudly. "Any questions?"

We all shake our heads, and Harvey, the driver, pops his head into the room. "Rule four," he says. "Be nice to your driver. I don't control the schedule, so don't get pissed at me if I can't drive through the night. You treat me good, I'll treat you good. You treat me like shit, I'll slam on the brakes a lot." I can't really tell if he's joking or serious. I like this guy already. "That reminds me, if you treat me like shit, make sure you sleep with your head toward the front of the bus."

We all get a good laugh out of that. My brother taught me that if you sleep with your head to the front of the bus and the driver has to slam on the brakes, your head crashes into the wall instead of your feet.

"A few other notes," Kylie says. She launches into bathroom protocol followed by the bus's temperature. It'll be set at a chilly sixty-seven degrees because apparently germs have a harder time living in the cold. I'm glad I brought a heavy sweatshirt, but despite that, I feel like Brody would do a better job keeping my body warm against his. "As a general rule," she finishes, "most of our performances will be Monday, Wednesday, Friday, and Saturday. As I said before, time off isn't always free time, so double check the itinerary. Band members, you'll also get text reminders from me for any PR promos I have booked."

"Thanks for all your hard work, Kylie," Brody says. "I know it's not easy organizing a bunch of fuck-ups like us."

She grins. "Only a handful of you are fuck-ups."

I laugh, and I suddenly feel an overwhelming sense that I'm home.

It's good I feel that since I pretty much don't have a choice at this point.

CHAPTER 24

BRODY

We've been on the bus less than an hour and I'm already antsy to get off.

I can't seem to lose my Jessa shadow, and it's driving me crazy. I glance at Zoey, but she's in her own little world as she stares down at the table. Maybe keeping this a secret was a mistake. I could be sitting with her by my side on this couch rather than Jessa.

Jessa's fine, and I would have fucked her raw by now if I'd had the chance before Zoey caught my attention.

But that's not how it happened, and so I feel like I'm constantly fending her off. I'm doing my best to send the *I'm not interested* signals, but in the spirit of keeping up the ruse that Zoey and I aren't into each other, I sort of have to pretend like what Jessa's doing is working. In a former life—as in two weeks ago—we probably would've broken in one or both of our bunks by now.

Instead, all I can think about is Zoey. Her lips. I haven't pressed my mouth to hers in a week, and I'm struggling for it. It's like the fuel I need to keep going, and before this tour even started, we only shared a few private moments. I need to get her alone, an impossible task on a bus.

Once the meeting is over, we stay in our seats and shoot the shit. "Remember what happened last time we were in Denver?" Kane asks, and we all look over at Rascal.

"What?" Rascal says, lifting both hands. "It's legal and it's a cannabis tourist's dream."

"He got so high he was convinced his phone was dirty and he tried to wash it in the sink," Kylie says, filling Jessa and Zoey in on the details.

"Kid can't handle his weed," I mutter. I shake my head as I earn an enthusiastic laugh from Jessa.

"I had to get a new phone," Rascal says. "That shit was fucking *strong*."

"It wasn't that strong," I say, and when I glance up at Zoey, she's suppressing a giggle. I wish I could piece together why Jessa's enthusiastic laugh annoys me so much while I wish Zoey wasn't holding hers back. I wish it was the sound of her laughter filling my ears instead of the grating dramatics beside me.

"No weed this time," Kylie warns.

"You're not my mother," Rascal says, which is his typical response to her because he's an immature asshole.

This lights a fire under Dax, who smooths everything over with a warning that we need to prove ourselves on this tour, and I do my best not to roll my eyes at how much my best friend has changed.

If our first headlining tour came before the days of Kylie, we'd already be drunk and maybe high too. I love the woman for all she's done for us, and I know she's good for Dax...but man, things have changed a lot.

I never wanted things to change.

But sometimes life happens and our only choice is to react. We've all settled into our roles at this point, but that doesn't mean I have to like it.

I sneak another glance at Zoey, and then I feel Kane's eyes on me. Kane has this strange, intrinsic ability to read people, and I'm positive without even looking over at him that he knows something's going on.

I'm not wrong.

It's much later that night, after we've shared our first dinner on a bus and almost everyone has gone to bed, that Kane asks if he can talk to me in the back office. When I meet him back there in the one semi-private place on this bus, he motions for me to sit. The office part of the bus has a built in U-shaped seating area across the back with little work tables that fold down to maximize space. It's a small space, and it's not super private since you have to walk through this room to get to the restroom, but it's the one area that offers a quiet place to talk—without cameras on us like in the forward cabin, a fact I've already forgotten about.

"What's going on with you and Jessa?" he asks.

Oh. I thought he was better at reading people. I chuckle. "Nothing," I say.

His brow crinkles. "Don't give me that shit. The way she was all over you at the meeting...something's going on."

I heave out a long sigh. "She's not even on my radar, dude."

He nods. "That's what I thought. You're letting her be the scapegoat while you try to hide the fact that you want Zoey."

Right. He *is* good at this shit. I shrug. "Maybe."

He shakes his head. "It's not a good idea, man."

"Why does anybody even care? If we do this and it fucks everything up, then she switches buses. Done. Easy fix."

"It's not just that," he starts.

I interrupt him by holding up both hands. "Dax has already given me the speech, all right? I know if I fuck with her, I'm jeopardizing our relationship with Vail."

"Exactly," he confirms. "You fuck around with her and fuck her over, and that fucks the rest of us over. Don't you get that?"

I pull down the little table built into the wall then push it back up—anything to keep my hands busy while we have this conversation. My knee starts bouncing wildly, but it's beyond my control. "That's not what this is. I don't want to just fuck around with her."

He's quiet a long time as he studies me. It's like he's silently judging whether he thinks I'm sincere or not, but I don't tend to have a lot of these genuinely vulnerable moments with the guys. I'm more of a keep it on the inside and make jokes about it kind of guy.

I keep pulling the table down and lifting it back up.

He finally breaks the silence with a warning. "Just be careful. Jessa seems like a lot to handle and it's obvious she's into you."

"I am being careful," I say. I lock the table back into place and grin as I try to lighten the mood back here. "Besides, it's not like we have a No Bang Oath anymore. They're all free for the banging."

He rolls his eyes. "There's the Brody I know."

"I guess I just don't know how to handle this. I want to get her alone so I can talk to her, but there's too many people on this bus."

"Want my advice?" he asks, and I nod. "Just act normal. Sometimes you and me talk here on the back of the bus. Sometimes you and Kylie get into a conversation up front. It's fine if you and Zoey talk to one another. You're making it more obvious by avoiding each other the way you are, and it's not just that. You're making it seem like you're interested in Jessa. Think about what that might be doing to Zoey."

The door to the office opens just then.

"Oh, sorry," Zoey says. She holds a small toiletry bag, and she nods to the bathroom. "I was just going to get ready for bed. I'll come back."

"It's okay," Kane says. He shoots me a smile as he stands. "I was just leaving."

He gets up and shuts the door behind him, and I wonder how much time we'll have back here.

"Hi," she says.

"Hey." I stand and walk across the small room. I think about locking the door, but *that* is one surefire way to make it really obvious what's going on back here. I lean in and press a gentle kiss to her lips. "I've wanted to do that all day."

"To me?"

I nod. "Of course to you."

"Not Jessa?"

I furrow my brows, and then I realize Kane was right. I've been playing the uninterested card so hard that I even faked Zoey out. I shake my head, and I move toward her. She matches me, moving backwards step for step until she's up against the door, reminiscent of our last kiss.

I pin her to the door with my hips and run my nose along her neck. I kiss the warm skin there, wishing I could have so much more than this little taste—hopefully a preview of what's to come for us.

"Not her, Zoey. Not anyone but you." I try to keep the wonder I feel out of my voice. I don't understand this. I've never wanted it to be just one woman, but I need her to believe me.

She lets out a tiny moan as I move my lips to hers, and it's all over too fast when we hear the door handle turn. I jump back and Zoey moves to the side.

It's Dax. "What are you two doing?" he asks casually, a little smirk forming on his face.

"Talking," I mutter at the same time Zoey defensively says, "Nothing."

Dax laughs. "Sure," he says dryly. He eyes the toiletry bag in Zoey's hand. "Anyone using the restroom?"

"You can go ahead of me," she says.

I sit back down as I try to think of something to calm the raging need in my dick. I look away from Zoey because that's certainly not helping.

She settles into the seat beside me. "If there weren't these...uh...*feelings* between us, how would you treat me?" she asks softly. The rumble of the bus allows us to share a private conversation back here even though Dax is in the restroom beside us.

I chuckle. "I probably would've tried to get you into bed by now."

"Why haven't you?"

I lift a shoulder and shift my gaze out the window, into the blackness of night in the middle of nowhere. "There are a lot of reasons."

"Name one," she says, issuing a challenge.

"It sounds like an excuse, but we've been a little busy. Between that and trying to throw everyone else off our scent, there just hasn't been an opportunity."

"Do you want there to be one?" She fiddles with her bag, and my eyes go to her hands. My first thought is what they'd feel like scratching down my back as I fuck her, but my next thought is what they'd feel like stroking my cock.

Neither thought is helpful in any way at all at this moment.

"Yes," I murmur, and my voice sounds husky even to my own ears. "And if you want it too, Zoey, I'll find us a way."

She nods. "I want it, too."

"Can I tell you one more reason?" I ask softly. I finally look over at her, and her eyes shine with some combination of attraction and lust and hope as she nods. "I don't want it to be just one night with you."

My stomach is a tangled knot of nerves as I say the words, and I study her as I await her reaction.

She presses her lips together then clears her throat before she speaks. "I don't, either."

"I've never done this, Zo."

"Done what?" she asks. She scoots over a little, just close enough to brush against my thigh without being obvious about it should anyone walk in, and there goes my dick again.

I heave out a breath. "More than one night. I've never wanted to."

"It's risky, and it's terrifying." She reaches over to squeeze my hand just for a second before she lets go. "But I keep getting this sense that you're worth it."

"I keep getting this sense that you're too good for me," I admit.

"You know, I keep thinking that, too." She grins.

"That I'm too good for you?" I ask.

She shakes her head. "That I'm too good for you." She giggles, and I can't help my laugh.

Adam walks in next, breaking up our quick moment of intimacy, but he doesn't look at us like we're doing anything wrong. "You guys seen Dax?" he asks.

I nod toward the bathroom, and he waves his thanks before heading out to his bunk.

"I like you, Brody. And I don't understand it because I feel like I hardly know you," she muses.

"Aren't the hours logged on a tour bus the perfect time to start?"

She shrugs. "Sure. Tell me everything."

I chuckle, and for some reason, the words I've never really spoken aloud to anyone but Dax fall from my lips. "I resent my father." Maybe it's because I just saw him when we celebrated the twins' birthday. He's at the forefront of my mind.

Her eyes meet mine with something akin to understanding. "I do mine, too. Why do you?"

"He works hard. His job is in Los Angeles, and our family is in San Diego. What he does when he's in LA is sort of the big secret elephant in every room of my childhood home."

"What does he do?" she asks, crinkling a brow.

"He stays during the week in LA at his apartment, a place where he's with a different woman every night." I say the words flatly, like I'm not talking about my *father.* "I've mostly learned to pretend like it doesn't happen. We all sweep it under the rug, but I see what it does to my mom."

"What does it do?" Her voice is soft and gentle.

"It kills her, Zo." I run my hand behind my neck and grip the skin there as I stare down at my shoes for a beat. "She loves him so damn much, and he doesn't treat her like she deserves."

"Then why does she stay?"

I shake my head. "I don't know. I've always thought it was just the price she decided she could live with, but when I saw her a few days ago, she looked worn down. It can't be what she thought it would be when she married him, you know?"

"Do you know that for sure?" she challenges. "Or is that something you've decided *for* her?"

My eyes whip over to hers. I wasn't expecting her to ask me *that* particular question. I was expecting some sympathy, to be honest. "I never thought of it like that," I admit. "Why do you resent your father?"

"He spent almost my entire life in prison and now he's gone." Her tone is flat now.

"I'm sorry," I say.

"He suffered a lot in the end. Maybe his whole time there. I don't really know. But I resent that he's gone and I never got to have a life with him, you know?"

I nod. "Do you think parents realize how much their decisions affect their kids?"

She purses her lips. "Good ones do, I think. But parents are still people. Some make bad decisions, and some don't. Some get caught, and some don't."

She's speaking from experience, obviously, but it's the wisdom behind her statement that really seems to speak directly to my heart.

It's the first door opening, the first time I've really let her see inside. She didn't run away. She shared a piece of herself with me, instead. That just confirms the way I feel about her isn't just some infatuation.

There's something real here, and I'm ready to sprint down that road to learn more.

CHAPTER 25

ZOEY

Brody: Do you have any idea how fucking painful it is to sleep literally on top of you yet you're so goddamn far away?

I giggle softly as I settle into bed. We'll be in Denver in a few hours, but I'm tired. The last twenty-four hours have been some combination of boring, exciting, and torture as I watch Jessa openly flirt with Brody from my spot on the bus. We've only had that one moment alone, unsurprising considering there are nine people crammed into six hundred square feet.

But that hasn't stopped him from texting me.

Me: Then get your ass down here.

Brody: Don't tempt me. I'm paying for my own room at the hotel in Denver. I need to be alone with you.

I hesitate before I reply. Even though we talked about it, I still want him to know I see what Jessa's doing.

Me: I bet you say that to all the girls.

Brody: Trust me when I say this: I don't.

I do trust him. He hasn't exactly been fending Jessa off, but we've had some good talks over the time we've been traveling so far. All except that one in the back of the bus last night have been in the company of others, which is fine. I'm getting to know all the guys in the band, and the more time we spend together, the more I like them. I even like Rascal, the kid who seems to be the scapegoat most of the time but only because he puts himself there.

I've learned about the band's origins—Brody, Dax, and Adam jammed through middle and high school together, and they met Kane and Rascal at music school one fateful day. I've learned the band name originated in middle school when Adam got detention in Mrs. Fenwick's math class and the boys couldn't stop talking about how Mrs. Fenwick's a Bitch...or MFB. When Brody's mom asked what it stood for, he somehow came up with "My Favorite Band" on the spot, and they laugh about how funny it is for fans to say, "I'm off to see My Favorite Band tonight!"

I've learned that Dax and Kylie have only been together about six months, that Kane has a serious girlfriend, and that Adam's relationship with his girlfriend is on the rocks. I've learned that Rascal is both the youngest and most immature, but he also has a big heart that he only allows to shine through once in a while.

The one person I'm sharing this space with that I haven't learned anything about is Jessa. I don't know if it's because I don't want to learn about her or if it's because she's staying low key under the radar as she does her best to take the seat next to Brody every single time he enters the room.

I tend to think it's more the latter. She hasn't really joined in the conversations apart from finding ways to flirt with Brody, and it's getting old by this point.

I've shared some of myself as well. There isn't too much to do apart from watching Netflix, playing video games, and talking as we travel to our first destination. Everything is taken care of in terms of preparation, so we just have to get there to get going. I used the back office earlier today to do some stretches and run through the trickier parts of the routine as best I could in the confined space. It would've been helpful for the choreographer to be there to offer some feedback, but she was too busy kissing Brody's ass to help.

I close my eyes and drift off to sleep with Brody's sentiment that he doesn't want some other girl fresh in my mind...and the sentiment that he's getting us a private room to share tonight in Denver.

When I wake up, we must be in Denver. The bus is quiet, which means we've stopped. A glance at the clock on my phone tells me it's a little before seven, and there's a good possibility that everyone else is still asleep. It's dark in my bunk—there aren't any windows in this section of the bus, and the black curtain I pulled across my bed keeps out the rest of the light. I slept with my earbuds in to block out any potential snoring, and I ended up with a surprisingly good night's rest filled with erotic and very dirty dreams.

We'll see whether those dreams come true tonight, I suppose.

I head out toward the forward cabin to see if anyone's awake, and I'm not surprised to find Kylie tapping away at a keyboard at the table.

"Coffee's hot," she says quietly without looking up from her screen to see who entered the room.

"Thanks," I say, mimicking her volume.

She glances up at me. "I figured you'd be Dax."

"Glad you just mentioned the coffee, then."

She giggles quietly. "Me, too. Did you sleep okay?"

I nod. "Surprisingly well for a bus."

"That rumble sort of just rocks you to sleep like a baby, doesn't it?"

I nod as I grab the top paper cup from the stack to pour in my coffee. "What does today's schedule look like?" I ask.

"I'm just finalizing it to get it on everyone's clipboards." She glances back at her screen. "Starting at noon, we have a pretty full day—dancers included. The roadies should already be at work setting up the stage, and we'll have a lunch meeting before we head into our final dress rehearsal before the show."

"On the actual stage," I finish for her.

She nods and claps her hands together. "Exciting!"

"What's it like to see your hard work come to life?" I ask, sliding into the seat opposite her.

She lifts a shoulder. "It's not my hard work. It's a team effort."

"But you're the one who worked with Mitch to arrange this tour, right?" I take a sip of my coffee.

"I forget that you have family in the business." She smiles up at me. "Yeah, Mitch and I arranged the dates and venues with the help of some promoters and Ashmark, of course. But it was MFB's talent that got them to this level—that got them the opportunity to even do this."

"You really love them," I note.

"A manager wears many hats, but to me, the most essential hat is that I'm the band's number one fan. I can't do this job with any authenticity if I don't support and believe in every facet of their talent." Her eyes shine with passion.

"I didn't even know what band I was auditioning to dance for," I admit.

"I know." She takes a sip of her own coffee. "We had to blind audition you because we knew you'd say no if you thought Ethan was involved. He wasn't."

"I know that now." I tap my finger on the side of my cup absentmindedly as I stare at the black liquid. I don't really like the taste of black coffee, but I like the rush of caffeine first thing in the morning. "I just wanted to prove myself on my own without someone else throwing my name into the ring, you know?"

"You've proven yourself by your talent, Zoey." Her voice is still low so as not to wake anyone up, but I think it's because she doesn't want anyone to overhear her next words. "As much as we all have mad, mad respect for Mark Ashton, we wouldn't have hired you without seeing you perform first on a recommendation alone. We had to be sure you'd fit with the band, and the second Brody ran after you to make sure you'd stay, we all knew you were something special."

I feel my cheeks warm at the mention of Brody. "Did he, um...did he say anything about me?" I ask, reducing myself to an immature teenager hoping the boy I like said something about me to his friends.

She doesn't hide a smile. "It really isn't my place to spread gossip about my band." I nod in understanding before she adds, "But yes, he did."

I hold my breath as I wait hopefully for her to spill some tea.

"It was the night you met," she says. "He was all twisted up over something, and he mentioned he felt like he had to go after you to make sure you didn't bail on us."

"He mentioned that to me, too," I admit.

"He likes you, Zoey, and he doesn't do the like thing. He does lust and he makes bad decisions...but I don't think you're one of them."

I'm about to respond when the door separating the forward cabin from the bunks opens and Adam steps out.

"Coffee's hot," Kylie says to him, the same words she said to me when I walked in.

I smile at her. "Thanks, Kylie," I say softly.

She shoots me a small smile and nods back, and then she gets back to the day's agenda.

I can't help but feel like I just had a breakthrough, though...and I think I might've even made a new friend.

* * *

Kylie wasn't lying when she said we had a full day ahead of us.

We have a working lunch at some restaurant near the venue where Kylie informs us of our schedule for the day as well as the rest of the week, and then it's time to work. Our first show is tomorrow night, so today is the last chance to fine-tune and get everything right. We'll have another short practice tomorrow, but this is the last time we'll run through the entire set with the band before we all take the stage together.

It's nerve-wracking and exciting at the same time.

After lunch, we're standing by our buses when Kylie introduces us to Marsha, her contact at the venue, who takes us on a tour backstage. I've actually been to this venue with Vail before, but I pretend like it's all new to me just to fit in with the other dancers.

And then I realize what I'm doing.

I said I would just be myself.

I said I wasn't going to pretend like I've had to my whole life.

And here I am, doing it again.

I brush it off and play it a little lower key.

We find our dressing rooms, and that's where we part ways. The band goes to one room, the dancers to another, and the roadies get back to work. Our dancing clothes are already hanging on racks and waiting for us.

"Practice will start in thirty minutes," Kylie tells us, and then she's off to tend to her millions of tasks.

"This is so exciting," Lauren says.

"It is," Jessa confirms with a complete lack of enthusiasm. "Now let's get changed into outfit number one." She claps her hands together with efficiency, and I hate her a little more.

I fight every instinct I have to roll my eyes as I pull outfit number one out of the garment bag.

A half hour later, we're practicing on the actual stage we'll be using tomorrow night. Kylie made sure the venue was available for our use today since it's our first show and we need a real practice on the real stage to ensure everything will run smoothly. It gives all of us the chance to work out the kinks.

We kill the opening number, and as I run into my place on the stage, a rush of adrenaline climbs up my spine. I haven't performed in front of a crowd this big since...ever. The venues where I performed in the past were much smaller, and they were dance recitals or musicals. They weren't concerts with ten thousand screaming fans—capacity for this venue, which has sold out tonight.

But the fans coming to these shows aren't here to see me. I'm just an added bonus to give the show more theatrics. They're here to see the talented boys performing all around me.

There's a different level of excitement in the air that was missing at the practice studio. It's palpable here on stage, down to the intercessions where Dax talks to the audience and we run backstage to take a quick break and sip some water.

It's not without its bumps, but we're ready for opening night.

I catch Brody's eye after we've taken our final bow and get set to run off the stage, and his are filled with heat. We're both ready for what comes next.

CHAPTER 26

ZOEY

Brody: Room 4312. There's a key for you at the front desk.

I gaze at my screen for a beat as I try to figure out how to tackle this. There's a dancer's room reserved with two queen beds for us to share, but I don't want to stay with the other dancers. I want to stay with Brody.

After dinner, we head back to the buses to get what we need for tonight's hotel stay. There's only one car taking us from the buses to the hotel, and Brody gets in on the first ride while I stall to give him time to check in. Jessa doesn't stall. She manages to slide into that first car. She probably rides on Brody's lap the whole way.

Just the thought makes me feel a little ill, but Brody's text makes it a hell of a lot better.

Jessa isn't spending the night sharing a bed with Brody.

But I am.

Denise, Lauren, and two of the roadies are in the final trip with me. The girls gossip about nothing important while I stare out the window. Their voices get louder and their laughs get more hyena-like every block we travel. If I hadn't been invited to this separate room with Brody, I get the feeling I'd need one anyway. These two are already irritating me and I've only been in the car with them for a few minutes. Maybe I'd get Ethan to pay for one.

Ethan.

Holy shit—that's a great idea.

"My brother treated me to my own room, so I'll see you guys in the morning," I say to Denise and Lauren when we pull up in front of the hotel.

"Ugh, she's so lucky," I hear Denise mutter to Lauren as I hop out of the car, grab my bag, and book it toward reception.

"There was a key left here for Zoey Fuller," I say to the clerk, who hands me the key. I can't help my smile as I stride toward the elevator, hit the button for the forty-third floor, and ride up by myself.

It's been a while since I've slept with someone new—discounting the whole fiasco that led to my spot on Single Life, obviously. I guess I relied on Sawyer or my vibrator to satisfy my needs for far too long.

I'm a little nervous about this whole thing—not that I won't be any good, because let's face it, guys are just happy to have a player in the game. I'm worried about how this is going to change things and how the dynamic of our secret will work once we've passed this physical barrier. We've only known each other a little over a week now, and very little of that time has been one-on-one. We're sort of forced into a confined space where one of the only options available is to get to know one another for the next two months.

I wring my hands nervously in front of me, and then I force myself to stop. I stare at the closed door for just a few seconds, and then I slide my keycard into the slot and open the door.

I find Brody sitting on a couch with the lights off. He's looking out the window over the view of Denver. He turns when he sees me, his eyes glowing in the reflection of the lights outside.

"Hi," I say tentatively.

"Hey," he says softly as he stands. He doesn't make a move toward me yet, and we stare across the dark room at each other until he speaks again. "Come here."

I set my bag down on a luggage rack near the door and move slowly across the room toward him. He holds out his hands, and I set mine in his.

He expels a deep breath, and I do, too. When I do, I realize this feels good. It feels right. With that exhalation, it's like I breathed out the nerves to make way for something we both really want.

It seems to flip a switch in him, too. "I was nervous for tonight. I thought all day about lighting candles or putting on some music or getting you some flowers. I thought about what you'd want to make this night romantic and special. But then I realized something."

I raise a brow as I wait for him to go on.

"We don't need any of that shit. It isn't us. You know what's us?"

I lift a shoulder without a word.

"Dirty jokes."

I let out a chuckle.

"So with that in mind, why did the walrus go to the Tupperware party?"

"Why?" My lips tip up as I wait for the answer.

"To find a tight seal."

I giggle. "I was nervous, too. All the way up here, I fought off those nerves, but you know what?"

It's his turn to raise a brow as he waits for me to finish my thought.

"The second I stepped into this room, I knew this was right. We are right, Brody. It may not make sense and there may be a hundred reasons in the wrong column, but I don't care. I want this."

I barely finish my sentence before his lips come crashing down to mine. He yanks on the hands he's holding in his until my body is flush against his while he opens his mouth to mine.

I wrap my arms around his waist the second he drops his hands, my fingers sliding under his shirt to feel the smooth, warm skin of his back. His arms go around me, too, and he hauls me as close as he can while he kisses me with all the pent-up passion and emotion we've both kept secret as we've each tried in our own way to fight it.

We didn't try very hard, admittedly, but when the chemistry is there, it's undeniably there.

He doesn't waste any time. As his tongue strokes mine and I find myself lost to the sensation, he unsnaps the back of my bra with one expert flick of his fingers. His hands slide from my back to my sides, up my ribs, and to the round underside of my breasts. I moan in appreciation to let him know I approve as he moves his hands up to cup my tits. He pinches my nipples between his thumb and finger before he runs a soothing finger over the tight peaks. All I can think is that I want his mouth off mine and on my tits. I want his mouth all over my entire body.

Patience, I remind myself. We'll get there.

We have all night.

Just the thought makes me a little giddy.

His fingers tease me as he lets go of my breasts and runs his hands down my ribs and around my back again before repeating the process. An ache starts to throb between my thighs with his gentle teasing. I move one hand to his thigh and scratch my nails up the denim fabric of his jeans, up and a little over, up and a little over again until I brush against his rock-hard dick. I run my hand across it, and he pumps his hips toward me just once with a little grunt, a purely animal instinct like he can't help himself.

I slide my hand under his shirt again, giving him a teasing taste of his own medicine. His mouth is still attached to mine, but I feel his lips form a smile above mine.

He pulls away long enough to pull my shirt over my head and help me out of my bra, which he tosses on the floor. He kisses me again and slowly backs me up until I hit the window. I squeal as my back makes contact with the ice-cold glass.

"I want to fuck you up against this window," he says, his voice deep and husky with lust. "And in the bed. And on the couch. Maybe in the shower."

"We have all night," I say, my eyes meeting his as my lips form a sinfully wicked smile. "Where do you want to start?"

His fingers dip down into my jeans. He teases my mound before he pulls his hand out of my pants. "Let's start right here," he says. He flicks the button on my jeans and pulls down the zipper, and then he's on the floor on his knees as he helps me shimmy out of my pants, throwing my shoes out of the way and taking my panties down so I'm standing completely naked and shivering against the window.

"Chilly?" he asks softly.

"A little," I admit, tangling my fingers in his hair.

"Let's fix that." He pushes my knees apart so I'm spread open for him, and then he tilts his head and jams his tongue into me.

"Oh!" I cry out at the unexpected jolt of total pleasure. He laps at me, his tongue dipping inside before coming out to flick my clit, repeating the process over and over. He flattens his tongue and slows down, lavishing my clit with attention. My knees start to shake as an orgasm pulls at me, and then he shoves two fingers inside me, sending me right over the edge.

I tug at his hair and squeeze my legs against his ears as he continues to lick me through an orgasm that absolutely shatters me. I scream his name as I pulse while my entire body throbs over and over with waves of pleasure.

When the bliss starts to wane, he shoves his fingers still harder into me, curling them as he continues to lap at my clit so erotically slowly that it should be illegal. It's too much, too fast and slow, too good as I explode into a second wave of bliss. I seem to lose control of my body this time as my legs give out, but Brody's there to catch me. He carries me over to the bed, where I lie for a minute in recovery.

I close my eyes and almost drift off when I feel his warmth as he moves to hover over the top of me. He's naked now, too, but I can't see him because of the dark and his proximity over me. His arms land on either side of me, and I feel the heavy weight of his cock as it settles between my legs.

"Are you ready?" he asks softly.

I nod as my eyes find his. Fuck yeah, I'm ready. He's already given me two orgasms, and the instinct inside me is to give him pleasure now. It's not some race to be even, but I want him to share in the bliss I feel.

He reaches down to align his cock with my body. He pushes the tip in and mutters, "Jesus, that's tight."

I can't speak, can't react, can't do anything but focus on how good he feels as he slides into me. We fit together like my body was made for his. He pushes his way in slowly then pulls his hips back, grunting as he moves. He drives in again, a little faster this time, and pulls back. He picks up the rhythm with each thrust in, and soon he's hammering into me with more passion than I've ever felt from a man before in my life.

"Oh fuck," he roars, and then he pulls out of me and everything stops. "Shit, it's too fucking good, Zoey. I need a second." He moves off me and paces in front of the bed for a second.

I stand up. "Are you okay?"

He nods. "I'm gonna fucking lose it but I can't let it be over that fast. I want to be inside you the rest of the night. The rest of the week. The rest of the fucking year. Jesus," he says, tugging at his hair until the ends stand up. He's a wild mess like this, full of all this carnal, primal desire that makes me so fucking hot for him I almost come on the spot just from seeing the pent-up passion he's carrying around.

For me.

I walk over to the window and face out. I set my hands on the glass and bend over so he can get the right angle to enter me again. "Come fuck me against this window," I say, and he doesn't waste a second before he's gripping my hips and shoving his way back into me.

He settles right into his rhythm again, and I should've known he could keep a beat based on the way he drums. He's hitting all the right spots in me, and my body starts to tighten again for the third time since we started this tryst. "Fuck, fuck, fuck, fuck," he grunts over and over, and then he thrusts up hard into me, pausing there for a beat and I know he's letting go. I let go, too, and he drives into me again as we both ride out our orgasms.

He pulls out and presses a soft kiss to my back before he helps me stand upright again. He pulls me up into his arms and carries me back to the bed, where he tosses me. He pulls off the condom I didn't even see him put on as he moves around the room, and then he disappears to the restroom. When he returns, he has a towel for me. I force myself up to clean up, but I don't bother getting dressed. I'd rather feel the warmth of his skin next to me—and besides, clothes will just get in the way when we wake up to do that again.

Whatever bond we just built was made to last, and that's my final terrifying and wonderful thought before I drift to sleep.

CHAPTER 27

BRODY

"What do you get if you cross an owl and a rooster?" Zoey asks me as she snuggles into my chest after my alarm goes off. I've snoozed it four times now and I really need to get up, but it's just so...perfect here with her.

"What?" I ask softly as I breathe in her hair.

She reaches her hand down and strokes my dick. "A cock that stays up all night."

I chuckle. "You want *more*?" I ask.

"The three orgasms before we fell asleep were nice, and the one you woke me up with at three in the morning was great, but I think I need just one more to really set the tone for this day."

I contemplate my decision for all of a nanosecond. My brain comprehends *you're gonna be late and*—before the decision is made.

The guys can suck it. I'm getting laid, and this won't take more than five minutes, anyway.

The shower we take afterward does, though. It sets me back longer than it should. I have a breakfast meeting with the rest of my band, and I was supposed to be in the same room as them last night so we could talk about tonight's show...but I feel like we're ready. I didn't need to rehash it all again for the millionth time. We're over-prepared, and I needed this night—and morning—with Zoey.

Once I'm dressed, I'm ready to head out. She's in the middle of applying something from a little container to her face when I walk up and slide my arms around her waist. I squeeze a boob for good measure. I don't know when I'll get to do it again. She giggles, and the sound is like a balm to my soul as I kiss her goodbye.

I'm falling hard for this girl. I wasn't expecting it—not on our first tour, not in a place where I could bag every single babe in the crowd if I wanted to...but last night only pushed me deeper into a hole I'm not sure I want to climb out of. I'm in this strange state of bliss I wasn't expecting to feel the morning after sleeping with a girl who I very much want to sleep with again.

I want to tell the guys. Fuck this secret bullshit. It's not fair to her or to me to sneak around. I don't want a secret hotel rendezvous, and I don't want to pretend like the very annoying Jessa has any chance with me when I'm interested in someone else.

I take a deep breath before I insert the key into the door of the room where I was supposed to sleep last night. I'm ready to tell them.

"Where the fuck have you been?" Dax demands the second I walk through the door.

The bliss that washed over me for a few private hours with Zoey seems to melt away like a blowtorch to an ice cube.

I don't answer as I slide into the only open seat at the conference table in the suite. I mumble an apology that I don't really feel and Kylie picks up as if she'd been mid-sentence when the door opened. Dax glares at me and shakes his head before taking a bite of the pancakes in front of him. I glance around. Everyone has a plate in front of them, mostly empty already. Apparently I missed the majority of this meeting.

"—and Kane, call Wyatt. He was missing something of yours. Any questions?" Kylie looks around the table at everyone, and her eyes land on me last. "You missed our entire meeting and I'm not repeating myself. If you're going to bow out to screw some random, that's your business, but when you're late and you miss band business, it affects everyone." She slams the lid to her binder shut and stands. "I need to meet with Mitch at the venue. I'll see you guys there."

Dax tugs on her arm, and she leans down for a quick kiss before scurrying out of the room.

Everyone except Dax gets up from the table and disperses to their bedrooms in the suite to finish getting ready for the day.

"Where were you?" he asks once it's just the two of us. He slides his last bite of pancake around his plate to sop up all the syrup before he looks up at me.

"I got my own room last night." I can't bring myself to say more.

"Why?" He finishes the last bite and sets his fork down.

I shrug. I feel like the naughty kid who's getting in trouble, but Dax doesn't have an ounce of authority over me.

"Dude, what's going on with you?" he finally asks.

I shake my head and stare out the window as the words finally pour softly out of me. "I never wanted what you found with Kylie. I never wanted to be tied down to a single woman. But I can't stop thinking about her."

"Zoey?" he asks.

I nod. "I'm tired of pretending. When I think about my life before I met her and now...well, I don't want to imagine my life without her."

"Then don't. Do what you need to do, and get your ass to band meetings on time."

I look over at him with surprise. I was expecting some sort of accolades for admitting my true feelings, and instead he's glaring at me. He usually doesn't lose his cool with me, but it wasn't just him and the other guys who were affected this time. It was Kylie.

My surprise dwindles quickly as I realize this isn't about me being late. It's about him sticking up for his girl.

And as much as I never would've understood that before, I'm still in a state of euphoria after last night. If this is what he feels around Kylie, then I guess I get it.

"Thanks for understanding," I mutter sarcastically.

He taps the side of his coffee cup absentmindedly. "This is our first night on our first headlining tour. Everything rides on this."

"We're ready, man," I say softly. Dax is the kind of guy who oozes confidence all the time, so to see this vulnerable slip is unusual. "We've been ready for this since we were thirteen."

He nods. "You're right. I'm sorry."

"We've got this."

And we do. The first show is a monumental success in no small part to the army of people we have in our crew. We start with a meet and greet then play to a sold-out crowd at the Pepsi Center. Between our roadies who are total pros, our gorgeous dancers, our stage manager and Kylie, and the way all five of us kill it on our instruments tonight, the show goes off without a hitch.

I'm focused maybe more than I've ever been in my entire life, and I'm completely on point. I catch Zoey's eye more than once, and the smile gracing her seductive lips is just for me despite the huge crowd gathered. It's a secret promise that there's more nights like the one we shared in store for us.

As soon as we've taken our final bow, the girls run off the stage to their dressing room and the five of us head together to ours, excited chatter filling the space as we move quickly down the hallway filled with people. Women call our names as we move, but our tradition is to get back to our dressing room, decompress, eat, and shower before we head out—sometimes to an afterparty, sometimes to a private performance at a club, and sometimes just to the bus if we need to get moving to the next city.

Kylie is waiting for us with a huge smile when we open the door. "You guys killed it!" she screams the second we walk into the room. She claps her hands and bounces up and down on the balls of her feet. We're all amped up on adrenaline. "Best. Show. Ever."

We celebrate with shots of tequila, and then we take turns showering as we dig into the boxes of pizza waiting for us. I don't know what awaits us after the show since I missed this morning's meeting and I never bothered to ask. It was a busy day filled with tasks and interviews and fans, and I'm fucking exhausted after very little sleep last night. But if we've got more on the agenda, well, I'll have to suck it up. Real rock stars don't bow out because they're sleepy.

And besides, as I caught Zoey dancing out of the corner of my eye more than once tonight, one thing became very clear to me. I'm done with the secrets. I'm telling the guys tonight, and we're going to stop pretending like there's nothing there.

"We are done for the night, but bus call is in one hour," Kylie says once everyone is showered and done eating. "This is where we usually let fans and guests in if you're ready."

"Can I just say something real quick?" I ask.

Everyone in the room—my four best friends, Kylie, and Mitch—all turn to look at me.

"Congratulations on a perfect first show," I begin. Everyone cheers in agreement, but I hold up my hands to stop them. I take a deep breath, because I need to get these words out now or I may never do it. "You may have already guessed this, but I've sort of been keeping a secret. Zoey Fuller and I are seeing each other." I hear a gasp, but I'm not sure who it's from. Kylie maybe, or Rascal. "We were keeping it on the down low, but I think it has the potential to turn into something serious, and I don't want to hide it from my best friends anymore." A weight lifts from my shoulders the second the words are out, and I hadn't even realized I'd been carrying it.

Adam lets out a low whistle. "Does Jessa know?"

I shake my head as a bit of the weight presses down again. "I guess I need to be the one to tell her."

"Congratulations, man," Kane says. "Is that where you were last night?"

My smile at the memory must give me away.

"You fucking dog!" Kane says, and everyone laughs.

"Let's keep it between us until he has a chance to let Jessa know," Dax suggests, and everyone nods in agreement.

And that's that. I told the guys, I'll tell Jessa as soon as I see her, and then Zoey and I will be free.

After we chat with some fans in our dressing room, I head out to the bus. We're off to Houston next, which is over sixteen hours from Denver by car. Our performance isn't until Sunday night, but with a driver break, it'll take until Sunday morning to get there.

When I board the bus, I find Jessa in the front cabin curled into one of the recliners. The guys are still back in the dressing room finishing up, but I bolted as soon as I could to take care of this. I'm not sure where Zoey is, but I realize this is my opportunity and I need to seize it.

"Hey you," she says flirtatiously, and I try not to roll my eyes at her predictability.

"Hey," I say. "Can we talk for a second?"

She raises both brows and waggles them at me like she wants to do more than just *talk*. In another life, maybe.

I sit across from her on the couch. I lean my elbows on my knees and clasp my hands in front of me, and she seems to sit up at attention as she takes in my serious posture.

I take a deep breath and then the words just spill out of me. "I like you, Jessa, and I think you're a great girl. But I'm seeing someone, and I need the invitations and innuendos to stop."

Her brows furrow. "Uh, first, there have been no invitations or innuendos. And second, you're *seeing someone*?" She puts air quotes around her last two words. "No you're not." She shakes her head in disbelief.

I don't need to explain myself to her, yet I find myself doing just that anyway. "It's new, but I know it's different. It's important. It's all the things I never thought I wanted, but when I think about my future, I see her in it. I don't want to see it any other way."

She sets her jaw like she's trying not to let her anger through, but the flare of her nostrils and glare in her eyes gives her away. "Who is this mystery woman?"

Zoey steps out from the bunk hall and into the forward cabin. Her eyes are sparkling as they fall onto me, and I give her a little nod of encouragement. "Me," she says.

Jessa's brows furrow deeper and her eyes widen. "You?" she demands. She looks at me with incredulity. "You're choosing *her* over *me*?"

For someone who hasn't offered me any invitations or innuendos, that's sure a defensive reply. "I'm choosing her over everybody," I say, and I flick my head to motion for her to sit next to me on the couch. She slides into the seat and I toss a casual arm around her. "I told the guys," I say softly to Zoey.

She turns toward me, her citrus scent attacking me and making me want her all the more. "You did?" Her words are a whisper of surprise.

I nod. "Just now. We don't have to keep this a secret anymore. And when we head to San Diego for our gig, I want you to come home with me and meet my family."

"Meet your family?" she squeals at the same time Jessa says, "Oh my God." She gets up with disgust, looks toward one of the cameras, and shakes her head before she bolts, leaving Zoey and me on the couch alone.

The cameras.

I realize now that they just caught our exchange, and no matter what happens, my relationship with Zoey will be chronicled in future episodes of *Rock on the Road*. The thought makes me excited—we'll be able to watch as our relationship develops. How many people can say they have an actual record of that?

"Isn't it a little soon for that?" Zoey asks.

I shrug. "Probably, but we've already spent a lot of time getting to know one another, and it feels right. Besides, it's still almost four weeks away. I wonder how much will change in the next four weeks."

There's no way of knowing that four weeks later, I'll be sitting in the home my parents own after introducing my girl to them when I realize exactly how much changed in four weeks' time.

In a word: Everything.

CHAPTER 28

ZOEY

I can't help my giggle at Brody's expression. We're snuggled up in my bunk somewhere in the heart of the US as we make our way from Cleveland to Detroit. I'm exhausted from another night of leaving everything I have up on that stage, but I'm not too exhausted to spend time with this enigma of a man who has managed to take over my every thought.

I'm not so naïve to think we're *meant to be*. I'm not sure that's true because that's just not something I believe in, fate and all that shit, but I'm immersing myself in the moment...and I'm wanting these moments to last longer.

We've got the bunk curtain open to prove we're not up to any shenanigans. Everyone else is awake and in the front cabin watching a movie as they wind down from tonight's show—everyone, that is, until Jessa passes through the bunks. She puts on her best flirty face for Brody, and as soon as she's past us, it's the slight roll of the eyes and the little snarl on his lips that forces a giggle from my own lips.

"Not a fan?" I ask softly.

He shakes his head and presses a kiss to my lips. "There's only one chick on this bus I'm a fan of."

"Chick?" I ask.

"Yep. C-H-I-C-K. A creative, hot, incredible, captivating, knock-out." He ticks off each word as he keeps count of the letters on one hand, and I can't help but laugh.

I narrow my eyes at him. "You came up with that really fast."

"Thank God my speed impresses you." He wiggles his eyebrows suggestively.

"Hey, speed wasn't an issue that night in Denver," I say softly, suddenly feeling the need to defend him from his own sex joke.

His hold tightens around me, and I feel warm and safe in his arms. "The only time issue I had that night was that there just wasn't enough of it."

"Thankfully we still have five weeks left on this tour together," I muse.

He hums in agreement, but we're both quiet for a minute. I don't know what he's thinking, but I'm suddenly struck with the fact that this tour *will* come to an end in just five short weeks. And then what?

Then I'm a dancer who wants to be on television but doesn't have a job, and he's still a rock star.

Do I go back to Atlanta?

I don't want to go back to Atlanta.

Do I go back to Ethan's?

I don't want to go back to Ethan's.

I want to stay right here, snuggled in Brody's arms. Forever.

"Hey," he says quietly once Jessa passes back the other way. "Where'd you just go?"

I shake my head a little and force a smile. "Nowhere."

"Tell me." His dark eyes are a little worried, and while I want to calm whatever apprehension he has, I also want to share mine with him. It just feels like a burden we could share so we could overcome it as a team.

A team.

I suddenly *want* to be a *team* with somebody. I've never wanted that before.

But with Brody, everything has changed.

I clear my throat and sit up a little, and his apprehension turns to alarm at my sudden movement.

"It's just...what happens when this is all over?" I wave my hands around at the bunk and the bus to indicate all of it.

The crease in his brow smooths out and his expression turns from worried to confident. "We have five weeks to figure that out."

"Yeah, but just mentioning that there's an end cap on this...I don't know. I feel it looming over us all the sudden." I draw in a deep breath as tension swirls in this little bunk.

"Babe, it'll be okay," he says, trying his best to cut through the tension. "We'll take it as we go. I'm HFU."

"HFU?" My brows crinkle as I try to decode his meaning.

"Hot for you."

I giggle, and suddenly it feels like things are going to be okay. "I'm HFU, too."

"Now let's cut the talk about what happens in five weeks and instead focus on you. I know you, but I don't *know* you. Tell me something nobody knows."

I press my lips together. The first thing that comes to mind is the fact that I slept with a Hollywood casting director to "earn" my spot on a reality television show. I didn't even admit that one to Kristen.

But I don't want to admit something that makes me look like an awful person, so instead I admit to something that isn't exactly my darkest secret. "I love to dance, but it's not my passion anymore."

"It's not?" His brows furrow and then his eyes take on a faraway look like he's picturing me dancing. "But you're so good at it."

I shake my head. "I want to be a television star."

"I know. And you will be."

"What makes you so sure?" I ask.

"*Rock on the Road*," he says, like the answer is obvious. "You'll be plastered on screens across America, and when the viewers see what I see in you, America is going to fall in love with you."

I shake my head. "The show isn't about me. Viewers are going to fall in love with MFB. With you and Dax. With Kane and Adam, and even Rascal."

He laughs. "Maybe not Rascal."

I giggle. "I've only been around you guys for a little over a month and even I love Rascal."

A momentary flash of something crosses his face—jealousy, maybe?—but it's so quick that I can't decode it. Maybe because I said the words about Rascal before I actually said them to Brody.

Love.

Do I love Brody?

I love all the guys in MFB, including Brody—but am I *in love* with the drummer?

I don't know yet, but I'm definitely on the track that'll get me there, especially if he keeps holding me here in my bunk, his lips whispering across my temple every so often as we talk and get to know one another on a whole different level.

"What would you be doing if you weren't the drummer for MFB?" I ask.

"I actually always wanted to work in medicine," he says. "I had aspirations to be an ER doctor until I picked up my first set of sticks."

"An ER doctor?" I ask, wrinkling my nose.

He nods. "Why? What's wrong with that?"

"Nothing at all. It's an amazing profession. I just could never do anything in the medical field."

"Why not?"

"Blood." I shudder. "Even just the word makes me a little nauseated."

"You can't handle blood?"

I shake my head. "Ethan fell off his skateboard when he was seven and I was five. I passed out cold when I saw the nasty wound on his knee." I make the mistake of picturing it and my stomach turns on me.

"Look at me," Brody says. I do, and the image darts out of my mind as his dark eyes bore into mine. "Don't think about it. Think about puppies."

"Puppies?" I giggle.

He nods. "Or a hot drummer hung like a horse with the calves of a god."

My brows furrow. "You know someone like that?"

He playfully nudges me in the ribs with a smile, but his distraction technique worked. "You need me to show you my calves again?"

"Maybe the other part."

"Well maybe when we get to Detroit and find ourselves a hotel room, we can participate in a little I and I."

"I and I? Don't you mean R and R?"

He shakes his head. "There won't be much rest, though I can provide you with some relaxation techniques."

"So what's I and I then?"

He grins salaciously at me. "Inebriation and intercourse, of course."

I giggle. "I think we can make that happen. I just wish we didn't have to wait until Detroit."

His lips find mine, and somehow we go from giggling and teasing despite our serious conversation to something much, much hotter.

I can feel it.

All these little moments are starting to add up to something big.

CHAPTER 29

BRODY

"What are you nervous about?" Zoey asks a week after the show in Detroit.

"I've just never done this." I run my hand through my hair for the hundredth time. It's a Monday afternoon as Zoey and I make the two-and-a-half-hour drive from Los Angeles to San Diego, and I feel more and more nervous with every passing mile. Our gig in town isn't until tomorrow night, so today is for seeing family and local friends—or, in my case, introducing the woman you've definitely fallen for over the last month to your family.

Maybe this wasn't a good idea.

"Never done what?" she asks.

I glance over at her. "I've never brought a woman home to meet my parents."

She reaches over to grab my hand, and she squeezes. Her hands are ice cold in my clammy, sweaty ones. "I'm the one who's supposed be nervous, not you."

"Are you?" I ask.

"If they're anything like you, I don't have any reason to be."

They're not like me, but I refrain from saying that. She'll be fine with my sisters and my mom, and even my dad, I'm sure. I just can't figure out why I thought this was a good idea. It's not. It's a terrible idea.

Even though we've gotten to know each other on every level possible sharing tight quarters nearly all day every day over the last month, it's still terrifying to do this thing I've never done before, to bring a woman home for my family to judge and dissect, for them to see our relationship and open it up for their comments and criticism.

But the two of us fit together like a glove. I'm convinced this is right, and introducing her to my family just felt like a natural next step.

And tonight, as soon as we lie down to go to sleep, I'm going to say the words that have been darting around my brain for weeks now. I'm going to tell her I've fallen in love with her. It feels like the right way to cap the day after family introductions.

Even so, I can't help when my father keeps edging his way into my subconscious. I've worked my entire life to impress him, to be someone who will make him proud. He's tough on me despite his support, and I never really know where I stand with him. I realize as we drive toward home that it's probably because I don't really know who he is as a person. I know him as the guy who was there on the weekends and who sent checks to cover the bills and college tuition. He wasn't consistently the family man I needed. He sometimes played catch out back with me or sat in the bars in the early days of MFB to catch our shows, but he wasn't the guy who was there for every single baseball game and every single performance.

Yet I can't say I never felt his support. We have a strange relationship where I always wanted more and he never really delivered.

"Why does a squirrel swim on his back?" Zoey asks, interrupting my thoughts.

I shrug as I keep my eyes on the road.

"To keep his nuts dry," she deadpans, and I huff out a courtesy chuckle.

I appreciate her attempt at lightening the mood, but each turn we make that brings us closer to home presses a heavier and heavier weight on my chest.

When we get there, though, he's not even home yet. He always parks in the driveway and leaves the garage spaces for my mom and sisters, and his car isn't there yet. He's probably wrapping up at the office—or maybe he's not even coming home until tomorrow night. Regardless, the weight lightens a little and I feel a little spark of excitement to introduce Zoey to my mom and sisters.

I cut the engine and pause in the driver's seat for a minute as I draw in a deep breath.

"I've never seen you like this," Zoey says.

I look over at her, and her concerned blue eyes provide some measure of comfort—the exact measure I need, in fact.

"My family will love you," I say. "Probably as much as I do."

Her jaw drops slightly open and her eyes widen. "You...you—"

"Love you," I finish for her. "I was going to wait to say it later, but—"

I don't finish my sentence because Zoey's mouth is hot on mine, and suddenly I forget where I am for a second just like I always do when she kisses me.

When she pulls back, she looks as dazed as I feel. "I love you, too," she says softly, and I lean over and press another kiss to her mouth. Somewhere deep down, I already knew she does, but hearing her say the words gives me every last ounce of strength I need to get through this day.

"Let's do this," I say softly, leaning my forehead to hers.

She links her fingers through mine. "Let's do this."

I have to let go to get out of the car, but as soon as she's out and standing beside me, I grab her hand again. We're a united front here, two people who just professed their love for the other, and I'm ready to do something I've never actually done before.

Abby throws the door open and Ally jumps me for a hug less than five seconds after I ring the bell. My fingers are still linked through Zoey's, and I don't let go.

"How's our big rock star brother?" Abby asks.

I laugh. "I'm not a rock star," I say sheepishly.

"Don't let him fool you," Zoey says. "He's a total rock star in every way." She lets go of my hand to hug Ally. "I'm Zoey."

"Oh my God, Zoey! We've heard so much about you!" Ally squeals.

"You have?" Zoey asks, giving me the side eye. "Only the good things, I hope."

I laugh. "Of course. I have nothing bad to say."

Zoey seems to melt a little, and both my sisters swoon. Abby squeals. They both tend to squeal a lot.

"Sorry, we've just never seen him like this," Ally gushes.

I roll my eyes. "Maybe this was a bad idea."

"Come in and meet Mom," Abby says, and she tugs Zoey down the hallway toward the kitchen.

I'm left behind with Ally, who says, "I love her already. I'm so happy for you, Brody."

I smile. "Thanks, Al. Me too." I practically run down the hallway so I can be there when Zoey and my mom meet for the first time.

"Mom, this is Zoey!" I hear Abby squeal just as I step into the kitchen.

My mom is chopping vegetables at the counter and she drops the knife with a small clatter when she sees us. "So lovely to meet you, Zoey," she says, stepping forward to give Zoey a hug.

It's a picture perfect moment with no dark clouds hanging over our little group. I just wish it could last a little longer than it does.

"How's my rock star son doing?" she asks, squeezing me next.

I laugh. "Did Abby tell you to say that?"

"We've seen the news articles, Brody. Your band is breaking records and impressing the right people. I'm so proud of you." She runs her hand over my hair like she's done since I was a child.

It's funny how I may be a *rock star* now, playing sold out venues to thousands of screaming fans who wish they could get on my bus or go home with me, but I'm still just a boy who is someone's son.

"Thank you," I say softly.

She turns to Zoey. "And you're a dancer for the band?" she asks.

Zoey nods. "I was lucky enough to be recommended when a dancing spot opened, and the rest is history." She smiles over at me in wonder for a beat, and then she adds, "I almost didn't take the position, but it was Brody who convinced me to stay. That was when the bond between us first started."

My mom looks at Zoey with stars in her eyes. She already loves her, and my sisters do, too.

My mom picks the knife back up to continue chopping as the five of us chat. There's only one person left for family introductions, and he should be home any minute.

CHAPTER 30

ZOEY

I freaking *love* Brody's family.

Brody's mom, Cindy, is the warm type of mom I always wanted growing up. She chops vegetables and puts them on cute little plates with a variety of dipping sauces.

I never had that. My mom was too busy with a new man every week, and my dad was too busy being in prison.

Cindy cuts little slices of cheese and sets them out with crackers.

I was lucky if my mom even remembered to buy cheese, let alone slice it for us.

We very obviously grew up in completely different households, but I love how easily I fit into this family just twenty minutes after stepping through the door.

"When will Dad be home?" Brody asks.

Cindy glances at the clock. "In the next hour or so," she says. "I thought he'd beat you home but he had a few things to wrap up since he's taking tomorrow off."

"He's *taking tomorrow off?*" Brody repeats with an edge of shock. "He never takes days off."

"He wanted to spend it with you and Zoey, and he wanted to help backstage if you need it," she says.

I wonder what his dad does for a living. It's not something we've ever really talked about. All I know is he travels back and forth from LA to San Diego a lot, and Brody indicated that he does some less than monogamous things when he's up in Los

Angeles. He's given me the sense that he doesn't want much to do with his dad, yet he's also given me the sense that he very much respects him and wants to earn his approval.

It's a complicated and messy relationship, but I can't really speak to parental relationships since my own were so very fucked up when they were alive.

Abby and Ally grab me and take me into the family room while Brody and his mom catch up in the kitchen.

"Is Dax still as hot as ever?" Abby asks.

I giggle. "He's definitely not hard to look at, but he's very happy with Kylie. And he's not even close to as hot as your brother."

Ally makes a face and Abby says, "Ew."

They grill me about the band and the shows and the set list. I share the gossip of Jessa and how Brody put her in her place all those weeks ago—plus how she's done what she can to make me miserable on tour. She doesn't have all that much control, though, and Brody puts a stop to her shenanigans as soon as he spots them.

"Ready for the tour?" Brody asks, interrupting me as I tell the story of the time I found Jessa planted firmly on Brody's lap. He holds out a hand to me, and I link my fingers through his as he pulls me up from the couch.

Abby and Ally are swooning from where they sit, both with wide smiles on their faces. They've obviously never seen their brother in love, but more importantly, they approve.

He takes me through their home, and I find myself in a boy's bedroom. "You stay here often?" I ask as I glance around. Posters of J Lo line the walls, a teenaged boy's wet dream I suppose. A few older photographs litter the dresser, mostly shots of Brody playing drums. I pick up one of him with a girl dressed up for some high school dance.

He shakes his head. "Not since I moved in with Dax almost nine years ago."

"Who's this?" I ask, showing him the frame.

"Mikayla—something that starts with a T."

"You don't remember her name?" I ask.

He shakes his head, takes the frame from my hands, and tosses it in the trash can. "That's how important she was to me."

I giggle.

"Come here," he says softly, and I comply. He wraps his arms around me. "I'm glad you're here."

"Me too."

He presses his mouth quietly to mine, and I give into the moment. He swings me around until I feel my knees hit the back of his twin mattress, and he's on top of me in a second, his hand finding my breast. He grabs it and kneads it, his mouth hot on mine as his tongue thrashes in my mouth until I get so damn hot for him that an involuntary moan escapes me.

He chuckles and pulls back. "I guess we should save that for tonight," he says. The plan is to go back to the house he shares with the guys in his band so he can sleep in his own bed at home for one night, and I don't blame him. If we were back by my hometown, I'd want to do the same thing…a gentle reminder that I'm not really sure where home is anymore.

I make a pouting face, and he laughs. "I'll give you something to pout about," he says lightly, and I giggle.

"We should get back to your mom and your sisters," I say. I don't want to—not really. I'd rather stay up here and mess around with my boyfriend, but we don't have a ton of time here and having sex on his childhood bed might just be a little disrespectful to the people who we're here to see.

When we exit his bedroom, he shows me the rest of the house. "This bathroom is quieter than the one off the kitchen if you need to use it," he says, nodding to the bathroom that three kids must've shared when they were growing up but that has now been taken over by twin twenty-three-year-olds.

"Do your sisters still live here?" I ask.

He nods. "They graduated college this past May. They both majored in marketing, and Abby started a job right after graduation. Ally is still looking, but they decided to stay here and save money."

"Smart," I murmur. If I would've been given the choice, looking back I can see how much sense it makes to move back in with mom and dad after college. I never had that option, not really. Mom was still alive back then, but Dad was in prison and Mom wouldn't have wanted me around anyway.

"You think so?" he asks. "I was ready to get the hell out."

Funny how I'd give anything to have what he had growing up, yet he still wanted to get out. Maybe it's just the normal and natural progression of life.

Brody leads me back toward the kitchen, where Cindy is prepping dinner despite the large array of snacks she set out on the counter.

"Can I help with anything?" I ask politely, though truth be told I'm a mess in the kitchen.

"Would you mind peeling these carrots?" she asks, nodding toward a stack of carrots sitting next to the sink.

"I'd be happy to," I say. That's easy. I peeled plenty of carrots when I was basically raising my two half-sisters, Bianca and Stephanie.

I haven't called the two of them in ages. To be fair, the last month has been a total whirlwind, and they probably don't even know I'm on this tour unless Ethan told them.

The peeler is next to the carrots, so I pick one up and start peeling the skins into the sink.

"Can I do anything?" Brody asks.

"I don't think so, hon. Go tell your sisters about the things you don't want to tell your parents and we'll have dinner cooking up here shortly."

I giggle as I think about all the things he really shouldn't tell his parents *or* his sisters, and then I lose myself in my thoughts and my work. The tour has been a lot of fun so far, in large thanks to everything Brody has done to make it fun. We snuggle in our bunks, we fuck in hotel rooms and anywhere private we can find backstage on gig days, and he doesn't miss a single moment to make sure I know how much I mean to him.

I've never had such an easy relationship. I've never had anything thrive so perfectly from the very beginning—despite keeping it a secret at first. And now that I've met his family and fit in so easily, it all just feels so *right.*

I can only think about what the future holds for us with a big smile.

"Dad's home!" Cindy calls as we hear the door to the garage slam shut. I'm on my last potato, so I peel a little faster...of course nicking my finger in the process.

"Shoot," I say, only just masking my curse word as I turn on the water. I run my wound under it then grab a paper towel to compress it. I don't look at it—not yet. I know it's bleeding. It's probably nothing, but I don't exactly want to get blood on the carrots I just peeled.

"Hey, honey," I hear Cindy say to her husband as he walks into the kitchen.

I turn around and see the backside of Brody's dad as he kisses his wife hello. I immediately see where Brody gets his lean frame.

Brody walks into the kitchen just as his father turns around to face us.

My eyes widen and I barely hold back my gasp as my eyes meet his.

I grip the paper towel a little tighter around my finger.

If I thought that little nick from a peeler was painful, well, that had nothing on this moment.

"Hey, Dad," Brody says, moving toward his father for a hug.

"Hey, Brode," he murmurs, his eyes never leaving me as he tries to send me some sort of silent signal.

Brody moves back to me and drapes his arm casually around my shoulders. "I'd like to introduce you to my girlfriend. Zoey, this is my dad, Derek."

Derek Jensen. The casting director I slept with to get my spot on *Single Life*.

Derek Jensen is Brody Jensen's dad.

Oh, fuck.

CHAPTER 31

ZOEY

"Nice to meet you, Zoey," Derek says as if we haven't met once before. He takes a step toward me and reaches out his hand to shake mine, but I'm glued to the spot where I stand.

My cheeks flush and I start to feel a little faint.

"Oh my God," Brody says, interrupting his father's movement toward me as he glances down to where I'm gripping the paper towel. "Are you bleeding?"

I follow his gaze, and then the little faint feeling I had a second ago gets worse.

I hold onto the counter to steady myself. "I just nicked it with the peeler," I say softly.

"Let's get you a bandage," Brody says. "Come with me."

He keeps his arm around my shoulders, obviously remembering a conversation we had once upon a time about how I can't handle the sight of blood.

That's not what this is, though.

This has much more to do with the fact that I slept with my boyfriend's father.

I slept with my boyfriend's father.

The words echo around in my head. I can't even process this.

Brody holds me steady all the way to a bathroom, where he lifts me up onto the countertop, stands between my legs, and reaches for the medicine cabinet. He pulls out various items but I can't concentrate on anything because I slept with my boyfriend's father.

"Close your eyes and let me take a look." His voice is warm and soothing, somehow calming my chaotic mind.

I do what he says, leaning my head back against the mirror above the vanity as I draw in a deep breath.

"You got yourself pretty good, Zo," he says tenderly.

If that isn't the goddamn understatement of the year.

He spreads some ointment on with a cotton ball. "But I think you're gonna be okay."

Will I be?

Will *we* be?

I listen to the sounds in the quiet bathroom as he rips off the paper wrapping from a bandage. It's just us in here. I should ask him something about his dad now that they've seen each other and the introductions have been made. It's what I would normally do, but my God there is nothing normal about this situation and I'm at a loss as to how exactly I'm supposed to handle it.

Do I tell him? Do I confess right away? Or is this something that goes to my grave with me?

It's not like I *knew* the man I slept with to get a place on some stupid, meaningless reality show was married and had a son I'd grow to fall in love with just a couple short months later.

God, is that all it's been?

I distinctly even remember thinking the casting director wasn't wearing a wedding ring. There weren't any photos of family vying for real estate on his busy desk. Sleeping with a married man is a hard limit for me. They took vows, and even though my parents never showed me how a real marriage should work, even I hold certain things sacred. Marriage is one of them...and it's probably why I'm thirty-three and single.

How was I supposed to know he was married?

How was I supposed to know I'd fall in *love* with Brody when that was the last thing I expected when I accepted the position as back-up dancer on tour with a band I didn't even know?

Derek's eyes in that one second look we shared back in the kitchen told me not to say anything.

But how can I not say anything? This is *Brody*. This is someone I see in my future. We're barely getting off the ground. I can't start all that on a lie. I just can't.

I draw in another deep breath, and I feel Brody's lips against my fingertip as he kisses it. "All better. You can open your eyes now."

I leave them closed for one more beat because I just know Brody is going to be too close, his brown eyes are going to be too focused on mine, and somehow he's just going to know. He's going to see that I have a new secret tearing me up inside, this huge thing I didn't even know.

When I finally open them, he's gazing at me with a brow furrowed in concern.

For me.

I don't deserve his concern, and frankly, I'm pretty sure I don't deserve him, either.

"You okay?" he asks. His voice is so tender and he cares so much about me and oh my God I slept with his *father*. It's all I can think about and it's been all of four minutes since his dad walked through the doors and turned my entire world upside down.

"Yeah," I say, avoiding his eyes as I focus on my finger. I hold it up. "Thanks."

He brushes his lips across mine. "Of course, Zo. I'll always take care of you."

I open my mouth to blurt the truth when his mom's voice interrupts us from across the house. "Brody? Everything okay?"

"Yeah!" he yells back. More quietly and just to me, he says, "Let's go eat."

I nod. "Just give me a minute, okay?" His brows furrow again, and I offer a weak smile. "I'm okay. Just need to use the restroom."

"Okay. Call me if you need me. I'll be in the kitchen."

I nod, and he helps me slide off the counter. I close the door behind him, turn on the faucet to run the water, and lean my head down into my hands as I give myself one brief second to grieve, because that's sure as hell what this feels like: grief.

What a fucking mess.

I lift my head and look into my own eyes. I'm still the exact same person I was when I walked into this house not too long ago, yet somehow everything has changed.

It was one bad decision.

I didn't even give it a second thought once the deed was done. I got what I wanted from it, and while maybe it wasn't the most morally sound way of earning my spot on a television show, it just didn't seem like that big a deal when I did it.

But now...now, it does.

Now it seems like the worst possible thing I could have done.

I've lived a long time doing whatever the hell I please, consequences be damned. I never cared enough about another human being to worry about how my actions might affect them, Ethan and my half-sisters excluded.

But I never could have anticipated this.

I flush the toilet even though I didn't use it and wash my hands, careful to avoid the spot where Brody bandaged me up.

I check myself in the mirror then open the door only to find myself face-to-face with Derek.

He grabs me roughly by the elbow. "Not a word of what happened to anyone," he hisses.

I can't make my mouth form words. Nothing, not even a squeaked out *okay*, comes out of my mouth. Instead, I simply nod in apparent agreement to his terms, rip my arm out of his grasp, and continue down the hall toward Brody.

I find everyone gathered around the kitchen table. Ally and Abby sit on a bench at a huge, square pub table. Cindy sits on one side of the table, and an empty chair is placed across from her, presumably for Derek. The open seat beside Brody means I'll be sitting right between him and his father.

Caught in the middle.

Trapped.

"Derek just went to change into something more comfortable," Cindy explains. "He'll be out in a minute and then we can get started."

He seemed comfortable enough to me in his business attire, but I refrain from dropping that little nugget. Instead, I nod.

"Is your finger okay, sweetheart?" Cindy asks. Her words have the effect of making me feel even worse. She's so kind and caring, such a good soul, and she's married to a monster who fucks women who want to be on television shows. Maybe she knows. Brody has indicated that she does, but I doubt she'd ever think for a second that I'm one of his lucky ladies...Brody either.

I nod and keep my eyes cast down on the table. "Yes, thanks."

Brody elbows me a little in the side good-naturedly, probably because he wants to know why I'm suddenly so quiet. Even if I could tell him, at the dinner table in front of the rest of his family doesn't feel like the ideal place to make the sort of confession lying heavy on my conscience.

A minute later, Derek saunters back into the kitchen and slides into the only open chair, the one that sits at the head of the table just around the corner from me. I squeeze my legs tightly together, refusing to allow them to fall open should his brush against mine.

I press a little closer to Brody, but that feels wrong, too.

This family dinner is suddenly the single most awkward encounter of my life.

Cindy gets up to grab a casserole dish from the counter, which she places on the center of the table. Everyone grabs for the dish closest to them and starts scooping food onto plates, but who can even think about eating at a time like this? The basket of rolls is in front of me, so I pick it up and set one on my plate. I pass the basket to Brody, and when I look to my right, Derek is holding out a bowl of mashed potatoes in my direction.

I take it from him, and of course our fingers brush in the process because why the hell wouldn't they, and I can't look at him because if he thinks this might happen again, he's sorely mistaken. I don't know what his intentions are, but the way he grabbed my elbow in the hallway was full of warning and maybe even a little anger, a little hatred, and suddenly I get the notion that maybe he thinks I'm here on purpose. What if he thinks I sought out his son as a way to get back at him? That show made me look like a complete fool, so I have the motivation for it, but God this is all such a mess.

I need to talk to him. I need to tell him that I met Brody by chance, fell in love with him, and had no idea the two of them were father and son.

I need to tell Brody.

I'll tell him tonight, after we leave. It's part of this new person I've become. I want to be honest, and I don't want any secrets between us. It's the only way we can move forward successfully. All I know for certain is that he needs to hear it from me.

Dinner is interminable.

I push my chicken around the plate with my fork while Ally goes on and on about the job she interviewed for this afternoon. I dip my beans in my mashed potatoes while Abby talks about her day at work. I pretend to eat a bite of salad while Brody answers questions about the tour.

I wish we could rewind the clock back to before the moment I discovered Derek Jensen is Brody's father. For once in my life, I felt like I fit in with a family. I saw a place for myself right here.

And now, that dream is shattered because of one mistake I made in the past.

Funny how that shit comes back to haunt you.

Somehow I make it through dinner. I avoid eye contact with Derek and I sit quietly in my spot.

"Delicious, Mom," Brody says, patting his stomach enthusiastically. He looks over at me, and I nod and murmur something about how great everything was.

"You okay?" Brody asks me.

I press my lips together. It's not an answer, but he takes it as a positive that I'm fine. He picks up my finger with the peeler wound and kisses it again, mistakenly assuming I'm quiet because I saw the blood on my hand earlier.

Oh, there's blood on my hands alright, but it's metaphorical...and there's no way to wash it clean.

We all bring our dishes to the sink, and I'm careful to act normally around Derek so as not to raise suspicions. I excuse myself to the restroom again once the table is cleared, and I barely make it down the hallway before I feel someone grabbing my elbow roughly again. I know who it is before I even rip my arm from his grasp.

"Are you just with him to get to me?" Derek hisses at me. He was sure much nicer to me that day in his office when he sent me all the signals before he fucked me. His eyes are full of hatred again, but there's something else in them I didn't quite notice before.

Fear.

"No," I hiss back, the anger creeping into my tone. "I had no idea you were his father."

"Some coincidence," he whisper-yells sarcastically.

He doesn't believe me, and I'm not sure I even care. I roll my eyes.

"Is this because of how you were edited on the show? Because I had nothing to do with that," he says, suddenly defensive—like I might be the one to tear down walls he has carefully erected around his personal time.

"I swear to you," I whisper-yell back, "I had no idea when I met Brody that his father was the guy I slept with to get a role on some stupid television show."

His glare deepens as I say the words aloud, but he doesn't have a chance to respond to me because a different voice interrupts us first.

It's Brody's voice, and it's sharp and horrified in the quiet hallway. Dishes still clang together in the kitchen as the twins and Cindy finish cleaning up, and despite Brody's next words, the fact that the other three weren't the ones to overhear this conversation provides some well of relief inside me.

"You slept with my dad?"

CHAPTER 32

BRODY

The world falls away from me as the only thing that exists inside this moment are me, Zoey, and my father.

A hum buzzes through my head as my heartbeat thrums in my ears.

"You slept with my dad?" I repeat, a little louder this time, because in this alternate world where truths are unveiled, no one else exists to hear my question except for the three of us.

Their expressions say it all.

They've been caught.

Dad backtracks first, but then he has a proven track record of back peddling. "This isn't what it sounds like."

Zoey draws in a breath, and it's as if the breath gives her the will to speak. "It's exactly what it sounds like." She glares at my dad. "I refuse to lie to Brody." She looks at me, her gaze softening as she holds up both hands in surrender. "It was before you and I met. I swear, I had no idea."

"Don't believe a word out of her lying mouth," Dad says, and she looks over at him in horror. "She's using you to get back at me."

"Oh my God, that's not true at all!" she says, her voice pleading, and I look back and forth between the two of them, wondering how this man who is supposed to be the pillar of my family, the patriarch, the man who I respect above all other men, has become so shallow and weak. Wondering how the woman I've fallen in love with could do this to me, whether she could use me the way my father says she did.

Wondering who the fuck to believe.

In this moment, I choose to believe neither of them...or maybe both, or some combination.

Whatever the case, neither of them is denying they had sex at some point, and that's the part that sends a dagger of ache through my chest and a bullet of pain through my brain.

My dad has been inside the same woman I've been inside.

My stomach turns on me. My mouth waters in that way it only does right before you vomit, but I swallow down the lump in my throat.

I don't know what to say or what to do or who to believe, and the words that fall from my lips are the only truth I know right in this moment. "You both make me fucking sick." I grab Zoey's arm. "We're leaving."

She looks surprised that I'm taking her with me, but what the fuck else am I supposed to do? She came here with me, and now she'll leave with me. And then...

I'm not sure what happens next.

"Thanks for dinner," I say to my mother, who is wiping down the counters. "We need to go."

"So soon? I was hoping to get a few minutes to chat." She tosses the towel next to the sink.

"Sorry. Emergency band meeting," I lie. I give her a hug. She deserves so much better than her bastard of a husband. I can't stand here a minute longer looking into her eyes and lying to her about who he is.

"Abby? Ally?" I yell. They walk in from the family room. "We're heading out." I ignore the disappointment on their faces because I can't take it. I hug each of them with all the ferocity a brother who won't see his sisters for a while can muster...but I realize as I storm out the front door that they'll be at the show tomorrow night. They all will be. My whole family. My cheating father, my forgiving mother, my clueless sisters, and the woman who somehow took my heart, smashed it into obliteration, and left me here with a gaping hole in my chest.

I'm quiet when we get in the car, but it's not because I don't have anything to say. It's because I'm seething with anger, and I'm a little afraid if I speak, I'll let out a tsunami of words. I'm not sure if now is the right time for that. Not while I'm driving, not while I need to focus on getting safely back to my band.

She's quiet, too, and it isn't until we're pulling off the highway that she breaks the awkward silence. She reaches over to take my hand in hers, but I fling it away. She settles her fingers on my thigh.

"He's lying, Brody. You have to believe me." She's pleading, and why wouldn't she? She's asking me to trust her words over my father's. She's asking me to take what she's saying at face value while I'm supposed to ignore the sentiments from the one man who was supposed to be on my side since my first seconds on this earth.

"I don't know what to believe," I say through gritted teeth. I bang an open palm against the steering wheel—probably not my smartest move considering I need to grip my sticks tomorrow night, but fuck it all. I'm pissed and I want to fucking hit something.

"You have to believe me," she says softly.

I bang my palm on the steering wheel again. "Shut up!" I yell. I can't help it. She's clouding my already muddled mind, and listening to her voice speak in the way it does in the glowing moments after we've fucked is only confusing me more. It's making me want to fuck her, but not in the way she would want me to.

I need to take my frustrations out on something other than her and my steering wheel.

When I'm mad, I usually turn to my drums. I pound out a beat, I slam my feet on the pedals and bang my sticks against the toms and let it all out and leave it there.

We're in the middle of a tour, but my practice set is still in the basement at the house where I've lived with the guys in my band for over a year now.

I was so excited to take Zoey there, to show her the place where I live, to let her into my bedroom, the private place few see in the daylight.

But now...

I reroute toward the hotel where the other dancers are staying.

I don't really know what any of this means, but I do know I can't look at her for another second. I can't sit in the car with her, breathing in the same air and sharing the same space she is.

She had sex with my father.

Some things are just clear deal-breakers, and that's one of them.

She's silent, and I see her brush away a tear from the corner of my eye as I turn right and am forced to allow her into my periphery. A pang stabs at my heart, just like it does any time a woman cries in front of me, but I refuse to let this one tug at my heartstrings. I'm too fucking pissed off, too unsure of what to believe.

And so I go with my gut.

We pull in front of the hotel and I stop the car. I stare straight ahead. I can feel her eyes on my profile, but I don't look over at her.

"Goodnight," I say, my voice firm and forceful.

She doesn't get out of the car, and I don't put it in park.

"Brody—" she starts, but I cut her off.

"Just stop. Get out of my car. I can't do this right now."

She draws in a deep breath but doesn't move.

I need her to go...even though I have no idea what my next move is.

CHAPTER 33

ZOEY

I can't leave. I'm glued to my seat in the car, and I just know if I leave, that means it's over. At least if I'm still here in the car, there's a chance for us. I need him to hear my side—to let me explain what I know to be the truth.

"What does this mean?" I ask.

He looks over at me, daggers in his eyes. He isn't just angry. There's a line of hatred mixed in, like even the mere thought of looking at me is painful for him. And maybe it is. I try to imagine what it must feel like to know the person you love slept with your parent, but the image somehow comes up short. I have no idea what he's thinking or feeling, but his father's words about me being a liar and using Brody to get back at him ring through my mind.

How do I get him to believe me?

"I don't know," he says. His teeth are gritted, just as they've been since he found out. It's like he's purposely trying to hold back right now, and a huge part of me just wants to feel the pain. I want him to dump all his words on me so we can figure out how to move past this.

Because not moving past this just isn't an option.

The thought itself sends a violent cramp through my stomach.

We've come too far to give up.

"All I know is that I can't be around you. I need you to get the fuck out of my car." He's back to staring straight ahead. He can't even look at me.

I decide to give him what he wants...for now. He needs space, and despite how well I *thought* I knew him, what we have is still in the newborn stages.

"Okay," I say quietly. I pull on the handle and the door opens. I unclick my seatbelt, and I've got one leg out the door when I turn back to him. "No matter what, Brody, just remember one thing. I love you."

He lets out a little snort of derision, and I get out of the car. He peels out of the hotel's entry before the door has even fully latched shut, and I realize a little too late that my overnight bag is still in the trunk of his car.

I let it go.

I have my purse with my wallet and my phone, and I can change clothes tomorrow on the bus. I don't really *need* anything in there anyway. All I need is a private room where I can spend the night lamenting everything I thought I had that was really just out of my reach.

As soon as I walk into the lobby, a familiar voice grates on my last nerve. "What are you doing here?" Jessa asks. "Shouldn't you be over at your fuckboy's house living the dream?"

I draw in a deep breath. *Don't let her get to you, don't let her get to you.* I chant the futile words over in my head. "I actually just came from meeting his family," I say snidely. "He had some band stuff to take care of so I volunteered to sleep here at the hotel." The lie falls from my lips before I can stop it.

She raises a disbelieving brow, but rather than respond and defend myself, I simply extract myself from the situation. I head to the front desk and thank my lucky stars that all the hotel rooms had been booked long before Brody and I hooked up, and I thank even more lucky stars that Ethan offered to spring for my own room at each hotel after I begged him not to make me share a room with Jessa.

I don't know where Jessa disappears to, nor do I care, and I find the elevator and make my way to my room. I open a bottle of wine from the mini-fridge, draw a hot bath, and slide into the tub, and then I spend the next two hours drinking wine, soaking, and fighting off tears.

Once the water turns cold and my fingers have long pruned over, I attempt to pull myself together. I wrap the hotel's fluffy robe around my body and fall into bed. I dial Kristen's number. I haven't spoken on the phone with her in weeks, and I just need to hear my best friend's voice right now instead of more text messages.

"Hey!" she answers. "How's the big dance star?" She's too enthusiastic for me right now, which tells me she's been drinking.

I don't answer right away because I'm afraid I'll choke out a sob. Kristen has never seen me cry.

"Oh my God! What's wrong, Zo?"

"Brody and I..." I take a deep breath and get my words out. "I think we're finished."

"What happened? I thought everything was going so well. Weren't you meeting his family tonight?"

"Yeah. That's the problem." I flip onto my back and stare up at the ceiling in misery.

"The family?"

"The dad, specifically. The sisters and the mom were everything I ever wanted in a family. All the things I never had, Kris. And then the dad walked in, and it was the casting director on *Single Life*."

"So you already knew each other? Big deal."

I never told her how I actually secured my spot on the show. I let out a heavy sigh. "We *knew* each other."

"Knew?" she repeats.

"Like in the carnal way."

I picture her mouth forming an O as she says, "Ohhhh. Oh shit."

"Yeah, exactly. The dad wanted me to keep it a secret from Brody, but I couldn't do that. We were arguing and Brody overheard us and then the dad lied and said I was using Brody to get back at him because of how I was portrayed on the show." The words tumble out of my mouth.

"What a dick!"

I love my friend for defending me. "But I don't think Brody believes me when I say he's lying. I was shocked when he walked in the door and I recognized him. I had no idea he was related to the man I've fallen in love with."

"Love?" Kristen repeats.

"Yeah, love."

"Oh Jesus, this is huge."

If anyone knows my history with men, it's Kristen. The only man I ever thought I loved never loved me back, and it took falling for Brody to finally accept that and move on. And now...this. I managed to fuck it all up without even realizing that's exactly what I was doing.

"What do I do, Kris?" I ask, my voice full of all the desperation I feel. "I'm trying to give him space. I was supposed to go to his house here in San Diego to spend the night. Instead he kicked me out of his car at the hotel where the other dancers and crew are staying."

"What an asshole," she mutters.

"He had every right to," I say, defending Brody. "He was pissed over what he found out and he doesn't know who to believe." I sit up and fix the pillow behind me to lean on the headboard.

"Did he end it with you?"

"Not exactly," I say. "But I wouldn't say we're on good terms at the moment. He kicked me out and basically couldn't even look at me. I'm afraid he'll do something tonight in his anger that we won't be able to get past." I use my finger to trace a design on the comforter as all my fears spill out of me. "But fuck, I don't even know if we'll be able to get past what I did. It's all such an epic mess and I don't even know how we got here when literally five hours ago we said I love you for the first time."

"I'm so sorry, Zo. Want me and Sawyer to come out there? Maybe travel around to a few shows and just be your buddy system for a few days?"

I don't hate that idea. It would be nice to see my best friends, to feel some of the comforts of a home that doesn't really exist for me anymore—maybe it never really existed for me. "I can't ask you to do that. You've both got responsibilities in Atlanta, and I'm traveling all over the place. It's too much."

"We're here if you need us," she says gently.

"Distract me," I finally say, giving up on tracing the pattern.

"I've got something real fresh," she says with a giggle.

"Hit me with it."

"Sawyer hooked up with Melody."

"His sister's best friend?" I ask, and Kristen giggles. "What's it like living with just him?"

"It's fine. We were never as close as you two were, and I don't find him as attractive as you did, so no worries there."

"I wouldn't care if you did," I say a little too defensively, and Kristen laughs.

"Friends don't hook up with other friend's hook ups," she says.

"But it was fine when you slept with my brother," I mock dryly.

"That was different. He's a fucking rock star, Zo, and I was in love with him for years."

I giggle, the first sign that maybe everything will turn around for me. "Okay, okay, I don't want the details. Not again, anyway."

"Deal." We're both quiet for a minute, and then she says, "Are you okay?"

"Better after talking to you. Thanks, Kristen."

"I'm always just a phone call away," she says.

"I know. Me too." I say the words because we've always said them to each other, but I realize they haven't really been true lately. "I mean it," I amend. "You need me, you call me. I'll be here."

"Okay," she says. "And with that said, I need to run. Someone's waiting upstairs for me."

"Who?" I demand.

"Gotta go! Talk soon!"

She hangs up before she can confess who she has waiting for her, and I can't help a little chuckle at the distraction. My life may be a mess, but at least I can always count on my best friend for a laugh.

CHAPTER 34

BRODY

"Dude, stop!" Dax demands, his arms locked tight around me in a full nelson hold as he attempts to keep me from hitting more shit in our home.

"What the fuck happened?" he asks as I fight to get out of his grasp. Adam is nearby, too, ready to help Dax if he needs to. No one's on *my* side, though. No one is here to fuck shit up with me. They're all blissful in their happy little relationships while I'm on the verge of total destruction—and I'm not talking about the couch cushions I just beat the shit out of in some effort to let go of the rage.

"She fucked my dad," I spit, the words foreign on my tongue despite the truth behind them.

"Tonight?" Kane asks from his perch on the chair across the room where he sits cuddling Sierra, who he hasn't seen since we got on a bus to start this tour.

I struggle once more to get out of Dax's hold, but he's got me locked in. I draw in a breath to prove he can let me go, and he does. "Before the tour," I say, collapsing on the couch I just beat up. "He was the reason she was on that reality show. I should have fucking known."

"Known what?" Dax asks, taking a cautious seat beside me.

"She was just using me to get back at him," I say, repeating the words my dad said earlier that have replayed in my head ever since.

"How does that even make sense?" Kane asks, always the fucking logical one.

I throw up both hands. "I don't know, man, but it's what my dad said and it's a fucking nightmare."

"What did *she* say?" Dax asks softly. Kylie straightens the cushion on his other side then slides down next to him when she sees I've calmed down enough to stop beating our furniture like some uncaring, immature asshole—exactly what I am at the moment.

"She denied it."

"Who do you believe?" Kylie asks.

I lift a shoulder. "The woman I barely know or the man who has a proven track record of lying? You tell me."

"I wouldn't say you *barely* know her at this point. Besides, what if it really is just a coincidence?" Dax asks, and I shake my head.

"Coincidences like that don't just happen. She was pissed about the way she was portrayed on that fucking show, so she figured out a way to get her revenge." I shake my head in disgust.

"By sleeping with his son? How is that revenge?" Dax asks.

"I don't know," I sputter, and I don't care. I leap up and head toward the fridge, where I'm about to grab a beer when I think better of it. I head over to the pantry and look for my old friend Jack on the liquor shelf, but we're all out. Fireball is my only whiskey option, so I swipe the bottle, unscrew the cap, and allow myself a large, scorching swig. It burns the entire way down my chest until it settles in my stomach, and then I help myself to another.

"I'm going to Emerson's," I mutter.

I watch as Kylie tugs on Dax's arm, and then as Dax and Adam exchange a look that says that's a bad idea. Adam opens his mouth to say something in protest, but he's either waiting on Bree to get here or she's already somewhere in the house.

Kane has Sierra.

Adam has Bree.

Dax has Kylie.

And I have nobody.

Noticeably absent from the room is Rascal, who's probably holed up in his bedroom playing video games and masturbating.

"Just stay here with us tonight," Dax says, but his words aren't enough to convince me. One more sip of Fireball does the trick, and I'm out the door before anyone else can try to stop me.

The air is warm on this mid-July evening, a balmy seventy-six, which is just about always the temperature in San Diego, but I don't really feel the warmth on my skin. I don't feel the humidity, either. All I feel is numbness everywhere.

I wish I would've brought that bottle of Fireball with me, but alas, I left it on the kitchen counter. I stalk into the bar that's a second home to my band and me and I'm greeted with a surprised gasp from Dinah, the bar manager.

"Where's the whole gang?" she asks in her scratchy voice that tells me she's smoked a lot of cigarettes over the years. Speaking of which, a smoke doesn't sound all that bad at the moment.

"Back at the house," I mutter.

She doesn't nod in understanding or sympathy. Instead, she says, "You want the usual?"

I shake my head because the usual is a bottle of Miller Lite, and I'm in a whiskey sort of mood. "A double Jack and coke."

Her brows furrow. She knows something's wrong. Rock stars don't return to their old haunts and have something other than the usual if everything's going peachy keen.

An unmistakably familiar shriek to my left has me pausing to consider whether coming here tonight was really the right move. "Brody Jensen? Oh my God, Brody Jensen is here!"

Leah's hands are sliding around my waist and trailing down to squeeze my ass before I have a chance to say the word, "Girlfriend." I snap my jaw shut as soon as I open it to spill the word.

I don't have a girlfriend anymore.

Well...maybe *technically* I do because we didn't *technically* break up tonight, but I can't be with someone who fucked my dad, so that relationship is as good as dead. I don't think we need to say the words for it to be officially over. It's over for me, and that's all that matters right now.

Dinah sets my drink on the bar in front of me. "Keep 'em coming," I say around Leah's grasp on me, and I pick up my drink and down half of it in two swift gulps.

"What are you doing here?" Leah asks. "Did you come back for me?"

I don't even try to mask my laugh. The arrogance of this girl...I once hooked up with Leah, but it wasn't just Leah. Her friend Emma was part of the equation, too. It was the night their third friend, Autumn, thought she might score with Dax for the second time, which didn't happen. I'm not so much a man who likes repeat business, and the thought of the commitment I made to Zoey flashes through my mind as Leah's hands trail down to my ass again.

Anger briefly replaces the numbness, but despite the rage burning inside me, Leah doesn't need to know.

Fuck commitment. Fuck relationships.

Fuck love.

Getting hurt like this is the exact reason why I've avoided this shit like the plague. A night with two women in my bed? Sure. A one-night stand with someone else? Absolutely.

But bring a woman back for more...let feelings get involved...tell her you love her, and it all goes to shit.

I never wanted anything serious. I wasn't in the market for it when it found me, and fuck if anyone thinks I'll ever do it again. Love hurts too much, and it's just not worth the pain.

But another night with Leah and Emma?

I think about that for all of two seconds. My mind flashes back to that night. My mouth covering one pussy while I drove my dick deep into a second one.

Pleasure upon fantastic waves of pleasure.

That's what I want.

I want pleasure to hit me so fucking hard that the alternating rage and numbness can't even stand a chance.

"Is your other friend here?" I murmur into her ear in the husky voice I use when I'm about to tell a girl I want to fuck her. And her friend, apparently.

"Emma?" she murmurs back, and I nod. "Yeah. She's at the table."

I take another bolstering sip of my drink. "Let's get drunk and go back to my place."

She grins widely, and instead of thinking how her smile lights her pretty face, I can only think about how good it'll feel to jam my cock between those smiling lips.

She presses a tentative kiss to my mouth, almost shy — funny after what we did the last time I took her back to my place, and when she breaks the kiss uncertainly, I grab the back of her head with my free hand and smash my mouth against hers. I slide my tongue between her lips, her tongue moves into my mouth, I thrash my tongue a little more wildly, and suddenly we're making out in the middle of the bar with the promise for more back at my place.

Her hands slide up and down my back, dipping down to cup my ass as our kiss deepens. I feel her tongue circling every crevice of my mouth, but I'm not quite drunk enough yet. All I can think about right now is how she kisses different from Zoey. This is fast-paced and too wet and not what I want, but I've already extended the invitation and I still want the Zoey thoughts to stop, so I keep doing it.

I break apart from her long enough to drain my drink, slam it on the bar, and signal to Dinah for another, and then my mouth is back on hers. The Fireball mixed with the first Jack drink is starting to edge its way into my consciousness, starting to dull the pain and blur the events happening around me. It's starting to make me think going home with Leah and Emma is a really, really great idea.

I bite down on her lip a little, and her yelp-moan of pain edged with pleasure fires me up. My dick is hard and ready to bust out of my pants and find a new shelter.

But it all goes to shit when I feel a palm pull on my shoulder. I break from Leah and spin around, ready to fuck up whoever is interrupting me despite the little ray of hope I have that it's Emma and she's here for her turn—but I'm sorely disappointed when I find myself face-to-face with my best friend.

"What the fuck are you doing?" Dax spits out at me.

There's a little ruckus in the bar when someone shouts something about Dax being here. I hear my own name and something else about MFB, and I only allow a split second to think about how much has changed in the past year. We used to play this bar all the time as local pseudo-celebrities, and now we're actual famous people. But I'm still the same guy, and right now I'm hurting. I just want a piece of home...or a piece of ass.

"What do you even care?" I spit back. I turn back around to Leah and spot my fresh drink sitting on the bar behind her, waiting for me. I mumble a quick apology to Leah then grab the drink and gulp half of it down in a single sip.

"This destruction, Brody. It's not you," Dax says.

"Well, I'm a changed fucking man." I drain the rest of the glass, slam it on the bar, and signal Dinah again. Her eyes slide beside me to Dax, who is surely giving her some signal *not* to serve me more alcohol, but I'm a paying adult in this bar and I deserve to be served.

"Don't interfere, Dax. This isn't your business," I hiss at him.

"Don't be a douche-poodle," he says, and I roll my eyes at his favorite new term.

"Fuck you."

He breathes out a visible sigh. "You know it's my business. We're in the middle of a tour and we have a show tomorrow night."

"I have plenty of time between now and then." I turn to look at the bar to see if Dinah's getting my drink, and Leah grasps me a little tighter around my waist.

"To what?" he asks close to my ear. "Fuck things up even worse for you and Zoey?"

"Hey," I say, turning back toward him and lashing out with a little shove against his chest. "*She* is the one who fucked things up, not me." I jab my finger into my chest.

"Who's Zoey?" Leah asks beside me, and I'm sort of surprised she cares. Of course she cares, though. Another woman means another obstacle in her way.

"His girlfriend," Dax says at the same time I say, "Nobody."

Leah looks confused for a second, but then she seems to buy my answer over Dax's. "It's over?" she asks me.

"Would you care if it wasn't?" I shoot back, and she giggles.

"No, not really." Her arms clamp tighter still around my waist.

"Don't do this," Dax pleads with me, just another symbol of everything that has changed. Before he got with Kylie, he'd have been all over this situation with me. And now he's being a fucking pussy and cock-blocking me all at the same time.

He throws two twenties on the bar. "That enough?" he yells to Dinah as he nods toward me.

"Too much," she yells back.

"You deserve it." He winks at her then turns back to me. "Come on," he says.

I shake my head and stand my ground stubbornly.

He sighs again, and then he sends a text. Within thirty seconds, Adam and Kane enter the bar, and the three of them practically drag me out of the place. A few of our fans follow us out, but I'm beyond the point of caring.

"Fuck all three of you," I say once we're out on the sidewalk in front of the bar.

"Don't cause a scene," Kane says, a clear warning in his tone. "Let's go."

Kylie's car is right at the entrance, and Dax gets in front while Kane and Adam corral me to the backseat.

"This is such bullshit," I whine once I'm in the middle bitch seat in the back.

No one responds, and I can't help but feel more alone than ever.

The walk to the bar is only about ten minutes, and the drive is about two. We pull into the driveway and everyone spills out of the car and heads back to their respective places, and I find myself alone. I grab the bottle of Fireball and head up to my bedroom.

When someone knocks at my door, I yell, "Go the fuck away," but the door opens anyway.

Adam steps in and shuts the door behind him.

"What the fuck do you want, traitor?" I ask.

He leans against the door. "I'm sorry about what went down. We all are, Brody. We just want you to think about what you're doing before you do something you'll regret."

"Let me live my fucking life and make my own bad decisions," I say, taking a swig of the Fireball.

He eyes the bottle for a beat. "Fireball?" he asks like he's about to tease me. We all know Dax keeps it in the house for Kylie.

The glare I send his way causes him to keep his teasing to himself. "It was all we had," I say, but I have to admit, the shit tastes pretty fucking good right now.

"We have to play in less than twenty-four hours. Don't get too fucked up."

"I've played fucked up before. I've played hungover, stoned, and half-asleep. I'll be fine."

He nods gravely and slides down the door until he's sitting on the floor. "Yeah, but you've never played heartbroken."

I don't have an answer for that because he's absolutely right.

"Neither have I," he admits.

My eyes shoot over in his direction, and it's the first time I realize that maybe I'm not the only one going through something.

I've known this kid since junior high. We've jammed together for over a decade.

As I study him from my perch on the bed, Fireball bottle dangling from my fingertips, I realize I've never seen him like this.

I toss the uncapped bottle across the room to him, spills on the floor be damned, and he expertly catches it one-handed with not a drop landing outside the bottle.

"What happened?" I ask while he takes his own swig, and then another before he answers.

"Bree broke up with me tonight." He stares down the bottle, not at me.

"I'm sorry, man."

Another swig, and then a lift of his shoulder before he focuses on me. "Four years down the drain. I thought she was the one."

That sort of puts what happened with Zoey in perspective. I lost four weeks of my life with someone I thought had the potential to be in my life long-term, but thoughts of marriage and children never even entered the conversation. Adam and Bree, though—we all thought they were in it for the long haul.

"Why'd she end it?" I ask. I nod toward the bottle, and he tosses it back to me. It's some *Cocktail* shit up in here, this open bottle flying around with no liquor spilling out. We would make some crazy ass fucking bartenders.

Except we're rock stars instead. And I think we do a pretty okay job at that, too.

"She couldn't handle the pressure of the tour. Couldn't handle the time apart. It came down to her wanting me to pick her over the band, over the success, over our career. And as much as I love her, as much as I *wanted* to choose her, I need to be with someone who would never force that decision on me."

"You told her you pick the band?" I ask. I notice the Fireball doesn't burn anymore as I swallow down a large gulp.

He shakes his head, and I toss the bottle back to him. I'm not sure which one of us needs it more at this point. "I told her I wouldn't make that sort of decision."

"And she took that as a no?"

He shrugs. "I guess. But, fuck, why can't I have both? Dax does. Kane does. Kylie and Sierra seem to get it. Why couldn't Bree?"

He's asking me sincerely, like I might have an actual answer for him. I don't. "Why did Zoey have to sleep with my goddamn father of all people?" I'm not comparing our pain, not vying for who has it worse—just letting him know he doesn't have to navigate this alone in my own fucked up way.

He nods sagely, and then I ask, "Why'd you fuckers stop me at Emerson's?"

He grunts out a mirthless laugh. "Because we all know it's not over with Zoey, man. You'll get past this. You two are meant for each other."

His words are tough to hear if only because they're totally wrong. "We all thought the same thing about you and Bree, man. And maybe you can get past this, too."

He presses his lips together and shakes his head. "Not after the things I said. I lashed out, and I can't take back the words, just like she can't take back the things she said. We're done, and no matter how I feel tomorrow about that once this shit's worn off," he says, holding up the bottle, "and the anger is replaced by some new feeling, it's over."

"I'm sorry, Adam," I say quietly, and his only response is another swig of cinnamon whiskey.

Despite everything, though, his words do make me wonder one thing: what feeling will replace the alternating anger and numbness when I wake up tomorrow morning?

CHAPTER 35

ZOEY

A full bottle of wine by myself might've been a bad idea. A bottle and a half was downright stupid.

I clutch my pounding head for a beat after I slap the alarm on my phone. Somehow I had the good sense to turn it on last night before I passed out, but I'm sort of regretting it this morning as the pain spears my skull.

I force myself out of bed and drag my hungover ass to the shower. The only reason I got any sleep at all last night was because of that wine, so at least I'm grateful for that.

But I'm terrified about what today holds.

I feel much better after a steamy shower and some ibuprofen, and I grab my phone to check Kylie's text with today's schedule. I have about an hour to spare before I need to head toward the venue, which is close by, so I call room service and order some breakfast.

My toes are underneath the comforter while I wait for my food, and I'm indulging in some trash TV, namely *TMZ*, when my stomach turns on me.

And it's not because of the wine.

"Brody Jensen from the wildly popular band MFB was spotted out last night in San Diego." The camera zooms in on a dark and grainy picture that looks like an amateur snapped it on a phone in some bar. The first image is clearly Brody, and some brunette woman with enormous tits and a slim waist is hanging on him. Nothing new—Brody has women hanging on him all the time. The second image, though, is a bit more telling. It's still obviously the same two people, but this time, Brody's mouth is smashed against Big Tit's mouth, and that's the one that turns my stomach.

On pure instinct, I shut off the television. I can't see more of that shit.

I know what these notorious gossip shows do. I've seen my brother and the other guys in his band deal with rumors and media making more of things and even misrepresenting times, locations, people...the list is endless.

But that was Brody. When I left him, he was wearing a black shirt and jeans. In that picture, he was wearing the same clothes. Same perfectly mussed hair. Same unmistakable scruff on the same perfect jawline.

It's anger first, and then disappointment that wash over me nearly simultaneously.

God, I hate his guts.

What a fucking coward. He ran at the first sign of trouble right into the arms of some woman. They kissed in a bar, and who the hell knows what else they did? My imagination takes hold of the worst-case scenario, that this bitch ended up in the bed that should've been *mine* last night.

Of course that's what happened. Why wouldn't it? This is *my* life we're talking about, after all. Nothing ever goes as smoothly as it should.

My food arrives, but I feel too sick to my stomach to eat it. I realize this is really messed up, but I still feel innocent in all this. I didn't know Brody back when I did what I had to do to nab my spot on *Single Life*, and the man gave no indication he was married.

Yet I don't really blame Brody for his reaction. It's gross, really, and I feel a little dirty and full of shame. The bath I took last night and the shower I took this morning weren't enough to scrub away the grime, and I'm not sure if anything ever will.

So how do we get past this? He sees what I did as a betrayal, and he betrayed me right back last night by running off to some other woman. I'm not sure where all that leaves us, but it can't be good.

I pack up my shit and grab an Uber to the bus lot, where I flash my credentials to get back onto the bus. I'm the first one back, but it feels just a little better to be back here, like I'm a little closer to him and everything we've built over the last month together. This has somehow become *home* for us, and maybe once he's back here, he'll feel it, too. Maybe everything will magically fix itself.

I wait nervously in my bunk for a while as I stare up at my ceiling to where he sleeps and think of everything that's happened. After forty-five minutes by myself, I hear the bus door swing open and slam shut. I peek my head out of my bunk to see who it is, and I'm less than thrilled to find Jessa, but I force myself out of bed anyway.

She grins at me as I emerge from the bunk hall into the forward cabin. "You catch the headlines?" she singsongs from across the bus.

I breathe out a heavy sigh and decide to play dumb even though I know *exactly* what she's talking about. "What headlines?" I drop down into a chair by the table.

"Brody was *all over* some girl at a bar last night. You didn't see?" She's positively *gleeful* over this, and my first instinct is to punch her in the face. I clench my fists by my sides, because the last thing I want right now is to get kicked off the tour because I started a fight.

I clear my throat as I try to come up with a witty response. It eludes me as I realize she's trying to get me to confess the truth in front of the *Rock on the Road* cameras. I won't do it.

"It obviously wasn't you," she says. "This girl had long, dark hair."

"I saw," I say quietly, my voice as lethal as I can possibly make it. "Can we drop it?"

She smiles as she plops into the seat across from me. "No," she says snidely. "I don't think so. You lied last night. You said he had a band meeting."

"He did," I protest.

"So you're saying he cheated?"

"I'm saying things went down between us that are none of your business, Jessa, and as we left it last night, we're still together. That's all you need to know." I refrain from adding that it's all she needs to know because it's all I currently know myself. "It doesn't matter, anyway. He's made it clear he doesn't want you."

A flash of something dark crosses her face before she smooths it over. "Well he isn't with you, either, now is he?"

I'm about to unleash a big old *fuck you* on her when the bus door opens again and Kylie walks in. "Good afternoon, ladies," she says in a clipped tone. She settles into one of the recliners and pulls out her tablet, where she starts tapping around and starting her day. I know the men can't be far behind her, and my heart pounds as I wait for Brody.

I don't know what this morning is going to feel like, but I'm terrified. He kissed another woman last night. My heart hurts just thinking about that, yet I'm trying to understand what he's going through. I'm just not sure I can.

Dax boards the bus first, followed by Rascal, Adam, who looks positively hungover, Kane, and finally, Brody. He looks like hell. His eyes have deep, dark shadows beneath them, and his clothes are rumpled like he just rolled out of bed and it was time to leave.

"Hi Brody," Jessa says when he passes by our table, honey in her tone that makes my stomach roll.

He offers her a tight smile and a nod of his head. His eyes dart past me as he carefully avoids eye contact on his way past the table and toward the bunks. I close my eyes and breathe out a heavy breath, and Jessa studies me through it all.

"What went down between you two last night?" she presses. "Because he didn't even *look* at you just now." She's purposely rubbing salt in my open wounds, kicking me when I'm already down, and I hate her even more for it.

"None of your business," I mutter, and then I stand because facing whatever wrath Brody has for me must be better than sitting here and taking it from Jessa.

When I head to the bunk section, Brody's eyes meet mine just before he climbs into his own bunk and pulls the curtain shut. I know he isn't sleeping in there, so despite bus decorum, I stand outside his curtain and say, "Can we please talk?"

He rips the curtain open and sits up, narrowly avoiding hitting his head in the process. "I have nothing to say to you."

"Who was the girl last night?" I ask, my voice weak to my own ears but goddammit, I need to know.

He looks mildly surprised I know about that, but he doesn't answer me. "I want you off this bus," he says. He climbs down from his bunk to square off at me. "Better yet, I want you off this fucking tour."

"You can't do that," I protest.

"Yes, I can, and as soon as I find a replacement, you're gone." He motions between the two of us. "This...this *thing* between us? It's over."

He storms toward the back of the bus, where he slams the door and leaves me a broken mess standing in the middle of the bunk hall.

CHAPTER 36

BRODY

"Dude, what the fuck are you doing?" Dax asks. I'm sitting in the back office on the floor, leaning against the bus wall as I contemplate what I just said to her.

But dammit, the second I saw her, the pain was ripped open again, as fresh as it was the second I overheard my father and her and their hushed whispers in what they thought was an empty hallway.

"Pouting," I say.

Dax spares a sharp laugh but slides down the wall and sits beside me. "Well stop. You're a rock star with a set to play tonight in front of a sold-out hometown crowd at the Pechanga. The fucking *Pechanga*, man, the place we sat in the crowd and watched more bands than I can count when we were in high school, in college, and making our way in our own right."

"I told her I want her off the tour," I blurt. Everything he just said is beyond my wildest dreams, but I can't stop thinking about Zoey and my father.

He looks surprised. "You did?"

I nod.

"And how do you plan to make that happen?" His voice is full of doubt. "Tonight is the halfway mark, man. Fifteen shows down, fifteen to go. You can't just kick off a dancer in the middle of it."

"If I can find a replacement I can," I shoot back.

"Because you're so schooled in dancers?"

I shake my head. "Because we have three pros on this tour and certainly one of them knows someone. No favors from our idols, just straight-up hiring a dancer to dance."

Dax blows out a breath. "I can't talk you out of this?" he asks, more doubt there in his voice because he knows, he fucking *knows*, that when I set my mind to do something, I'll make it happen.

I shake my head.

"You're a dumbfuck, you know that?"

I nod a bit, pressing my lips together. "Thanks, man. Way to hit a guy when he's already down."

He chuckles. "I told you not to fuck things up with her. This is Ethan Fuller's sister, and—"

I cut him off before he can dig into a lecture. "I know who she is, all right? And for the record, *she* fucked things up, not me."

"But you love her."

I lift a shoulder. "We all know how overrated love is, don't we?"

He shakes his head. "Not anymore. Not since I found the right woman."

"You're the dumbfuck, then, if you believe love doesn't always equal pain and suffering. You enjoy that shit when it comes to an end."

"Hey," he cuts in sharply. "Just because you're going through something doesn't mean you're allowed to lump us all in with you. I'm happy, Brody. Happier than I've ever been in my life. And I refuse to let you bring me down or make me feel bad that Kylie and I wound up together. I came in here to try to listen, to try to lend a shoulder, but you don't want that." He stands up and brushes his hands on his thighs. "You want to lash out and try to get everyone to commiserate with you, but fuck that. I won't be a part of it. You wallow and do what you need to do to get your ass on stage tonight. Pull yourself together. If you're pissed at Zoey, be pissed at Zoey, but don't make everyone around you miserable."

"I want her off this bus," I say quietly as he turns to leave.

He blows out a heavy sigh and doesn't answer when he walks out the door and toward the bunk hall, the door slamming shut behind him.

* * *

Relax, I tell myself. *Just relax.*

But I can't.

It's all wrong. Everything's off. The sticks feel foreign in my hands. I banged out a practice set backstage during the opening band, and I missed hitting a cymbal—if that fucking happens tonight, I don't know what I'll do.

I go the safe route. I play simpler. I bang out the beats I'm trained to bang, and nothing more. I can't help when my eyes edge to Zoey.

I still play, but the sticks feel too small in my hands. Or maybe too big. Or maybe it's my hands—they're too big for the sticks. Between songs, I grab a different pair out of the bag I keep behind me. Something's gotta give, but I know what it is.

It isn't the sticks or my hands or my drum kit.

It's fucking Zoey.

It's her tight little body dancing in front of me the way she's done for fifteen shows, but before when I watched her out of the corner of my eye while I played, I felt happiness. I was thrilled at the prospect of taking her home to my bed—or back to the bus, anyway. I knew I'd spend the night with her in my arms, and we'd find a time and a place where I'd get to touch that gorgeous body, where I'd get to fuck her and feel her and smell her citrus scent and bury myself in her.

But now, all I can think about is the fact that she had sex with my dad—who is somewhere backstage with my mom and my sisters.

Dax introduces the members of MFB, and that's when I'm supposed to fly into a little drum solo. I take it easier than I've ever taken it. Fuck throwing a stick up into the air and watching it twirl four times before I catch it. I want to impress my sisters and my mom—and I *wanted* to impress my father as well, but that was before I knew the truth. And now, well, hopefully my mom and sisters will just be impressed that I'm up here in front of a sold-out crowd. Fuck my dad and whatever he thinks about any of it.

Zoey dances and I play. I play and Zoey dances. This is my reality, and this is exactly why I need her gone. I can't concentrate, and it takes every single ounce of my willpower to complete the set, to finish the job I'm here to do, to not fuck everything up royally the way the rest of my life seems to have gone.

We meet backstage just before the encore. "Safe tonight, Bro," Kane says to me, and I shoot him a look that clearly tells him to fuck off.

Dax shakes his head. "We're fine. We got the job done." He's breathing heavily, and Kylie tosses him a fresh shirt. He changes and tosses the sweaty one back to her, and I catch a glimpse of Zoey out of the corner of my eye. She's avoiding eye contact as she stretches, keeping limber until she has to run back out on stage. I see our families standing to the side. Rascal's parents. Kane's parents, two brothers, and Sierra. Adam's parents and sister. My own family. Noticeably missing is Dax's family, but he doesn't talk to them. Even Kylie's parents are here with her younger brother.

I don't make eye contact with any of them. I focus on our huddle, but Dax breaks it early so everyone can run and say hi to their family members for a brief second before we have to return to the stage.

I don't run over to mine.

I stand rooted to the spot, scared to look over at them, scared to look at Zoey, scared that I'm going to fuck the rest of this set, scared about these feelings flitting through my chest.

Fuck it.

I run back out on stage. It's dark enough up here that no one sees me, and I take my spot on my throne, the name for the stool where drummers sit.

I look out over the crowd. It's pitch black save for the flashlights of cellphones lighting the entire arena as the crowd whoops and cheers and screams for more MFB.

And that's what lights a fire under my ass. That singular moment where I'm on stage and the crowd is waiting for more of the music I created with my band—that's what I live for. Not some woman who'll only fuck me over in the end like every other woman. Not earning the respect of a man I don't respect myself.

This is for me and my band. This is my life, and I'm content to live the way I lived it before fucking Zoey came along and ripped it all to shreds.

We finish without a hitch, Kane's words of me playing too safe in my mind the entire time. I kick it up a notch as I focus on the crowd, the fans, the people who are paying to watch us play tonight. I fucking slay the final song, and then we take our bows and rush off the stage.

We've got two more nights here in San Diego, and our next show is in Oakland, not terribly far away. So I've got two free nights to figure out how the hell to get Zoey off this tour so I can breathe again.

But first...first I have to face my family.

They're waiting in the dressing room when we get there. My sisters gush over me and turn their attention almost immediately to Dax, who is free only because Kylie is settling up finances with the arena.

"That was wonderful, Brody. So much talent." My mom hugs me despite the sweat-soaked shirt I'm wearing. "I'm so proud of you."

"As am I," my father booms, like I give a royal fuck. "Can we talk privately?" he asks.

I shake my head. "I need to shower and we have a band meeting back at the house tonight," I lie.

"It'll only be a moment."

My jaw clenches and my teeth grind together, but I cave. "The room next door is empty."

I lead the way, and once we're inside and I've flicked the light on, I can't help but notice how contrastingly quiet this room is compared to the party going down right next door.

"I'm sorry for what I said," he begins. "I panicked."

I raise a brow but don't otherwise respond.

"I'm not a good man, Brody," he says, and I snort in agreement. "I've done things I shouldn't, and I've taken advantage of my position. But the worst thing I did was lie to you."

"About?" I ask, pulling off my shirt and mopping the sweat on my forehead with it. Might as well be completely exposed for this conversation, right?

"When I said she was using you. I have no idea if that's true or not. I just couldn't take the way you looked at me like you hated me."

"I do hate you," I say, and disappointment shadows his eyes.

"I have no one but myself to blame for that, but it all changes today. I will find a way to earn back your respect. I will find a way to make things right."

I shake my head. "Don't you see, Dad? The damage is already done. You fucked the woman I love, and it doesn't matter *when* or *how* it happened. The fact is that it did happen and you have a wife you vowed to love and honor. You've loved and honored nobody but yourself, and that's not something you can just make right with the snap of your finger."

He gives me a pleading look. "I understand. Just please, please don't tell your mother."

"You think she doesn't know?" I yell. "We all fucking know, *Dad*." I say the name given to him by my birth with pure venom in my tone.

He nods, defeated, and it's the first time in my life I see him as another human who just really fucked up. But his mess isn't mine to fix, nor is it any of my concern anymore. "I have a celebration with my band to get to." I turn to leave the room, and I can't help one last parting shot. "Fuck off and go to hell."

It's not the nicest thing I've ever said to my father, but I don't regret the words as they leave my mouth.

CHAPTER 37

BRODY

It's strange sitting here in the middle of a huge party in my house but not really being present at it.

Familiar faces mill about our family room and kitchen, and I sit on the couch in a bit of a daze. I need to snap out of it, but I'm not sure how. It's some combination of hurt, disgust, heartbreak, and brooding while I pound beer after beer.

After all, we have no gig to perform tomorrow night. No concert in front of thousands of screaming fans. That means I have a full twenty-four hours of recovery ahead of me, and the beer helps numb the searing pain in my chest, so I keep drinking more of it as I hope for reprieve.

I spot Jessa when she walks through the doors, and I wonder if Zoey will have the nerve to show her face here tonight. Her eyes find me to no one's surprise, and I nod her over in my direction. She saunters over like she's on a fucking runway, and I force my eyes to remain focused on her despite their natural inclination to roll upwards.

I'm not interested in her, not even a little...but that doesn't mean she can't be useful to me.

She slides into the small space beside me, and I move over a little to accommodate her.

"I need a favor," I say.

She nods as her brown eyes gaze up adoringly at me. "Anything."

"I need you to find a new dancer for the tour." My words are succinct, and I expect her to look a little surprised, but she doesn't. Instead, she looks a little nervous.

"Oh, Brody, I can't do that," she says, contradicting her last word to me. "It would be impossible to train someone mid-tour like this."

I move back toward her so our thighs are pressed together, and I lean in close to her ear. I'm sure my breath reeks of beer, but I have zero fucks to give. Jessa wants me, and I'm using that to my advantage. "What about you? You know every single dance. You invented them. You don't need to watch Denise and Lauren because they've got it down pat by now."

She raises a brow. "Denise and Lauren? Does that mean Zoey's out?"

I lift a shoulder. "If I have anything to say about it, yeah, that's what it means."

"What happened?" she asks, using this baby voice that nearly makes me wince. It's about as appealing as nails on a chalkboard and I'll never understand why women think it's sexy.

It's not.

"It doesn't matter. All you need to know is that it's over."

Her hand snakes its way onto my thigh. When I glance down at her, her bottom lip is sticking out in a petulant pout. "I'm so sorry, Brody." Her hand slides a little higher, but it's not anything I haven't felt before. If she was someone else, maybe. Fuck, in a few more beers...*maybe*. "What can I do to make you feel better?"

"Dance for us. Get her off the tour so I don't have to be reminded of the total shit show it turned out to be."

She considers it for a few beats, and then she nods. "Okay. All right. I'll do it." She lifts her hand and taps my nose with a pointy nail. "For you."

I get the feeling that she thinks I owe her one now, and indebted to her is not really the place where I want to be—but if it gets Zoey out, I'm in.

"Thanks, babe," I say, forcing the term of endearment out of my mouth for someone who isn't very endearing to me.

"I'd do anything for you. Haven't you figured that out yet?" Her voice is low and sultry, and combined with the beer I've already had, it's almost enough to convince me. Almost.

Not quite.

And then something happens that flips everything on its head.

I spot Denise and Lauren walk in. Trailing just a few steps behind the two other dancers, Zoey Fuller steps foot through my front door.

"Oh fuck no," I mutter, and Jessa's head whips toward the direction of the door.

"Take me up to your room," she demands.

I give her a look that clearly tells her she's fucking crazy, and she relents a little.

"Just to get you out of here." She lifts a shoulder. "And make other people think maybe there's something else going on."

My eyes meet Zoey's over Jessa's head, and the beer clouding my brain tells me Jessa is exactly right. What a brilliant idea.

I drain my beer, grab her hand, and pull her along behind me. The first stop is the fridge, where I grab two beers—both for me even though it'll look like one's for her—and then the next stop is up the stairs into my bedroom, where I slam the door behind Jessa.

It's still loud in here with the music and the voices blaring a floor below us, but closing the door gives us a little bit of semi-quiet.

She's in my most private space now, this girl who I'm not at all attracted to but who wants me for reasons beyond me when I feel like we barely know one another, and I'm not sure what my next move should be. I set the two beers on my nightstand and collapse on my bed, and Jessa gives herself the tour.

My walls are mostly bare except for a drumhead with MFB's earliest logo on it. I have one dresser and one nightstand, and since we just left for tour, my room is fairly clean. I'm a simple guy. I don't like a lot of clutter, and my room shows that.

"This room doesn't tell me anything about *you*," Jessa says. "Except that you don't decorate."

I shrug. "It's a place to sleep. Sometimes a place to fuck. Does it need to say more than that?" I drink down half the fresh can of beer I brought up with me.

She gasps a little at my mention of fucking in here, and her eyes narrow a little like she can't really get a good read on me. Good. I don't want her to.

"My bedroom walls are full of dancers and bodies. I feel like it seeps into my brain while I sleep and it helps me live my career, you know?" Her eyes take on a dreamy and faraway look.

"I live my career by sleeping on a tour bus." I realize my tone is rude, but I'm trying to throw her off the scent, not come begging.

I drain the can and smash it on my nightstand before popping the tab on the next one, and she stops pacing my room and settles in beside me, propping up a pillow and leaning against my headboard. "Do you like touring?"

"I get paid to play drums. There's something pretty fucking epic about that."

"But the buses, the bunks, the lack of a shower..." She wrinkles her nose as she trails off.

"None of that shit bothers me. I love traveling and jamming with my best friends." I omit the fact that it'd be more fun if it was just the five of us on our bus and not a couple dancers and our manager tagging along for the ride. I feel pretty damn chivalrous leaving that part out.

She nods. "It would probably be different if I felt like I had friends on this tour," she muses, and it's the first time I sort of feel for her. She's the boss of the other dancers, but she doesn't quite fit in with the band. She's stuck somewhere in the middle, which is probably a tough spot.

"I'm your friend," I say if only because the silence stretches a little too awkwardly long. I want to add that I'm *just* her friend, nothing more, but I don't.

She bumps my shoulder with hers. "Thanks, Brody." We're quiet for a few beats, and then she asks, "Who is the most fascinating person you've met?"

It doesn't take me long to come up with an answer, but I can't manage to spit it out.

There's one person who has the career I want, who I've modeled my own talents after since I was fifteen-years-old, and somehow I ended up falling in love with that man's sister.

"Mark Ashton," I say instead of Ethan Fuller. I have to. I can't risk admitting how much I admire the brother of the woman I just ran away from downstairs.

"He's dreamy," she agrees.

I chuckle. "That's exactly why I chose him." I have another sip of my beer. I feel like social etiquette tells me I should ask her who the most fascinating person she has met is, but I can't bring myself to care.

"For me, it's Gianna Murphy, the judge on that show *You Can Dance*. I appeared on the first season as a back-up dancer, and Gianna just has this career that I admire so much."

I didn't ask, I almost say, but because she's letting me use her right now, I'm not quite that big of a dick to say the words. I let out some grunt of agreement, like I listened to what she said.

"Are you more indoorsy or outdoorsy?" she asks next, like she's checking off some getting to know you questionnaire.

"Outdoorsy except when we're playing. Acoustics suck in outdoor venues."

"You just need louder speakers," she says, and she giggles like it was a really clever answer. "I'm more outdoorsy, too. I love camping and nature and hiking."

And now I know she's full of shit. A girl who wears as much make-up as her and who spends as many hours curling her hair as she does can't possibly love nature and camping. I hate when women say what they think men want to hear, and all this is doing is making me like her less. "I hate camping," I say, which isn't really true but it's an experiment to see what she'll say.

"Oh, I've only been a couple times. It was okay."

I shake my head and ignore the fact that she just flat-out lied to me. I finish the second can of beer and crush it on my nightstand again.

She turns to look at me, and I stare up at the ceiling. And then she's suddenly climbing over me, like I gave her some signal or indication that this is what I want, and she's straddling my lap. She leans down and her hair tickles my face before she presses her lips to mine.

I'm drunk and I'm stupid, but I'm not completely powerless.

Just as I'm about to push her off me, the door to my bedroom bursts open.

I pull my head to the side to see who it is, and a flash of blonde hair flies out of the room before I can even tell it was Zoey.

But it was Zoey. The blonde hair and the little glimpse of her perfect body gave her away.

Good.

This is exactly what I want her to think—that I'm up here hooking up with Jessa. That's why I dragged her up here with me.

What perfect timing that she happened to walk into my bedroom at the very same second Jessa tried to seduce me.

I push her off me. "Jessa, you're a gorgeous woman, but this can't happen."

She looks defeated, but not as embarrassed as I expected. "Why not?" she challenges.

"Because I just ended things with Zoey." And then, just like she lied to me about camping, I lie to her to make her feel better. "If I'm going to get involved with you, I don't want it to be on a rebound." I run my knuckles down her cheek, and that seems to do the trick.

She nods. "I'll wait until you're ready," she says softly, and then she stands, brushes the front of her shirt down, and heads out the door, leaving me alone in my bedroom.

CHAPTER 38

ZOEY

I think there are defining moments in every person's life. Moments that tell us what we're really made of. Moments that break us and moments that piece us back together.

Seeing Jessa on top of Brody, her mouth on his—that's a moment that caused some damage. My chest hurts, and I rub at it as the tears blind my eyes while I try to find my way through the house.

I try to remember all the reasons I never should've fallen for him in the first place, but none of them matter now.

All that matters is that he kissed my mortal enemy.

Maybe that's dramatic, but it also really defines the heart of the matter.

He knows I can't stand her. He knows the level of jealousy I feel whenever she flirts with him.

Yet he allowed her into his bed.

This hurts way more than the damn photographic evidence of him kissing some random girl in a bar. That was a mistake...but this damage is permanent.

"Zoey!"

A male voice—not Brody—calls my name as I storm through the living room, swiping angrily at the tears I so hoped would've waited to fall until I got outside. I don't let my vulnerable side out often, but fucking Brody broke me.

I ignore whoever it is. I'm humiliated, hurt, and alone, and I'm in no mood to explain why to whoever is trying to get my attention.

Once I'm on the front porch with the door slammed shut behind me, my head buzzes and my ears ring from the loud music I subjected myself to as I wondered what he was doing upstairs. It was Dax who told me it'd be okay. Dax was the one who said I should go knock on his door and if he didn't answer, it was just because he couldn't hear me knock over the music.

Dax. It was him who told me that it's not really over for Brody and me.

He gave me hope when I wasn't sure there was anything left to cling to, and the second I opened my heart back up to the possibility, Brody kissed Jessa and my entire world imploded.

Maybe in the same way Brody's did when he found out about his father and me.

I push the thought away. I refuse to allow any inklings of logic into my head right now. Instead, I put all my focus into opening the Uber app and requesting a ride from my current location.

The door opens behind me as I tuck my phone back into my pocket. I hold onto the handrail surrounding the porch and stare out into the dark night lit only by the streetlights a few houses down the block in either direction.

"Are you okay?" It's Dax's voice, and I don't turn around.

"Fine," I mutter, but even I can hear the lie in my words.

"What happened?" His tone is soft and gentle, and a dart of jealousy rushes through me that Kylie gets this good man while I somehow ended up with the guy who runs out of the room the moment he spots me so he can kiss Jessa on his bed.

The same guy whose dad I slept with.

"Nothing," I mutter.

"Hey," he says, touching my shoulder softly. "I'm not letting you get away with that."

I turn around and cover my face with my hands as the tears start to fall. Strong, warm arms wrap around me, and it strikes me suddenly that I've forged a valuable friendship with these guys just from being on the road with them on their first headlining tour.

No matter what happens with Brody, I'll always be a permanent memory of this trip. In fact, I keep forgetting that this is all documented and will be hitting the air in a few months. I wonder how *Rock on the Road* will explain my sudden absence if Brody finds a replacement dancer for me. I wonder if I'll have to watch Brody as he falls in love with Jessa after he fell in love with me first.

I start sobbing uncontrollably at the thought, but Dax doesn't react. He just holds me as I let it all out, and once I'm able to draw in a shaky breath, he lets go. He studies me for a few beats as I wipe under my eyes, and then he finally asks, "What happened up there?"

"Jessa was on top of him. They were kissing."

Dax's brows furrow and he shakes his head. "No..." he says, trailing off. "No way. That's not possible."

"He doesn't want me anymore, Dax." I sniffle and turn around. I grab hold of the handrail again, because if Dax isn't holding me up anymore, something has to. "I messed everything up before I even met him."

"He doesn't like her, Zo. Something's off here. I'll get to the bottom of it." He's so sure of himself, but I don't believe him. I know what I saw.

I shake my head. "It doesn't matter. He doesn't want to be with me, and that's that. He'll find someone to replace me, and I'll go back to my life."

I'm not sure if I mean he'll replace me on the tour or replace me in his life. Both, maybe. But I say the words to Dax to save face even though I have no idea what, exactly, that looks like. I left Kristen and Sawyer and they're doing their thing in Atlanta. Indie's made it clear I'm not welcome back at my job at Indigo Beauty.

So where does that leave me? I guess I could go back to Ethan's to regroup.

Ethan.

I think about my brother for a minute. Is he the reason Dax is out here right now—because he doesn't want to rock the boat with one of his rock star idols? Does Dax *really* care about me? Or is he just making sure everything is smoothed over?

God, I just want to go home.

I just don't know where that is anymore.

Do I even want to return to Atlanta now?

I wanted to be on television. That was my goal. I can't do that from Atlanta...but I might have a shot here in Los Angeles.

But Los Angeles just reminds me of the failed reality show I went on that led me to this very moment of misery.

I don't know if I can stay here, but I'm not sure I can leave, either.

"Your life is on the road with us now," he says, still brimming with all that confidence.

"It's been a fun ride," I say, already resigned to my fate. "But I know that when Brody wants something, he'll stop at nothing to get it. And he wants me off this tour."

The door opens just as a car pulls up to the curb. My ride.

Dax and I both glance over at the figure stepping through the front door. Lo and behold, it's the devil himself.

Dax doesn't say anything. He waits for Brody to speak first.

"Jessa agreed to dance as Zoey's replacement for the remainder of the tour," he says flatly to Dax, not to me.

The final stab to my heart cracks it before it shatters in a million pieces on the ground.

I don't react—not immediately, and not in front of Brody. He turns to go back into the house.

"I—shit, Zo. I don't even know what to say," Dax says. "I'm sorry. He's hurting and—"

I cut him off. "Don't make excuses for him. It's pretty clear where his head's at. Thanks for trying. I will clear my stuff off the bus tonight." I step forward and give him a quick hug because this is goodbye. "Tell the rest of the guys and Kylie bye for me. Thanks for everything, Dax."

I push out of the hug and rush over toward the car.

"This isn't goodbye, Zoey," Dax calls after me.

I don't say anything back. Between the emotions squeezing the back of my throat closed and the fact that he's completely wrong about that, I have nothing more to say.

I give the Uber driver the address for our bus lot, and then I quietly cry to myself in the back of the car while I head toward my mobile home on wheels where I'm not so welcome anymore.

I fire off a text to Ethan asking if I can stay the night. He responds nearly immediately, and I'm grateful for the feeling that *someone* in my general vicinity is on my side.

CHAPTER 39

ZOEY

"What's going on?" Ethan asks when I walk through the door with tears in my eyes. He folds me into a hug. "And who do I need to fuck up for doing this to you?"

I shake my head. "I did this to myself." I almost add that it's Brody who he needs to fuck up, but as much as Brody's actions where Jessa are concerned hurt me, it's my own fault. He was only doing what he had to do to protect himself.

Either that, or I'm giving him way too much credit. He did kiss her, after all, and he did replace my spot on the tour with her. I wonder for a beat why they didn't just have her step in when their other dancer dropped, but I realize she had a key role in making sure the dancing went off without a hitch. But by now, all the hitches are well worked out.

Maci appears behind him, baby Eli asleep in her arms. "I'm so sorry, Zo," she whispers. "I'll get the baby down and I'll be right back."

I stare at the baby and feel a little twinge of something I've never felt before. Some unfamiliar and completely foreign feeling. What's it like to be a mother? What's it like to hold a sleeping baby who you created in your arms? What's it like to love and be loved unconditionally in return?

I guess not all parents love unconditionally. My own really didn't with Ethan and me, and maybe that fucked me up so much that I thought it was no big deal to sleep my way onto a television show. Maybe if my parents would've been more like

Maci and Ethan are to Eli, maybe then I would've learned right from wrong. I would've learned there are consequences to my decisions—something that was never really true until about twenty-four hours ago when everything came crashing down on me.

It's amazing how much you learn about yourself when your heart is shattered. I can only imagine how I'll learn what I'm made of as I try to pick up the pieces—something I'm not sure I'll be ready for any time soon.

I blow out a breath and force myself out of my brother's comforting arms. "I think I'd just like to go to bed tonight if that's okay."

It's late. We had a show tonight, and then the party, cleaning out the bus, and then the drive to LA from San Diego, and now it's after three in the morning. I'm not surprised my rock star brother and his rock star wife are still awake and looking refreshed with their infant child, but I'm ready to crash for at least a week after everything that's happened.

"Of course it's okay, Zo. Whatever you need, I'm here." My brother touches my shoulder tenderly, and it reminds me a little of when Dax did that on their front porch less than three hours ago.

Ethan picks up my bags and carries them down the hall to my room, and I can't help but pause and stare at the drumsticks hanging on the wall as I follow him.

I shake my head.

It was so stupid to fall for the *drummer* of all people. Reminders hit me everywhere, and I'm afraid they always will. I'll be struck with sadness every time I hear a drum beat. I'll feel a squeeze in my soul every time I spot the wooden sticks or a floor tom. I'll remember how freeing and easy it was to dance in front of the man I was falling for as he kept the beat behind me.

I blow out a breath and force my gaze away from the wall of Ethan's accolades that suddenly means something very different to me than it did before.

"It was the drummer?" he asks softly once I've entered the room where I'll be sleeping.

I nod, but I don't otherwise change my expression.

He shakes his head. "That fucking asshole. I'll rip him a new—"

"Don't," I say, holding up my hand and cutting him off. "Not now. I'm not ready."

He nods and heads toward the door. Just before he steps through it, he leans one hand on the frame and turns back toward me. "I love you, Zoey bear." His childhood nickname for me warms my dead heart just a little.

"Love you, too, Ethan heathen," I say, tossing my own endearment back at him.

He chuckles, knocks lightly twice on the door frame with a closed fist, and leaves the room.

And finally, after everything that's happened tonight, I collapse into bed and cry until sleep takes over.

* * *

It's the bacon that gets me every time.

I stayed in bed through the pancakes, but the second the smell of bacon wafted through the entire house and up to my nostrils, I had to get out of bed.

My brother knows me well, and I'm suddenly totally grateful for that.

I scrub my face and brush my teeth, hoping the huge puffy bags under my eyes will magically disappear before I get over to the kitchen. It's just another thing I'm wrong about, I guess.

"You look like hell," my brother greets me.

"Back at you," I mutter, and he laughs.

"Bacon?" He flips two crispy pieces out of a fry pan and onto a plate for me.

"I'd still be in bed if there wasn't any bacon." I take the plate and plop into a seat at the kitchen table. "Where's Maci?"

"Playdate over at Steve and Angelique's," he says, naming one of the guys in his band and his wife. He sits next to me. "You ready to talk?"

I lift a shoulder. "Shouldn't I just wait until Maci gets back so I only have to tell the story once?"

"Zo, this is me." He links a pinky finger through mine like we did when we were kids and we both instinctively knew we were all the other had. "Just you and me."

"Just you and me," I mumble back, and then I spill my guts in between bites of bacon. "I didn't want to, and I tried to avoid it, but I went and fell for Brody Jensen."

"MFB's drummer," he says flatly.

"Yeah. And he fell for me too. Everything was perfect. He introduced me to his family, and when his dad got home, things got a little complicated."

Ethan's brows furrow and he nods for me to go on.

I clear my throat and stare down at the grease gathered on my plate. "I'd, uh, actually met him before."

"So?"

I look up at him. I guess the only way to do this is to just spit it out. "He's the casting director I slept with to get that role on *Single Life*."

"Jesus Christ, Zoey," he mutters, scrubbing a hand along his jaw. I know he's really trying not to look at me with disappointment, but I feel it all around me like a cloud.

"Brody found out, not that it was something I could've kept from him anyway, and I guess it was something he couldn't get over. Basically he found a way to replace me and kick me off the tour."

He lets out a sigh. "So now what?"

I shrug. "I didn't know where else to go. I haven't really thought about the next step."

"Good thing your big brother is here to the rescue." He pulls out his phone and taps a few keys.

"I don't want you to rescue me," I say, and I grab his arm. "What are you doing?"

"Nothing," he says, tapping some more. He doesn't care that I don't want his help. I didn't ask for it—well, other than asking to stay here at his house. I want to save myself for once, but I've never had to do that and I don't exactly know how.

"Ethan." I say it firmly, but he ignores me. "Ethan," I say a little louder, but he still ignores me. He's such a stubborn butt. "Ethan!" I practically yell, and he finally looks over at me.

"What?"

"What the hell are you doing?"

He shoots me an angry look. "Getting you a job."

"Here?"

He shrugs. "You don't have a plan, and you need a distraction. Ashmark recently revamped their marketing department and we're in need of someone with some marketing experience."

"What would you have done if I hadn't shown up on your doorstep?"

He looks at me like I asked a stupid question. "I would've waited another month until your tour was over before presenting you with the idea."

"And what if I don't want the job?"

His patronizing look deepens. I guess that sort of *is* a stupid question. I'm dealing with stubborn Ethan here. It doesn't really matter if I want the job or not—clearly it's already mine, and my only way out is to fuck it up or quit.

But the more I think about it, the more I realize how perfect this could be. Ashmark is Mark Ashton's record label, a hugely successful endeavor run by the god of rock himself.

I ignore the fact that MFB is also signed to Ashmark and might make an appearance at the label once in a while.

"Okay," I finally agree. "I'll do it. When do I start?"

He glances at his phone. "Tomorrow if you're up for the challenge. I need to head in to get some work done myself and I can take you with me to fill out the paperwork and start your training."

I nod, warming up more and more to the idea of having something permanent that's just mine here in Los Angeles. "Let's do this."

CHAPTER 40

BRODY

It's a completely different experience watching Jessa prance across the stage than it was watching Zoey. Even though technically Jessa was above her in terms of rank, her moves aren't as fluid. Or maybe it's her body. I can't put my finger on it, but I'm very aware it's not Zoey.

And it fucks with me while I play. I'm back to the basics like two nights ago in San Diego. We're up in Oakland, and I can't help but wonder if she's still in the same state as me. Did she head back to her brother's place in LA? If she did, she might be as close as a six-hour drive.

Not that it matters.

Kicking her out was the right decision, even though the vision of her on the porch hunched over in disappointment and sadness as she talked to Dax haunts my dreams.

Even the after show is a completely different experience. I'm not in the mood to party and celebrate with my best friends and a handful of our fans after tonight's show. It was an average performance for me at best, and I'm tired and nursing a roaring headache—possibly from the scotch I downed last night alone in my room.

I'm sitting by myself on some couch, my elbows balanced on my knees and my hands clasped in front of me, when Adam drops onto the cushion beside me.

"You up for your three Bs?" he asks me as music blares and beer can tabs are popped all around me in the dressing room after the show—our apparent location of choice for tonight's after party.

I can't even manage to force out a laugh as he throws my own acronym at me—the three Bs meaning, obviously, bar, booze, and boobs. Sometimes it means babes, and sometimes it means blowjobs or banging, and tonight, I guess it could mean any of those.

I shake my head. "Nah, man."

"Look, dude, we're in the exact same boat right now." He glances over at me, and when I look back, I see the fire in his eyes. He's angry—not at me, but at his recent break-up, and it's clear he wants something to help him forget, even if it's just for tonight. "Fuck these bitches who are making us miserable. We're rock stars, so let's drink until we're numb and find someone new to fuck."

I stare straight ahead. There are women dancing in front of me, but I don't really *see* them there. I just stare blankly for a minute, mulling over his words.

Let's drink until we're numb and find someone new to fuck.

I slowly nod my head. "All right," I finally say. "Let's do it."

The melancholy look on Adam's face is replaced with one of challenge. He's up for this, and he's ready to hop right back into the pool after he's been out of it for years.

I've only been out of it for weeks, and yet I'm finding it a little harder to jump in. I'm only doing this because I need to get Zoey the fuck out of my head for a night. Maybe one night with someone else will be just what I need.

Or maybe not.

Only actually doing something about it will answer that question.

Adam grins and nods toward one of the women dancing on the other side of the room. She's Bree's opposite with her long, dark hair and dark eyes...and come to think of it, she's

Zoey's opposite, too. I'm not sure if he's nodding toward her as an option for me or for him, but I'm not feeling particularly picky tonight.

As long as her eyes aren't blue and her hair isn't blonde, I'm up for pretty much anything.

Scratch that. Maybe a blue-eyed blonde is exactly what I need to replace the memory of Zoey.

Replace the memory.

Is that what I've done my whole life?

Did it take seeing my best friend fall in love to realize that it's not something so bad—that I could have that life, too?

It all hits me in the split second it takes me to look around the room for tonight's bait. I think of my six-year-old ballgames my dad wasn't able to show up to because he was in Los Angeles. I haven't thought about that in years...instead, I tend to remember the few times he *did* attend our gigs at Emerson's when he was home. I replaced those memories when he didn't show up for me with ones where he did.

I think of the revolving door I've had on my bedroom since I lost my virginity at the ripe age of seventeen. I lost count somewhere along the way of exactly how many women I've been with—though I've always been safe, even with Zoey—because each woman just wiped away the memory of the one before her.

And I'm doing it again.

It's a pattern with me, apparently, and not one I'm open for breaking today.

"Question," Adam says, breaking into my thoughts just as my eyes land on a gorgeous blonde across the room. Perfect—for tonight, anyway. She looks different enough from Zoey but has the characteristics I'm looking for this evening. Blonde hair, eyes that look blue from this angle, and tits big enough to bury my face in.

I glance over at the kid I've known since junior high with curiosity. He has this look of anxiety about him, like the time just after we met when I made him pick up a worm and chase my sisters with it after it rained. He didn't think it was a good idea, but I talked him into it anyway. I was right—we made my sisters scream with terror, and we spend the afternoon laughing about it.

Oh, to be eleven again.

"How, exactly, do we do this?" he asks. "I've, uh, been out of the game a long-ass time."

I laugh, and then I arrogantly lace my fingers together and mock stretch my hands outward. "Watch the master at work."

I stand and beeline toward the blonde. She looks at me with some mix of confidence and lust as I approach. "Dax told me there'd be gorgeous women in here after tonight's show, but I never expected someone as incredible as you."

She grins. "Is that a line?"

"Only if it worked."

She lifts a shoulder. "I'm Samantha, and I'm into drummers."

I laugh. "Ready for another line?"

She lifts a brow and shoots me a sly smile as she waits.

"I bang on things for a living. Want me to show you how good I am at my job?"

She lets out a little tinkling laugh, and for some reason it takes me back to a memory not so long ago when I was in my bunk with Zoey and she was laughing at something I said. I shake the imagery out of my head.

"Does this mean I get to see your tour bus?" she asks.

I think about that for all of a split second. In the spirit of replacing memories, I nod. "It means I'll show you the inside of my bunk."

It won't be the first time I've brought a woman back to my bunk to fuck, and I suppose it won't be the last time, either. I haven't fucked on a tour bus since Kylie's been with us out of respect for her—and for Zoey, if I'm being honest, because she deserved better. I don't know Samantha here from anyone else, and tonight will be the last time I see her. So I'll give Dax the heads up to stay off the bus for the next hour, and I'll be good to go.

Unless, of course, Adam wants to bring his bait back to the bus.

I glance over at my pal to find he's no longer on the couch but chatting up the brunette he motioned to earlier. Good on him.

I grab Samantha's hand and head over to Dax, who's in the middle of a conversation with some guy in a suit. I whisper in his ear, "Stay off the bus for an hour."

He shoots me a dirty look and says, "Excuse me," to the suit. Then, more quietly to me so only I can hear him, he says, "What the fuck are you doing?"

"Moving on," I say thinly.

He raises a brow and gives me a look like it's a dumb decision, but fuck him and his perfect little relationship. He finally cracks a small smile even though his eyes still reek of disapproval. "And you need an hour? We'll give you ten minutes. Should be more than enough time for the grand bus tour and whatever you have planned."

I punch him in the arm, and then he turns back to the suit. I take it as my cue to leave. I catch Adam's eye on the way out the door, and I raise a brow. He grins at me and turns back to the chick he's chatting up, and I'm home free to seduce the titty-licious Samantha.

We weave through the back halls of the venue, dodging fans who recognize me as I make my way toward the bus lot. I'm not a total dick—I stop to chat or sign concert tickets or take selfies, even though I know it's burning the small window of precious time I have to do what I need to do tonight.

And yes, I *do* need to do this. I need to feel a woman, a *different* woman, and I need to try to move forward. I'm not some pussy who needs time to grieve the loss of what might've been the most important relationship of my life. I'm ready to take the bull by the horns, or rather Samantha by the tits, and find a way to smile again.

I don't want to play safe tomorrow night. I want to leave everything I have out on the stage like I always do, and it starts with this. Harvey, our bus driver, stands outside chatting with bus two's driver, and I punch in the code to let myself into my home on wheels. The door's barely shut behind us when Samantha slides her hands around my waist and clutches onto my ass, her breasts pressed into my chest and her lips inches from mine.

"So this is your bus?" she asks, her voice dripping with seduction.

"This is it," I say back with a husky voice, and I close the gap between our lips by pressing mine to hers.

She gives into the kiss quickly, and she tastes like tequila—the perfect taste for a woman, if you ask me. I pretend it doesn't remind me of *her*. It means she may be drunk, though she seems lucid enough to know what she's consenting to by being here with me right now.

She moans into me, and it's different from Zoey's moans. It's thicker, longer, more dramatic. I can't seem to help the comparisons in my mind.

Samantha isn't Zoey...but I wish she was.

Samantha's hand moves from my ass around to the front, where she grasps me. Her hands are bigger and she's more aggressive than the more delicate Zoey—a word I never would've thought to describe her before Samantha. She moves to unbuckle my jeans and though I know I should stop her, I also can't help but think she knew what she was signing up for when she accepted the invitation back to my bus. If she didn't want my cock in her hand, she certainly wouldn't be reaching in my pants to take it out.

And if she didn't want this, she wouldn't be moving her hand up and down my shaft, squeezing and applying pressure when she gets to the tip before twisting her fist around me and stroking back downward.

She wants this. She wants *me.*

Zoey wants you, too, a voice in my head whispers.

But I ignore it because even if Samantha isn't the one I want to be here with right now, she's a woman who's giving me a hand job and I'm not about to stop her when I'm seconds from coming.

My balls draw up and a grunt heaves out of my chest as I come all over Samantha's hand, and I'm just proud of myself in this moment that I remembered her name.

It's the small victories, I guess. I direct her to the restroom on the bus in case she wants to wash her hands, and I clean myself off with a tissue before tucking my dick back into my jeans.

It gives me just enough time to really think about what I'm doing—and what I shouldn't be doing.

A cloak of guilt seems to wash over me.

I knew it was wrong, and I did it anyway. I went through the motions and did what I thought I was supposed to do because that's what we do when we're heartbroken, isn't it?

But this is all wrong. I can't keep kissing a woman I care nothing about when Zoey's still in my head and my heart.

Samantha emerges from the bathroom, a lusty smile gracing her lips. "Let's get you back to your friends," I say.

Her smile slips as her eyes narrow. "You got yours and that's that?"

I lift a shoulder, a little surprised that she'd fire back at me even though I deserve it. "I'm sorry. I just realized that as much as I like you, I'm not over my ex."

It's the simplest explanation for a very complicated problem.

She huffs her way past me and off the bus, and I don't even care that it's probably the last time I'll ever see her.

CHAPTER 41

BRODY

I step outside to breathe in some fresh air, but all I get is bus exhaust—the pleasures of life on tour. It's only when I'm leaning up against the side of the bus, looking up into the sky at the stars I know are there but that I can't see because of the lights of this city that I notice the cameraman standing a few feet away.

Of course.

They're always there, always watching. It got to the point where I *almost* forgot about them, but it makes sense they'd catch a girl storming angrily off the bus minutes after the bus was rocking.

I can only imagine how producers will want to portray this moment for the viewing audience—whatever gets the best ratings, right?

But then I remember this isn't the fixed dating show Dax went on. This is Dax's pet project with Mark Ashton. If I demand they cut this scene from production, they will.

At the same time, I can't help but think it won't make me really look all that bad. Maybe it'll even look like I did the right thing for once. Maybe my actions will show that she wanted me, and I put a stop to it.

It's not like they'll air footage of me getting a handy from a random.

Probably not, anyway.

I blow out a breath with a muttered, "Fuck."

"Having a rough go, Mr. Jensen?"

I didn't even notice our bus driver approach me, but his voice breaks my second of solitude. I press my lips together and nod slowly as I stare up at the sky.

"Being a rock star," he muses quietly. "It's not all fun and games, is it?"

I shake my head with another resigned sigh. "It seems like it should be, doesn't it?"

He chuckles. "I've been driving buses for bands long enough to know it never is."

I wonder what sorts of things he's seen over his career. Probably more of the bad and the ugly than the good.

"The worst part's the loneliness," he says. "You're here among your best friends, surrounded by adoring fans and women who want nothing more than *you* for the night, but there's still a hole." He clears his throat and looks embarrassed when my eyes meet his. He backpedals a bit. "At least that's what some of the guys have told me."

I shake my head. "Nah, man. You've got it exactly right. But I didn't feel that sting until...well, until the last forty-eight hours, I guess."

"The blonde gal?" he asks knowingly.

"You know it."

He nods sagely. "Is there anything you can do to win her back?"

I look up at the sky again, like I might find the answer there. "It's not that simple, Harvey."

"With women?" He snorts. "Nope, it never is. It's why I gave up on them and dedicated my life to the road."

"Are you happy on the road?" I can't help the question before it slips out. It's not my place to ask a man I've spoken to only a handful of times over the last month of this tour, but he seems somehow more worldly than I've given him credit for.

He lifts a shoulder and his lips twist into a sort of wry smile. "Depends what you mean by happy. I'm happier not fighting with my first wife. I'm happier not being in the home where my second wife died. I can't say I'm happier than I've ever been, but I'm happier than I was when I was stuck in a rut."

I nod, not sure what to say at his confession. This break-up with Zoey seems so minor in comparison to the life he's lived—divorcing one woman and losing another to death. The air is suddenly heavier around us. "I'm sorry about your second wife."

He chuckles. "And I'm sorry about the first." He grows serious after the joke he clearly makes as a defense mechanism. After a tight-mouthed smile, he says, "Thanks. I miss her every day."

And that's that. The other bus driver steps up to interrupt what he doesn't know is a pretty deep conversation, and the two drivers resume their conversation from earlier.

But I'm left with Harvey's words. Will I eventually look back and realize that complacency doesn't make me happier than I was when I was with Zoey?

I don't know the answer to that, but it's only been two days. It's difficult to base any real decisions on that. Emotions are still running high, and the wounds haven't even started to scar over.

I just need some time.

I need time to get Zoey out of my head. Time to move forward. Time will heal this like it's supposed to heal everything, and then I'll be able to kiss another woman without thinking of her. I'll be able to touch and be touched without comparing her to Zoey. I'll be able to get past what feels like the ultimate betrayal so I can be with a woman again—not out of revenge or some sick need to replace what I had with someone, but because I want to live in the moment and feel the pleasure again.

I get on the bus and start drinking. The other guys come out from the dressing room party and join me, and then we end up at some bar.

An hour later, I'm fucking plastered, and I have a feeling I'm not going to remember much of what happens tonight.

In fact, it only takes one more beer to push me over the limit, and then everything becomes snippets.

A snippet of myself gyrating against some girl I've never seen before while a Beyoncé song drowns out all the noise around us.

A snippet of a conversation with Kane and Adam...possibly about Zoey.

A snippet of Dax asking me if I'm all right.

A snippet in a dark alley. Am I behind the bar? Am I throwing up behind the bar?

And then it's morning, and the searing light of a new day streams in through the bus window. I have no idea how I got back here last night, but at least I awake alone.

I shake my head at my-damn-self as I realize how I've got to get a handle on my life. I'm in my late twenties now, and I should know better than to turn to alcohol. I realize far too late that shaking my head at myself was a terrible idea as a searing pain stabs my skull.

God, I'm a fucking idiot.

I head out to the forward cabin to see if anyone's up yet, and Adam sits on the couch with his phone in his hand.

"How are you this morning?" he asks with a grin.

I glare at him. "About how you'd expect. How bad was it?"

He lifts a shoulder and tosses his phone on the couch beside him. "Not that bad. Kane took some video he's desperate to show you."

"Oh Jesus," I mutter, starting up a cup of coffee for myself. "How was your night?"

He sits up. "I've had worse."

Kane steps into the forward cabin, cell phone in hand. He holds it up and wiggles it around a little with a shit eating grin on his face, and I find myself suddenly a little nervous for whatever his phone holds.

"How bad is it?" I ask.

He laughs. "It's not the debauchery of the past, Brody. I just happened to catch something I think you really need to hear."

"Lay it on me," I say, collapsing into a chair.

He pulls up the video, turns up the volume, and hands me his phone.

"I miss her so goddamn much," I hear myself say over the loud din of the bar. This time, it's a Justin Timberlake song in the background. It's dark in the bar, and Kane was a little drunk, too, as evidenced by his terrible camera work. Still, though, it's obviously me. "I was an idiot. I don't care who she was with before me. I don't care that she'll forever make comparisons between my dad and me. I'm sure I win that battle anyway. I just want her back. I love her and I always will. No one will ever measure up to her."

It's all the thoughts I've pushed out of my mind, and it just took a little truth serum in the form of Miller Lite to force the admission from my lips. And now there's video evidence of what a heartbroken, lovesick fool I really am.

Kane flips to the next video, and sure enough, there's me vomiting in the alley behind the bar.

Classy.

This whole Zoey thing is fucking with me hard core. Add the video Kane took to that equation and I'm a volcano about to erupt.

I just don't know what'll happen once the lava starts burning up everything in sight.

CHAPTER 42

ZOEY

four weeks later

"I want to find a way to get in touch with his mom," I say. "Maybe explain what happened."

Ethan shakes his head as he maneuvers the car onto the highway. "I'm telling you, Zoey, don't do it. Not one single good thing could possibly come from that."

"It could lead me back to Brody," I counter.

"Or you could be breaking up an entire family. You may be part of the equation, but all you'd be doing is detonating a bomb that isn't yours to detonate."

I stare out the window at the traffic whizzing by us as we make our way together toward the Ashmark offices. I'm still staying with Ethan, and he had some work to do at the label today and offered to carpool with me.

He's right, I guess. And I hate that.

"You know what you should do instead?" he asks.

I glance over at him.

"Talk to Brody. Confront him. Make him listen to your side."

"How? I tried texting him and he didn't answer."

He blows out a frustrated breath. I'm sure he's tired of rehashing the same conversation six ways from Sunday, but it's too damn bad for him. This is my life, and he opened the door to all of me when he invited me to stay at his place.

Okay, admittedly that's an immature view, but it helps me to talk about it...even if everyone around me is getting really tired of it.

He glares over at me. "What are you, a fucking millennial?"

I frown at him. "What's that supposed to mean?"

"You don't *text* your way through a break-up." He's focused on traffic, but his voice is passionate. "You fucking pick up your phone and talk. And if he doesn't want to talk, you leave a voicemail. You show up at his door. You find a way. You fucking *fight*, Zoey. You don't just roll over and die."

"Is that what you think I'm doing?"

He lifts a shoulder. "I certainly don't see you fighting. I just see you wallowing and whining, two things I'm not going to allow much longer in my house."

"Are you telling me to move out?"

"God, you're annoying." He sighs with frustration again. "No, that's not what I'm saying. I'm saying it's been a month, Zo. It's time to get back on your feet."

"I'm trying," I say, my voice small.

He glances over at me and shakes his head a little sadly. "No, you're not."

We ride in silence the rest of the way to the office, and then I run to the conference room for my Friday morning marketing meeting with his words playing over in my head.

I'm largely not paying attention during the meeting, but Jay, Ashmark's head of marketing, has become one of my closest friends in Los Angeles in the weeks since I left the tour. He knows everything—including why I refuse to date anyone. He's running the meeting, and he'll fill me in on what I missed.

I'm just not over Brody yet, and I haven't been able to puzzle out *why* I can't get over someone I was only with for a few weeks.

"I need an ideal buyer profile for Sole Storm," Jay says, referring to a new band Ashmark just acquired a few days ago. "I need everything from where they live, shop, eat, sleep, and fuck to what devices and services they use to stream music. Ashleigh, you'll take the lead, and I want Gabe and Caleb on your team."

Jay glances around the room, and I silently hope he doesn't choose me. I can't stand working with Gabe on anything. He's a nit picky control freak, and it's sort of like being back in school doing a group project. "And Claire," he finishes, and I let out a tiny breath of relief. "I'll need it first thing Monday morning. Zoey, where are we at on the Youtubers?"

"We're in talks with Andre Cooper, a twenty-four-year-old music videographer with over twenty million subscribers." I recite his demographics from memory. "His price tag will be astronomical, but Vail is his favorite band and he's extremely interested in partnering with Ashmark."

I glance over at Mark, who doesn't normally come to these meetings. He's nodding the go ahead to Jay.

"Get Mark a full report on Andre before you leave today and we'll move forward on the proposal." Jay glances around the room once more. "Anything else?"

When no one has anything to add, Jay dismisses the group with a forced, "Have a good weekend."

"Zoey, can I have a word with you?" Mark asks as the room starts clearing out.

I feel nervous, but not the sort of nervous this would've made me in the old days when Mark wanted one-on-one conversations with me. This feels more like I'm in trouble with the school principal.

After a look that I can only describe as *meaningful* from Jay and the room has cleared out except for Mark and me, he clears his throat as he stands. "I'm really impressed, Zoey. It's kind of hard to believe you were on tour dancing just a few weeks ago and now you're such an integral part of our marketing department here."

"Thanks, Mark. And thanks for the opportunity to prove myself. I didn't realize how much I enjoyed the marketing stuff until Ethan forced this job on me."

"Are you doing okay?" he asks.

I lift a shoulder.

"Still Jensen?" he pries.

I close my eyes because I feel heat pricking behind them at just the mention of Brody's last name.

It shouldn't still hurt this bad after all these weeks have passed...should it?

"You know," he begins, "their last tour date was a few nights ago in Nashville."

I wonder what that means.

Is Brody back in California? I tried to get in touch with him right after he kicked me off the tour. I sent text messages every day for the first week asking if we could talk, and when they went unanswered, I was hurt, but I understood. He didn't want to talk to me, and I'd fucked up enough stuff for the time being. I chose to leave him alone to finish out his commitment to the tour even though he stripped that same chance away from me.

But now the tour's over, and the more I think about my conversation with Ethan this morning, the more I realize I deserve my chance to explain my side of the story.

He cut me out without so much as a word out of me, and the more that pulls at my thoughts, the more I start to feel anger pulsing through me.

And it only took one sentence from Mark to help me finally understand why I can't get over him.

The tour's over, and we're over, but I never got to say goodbye.

I never got the chance to make him understand that I had no idea he was related to that casting director I foolishly decided to seduce to get on some stupid television show.

I have no closure on what happened between us. He found out something he didn't like, and he cut me out. And that's not fair.

Come to think of it, I lost both my parents before I had a chance to say goodbye. I guess that's something that affects me much more deeply than I ever realized.

My dad might've been a shitty human being, but he was still my dad. I knew it was coming, and while I spent more time with him in the end than I did the entire rest of his life as he rotted away in prison, I still never really said any of the things you're supposed to say when one of the two people who gave you life is ripped away from you—regardless of the relationship we shared. One day he was there, and the next day he was gone.

Same with my mom, except we were fighting when she died. I told her I didn't like her boyfriend, and she yelled at me that she didn't care. She left the house for his place, and she never came back.

So goodbyes, closure, whatever you want to call it...I suppose I'm starting to realize they affect me in deep and infinite ways.

And I didn't get any of that with him.

I blow out a breath before I form words to reply to Mark's statement that the tour's over.

He clears his throat. "They're scheduled to be here at two this afternoon for our first post-production meeting for *Rock on the Road,* and we're viewing the rough edit of the first episode."

"He'll be here?" My voice is small and unsure—words I'd never use to describe myself.

"Yeah." He nods. "He will."

"Can you get me a few minutes alone with him?"

"I'd do anything for you, Zoey." He shoots me a small smile, and those words paired with that smile would've melted my teenaged heart. But now, especially after everything that happened with Brody, I appreciate his sentiment coming from nothing more than my big brother's best friend...oh, and my boss.

"Thank you." My voice comes out in a whisper.

"Now go get that Youtuber." He winks, and I can't quite muster a smile back in my nervousness, but at least I have work to focus on for the next few hours.

CHAPTER 43

BRODY

I drove up separately from the other guys after a text I received this morning.

Ethan: *Meet me for lunch before your meeting with Mark.*

He wasn't asking, but when the man you've idolized for well over a decade carves out time to do lunch with you, you don't reject him. We're doing a late lunch at one o'clock at the café in Ashmark's building, and the solitary drive up to Los Angeles from San Diego gives me plenty of thinking time.

Time I don't really want, but time that's there anyway.

Even though he's a separate entity from his sister, I can't help but think of her anyway...just as I do every time I hear the mention of Vail or Ashmark or back-up dancers or blue eyes or blonde hair.

I convince myself I've made a terrible mistake, but then the image of her banging my father forces its way back in and I know it wasn't a mistake.

I've been living in limbo for the last month, avoiding women and focusing on really honing my Fortnite skills as I try simply to get through each day. At least when we were on tour, I had something to occupy my attention.

But now the tour's over, and with that comes a little bout of depression. It's weird trying to reacclimate to the real world after living a fantasy life for eight weeks, yet we're back home and talking about our next album as we wait for producers and editors to finish our season of *Rock on the Road.* I assume

Ethan's lunch meeting today has something to do with that—the entire reason we're heading up to LA anyway. Maybe he wants me to cut Zoey out of our season completely.

I promised her once upon a time she'd get a spotlight, though, and I plan to hold true to that promise despite what happened.

I know what the chance to get on television means to her, and as much as I hate what happened, I don't hate *her*.

I ignored her texts. It was hard, but I knew if I played the game, she'd eventually stop. I was right, and it only took a week.

I haven't spoken to anyone in my family since our show in San Diego—the night after I overheard something I never really wanted to know.

My sisters deserve better, and so does my mom. My dad, however, can suck a giant dick for all I care.

Now that the tour has wrapped and I'm back home, I know I need to make time to visit my family. They're geographically close to the home I share with the guys in my band, and I don't really have any other excuses...other than the fact that I don't know how I'll face any of them knowing what I know.

I pull into an underground spot at the label and head to the café Ethan wanted to meet me at. I'm ten minutes early, but I just avoided the lunch rush. Ethan's already there with earbuds and a laptop, and I settle in across from him.

"Hey, man," he greets me, slipping his earbuds out. "How've you been?"

"Shitty," I mutter.

"Post tour spiral?" he asks, and I've never heard it called that but I absolutely get it.

I lift a shoulder. "Part of it, I guess."

"My sister?" he prods.

I nod and purse my lips. "Yeah, that'd be the other part."

He chuckles. "I thought as much."

I wait for him to go on, and when he doesn't, my manners—and my curiosity—win. "How's she doing?"

"Shitty."

I nod. "Sorry about that, man, but there's nothing I can do."

He presses his lips together and makes a questioning face. "Really? Or is it just that there's nothing you *want* to do?"

I run a hand along my jaw. "Look, what happened between us is complicated."

"I know everything," he says, cutting me off. "And I get it, man. It's complicated. You're right. But the two of you are fucking miserable wretches without each other. At least give her the chance to explain. Don't fucking ignore her texts. Let her give her side of the story before you write her off."

"Is this why you wanted to treat me to lunch?" I ask.

He chuckles. "I said meet for lunch."

"I know what you said."

He outright laughs this time, and a waitress stops by with menus and water. "Alright, this is on my dime, and yes, this is why I wanted to meet you. Among other things."

"Can we talk about the other things for a while?" I'm not quite begging, but I'm not too proud to, either.

"Nah, I've got an agenda here and I need to stick to it."

This time I laugh as I finger the menu. "Lay it on me, then."

"From an outsider's perspective, what happened was a genuine mistake. But you didn't give my sister the chance to tell you that." Ethan is poised and confident as he speaks, and I'm still fidgeting with the goddamn menu. My knee bounces up and down and I'm seconds away from drumming my fingers on the table.

"Does it really matter if it was a mistake or not? What happened happened, and it's not something I can get past." I tap on my menu a little as the urge to drum takes over.

"It does matter." He glances down at my fidgeting, and I try to stop just as the waitress comes by to take our order. He continues talking about her when the waitress leaves like we weren't even interrupted. "She had no idea, dude. She's got this strict no dating a married man thing. She would *never* have done that had she known who he was. And it was long before she even met you. She had no idea who she was auditioning for when that agent contacted her. Remember?"

Of course I remember. They're details I've gone over ad nauseum the past month, both with various members of my band and in my own head. But it doesn't change the fact that my father will be present in the room every time I look at her.

How do I get over that?

I don't say any of that to Ethan, obviously. Instead, I mutter, "Yeah, I remember."

"So give her a chance to tell her side. That's all I'm asking."

"Is she back in Atlanta?" I ask, the smallest part of me starting to relent.

He shakes his head. "She's been staying with me, actually. And she's been working."

"Working?"

"She took a job in marketing."

"What she was doing before the tour," I murmur. Good for her.

"Yeah. But not marketing some beauty line. She's working for Ashmark."

Oh Jesus.

So she's here in this building, probably right now, maybe a few floors above me.

I blow out a breath.

I'm not ready for this.

I prepared myself to meet with Mark, and last-minute to have lunch with Ethan. I knew the reminders would be here, haunting and taunting me, but I had no idea *she* would actually be here.

"And that's the other thing I need to tell you," he says.

My brows furrow as I wait for him to continue.

"I actually already ate lunch. That food I just ordered is for her. She's on her way down right now."

I glare at him. "Are you fucking kidding me?"

He looks toward the door, and I know she's here. It's like something in the air changes as it charges with tension and electricity.

"Dude, we all know you wouldn't listen to anybody but potentially me. Give her a chance to tell you her side. That's all I'm asking."

I feel blindsided. Sucker punched. The air whooshes out of my chest.

She's on her way down right now.

I didn't even know I'd be seeing her today, and now it looks like I don't have a choice.

CHAPTER 44

ZOEY

With shaking hands, I open the door to the café. I see my brother right away, and then I see Brody with his back toward the door. I pause and draw in a deep breath.

This is my one shot, and I can't blow it.

I stand up a little straighter and repeat my dancer's mantra.

Be daring.

Be expressive.

Be bold.

It's the chant that has helped me through my nerves more times than I can count, but today those nerves are for an entirely different reason.

Ethan's eye catches mine, and then he stands as I approach the table. He leans in to kiss my cheek, and then he claps Brody on the shoulder. "Nice talking with you, man," he says, and then he leaves.

I slide into the seat he vacated and look across at the man who still holds my broken heart in his hands. Despite that pulsing flash of anger I feel, love seems to be the predominant feeling right now. He's as handsome as ever with that scruff on his face and that perfect hair and those dark eyes that are a little more shadowed than I remember them. I could stare at him all day, but I'm here to talk, and I know my window is small.

"Hi," I say.

He doesn't respond. He just stares out the windows behind me...or, rather, he glares out them.

"Can you please look at me?" I ask softly.

His eyes finally move reluctantly toward mine, and his immediately soften just a bit.

The waitress picks that exact moment to drop off the food. I look at it as good timing—at least I wasn't in the middle of the speech I've been planning for the last two hours.

I'm not getting much work done today.

Once the waitress leaves, I find I can't eat the salad. Brody, however, loads ketchup and mustard onto his burger and digs in.

"I've missed you so much," I begin.

He grunts around the food in his mouth.

I charge on since he can't be bothered to make words. "I'm having a hard time getting past whatever this thing was between us, and I finally figured out why just this morning."

He raises a brow of curiosity—which is monumental in my book. It's showing he's interested in what I have to say, and that interest was the one thing I was really scared I'd have to fight for today.

I push my salad around my plate with my fork, focusing on anything other than his dark brown eyes as I confess the words that seem to bleed straight from my heart. "I didn't get my shot to tell you *my* side of the story. I have no idea what you've been up to the past four weeks, or who you've spoken to or what they've told you, or who or what you believe at this point. But I do know one thing for certain. You kicked me out and never even let me defend myself. I can't get over you because I don't have that closure."

"I thought I had my closure, but I still can't get over you."

My eyes whip up from the chopped greens on my plate to those dark brown orbs as they gaze across the table at me.

"You can't?" I ask.

He shakes his head. "No, Zoey. I fucking loved you with everything I am, and then I overheard a whispered conversation that never should've happened. You broke my heart. *He* broke my soul."

I know who he's referring to without naming names. I'm about to defend myself, to tell him I was going to explain it all as soon as we left, but instead of hopping to the defensive, I backtrack to the beginning.

I set my fork down and force myself to look across the table into his eyes as I speak. His dart around, back and forth from my own eyes to the window to the waitress walking behind me, but I keep mine focused. "I've spent my entire life in Ethan's shadow. When we were kids, he was the troublemaker, so any attention my parents had to spare always went to him. When we got a little older, he was the rebel bad boy of our high school. Everyone knew he and Mark were going to make something of themselves someday, and nine times out of ten, the friends I made only wanted to use me to get close to him. And then Vail formed, and Ethan always wanted to save me." I can't help my small laugh. "Even today, with you. He got you here so I could talk to you. He stepped in to save me again."

"I already know your history with your brother, Zoey," Brody says with a touch of exasperation, as if I should get to the damn point already.

"I know you do, but I don't think I ever made it really clear how very much I want to step out of his shadow and into my own light." I glance down when I see his fingertips as they drum on the table—a sure sign I'm making him uncomfortable, but I don't care. I'm here to say my piece, and then he can take it or leave it. It's the only way I know how to move on.

"You saw how angry I was that first night when I realized he had a hand in getting me on stage with MFB," I say, and he nods. "But what you didn't know was the internal rage that burned because of it. I've never, not even once in my life, even had the ability to find success on my own merits without Ethan somehow stepping in to save the day like some superhero. By the time I got to the audition for *Single Life*, I was desperate. I'd heard of the casting couch, and I'd made up my mind on the way there that I'd do anything, and I mean *anything*, to get that spot on the show."

His fingertip drumming seems to increase, as does the bounce in his knee...but those eyes of his—they're his tell. He's softening as he listens to my story. He knows me well enough to know how sincere I was in making my own way, and everything I'm doing today is *still* somehow because of Ethan, right down to this very conversation.

"When I walked into that office, there was no sign of a family. I checked his ring finger. I took stock of the desk and credenza. Nothing that told me he was married, which would have been the one thing that could've changed my mind."

Brody runs a hand along his jaw, and I wish it was my hand feeling those rough whiskers there, my fingertips smoothing the crinkle of his brow, my lips touching his as we figure out a way past all this.

"It was only a few days later that I got the call I'd made it. Production was about to start, so I quit my job and came here to Los Angeles with the expectation I'd be here at least a month. I was wrong. You saw how I was kicked off the first night, how the producers made me look like a drunken idiot on national television. When a talent agent contacted me the next day, I should've known it was too good to be true. I should've easily guessed Ethan was behind it. But I didn't, and I came back to LA and met you, and the rest is, well, history. I didn't have any clue who you were before I met you."

"I believe you," Brody says, and I'm sort of shocked that he admits that.

"Thank you." I hold his gaze for a beat before he breaks it. "I swear to God, Brody, I had no idea he was your father until he stepped foot into your house. He grabbed me and told me not to tell you, but I couldn't lie to you. I was going to tell you on our way home. I didn't want to do it in front of your mom and your sisters. I didn't care if he wanted to keep up the charade. I wasn't going to be a party to that, and I'm so sorry you found out the way you did."

"Finding out from you an hour later wouldn't have made it any better," he says, his voice full of venom.

"I know it wouldn't have, but at least you might not have felt so betrayed by overhearing it." I look down at my salad again. "I didn't know at the time that what I was doing was going to have such far-reaching effects. I didn't know it would affect every facet of my being, and I really didn't know it would lead to the type of heartbreak no person should ever have to endure in a lifetime."

He blows out a breath. "So now what? Do you have your closure?"

My eyes meet his again, and his still aren't as forgiving as I'd hoped. Mine, I'm sure, are full of hurt.

"No," I say, shaking my head. "I don't feel any better now that I've gotten to share my side. We haven't talked about you kissing Jessa and how much that hurt me. We haven't talked about how angry I am at you for kicking me off the tour."

"Then say it," he says, holding out his hands like a challenge.

"Okay, I'm fucking pissed that you didn't let me finish the job I came to do."

"I'm sorry." His voice is quiet. Sincere. And frankly, I'm shocked.

"Are you with her?"

He shakes his head. "She came onto me, Zo."

I soften at the nickname.

"She kissed me at the exact moment you opened that door. I was using her to make you jealous, and while I will admit we became friends, it was never anything more."

I raise a brow. "Big of you to admit that."

He shrugs. "It's the truth. And I kicked you off because I was there to do a job. I couldn't do that job with you there. As it was, I played like shit for the back half of the tour."

"I highly doubt that," I say softly, coming to his defense even though we're talking about one of the things that hurt me the most. "I don't know, Brody. I was hoping by telling you all this, you'd get it, that you'd maybe find a way to forgive me or that we could move past this and find a way to be together, but that's obviously not something you want."

"It's everything I want," he says, his voice an emotional whisper. My heart races with his admission. "I just don't know how to get past this."

"Then let's try together," I suggest with a voice full of hope. "Let's navigate this thing and stumble together and find our new path."

He clears his throat and focuses his gaze behind me again. "I don't know if I can, and I know for certain I won't make it past losing you again."

I don't tell him how much I feel exactly the same way, but I have to take this chance. It might be my only one I have to get him back. "Then don't lose me."

He blows out a breath. "I wish I could say it would be that easy, Zo, but—"

I cut him off with some begging. "Please don't *but* me."

He gives me the saddest smile I've ever seen. "I have to." He sets down what little is left of his burger and stands. "I can't do this. Not today, and not with you." And then he turns and walks out of the café.

CHAPTER 45

BRODY

I've made a lot of mistakes in my life, and as I step onto the elevator to take me up to my meeting with Mark, I can't help but wonder whether leaving Zoey behind in the café was one of them.

I think for once in my life, I went with the more difficult choice. It would've been so easy to give in and say yeah, let's do it. Let's give it another try. Everything inside of me screamed those exact words, but something malfunctioned on the way from my brain to my mouth.

Seeing her today told me that playing video games and avoiding sexual encounters for the last month was the right choice. I'm not ready to date again. I'm not ready to get involved again—not even for a single night.

Because none of those women are Zoey.

I'm happy for her that she figured out how to get her closure...but I can't say the same thing for myself. I have no idea how to get over her.

I push away all thoughts of pleading blue eyes and those silky strands of blonde hair. I'm here for a meeting with my record label, and I need to focus.

It's a quarter to two when I arrive in the lobby, and I find the rest of my band already there.

"What did Ethan say?" Dax asks in passing as I sit beside him.

"It was a goddamn set-up."

Dax looks over at me with furrowed brows. "A set-up?"

I speak through a clenched jaw. "He got me here early to trap me into talking to his sister."

Dax lets out a low whistle. "Smooth."

I shake my head. "She broke me, Dax. Don't you get that?" He looks surprised at my admission, and I charge on. "I wasn't ready to see her and certainly didn't want to sit there listening to her tell me every sordid detail that she never got to tell."

"But you did, and now..." Dax raises his brows encouragingly. He's been rooting for me to get back together with her all along.

I stare straight ahead and speak the words quietly. "And now we're exactly where we were an hour ago, except I got to hear from the source herself that she was so desperate to get her shot on television, she slept with the casting director who happened to be my father. Oh, and apparently she needed to give me her side of the story to find her closure."

"Mark is ready for you," the receptionist says, effectively ending our conversation.

Or so I thought.

She leads us back to the conference room, and Dax grills me the entire way. "So how did it feel to see her again?"

"Fine," I mutter.

"Don't you want to get back together with her?"

"No." It's a lie, but one that rolls off easily.

Of course I want to get back together with her. It's all I've thought about for four long weeks. But how do I do that knowing what I know?

Dax is quiet once we enter the conference room, and our meeting starts.

The producers talk first about their vision for the show, and then they pull up the first episode.

It's completely surreal seeing ourselves on television, and excitement builds inside me that we're really doing this. The premiere is a week from Sunday, and all five of the members of MFB leave the meeting with a feeling of excitement and optimism.

Kane drove the rest of the band, so Dax volunteers to ride with me back to our place in San Diego. I'm hesitant because I just want some time alone, but I don't admit that to my best friend.

"You want to talk about what happened with Zoey?" he asks before I've even pulled out of the Ashmark lot.

"Not really."

"What did you think of the rough edit?" he asks instead.

"I thought it was perfect." I turn out of Ashmark's lot. "It was fun reminiscing the album drop and the tour prep. And the intros of each of us were spot-on. It's maybe the one reality show I've ever watched where I felt like there wasn't any manipulation behind the scenes."

"I thought so, too." He's quiet after that, like he wants to ask me something else about Zoey but isn't sure how to phrase it. He changes the subject again, and it's weird having this choppy sort of conversation with the one guy I've been able to talk to about anything since I was eleven. "I recorded a new bridge the other night. You wanna hear it?"

I nod and switch my input to Bluetooth so he can play it for me.

Before he hits the play button, he says, "I was thinking something like this for 'Epic Wonder.' I tweaked the first verse again, as you'll see."

He plays it, and it's so perfectly MFB. It fits our sound but it's fresh and original. I tell him that, and I sense a bit of relief on his part.

"Were you nervous to play that for me?" I ask, my eyes focused on the road as I merge onto the busy highway.

"You've been...I don't know, man. Different lately, I guess. I never know which Brody I'm gonna get."

"Different how?"

He thinks for a minute. "Volatile."

"Volatile? That's a big word, Hunter."

He chuckles. "Hot and cold. Is that a little more *Green Eggs and Ham* for you?"

I don't laugh back because I don't find it funny...and it's only then I sort of get what he means.

"One minute you're back to your old self. Laughing, making jokes, the life of the party. And the next minute you've retreated so far into yourself I'm not sure who you are anymore." He's quiet when he talks, like he's admitting something he's been chewing on but hasn't been able to say to me. As soon as the words are out, I realize this was his motive in riding home with me.

I blow out a breath. "To be honest, man, I'm not sure who I am anymore, either. I was the same guy my entire life, and it only took one girl to change everything."

"Then what are you still doing without her?" I feel his gaze on me, but I keep my focus on the cars in front of me.

I don't answer. Maybe he's right.

Seeing her today sparked something in me that I hadn't felt in a month. I want to be with her, but I'm cautious because the last month has been hell. If I pin my hopes back on her only to be let down in the end, I'm not sure the *old self* Dax referred to will ever have a shot of coming back.

I wonder if she got her closure today. I wonder how she's feeling knowing that my words to her that I can't do this might be the last ones we say to one another. I wonder if she feels like the book is closed now when I'm still not sure whether there are more chapters to be written.

The rest of the car ride home is filled with a lot of silence as I mull over Dax's question. We change subjects and talk a bit about our next album, but all my thoughts still lead back to her.

We stop for gas and beer, and when we get home, we find Kane, Adam, and Rascal at the kitchen table with beer, a box of poker chips, and a deck of cards.

"No chicks tonight," Rascal says. "Get your money because I'm about to take it."

Dax laughs, and I continue to brood, but I grab a couple cans for Dax and me.

He's right. As I sit here with my friends having a poker night, watching Dax and Kane smoke cigars because they decided a few months ago cigars and poker go together, watching Rascal make stupid, immature jokes, watching even Adam get in on the laughing, I can't help but feel like I'm an outsider looking in. I'm here, I'm laughing when I'm supposed to, but I don't feel it on the inside.

I'm going through the motions, and the only thing I've really *felt* in a long time is Zoey's words when they hit me square in the chest today. Zoey's face when she first came into my view in the café. Zoey's eyes as she asked me to look at her.

Zoey.

I can't get back to myself until I have her back in my life.

As I win the hand of Texas Hold'em after bluffing out Kane, I don't even crack a smile. We just get to the next hand and I take more money from my friends.

I'm still sitting up in my bedroom contemplating what to do well into the darkness of night. It isn't until after too many beers and everyone else has gone to bed that I finally pick up my phone, type out a text, and hit the send button before I lose my nerve.

CHAPTER 46

ZOEY

I should be sleeping when my phone buzzes with a text, but instead of actual sleep, I've been tossing and turning as my meeting with Brody today plays over in my mind.

It's everything I want.

He still wants to be with me.

I can't do this. Not today, and not with you.

But he won't allow himself to.

I can't get the image of those shadowed eyes out of my head. They haunt me while I try to sleep. I'd wanted to make him see that this was purely a mistake—and one that we can get past—but I don't think I succeeded.

I glance at the clock. The bright red lights scream at me that it's 2:18.

Good texts never come after two AM.

Well, at least that was my belief before tonight.

Brody: *I can't stop thinking about what you said today.*

My response is immediate.

Me: *I said a lot of things. Which part?*

Brody: *You said you wanted to stumble together and find our new path. You said not to lose you again.*

I'm not sure exactly what he wants me to say.

Me: *Yes, I did say those things. And I meant them.*

Brody: *I shouldn't have walked away today.*

Me: *What would you have done differently?*

Brody: *I would've kissed you like I wanted to the second I saw you. I would've said okay instead of no.*

Me: *So where do we go from here?*

Brody: *I don't know.*

Me: *I want to be with you. I want to try again, and if I end up with a broken heart in the end, at least I can say I gave it everything I had.*

Brody: *Then let's try.*

Those unfamiliar pricks of tears heat behind my eyes again. I was never an overly emotional person...not until I lost the one person who ever really mattered to me.

Me: *Do you really mean it?*

Brody: *Yes. I need to see you. I need to hold you and kiss you again.*

Me: *Where are you?*

Brody: *San Diego.*

It takes me all of two seconds to come up with a plan.

Me: *I'm at Ethan's but I can cancel my plans tomorrow and get to you first thing in the morning.*

Brody: *No. I'll come to you. But not at your brother's. We need a neutral place.*

Me: *The Sheraton?*

Brody: *Where it all began. I like it. The Sheraton. Tomorrow at 5.*

Me: *I can't wait.*

Brody: *I'll see you then.*

My heart went from shattered to completely full and happy in a matter of seconds.

Holy shit...he wants to try again. He apologized earlier for kicking me off the tour, he explained away the Jessa incident, and now he wants to *try again.*

When I first got to work this morning, I never thought the day would end this way. For the last month, I've wanted something that was no longer in my reach, but now he is. And this time, I'm not going to fuck it up.

I drift into a sleep filled with dreams of what might happen tomorrow night, and when I wake, it's much too early but I have some major primping to do to get ready for tonight.

By the time I've been waxed, polished, buffed, and scrubbed, it's time to toss some things into a bag and get my ass over to the Sheraton.

I pull my car out front and give the keys to valet, sling my overnight bag on my shoulder, and head into the lobby.

I spot him immediately as he checks into the room he booked for us. I take a few seconds to really live in the moment. I allow my eyes to trail down to that ass, and back up the hard planes of the back hidden under his shirt, the arms that are solid and muscular from drumming and working out. My arms will be around that body tonight.

I tentatively step toward him, and just when I'm a few steps away, he turns around and our eyes meet. Gone are the shadows that were there yesterday during our lunch meeting, replaced now with something along the lines of hope.

"Can I interest you in a beverage in the lobby bar?" he asks, and I can't help my giggle at his formality.

"I'd love one."

He takes the bag from my shoulder and hands it to the bellman, and then we make our way over to the bar.

"Mule?" he asks, and I nod. He looks at the bartender. "Two Mexican mules."

"Two?" I ask, raising a brow.

He shrugs. "I've sort of gotten used to them now."

"You've been drinking them? I thought you hated them!"

"I did. But they remind me of you."

His statement is so simple and so sweet that I nearly rip my shirt over my head and toss my jeans next to it. But I don't. We're in public, and I actually sort of appreciate that he wants a *date*—or, at least, some time to talk—before we head up to the room.

I mean, we both know what the room is for. It's not like he chose a hotel as our meeting place because he wants to hold hands across the table in the lobby bar.

Despite that, though, I prefer a little wining and maybe even dining while we catch up on the things we missed and make sure that this is going to be the right fit for both of us.

We find an empty table—there are lots of them at a little after five—and we sit. He holds up his glass, and I clink mine to his. "To trying again."

"To trying again," I echo, and then we both take a sip.

"Why did the semen cross the road?" he asks.

I raise a brow and give him a little smile. "Why?"

"Because I put on the wrong sock this morning."

I laugh. "Gross."

He reaches across the table to take one of my hands in his. "Absolutely, but also accurate. I, uh, haven't been with a woman since you."

"You haven't? Even on the last half of the tour?"

He shakes his head. "There was one...*indiscretion* right after you and I broke up, but it wasn't sex and I realized pretty quickly that she wasn't you and I wasn't ready."

I'm a little hurt by the admission, but he had a right to be with whoever he wanted. The fact that he hasn't had sex since he was with me tells me something about how deeply all this has affected him—especially since I sort of get the feeling he slept with whoever, whenever before he met me.

I don't want to ask, but the question slips out anyway. "What made you change your mind about trying again?"

"Something Dax said, actually."

I'm surprised at that. I thought maybe it was something *I* had said to him. "And what was that?"

"He told me I haven't been myself, and I realized it's because I can't be myself without you."

My heart warms at that. My entire chest warms, actually, and it's not just from the tequila. "That's a really sweet thing to say."

He squeezes my hand. "It's the truth. I've been in this crazy limbo as I try to sort out my feelings, and I just don't think there's any way to sort them. Will this be difficult?" He motions between the two of us. "Probably. I might need some time. I might stumble a lot, and I'll need your patience while I figure shit out. But, God, do I want to try again. I want to be *me* again, and I can't do it when a piece of me is missing."

"I love you," I say softly, squeezing his hand back, and suddenly I wish we'd gone right up to the room.

He closes his eyes and presses his lips together, a visceral reaction to my words, and when he opens his eyes, he nods. "I love you, too."

I feel his words through my entire being as they send a shock of hope through my spine that this might actually work for us this time.

We look at each other in tense silence for a beat. So we both love the other, but where does that leave us?

I break the tension with a joke. "What should a man do if he comes across an elephant in the jungle?"

Brody's lips turn up. "What?"

"Wipe it off and tell it you're sorry."

He laughs. "Good one. What did Cinderella do when she got to the ball?"

I shrug.

"She gagged."

This time I accidentally spit my tequila drink out all over the table as I laugh. This makes him laugh, too, and then I'm suddenly wiping away the tears of laughter as they stream down my cheeks. My stomach hurts, and this all feels so damn *good.* So *right.*

I missed laughing with Brody even more than I realized.

We order more drinks and fill this round with conversation.

"What's next for MFB?" I ask.

"Well, we've got the premiere of *Rock on the Road* a week from tomorrow night, and we're heading to New York for a few days next week to film promos. We've got Fallon, Meyers, and GMA scheduled. Then we come back to LA for Ellen, Kimmel, and Conan."

"Wow," I say with a little whistle. "You guys are gonna be everywhere."

He nods. "Pays to have Mark Ashton at the helm of your label."

"Congratulations on all that, Brody. I'm proud of you and the rest of the guys."

"Thanks," he says almost shyly—like he can't quite grasp that this is his real life now.

I switch gears to take some of the spotlight off. "So you mentioned you played like shit for the second half of the tour. What else went down?"

He shrugs. "I couldn't focus when I didn't have you in my periphery. Sort of mirroring my life, I guess."

"How'd Jessa do?"

"Fine. She wasn't as fluid as you, not that I know much about dancing." He takes a sip of his drink and taps the side of the glass absently. "I found myself watching her less and looking out into the crowd more. I kept looking for your face. I didn't expect to actually see you, but I still looked."

"You did?" My insides turn to a melted gooey mess.

He nods thoughtfully and his knee starts bouncing. "I didn't sleep much. Instead, I stared up at the ceiling and wished you were still in the bunk underneath me. I spent a lot of time wondering if I was doing the right thing. I still think what happened is weird, but I'm cautiously optimistic that we can get back to where we were."

"I'm throwing caution to the wind." I grin and raise my brows, and he laughs.

"I'm not generally a cautious person, as you might've learned about me, but I still think we need to take this slow."

"Slow as in..." I trail off and wait for him to fill in the blanks.

"As in...okay, not the sex part. We can fast forward to that." He grins, but it fades quickly as he turns serious. "But the feelings part. It may take me some time to be ready to open back up and trust that what we have is real."

"I never gave you a reason not to trust me." My voice is passionate.

"You're right. You never did, yet I still felt betrayed for the entire second half of the tour."

"It's because you never let me explain. I could've made you understand the night you found out, but you dropped me off at the hotel and made me get out of your car. And then you made out with some bimbo that night and it was all over the tabloids and I knew you were done with me."

"Not done," he says sharply. He rests his hand over mine. "Never done. Even if we try this and it doesn't work, I can't say my heart will ever stop loving you."

I feel my eyes mist over a little at the sentiment, but before they can turn to actual tears, he says, "I want to kiss you."

"Then kiss me."

He shakes his head. "I want to do the fast forwarding. I've said some things I needed to say, and you said your things. So now—"

"We can finally get to the make-up sex?" I ask, interrupting him.

He chuckles. "Something like that."

"Take me up to the room."

He pulls out his wallet and leaves some cash on the table for our drinks, and then he grabs my hand and leads the way up to the twenty-fourth floor...the same floor we were on the last time we stayed here.

CHAPTER 47

BRODY

The door is barely latched shut behind me when my body acts on pure instinct. I push her up against the wall with my hips and pin her there, holding her two hands in one of mine above her head as my mouth melds with hers and my fingertips skim her torso.

I thrust my hips against her so she can see how fucking hard I am for her, how crazed with lust she makes me. Part of me wanted to take this a little slower, but Jesus I can't do that when the sexual attraction between us is so palpable.

Her tongue thrashes against mine just like it always did, and it's like riding a bike...so to speak. I remember every nuance of her body, every spot that makes her shiver and every touch that makes her moan.

I reach down to pull her shirt over her head. Her bra's still on, and I bury my face in those perfect, gorgeous tits of hers for a beat before I move my mouth back to hers.

Her hands skim up and down my back, and then she yanks my shirt over my head. She runs her fingertips along the cuts of my abdomen, and I gaze at her with hooded eyes. She takes her eyes off my stomach to glance up at me, and there's so much hope and adoration listed there in her eyes that something twinges inside me.

Is that how she looked at *him*?

Or is this reserved for me?

I shake off the thought as I force my lips back to hers.

I shouldn't have to *force* anything in this situation, but I find myself suddenly distracted.

I break the kiss and move toward the bed. Certainly sex will get my mind back in the game.

Except it doesn't.

I've got her stripped to nearly naked, just lying on the bed in some sexy black panties with material so thin I could rip them off with my teeth, and the vision pops back to me again.

Was she wearing these panties when she was with *him*?

I hover over her, still clad in jeans, and thrust my hips against her. She moans as she leans her head back. Did she expose her neck for *him*?

I want to pump my cock inside her over and over, but is that what *he* did?

It's too vivid. It's too close. Images of her and him together flash through my mind.

It doesn't matter that they happened months before the two of us met. It doesn't matter that she had no idea I'm Derek Jensen's son...no matter how much I regret that fact.

The fact is it happened, and it's still not something I'm over.

I thought I could get there, but it turns out I can't...not with him here in this bed with us.

I sigh in frustration as I roll off the top of her. I sit on the edge of the bed as I contemplate my next move even though I already know what it has to be.

"What's wrong?" she asks, still lying back like I'm about to work her over...and I wish with everything inside of me that I could.

I don't know what to say. I wanted this to work. I wanted to get back to myself again. I wanted a lot of things, but my cheating, asshole father took every last one of those things away from me when he decided it was okay to fuck a potential castmate on one of his shows.

"I...uh." I try again. "I never stopped loving you, Zo. I never will. But that doesn't mean this is gonna work."

Her jaw drops open slightly as a flash of fear runs through her eyes. "What are you saying?"

"I'm saying I can't do this. I thought I could, but I can't."

"You...you what?"

"I can't stop seeing him and you. When I kiss you, when I close my eyes, when I think about my dick inside you. He's right there in the bed next to us."

I stand, grab my shirt from the floor, and pull it over my head. I'm still wearing my jeans and I hadn't bothered to kick off my shoes yet.

"I'll see you around," I say, and then I hightail it the fuck out of that room, leaving behind what I'm sure is a very confused and very heartbroken girl.

I get in the car because I don't know what else to do and I start heading toward home.

I feel like shit. I shouldn't have left her like that.

But, like a coward, I ran.

I don't want to be alone right now, but I certainly don't want to hash this out with anybody, either. So instead, I decide to call the one person who always makes me feel better.

"Brody!" my mom answers, exclaiming my name like she always does when she gets a call from me.

"Hey, Mom," I say. I usually mirror her enthusiasm, but I can't muster it today.

"How's my boy doing? How was the rest of the tour? How's that beautiful Zoey?" She tosses out the questions without giving me a chance to answer.

I wait a full four seconds to respond, just to make sure she's done. "Okay, good, and probably not great."

"Zoey's not great? Why not?" Her voice is all full of anxiety, and I hate that I put that there.

"We broke up, Mom."

"You broke up? But why? You two seemed so perfect for each other!"

I can sense her disappointment in our decision to end things, but that's not the thing that sends my heart up into my throat. I can't tell her why we broke up.

"She did something I can't get past." Those are the words I choose because they're the truth, but they're also the least revealing.

"Come to dinner," she says, her voice full of hope. "Tonight. I'll make your favorite. The girls are going out with some friends and Dad is out of town, so it'll just be you and me."

I don't want to go, but I know I should. Plus, she'll be making tacos. How can I say no to that? "Okay. I'm just leaving Los Angeles but I'll come straight there."

"Drive carefully and I'll see you soon."

"Bye, Mom." I hang up and wonder what the fuck I just agreed to do.

The ride is some mix of endlessly interminable and ridiculously fast. I'm pulling into the driveway of my childhood home before I've really had a chance to decide what I want to say to my mom...if anything.

I don't really know what led me here instead of anywhere else in the world, but somehow going home feels like the right thing to do.

I let myself in and call her name as I walk in.

"In the kitchen!" she yells back, and I head that direction. She's sautéing ground beef at the stove when she spots me. "Brody boy!"

She wipes her hand on a towel and comes over for a hug. I cling to her a few seconds longer than I should.

"Get yourself a drink and then sit and tell me everything I've missed. Dinner will be ready in ten minutes."

I chuckle, but I follow directions. Once I'm seated with a can of Dr Pepper, she asks, "You said you're just okay on the phone. Is it because of the break-up?"

"Yes and no." I take a sip from the can. "It's hard coming back from tour and trying to pick up your life where it left off."

"I can only imagine." She steps away from the stove long enough to pat my shoulder. It's such a simple gesture that lets me know she's here for me, and the guilt of knowing what I know presses down on me. She deserves so much better than my father, and she deserves to know that. "How did the rest of the tour after we saw you in San Diego go?"

"It went fine." I think for a beat, and then I add, "Zoey left the tour."

"She left?"

I clear my throat. "I found a replacement and kicked her out."

She leaves the stove and sits across from me. She sets a hand over one of mine. "Why?"

"Can we talk about something else?"

"Yes, of course. Whatever you want, Brody." She squeezes my hand and gets up to stir the beef again.

I draw in a deep breath for strength. "Can you maybe turn off the stove for a while? I have some things I need to say."

She looks at me with brows drawn down low, but she does it and sits across from me. "What's going on?"

"Do you love Dad?" I ask, blurting out the question. I didn't think I was going to do this until I got here. I see how genuine and kind my mother is, and as painful as the truth may be, I want her to know that she doesn't have to be with someone she doesn't love.

"Why would you ask me that?" She looks genuinely confused.

"You've been married to him for, what, thirty years?"

"Twenty-nine," she amends.

"But do you *love* him?"

"Where is this coming from?" she asks, and I realize she's not answering the question.

"Why doesn't he come home during the week?" I ask, trying a different angle.

"He works late nights and it's too long a commute for him. We agreed when we had kids that we didn't want to raise them in Los Angeles, and this was the compromise."

"What do you think he does in that apartment of his? Or even in his office?"

"I think he works hard all day and then goes to his apartment to sleep before he gets up to do it all again the next day." She says the words like they're rehearsed—not like they're what she really believes.

I narrow my eyes at her. "Are you really that naïve?"

"What are you trying to say to me?" Her brows draw further down.

I take both her hands in both of mine. "I'm saying I love you, Mom, and I want more than anything for you to be happy. Are you *happy* with Dad? I mean *really* happy?"

She doesn't answer for a long time, and when she does, her voice is quiet and her eyes are focused on our hands. "I haven't been *really* happy for a long time, Brody. I'm not naïve. I know what he does. But it's the price I pay for forcing him to work so far from home."

I shake my head. "Don't you dare say that," I say sharply. "No one, and I mean *no one*, deserves to be cheated on and disrespected the way he's always done to you. Marriage and love, commitment, children—none of that should ever come with a price. If the compromise was to live in San Diego and work in Los Angeles, fine. The compromise was never for him to sleep with the women he's casting on reality shows like *Single Life*."

My eyes widen as I realize what I just said. The words are out before I can stop them, and it doesn't take a genius to connect the dots.

"*Single Life*?" she repeats, and the truth finally dawns on her.

I pull my hands back and look away from her because the confusion on her face physically hurts me to see. It makes me want to kick my own father's ass for the betrayal.

"Wasn't Zoey on *Single Life*?" she asks softly.

I blow out a breath. "Yeah," I mutter.

She folds her hands together primly. "Oh." It's a single word, a grunt really, and that's her only response. "Well, let me finish up those tacos."

She moves to get up from the chair, but I grab her arm. "Mom, it's okay. You don't have to brush this under the rug like you've done my entire life. I know. We *all* know."

She swipes at a tear that seems to have escaped her lid much to her annoyance. "Fine. So I'm a coward and a loser who allowed it all these years. Is that what you want me to say?"

"Why do you stay with him?"

"For you." She lifts both shoulders helplessly. "For your sisters. Because we're a family and that's what family does."

"Not at this cost. You deserve better than that piece of shit."

"Hey," she warns abruptly. "That's your father."

"Yeah, and he fucked a girl who was desperate to get on a television show two months before I met her and fell in love with her."

She gasps at my admission. Before, it was the mere hint, but to hear the harsh and grating truth actually come out of my mouth is...intense.

I blow out a breath. "He may be the man who donated sperm for my life, but that's all he is to me. He's not my father. Not anymore."

"Oh, Brody," she says, and she finally breaks down. I don't know if it's because of Zoey, or if it's because I've written him off, or if it's because we're finally talking about all the dirty laundry we've always pretended didn't exist, but she cries.

I hug her, and I soothe her and tell her that she deserves better and I will stand by her side no matter what she decides. But I hope she decides to leave him, because I can't stand the thought of her staying with someone so fucking vile.

"I'm so sorry," she finally says, and she backs away from me and grabs a tissue from the counter.

"You have nothing to be sorry for."

"Yes, I think I do. I've been too scared to admit the truth, too afraid of ripping apart our family, but now that I've had a chance to see how deeply this affects the very people I've been trying to protect, I can't allow it to continue." She blows her nose again.

"Mom, I will be here for you no matter what you decide." I stand and walk over to her and squeeze her hand. "If you want to leave him, I'll buy you a new place to live. If you want to divorce him, I'll hold your hand through it all. So will the twins. You've got us."

She nods. "I need some time to think about all this. Is that okay?"

"Of course. You take all the time you need."

She squeezes my hand back. "I raised a good boy. I love you, Brody."

I kiss her cheek. "I love you, too. Now let's eat some tacos."

She laughs, and I help her finish cooking and prepping.

Once we're seated for dinner, she breaks the easygoing silence that took over while we worked. "So you ended things with Zoey because of him?" she asks tentatively.

I nod. "I found out that night we were here for dinner. Zoey had no idea he had a family. She had no idea who he was or who I was or that we were related until he walked in the door." I find myself defending her when I don't mean to. "I kicked her out and didn't even bother to listen to her side of things until I was forced to sit down with her yesterday."

"Wow. You ended things almost a month ago and didn't talk to her until yesterday?"

I nod.

"What's that been like?"

"Tough." I dip my taco in some salsa.

"Have you spoken to your father?"

I shake my head and chew my taco before answering. "Not since the night of the show in San Diego."

"Is that why you've been avoiding us?" she asks softly.

"I didn't mean to avoid *you.* I just didn't know how to face you knowing what I knew," I admit. I take another bite of taco.

"That couldn't have been easy, but you can always talk to me about anything. *Anything.* You know that." She pauses to take a bite of her food, and then she continues. "But what about Zoey? I mean, I hate that she did what she did, but sometimes desperate people act how they think they need to act, and there's a pretty public history in Hollywood of all the ways women have earned roles."

"I can't look at her without seeing what she did, but I also can't get over her." I reach for a tortilla chip.

She's quiet for a beat, and then she says, "I saw you with her, honey. You love her. Maybe more than you've ever loved anybody."

I nod. "She finagled her way to get to me yesterday and said she needed to give her side of the story to get some closure. She told me he wasn't wearing a ring and there weren't any family photos and she had no idea. I saw her again today, and I was willing to give it another try. I thought everything was going to be okay, but as soon as I kissed her, all I could see was him. Mom, I don't know how the hell I'm supposed to get *my* closure."

She closes her eyes. "Do you think telling me will provide some of that for you?"

I shrug. "No. Maybe. I don't know. It's hard either way. I feel like shit you know, but I felt like shit when you didn't."

"Don't." Her voice is adamant and calm. "What happened was your father's fault, not Zoey's. He was the one in the power position, and it's as simple as that."

"But what if she came onto him first?"

She shakes her head. "Doesn't matter. He should've been strong enough to tell her he has a family. He should've been wearing his wedding ring and he should've been bragging about his wonderful children by littering his desk with pictures of you. He should've told her that this isn't how things work. None of that happened, though."

"So now what? How do I move on? How do I get past this and either get back with Zoey or get over her?" I'm practically begging for an answer because I have no idea what to do here.

"Do you want to move on?" she asks.

"No. But I don't know how to get the image of her and him out of my mind."

"Simple. You need to make amends with your father."

CHAPTER 48

ZOEY

I stayed the night in his hotel room.

A little part of me thought he'd come back. I couldn't just get up and leave because what if he came back and I missed him?

So I slept in the bed we should've woken up together in—or, rather, I tossed and turned in it—and I wake up far too early on a Sunday morning with the same familiar cracks in my heart. Cracks that were filled with hope after a late-night texting session. Cracks that were starting to heal after we drank Mexican mules in a lobby bar last night.

Cracks that are deeper than ever before. Cracks that will never heal again.

I suddenly feel like the down comforter is suffocating me. I throw it off, get up and get dressed, and sling my bag over my shoulder. I glance around the room once more, my eyes focusing in on the spot where he paused to kiss me with so much passion just inside the doorway. If only we could get back to that point.

At least I don't feel like he blames me in any of this anymore. That's one bright side to this whole mess. I hope by explaining my side to him, he could see that I acted out of a desperation that was so extreme I felt as though I was out of options. I hope he can see that it was his father who took advantage of the young woman who wanted some air time.

I feel horrible *hoping* that. I don't want a divide in his family. But I'm not the one who caused that divide.

I head back to Ethan's, and the house is quiet when I let myself in. I really need to move out of here and get my own place, but it's hard to think about that when I don't feel settled.

I know Los Angeles is where I want to stay now. I'm done with Atlanta. I've started a life here. But Ethan and Maci deserve their privacy—just as much as I do.

I really thought today would be different. I thought I'd be celebrating a reunion with the man I love with all my heart. Instead, I'm walking down the familiar hallway to my room in Ethan's home as I try to erase the memory of the last day and a half.

"She's back early." A quiet female voice interrupts me mid-stride back to my room.

I turn around and face my sister-in-law. "Yeah, she is. Earlier than she thought she'd be."

Maci must sense my internal turmoil because she ushers me into my bedroom. She sits on my bed while I toss my bag on the floor and collapse beside her.

"How'd it go?" she asks cautiously.

I toss my arm over my eyes. "Not great."

"I'm gonna need more than that, my friend."

I sit up and blow out a breath. "It seemed like everything was fine. Like *we* were going to be fine. We had a nice time with a couple drinks in the bar, and then he took me up to his room, and we started kissing. I sensed a hesitance from him, but then he got me practically naked and we were about to get busy when he stopped. He told me he couldn't do this feeling like his dad was right beside us in the bed, and then he left."

"He left?" she repeats.

I nod.

"Fucking coward."

I shrug. "I can't really blame him, Mace. He sees his *dad* when he kisses me. It's just...I don't know. It's too weird."

"How did *you* feel?"

I settle back into my pillows and stare up at the ceiling. "I felt like I was back with my other half. Like I could finally be myself again."

"And now?"

"I guess I figure out how to move on."

She grabs my leg and shakes it a little. "Haven't you been trying to do that for the last month?"

I grunt in agreement.

"And how's that working out for you?"

I nudge her leg with my foot. "What do you suggest I do, then?"

"I don't have the answer for you, Zoey. I just hate seeing you like this. I hate that he led you on and dropped you again. I think he's a coward and an idiot for letting you get away."

I sit up a little again as some of his words ring back to me. "Yesterday he said something."

She waits for me to continue, but I'm too busy chewing on his words.

I might stumble a lot, and I'll need your patience while I figure shit out.

"Are you going to finish that thought?" she finally asks.

"He said something about how he may need my patience while he figures his shit out." I grab Maci's arm. "Do you think that's all this is? He needs some time?"

She pulls her arm from my grasp. "Ow."

"Sorry."

"And maybe." She shakes her head. "I don't know, Zo. I don't want to give you false hope because I don't know him well enough to predict what he meant by that. But maybe those words can tell you that not all hope is lost just yet."

It might be, but it might not be.

I need to be patient, like he said.

I can't give up hope on us. Not yet, and maybe not ever.

He said he was going to New York for his *Rock on the Road* press junket. Maybe once he's through that and back in California, we can figure out our way back to each other.

I've never been a particularly patient person, but something tells me he's worth waiting for.

CHAPTER 49

BRODY

After a very successful whirlwind trip to New York, we're back in California for our west coast press. The show premieres in three days, and I have a rare two-hour window a little before lunchtime on a Friday afternoon.

My mother's words that the way to get my closure is to make amends with my father have played on a loop in my head for nearly a week now, and as I stand outside the large office building where my father's office resides, I can't help but think she's right.

But, then, mothers are *always* right.

I draw in a deep breath for strength then enter the building and stride across the lobby right past the long line of people waiting at the check-in desk. I don't need to check in. That's something my dad told me years and years ago. The people here know who I am, and that gives me certain access the general public doesn't have. I move toward the elevators with confidence and hit the button for his floor.

He isn't expecting me, but I feel like that's just part of the fun.

When I get to his floor, the pretty, young brunette receptionist greets me and tells me to have a seat, and I ignore her as I breeze past her without even stopping to consider how many times my dad's banged her.

I'm on a mission, and right now, nobody's going to stop me.

"Mr. Jensen, you can't just walk in there!" the receptionist, whose name is currently escaping me even though I've met her several times, yells after me.

I march right up to his closed office door and grip the handle for a split second. I have no idea what I'm about to find behind this closed door, but it's the entire reason I'm here.

I grip the handle tightly, pull down, and push open the door.

And I find my father, pants around his thighs as he pounds into some poor, young woman from behind as she bends over his desk.

A sickening feeling rises up in my throat as my stomach lurches.

We all know this is what he does. We all know he's a lying, cheating, piece of shit.

But I've never had the misfortune of witnessing it firsthand.

As vile and disgusting as this moment is, something propels me forward. Something intrinsically whispers to me that I need evidence of this very moment. Not for the woman—I'd never embarrass her like that—but against the piece of shit currently fucking her.

I snap a quick photo, making sure to keep the woman's face—but not her dark hair—out of the shot.

I slam the door behind me, and she gasps when she hears the sound. Her eyes widen as they focus in on me, but it isn't her I'm concerned with.

My dad eyes me. He has the dignity to pull out of her immediately and tuck himself in as he zips up his pants, but he knows he's been caught.

She straightens and smooths down her skirt before retreating back to the chair facing his desk. She won't even look at me because she's too embarrassed, but I don't want her to be.

"What are you doing here?" my father demands, and for the time being, I ignore him.

"Hey," I say softly to the woman as I kneel down beside her. "This isn't your fault. Don't be embarrassed. What he failed to tell you is that he has a wife and three children who've lost all respect for him."

She looks like she's about to cry.

This poor girl. She's a victim of his disgusting behavior, just like every other girl who has been in the exact same position she was mere seconds ago.

"What's your name?" I ask, squeezing her shoulder gently as a way of showing her she can trust me.

"Mandy Jacobs." Her voice is quiet.

"Okay, Mandy. I'll make sure you get the part you're auditioning for, okay? Now if you could give me a minute with my father, I'd appreciate it. Just wait in the lobby because I'll need to get some more information from you."

She nods, and then the tears really do start falling as she stands and practically runs out of the office.

"You didn't have to embarrass her like that," my father says to me once the door latches shut behind her.

"Are you fucking kidding me? That's what you have to say for yourself right now?"

He shrugs like he can't be bothered with more words, and that's when it all clicks.

He didn't have *feelings* for Zoey. He didn't care about her. She was just one of the hundreds of gorgeous women who traipse through this office thinking they have a shot at stardom at the hands of this fucking monster.

She was *nothing* to him.

But she's *everything* to me.

And after seeing him with this other woman...well, those images of him with Zoey will now be replaced by the real thing.

The meaningless, revolting act that he gives into probably more often than I ever considered.

The man has a real problem, and now that I have evidence, I have a feeling that he's about to have a few more.

It's time for him to pay for his sins.

Mothers may always be right, but my mom was just a little off on this one. I didn't need to get past what happened between my father and Zoey by making amends with him. I just needed to come here today and see what I saw. I needed to witness the fact that he doesn't give a shit about what he does—that he fucks whoever he wants and then determines whether or not to give them the roles they humiliated themselves for...based on what? How good a fuck they are? How quick they are to let him in?

Who knows, but it all stops here.

"Thanks for doing this today," I finally say.

His brows furrow in confusion.

"It just proved to me that you were nothing more than a stepping stone for the woman I love. You're nothing more than that to *all* the women who walk in these doors, and I hope you realize that Mom knows. Abby and Ally will know soon enough, and I hope losing the people who should've meant everything to you was all worth it when you end up alone."

He lets out a menacing little laugh. "Oh, Brody, that's fresh. But your mother has known for years and doesn't care. Nothing's going to change just because you walked in on me today."

"You don't think so?" I raise both brows and flash him the photo on my phone. "Even with photographic evidence?"

"Photoshopped," he says flippantly.

"I can't believe how little you actually care about your actions." I also can't believe how unbelievably arrogant he is about this whole thing. He should be freaking the fuck out, but instead, he thinks he can just continue to do what he's always done.

And maybe that's where my *closure* in this whole thing comes in.

Mandy Jacobs, Zoey Fuller...and how many more women could we find who got fucked over this very desk in order to land a role in one of my dad's shows?

He's going to pay, and I'm going to smile as I stand by helping to collect.

But first, I have to take care of some penance of my own.

CHAPTER 50

ZOEY

I stare out the window of my Ashmark office listlessly, just like I've done nearly every day this week for large portions of my day. I wonder if he's back from New York. I wonder how the press tour is going. I wonder a lot of things, but most of all I wonder when things will ever get back to normal for me.

Maybe I need to get out of LA and go back to Atlanta. There are too many memories here in California, and knowing he could be as little as two and a half hours away might be a little too close for comfort. I don't want to leave Ashmark. I like my job here, even though I don't plan to stay here forever. I still have a goal. Dreams don't die just because we're going through something, and I like the fact that I'm in Los Angeles for when I'm up to auditioning for small parts and working my way to the top.

A small knock sounds at my door, and I glance away from the window to find Mark standing there.

"How's it going?" he asks.

I shrug, and he shoots me a small smile as he steps into my office and takes a seat across from me. He clears his throat and gets right to the point. "The *Rock on the Road* premiere is set to air this Sunday. You know about the launch party, right?"

"Will he be there?" I ask softly, my voice filled with the sort of pain that comes from a break-up. I'm trying to be patient—really, I am—but I also realize he needs his space while he works out whatever it is that he needs to work out.

He nods. "Yeah," he says quietly. "He will. You're invited, but I would never want to put you in a situation that would make you uncomfortable, Zoey. This is one-half my project—well, technically more than half financially—and you're important to me." He lowers his voice to that rasp that I dreamed about for years. "Not just because you're Ethan's sister. We all love you, and we just want you to be happy."

"Someday I will be," I say, even though I don't really believe the words.

"I have a buddy who I think you'd really get along with," he says.

"Oh, God. Stop right there." I want the ground to open up and swallow me at his words. "The day I let Mark Ashton fix me up on a date is the day I die of embarrassment."

He chuckles and holds up both hands. "Okay, okay. Forget I said anything."

"I don't know if I'll ever forget this moment."

He laughs. "Well, I just wanted to invite you. You have as much a right to be there as anybody. And there will be plenty of free booze."

"I appreciate that, Mark." I return my gaze to the window. "I just don't think it's a good idea."

"You're welcome if you change your mind." He abruptly changes the subject. "Did Andre sign the contract yet?"

I nod. "This morning."

He raises his brows. "Impressive work, Ms. Fuller."

I allow a small smile. "Thank you, Mr. Ashton."

He nods, and then he stands. "Make sure the signed contract is in my email by the end of the day."

"It's already there."

He shakes his head a little on his way out and murmurs, "Man, I knew hiring you was going to be a good idea."

No sooner have I returned my gaze out the window than I hear another little knock on my door. I expect it to be Mark again, back with one more question, but when I look to see who's standing there, I let out a little gasp of surprise.

"What are you doing here?" I ask.

"Can I come in?" Brody asks. His eyes have a new fire behind them, and I can't get over how shocked I am to see him here.

I nod stupidly, and he closes the door before he walks in and sits across from me.

Closing doors. I can't tell if this is a good thing or a bad thing, but a closed door screams one or the other.

"I figured something out today," he begins.

I'm silent as I wait for him to hit me with it.

"Maybe I'm a complete idiot, but I went to my dad's office less than an hour ago." He sits back in his chair and crosses his leg so one ankle rests on the other knee, and I can't help but think I've never seen him look so...*relaxed.* "I barged right in without giving a single fuck."

I wince a little as I wait for him to hit me with it.

"Any guesses what he was doing?"

I shake my head even though I know exactly where this is going.

He nods. "Some poor girl was bent over his desk while he banged into her from behind."

I press my lips together but don't say a word.

"And you know what?"

I raise both brows.

"Seeing it in person for myself...well, as weird as it sounds, it was everything I needed to get over what he did to you."

"What he did to me?" I ask.

He nods. "Yeah, Zoey. It wasn't your fault. You were desperate, and you did what you thought you had to do, just like every other woman who walks through his office. I hate, *hate* that he did that to *you* of all people."

"Brody, I was a willing participant," I say, not because I'm defending his father for what happened between us, but because I don't want Brody to believe something that isn't true.

"I know you were, but that doesn't change the fact that he was in a position of power and he took advantage of that. And Zoey, I have proof now." Something changes in his expression, and he turns downright passionate. "I have the name and number of the girl he did this to today, and I have you, and we're going to hunt down all the other girls and bring a lawsuit so fucking huge against this asshole that he won't be able to afford the desk calendar he fucked all those women over."

"Oh...I don't know about all that," I say. What happened is beyond mortifying, and this type of thing would get a lot of attention in the press. People would know that I was with Brody's father and then I was with him. People will judge me. They'll judge Brody. They won't have all the facts and our lives will be under a microscope. I'm not okay with any of that.

He stands, walks around my desk, and kneels on the floor in front of me. He takes one of my hands in his.

"Babe, I want to protect you and take care of you. I want to love you and be by your side. I want to hold your hand through all of this, just like I'm going to hold my mom's."

"Your *mom's*?" I practically squeal.

He nods. "Yeah. She knows."

"She *knows*?"

He nods. "And she pointed out to me that this is his fault, not yours. He has taken advantage of desperate women for years, and I want to be the one to make him pay."

I lean my elbow on my desk and cover my eyes with the hand he isn't holding. "She must hate me."

I feel his warmth as he moves in toward me. I open my eyes, and he's shaking his head. "No, Zoey, she doesn't. This is what's going to convince her to leave him after all this time. Seeing how much his actions affected *me*—that was the final straw. She's the one who made me see that I *can* get past all this. And I will. I took a huge leap today, and it paid off. And now I'm here begging for you to give me another chance. To take me back. To be mine in all the ways that matter."

I stare at him for a minute, completely dumbfounded. I don't know if this is another test of my patience or a sincere effort, but as I look into those eyes so heated with fire and love and lust and everything in between, I have to believe that he's ready to give this a real shot with me again. I place my palms on his scruffy cheeks, and I feel like I'm home again. "Brody, I've been yours in all the ways that matter since the first time you kissed me in a hotel hallway."

He leans his face down and touches his lips to mine, and it's reminiscent of that very first kiss in a hotel hallway all those months ago. He brushes his lips across my bottom lip first before he moves to my top lip. I push my tongue into his mouth, and his hand finds the back of my head and then we're kissing like we need it for our very survival...which, after everything we've been through, maybe we both do.

CHAPTER 51

BRODY

I had some obligations to get to with the band, so all we had was one heated kiss. But, man, it felt good to kiss the woman I love with my whole heart again...and to be free and clear of the demons of the past.

I swing by the hotel and grab my own room rather than the suite I'm sharing with Adam, and then I meet the guys for the next stop in our media tour. I'm ready for the premiere, and even more excited now that I'll have Zoey on my arm as my date for it.

And that reminds me...we have some final interviews to refilm. I think back to my words in the last interview I did, and I didn't speak kindly about how the tour was ruined for me by the actions of a single person.

I suppose that's true, but the single person wasn't who I originally thought it was. It wasn't Zoey at all. It was my father all along…and I realize only now that I'm also partly to blame.

Once our final Friday night interview is over, Dax pulls me aside. "What's going on with you?"

"What are you talking about?" I ask.

"You're...different. Dare I say back to your old self?"

I chuckle, and then the chuckle turns to a grin. "Some things went down today, and, well, I think I'm gonna be okay."

His brows crinkle, and he asks quietly, "Zoey?"

I nod. "I stopped to see my dad around lunchtime. Barged right into his office and caught him in the actual act of what he does to these women. And it made me realize she was just one in a line of them. She never mattered to him, but she matters to me."

"Yeah?" Dax asks, a grin spreading across his own face.

"Yeah. I went to Ashmark and talked to her. And then I got us a hotel room for tonight...so I hope you don't mind, but I'll be skipping out on dinner."

His grin widens. "I don't think any of us will mind, Brody."

An hour later, Zoey pulls her dress over her head and lets it dangle from her fingertips for a second before it drops to the floor. She wears a black bra and panty set, and even though it's dark in here, I see her in all her perfection. I see the body I've missed on the woman I've ached for. I see everything I need to live again as she stands here in front of me.

I take a step toward her, and then another and another, closing the gap between us. I don't touch her, not yet, because I'm allowing her to make the first move. And she does. She places her palm on my cheek, and I lean into her hand as I close my eyes, the vision of her loveliness locked in my mind's eye.

Her skin is warm and she smells something like a citrus heaven might smell. I can't wait any longer. I grab her hip and pull her against me, shoving my rock-hard cock against the little scrap of fabric covering her pussy.

A sexy little kitten moan escapes her lips at the feel of me, but I want to make her roar.

Her hand comes between us to skate down the ridges of my abdomen before she lands on my dick. She rubs me on the outside of my pants, and I'm about to blow my load after a few strokes. It's been way too long since I felt the warm skin of a woman's hand on me. It's just been me and my own calloused, rough drummer's hands for a long time.

But not anymore.

I grab her up in my arms and carry her over to the bed. I toss her down, pull her panties down her legs, throw them beside us, and dive face-first into the sweet pussy that I've missed more than I realized.

"Oh my God," she shouts over and over, fisting the sheets on either side of her legs. It's like my tongue's muscle memory remembers every nuance of her as I give her the pleasure I remember giving her so many times back when we were together.

I lick and suck, add in a finger or two, and lick and suck some more, and it isn't long before her legs draw tight against my ears and her body contracts tightly before her hips jerk every which way as waves of pleasure wash over her body.

It's a long orgasm for her as orgasms go, and it seems to go on and on as wave after wave continue to pulse out of her. I ride it like a goddamn champion surfer, though, my tongue pressing against her clit as I continue to thrust my fingers in and out of her.

Eventually the pulses subside and her fists loosen on the sheets. Her moans and shouts soften to heavy breathing, and she relaxes back into the mattress.

I wipe my mouth with the back of my hand and crawl up the bed until I'm hovering over her. She's still wearing her bra, and I pull each tit over the cup and lavish them with attention. I cup them with my palms and pinch her nipples, and then I put my mouth on them and taste them until she comes to life again.

"Mm," she moans, quietly at first, and then she says, "I need you. Inside me. Now." Each phrase is punctuated with a moan as I suck a little harder.

I give the lady what she needs.

I'm out of my jeans and securing a condom before she can ask again, and then I'm thrusting into her tight pussy like she might change her mind. She won't. I won't. We're in this together—for tonight and for the long haul.

I feel a spark of unfamiliar emotion in my chest as I drive in and out of her. It's something I've never felt, not even when we were together before. I push it away as I focus on the feeling of being back where I belong, our bodies connecting on the most intimate level as my balls draw up and tighten. I don't want to come, don't want this to end, yet I want to feel the relief that comes with an orgasm.

She contracts around me, and that's when I let go. The two of us come in sync, like a team, together like we're meant to be. She screams her moans, and I shout incomprehensible obscenities as I come.

When it's over and I pull out of her, I collapse on the bed beside her when it hits me what that unfamiliar emotion was.

It was relief that poured through me and met with all the love I have for this woman.

It was a rough road getting here, and the path isn't totally clear quite yet, but she's back in my arms and I can't think of anything that's more relieving than that.

CHAPTER 52

ZOEY

I'll always look back on tonight as the night we officially got together. Not *back* together...just *together.*

What we had on tour was completely different from what we're starting now. We had day in and day out together in this sort of fantasy land that had to come to an end regardless. Our reboot now, though, is based in reality. I have to go to work Monday. He has his own shit to do, whatever that is. The tour's long over, and I'm ready to put the past to rest so we can start looking toward a future together.

After our fast-paced make-up sex, we lie naked and spent in each other's arms.

"What's your biggest fear in this?" he asks me softly.

I turn so we're still holding each other but now I can look into his eyes while I talk.

"That you'll push me away. I can't go through that again, Brody."

"You won't have to. I'm sorry for how I handled things." He presses his lips tenderly to my forehead as he thinks through his words. "I think part of me always knew we belonged together, but I had to find my own way past what happened."

"In the spirit of full disclosure and no secrets between us, I feel like I need to confess something." My heart rate picks up speed as I prepare to drop one final bomb, but once I get this off my chest, I'll feel so much better.

He eyes me warily as he waits for whatever it is that I'm about to hit him with.

I clear my throat. "I, uh, just want you to know that Mark and I used to date."

"Mark Ashton?" he asks.

I nod.

"Isn't that common knowledge at this point?"

I expel a breath of relief before I giggle. "Is it?"

"Dax told me ages ago."

"He did? And you're not mad?"

"Why would I be mad?" He leans up on his arm and looks down at me with so much love in his eyes.

I lift a shoulder. "I don't know. I guess because Mark and I are close now."

"He's married, babe. And has a kid and another on the way. I've seen the way he looks at his wife. It's the same way I look at you."

I look up into those brown eyes of his and see exactly what he's talking about.

He's quiet for a minute, and then he adds, "After what we've been through both together and apart, there's nothing that'll drive me away. I want to be with you, faults and scars and history all."

I nod. "That's what I want, too."

"Then let's forget the past and start from the beginning again."

I shake my head. "Let's start from the middle. The beginning was hard. We had to hide our feelings and couldn't celebrate what we were feeling out loud. The end was tragic. But the middle? The middle was fucking perfect."

We talk more about the things that scare us moving forward, the things we want to leave behind us, and the things we missed in each other's lives when we were apart.

After we're all talked out and nearly asleep, Brody climbs over the top of me again and kisses me, and my body jolts awake at his proximity as I gear up for more.

This time, though, he takes it slow.

He kisses me forever, my body heating up as I start to push my hips toward his to give him the hint that I want this. Him. More. Now. I feel his dick as it grazes against my bare skin, and the only thought in my head now is taking him inside me completely bare, with nothing between us. I get the birth control shot, so we're good to go on that front. I've never had sex that way. I've always insisted on a condom, but I don't know how to tell him it's okay when he's kissing me other than to just guide him in.

He ignores my hips gyrating toward his, though, and keeps kissing me. For now. He's slow and sensual, his hands still as mine skate up and down his back, sometimes clawing and other times gentle. Eventually he thrusts his hips toward me, and again I feel the tease of his bare skin against mine, the heat of his cock so close to me as he sends pulses of need through my entire being. He reaches down to fist himself, and then he pushes his dick against my clit. I cry out and my eyes roll back in pleasure at the feel of him so hot, so close, so completely naked and exposed.

In my mind, I'm chanting, *do it, do it, do it*, and when he swipes teasingly through me again, I whisper, "Do it."

His eyes meet mine with a question, and I nod my consent. That's all he needs. He enters slowly, both of us groaning as my body pulls him back in. He doesn't pull back right away, simply seats himself all the way inside me and holds steady for a few blissful beats.

When he does pull back, he does it slowly, carefully, tenderly. Everything about what he's doing right now shows me through his actions how much he loves me and cares for me...how right this is and how much we both know it now.

He makes *love* to me in a way no man ever has before. He's sweet and tender, slow and sensual, like he never wants this to end. I don't, either. The feeling is unbelievable as he moves inside me with no barriers and no limits.

This is it. This is the love I never thought I deserved, the love I never knew could exist for someone like me.

It took a whole lot of bad decisions to get here, but in the end, every single one of them was worth it. After all, it paved the way to our happy beginning.

* * *

The premiere party is at the Ashmark offices in the special sixty-seat theater Mark built. Typically it's used for video viewing parties, but tonight it'll be used for all of us to gather together to watch the very first episode of *Rock on the Road.*

Mark stands just inside the lobby when our group emerges from the elevators, and his eyes light with a smile when he spots me, my arm linked through Brody's. "Zoey," he says, and he walks toward me with outstretched arms for a hug. "You look gorgeous tonight."

"Thanks, Mark," I say.

"Congratulations on the premiere," Mark's wife, Reese, says next. She hugs me, and once again I feel a rush of happiness for Mark. The first time I met her, I assumed she was a nobody as I plopped down on Mark's lap like I owned him back when they first started dating. Little did I know how serious they'd already become, and now they're married and have their own family.

Crazy how life works.

"Stop in the conference room next to the viewing room first for drinks and hors d'oevres," Reese says with a smile, and we head off toward the conference room. We're the first to arrive, but Denise and Lauren show up next. I hug both of them, and they're thrilled to see me back with Brody. Denise makes some comment about how she'd never have taken him back after he kicked me off the tour, but she doesn't know the whole story—including the fact that we've talked through it all.

We snack a little, drink a little, and get ready to watch the final product.

Everything seems to be going smoothly...until Jessa walks into the room.

It's like all the joy is immediately sucked out of the air.

I'm the one who ended up with Brody in the end, so I shouldn't feel this way...but when she walks in, she beelines for him when he's at the bar and I'm clear across the room talking to Dax and Kylie. She probably has no clue we found our way back together, and I watch as she slides her arm around his waist. He turns to look at who the offender is, and he gives her a tight-lipped smile.

I watch as she notices he's carrying *two* drinks—a Miller Lite for himself and a Mexican mule for me.

She eyes the second drink, and I watch her ask him a question. She has to be asking who it's for, and a single word drops from his lips that I can read even from here: *Zoey.*

He locks eyes with me from across the room, and I can't help but glance over at her as her eyes follow his.

Her face turns positively sour, and for me, it's the cherry on top of what's been a pretty damn perfect two days.

Mark saunters into the room with all the swagger of a true rock star. "Fifteen minutes to showtime," he announces. "Now is a good time to make the move toward the theater. Drinks are both welcome and encouraged in there."

His words are met with a laugh from the group gathered, and Brody makes his way across the room toward me—sans Jessa, much to my total and utter gratitude.

Brody's arm slides around my waist as he presses my drink into my palm, and then his lips skim my temple. "Ready to go watch the show?"

I press my lips to his, and when I break apart from him, I smile. "Ready. Break a leg."

He grins, and we make our way to the theater. I'm sitting between Brody and Kane, and Dax is on Brody's other side. Everything feels just as it should.

The lights go down and MFB's last album cover fills the screen as a whoop rises up from the crowd gathered.

The scene cuts to one of MFB's early practice sessions in black and white. "No, man. It needs to go like this." Dax plays a riff on the guitar, and the other guys all nod in agreement. Brody hammers out a beat on his drums, and Kane watches thoughtfully. They all agree on the sound, and then it cuts to the title screen. *ROCK ON THE ROAD: Season 1.* And then the subtitle: *STARRING MFB.*

The whoop in the crowded room turns to an actual cheer, and then we get into the meat of the episode.

The first segment is introductions of each of the band members. We get a glimpse into their personal lives—Dax is with Kylie, Adam is with Bree, Kane is with Sierra, and Brody and Rascal are single.

After the introductions, we watch segments on MFB's time in the recording studio, organizing tour dates, and the album launch. The show ends with the auditions for the dancers with a lead into next week's episode when the voiceover asks what will happen when one of the selected dancers is unable to make it to the tour. A brief snippet from my audition tape appears in the previews for next week, and then I see a flash of Brody kissing me and I wonder how much of the show will focus on our relationship.

I'm so proud of the MFB boys and I'm beyond excited to see where all of this will take us during the rest of the season.

The afterparty is held at a bar owned by Vail's bassist, James. We get drunk, we laugh, and we have an incredible time celebrating the success of Mark and Dax's passion project.

A week later, the second episode doesn't disappoint in the amount of airtime I get. There's an entire profile on me, including the fact that Ethan Fuller is my brother plus a snippet of the phone call that landed me the job in the first place. The other dancers don't get even close to the same amount of attention placed on me, and it has to be because Mark is the show's creator. The majority of this content was created when Brody and I were apart, and I'm forever grateful to Mark for giving me this shot of potential discoverability.

After the profile on me, the show cuts into what would look to anyone else like an actual love story: secret looks between Brody and me before the tour even launched during our practice sessions, a stolen moment in a bathroom hallway interrupted by Mark Ashton, a private conversation between Brody and Dax where Brody admits he's starting to have feelings for me.

All the ingredients that add up to our own love story.

The cameras are almost always watching. Kylie's words from our first day on the bus come back to haunt me, and I wonder what other secret moments aren't really so secret.

I can't help but think week after week as I watch with Brody beside me how very different this would be if we hadn't gotten back together. Would I even be able to watch it without him by my side? I doubt it.

But he's here, holding my hand or slinging his arm around me, and we're watching together before we go out to celebrate together and then come back home...together.

CHAPTER 53

ZOEY

"I need you to do something with me," Brody says.

"Anything," I murmur. I'm naked, and I've just been fully worked over, and I'd probably agree to pretty much whatever he asks at the moment.

We're back at the Sheraton, the place Brody always stays when he comes to LA for a few nights. Ethan doesn't care when we stay there, but for the really loud sex I want to participate in with my boyfriend, I prefer the privacy of a hotel versus the house with a toddler in it.

"I need you to come see my mom and my sisters with me tomorrow for dinner."

That euphoric feeling I was just having a minute ago seems to whoosh out of my system. I sit up quickly—too quickly, and I feel a little dizzy. I hold my head in my hands for a second as I ask, "You what?"

"You said *anything*," he accuses, glaring at me.

"In my defense, I was in a post-orgasmic state of bliss. You can't do what you just did to me and follow it up with something this serious."

He laughs. "Fair enough. But will you?"

"Go with you to see the woman whose husband took advantage of me right before I fell in love with her son? Yeah, sounds like a real party."

His gaze softens at me. "You're going to be a permanent part of my life, and I need you to find a way to face her. I need the two most important women in my life to get along, and I've already told you, she doesn't blame you in any of this."

"I don't deserve someone like her." My voice is soft as I stare down at the comforter.

"Stop it," he says sharply. "You made a mistake, and everyone gets that. Even my sisters. This had very little to do with you and everything to do with him."

I stare at him a long time before I finally commit. "Fine."

He grins. "Yeah?"

"Don't ask again or I might change my mind."

I don't, though, and less than twenty-four hours later I'm standing on the front porch of the Jensen house in San Diego, a fresh *For Sale* sign planted in the front yard. I grip Brody's hand tightly in mine as I fight against the nerves so they don't get the better of me. In the other hand, I clutch a bottle of wine—something Brody says always wins his mother over.

It's Abby who opens the door first, and her demeanor is much different from the last time I was here. She hugs her brother and barely says hello to me, and I can already see this was a mistake.

Ally, however, gives us both hugs once we're in the entry, and then Cindy peeks her head around the corner. "Hey, you two," she says. She gives Brody a hug, and before she can give me a hug, I hold out the bottle of wine like a peace offering.

She offers a small smile as she takes it from my hands. "My favorite," she says, and then she hands the bottle to Brody. "Give us a minute," she says to her kids as she looks at me, and a stab of fear pulses down my spine.

This is it.

This is the part where she tells me she fucking hates me and I'm not good enough for her son.

I don't blame her because I agree with her. I'm not good enough for him.

"Come here, you," she says to me. She wraps me in one of the warmest, most comforting hugs I've ever felt from a motherly figure, and somehow I believe things are going to be okay as my fears start to slowly melt away.

"It wasn't your fault, Zoey," she says softly in my ear.

"I'm so sorry, Mrs. Jensen."

She squeezes me tighter. "It's Cindy. Or Mom. But never Mrs. Jensen. Not ever again."

I pull back from our hug and look at her in confusion.

"I filed for divorce yesterday," she says.

Tears fill my eyes. "You did?"

She nods. "And I wouldn't have been strong enough to do it if I hadn't known how much his actions hurt my son. I'm sorry you got caught in the middle. I'm sorry for what he did."

I can't believe this woman is apologizing to *me* after what happened.

"And I want you to know that I don't blame you. I never could do that, not knowing how much my son loves you. I'd like to start fresh with you and leave the past behind us if that's okay with you."

I hug her again. "I want nothing more."

She squeezes me. I wonder what it's like to have a mother who loves you *this* much. I never had that, but I feel it deep down that this is my family now.

Abby might be mad at me, or maybe she's just having a bad day. We never really know what's going on inside someone's head. She might be upset her parents are getting divorced, and she might blame me. But, on the other hand, maybe she'll come around someday. Maybe her sister and her mom will help her to see what they all can see.

Even so, I'm overwhelmed with the gratitude I feel. I'm grateful for Cindy, who feels like a mother to me now. I'm grateful to Brody for loving me. I'm even grateful for the road that got us here, because everything's coming together just as it should.

CHAPTER 54

BRODY

"Holy shit, Brody," Dax says. He whistles between his teeth as he checks out the rock in the black box. "That looks expensive."

"It was," I say.

"I can't believe you're really doing this." He shakes his head in wonder.

"Just gotta stay on par with my best friend." I laugh, and he does, too.

"Yeah, that's a great reason to get engaged. Because I did it first."

"There's just a little more to it than that," I say, thinking of everything I found the day I found Zoey.

"What's that?" Kane asks, interrupting what I was hoping would be a private moment with my best friend. I didn't even hear him come in.

I snap the box shut and shove it into my pocket. "Nothing," I mutter.

"Liar. You're proposing?"

"Maybe," I say, drawing out the *ayyyy* sound.

"Damn," he says, shaking his head. "If you would've asked me a year ago who was getting engaged before Sierra and me, I wouldn't have believed it. First Dax and Kylie beat me and now you and Zoey."

I nod. "Trust me when I say I wouldn't have believed it, either. It just took the right girl and a little bit of luck."

"Let me see the ring," Kane says.

I take the box out since the cat's out of the bag now anyway, and he whistles when he sees it, too. "Damn, dude. She's gonna love it."

"I saw it and knew it was the one. Sort of like my relationship with her."

"Yeah, sort of," Dax says sarcastically. "Except for the whole break-up thing."

I laugh. "Yeah, except for that."

"I'm happy for you, man," Kane says.

"You gonna do this someday soon?" I ask.

He shrugs. "Sierra wants me to. I'm not ready yet. You know, that old chestnut. Does Zoey know it's coming?" he asks, deflecting the topic back to me.

I shake my head. "She has no idea."

"When are you doing it?" Dax asks.

"I have a plan. But I have some things I need to take care of first." And one of those things is something I'm nervous as fuck about.

"Well, we'll leave you to it," Dax says, nodding at Kane. "I need to go pick up Kylie for this dinner thing I promised I'd go to with her."

"Not a word about this to your women," I warn, and they both laugh and hold up their hands in surrender on their way out the front door.

We're a little over a week out from the *Rock on the Road* season finale, and that's where my idea comes in.

I pick up my phone and shoot off a text to Mark Ashton.

Me: *Is it too late to re-tape my final interview?*

Mark: *You've got a little time. What did you have in mind?*

Me: *It's a lot to explain. Do you have time to talk this afternoon?*

Mark: *I'm at Ashmark all day. I have a meeting until two but I'll call you after that.*

Me: *Thanks, Mark. I owe you one.*

Mark: *You owe me way more than one.*

I laugh at his text. He's certainly not wrong about that.

When my phone rings later that afternoon, I fill him in on my idea.

Not only does he encourage me, he tells me he'll arrange everything. It's not the first time I see how much he loves Zoey Fuller, but I appreciate it nonetheless. She's like a little sister to him, and we're both lucky that he's a part of our lives...and that he's willing to step in and help the way he's going to. I owe a debt of gratitude to him for giving me this life.

We all do, really.

Drumming for a living, traveling the world with my best friends...it's been an amazing ride so far, and it's only just beginning. I can't imagine the sorts of things that'll change once I'm married. I'll still tour, obviously, and I wonder if Zoey will come with us or stay home. We've been talking about renting something together in Los Angeles, but we've both been busy and haven't had a chance to really find our own place. When I don't have responsibilities with MFB, I've been staying at her brother's place in Los Angeles with her—or sometimes at the hotel where it all began—but she deserves a place she can call home. And soon we'll be planning our next tour...and then what?

She's still loving her job at Ashmark, and just last week she auditioned for this role on a soap opera. She'd be perfect for it, and it's just the sort of role she's dreamed of her entire life. It could be the very thing to kickstart her entire acting career. Because of her appearance in *Rock on the Road*, she's been contacted by a few different talent agents for spots in commercials or guest spots on television shows.

She's fucking amazing in everything she's ever been in, and that's not just my own bias talking as the person who loves her most in the entire world.

There's only one person who could even try to compete for that title with me, and that's the thing I need to do before I propose to my girl.

Her dad's not around for me to ask permission, but I don't think she'd care about that anyway.

Her brother, Ethan, though—my rock star idol who will someday soon (hopefully) become my brother-in-law...well, I want to know he's on board with this before I ask.

And so, with shaking hands, I pull up his number. Instead of calling, I send a text.

Me: *Zoey is working late tonight and I'm heading up to LA in a bit. Want to grab a beer with me?*

Ethan: *Sure. Name the time and the place.*

I'm not surprised he's so quick to answer. We've become actual friends over the past couple months that Zoey and I have been together. That'll happen considering the pure amount of time I've spent at his house because of her. It turns out Ethan and I have a hell of a lot more in common than just the fact that we're drummers.

Me: *Seven, your place.*

Ethan: *Deal. You bring the beer.*

I laugh.

Me: *That peach stuff you liked last time?*

Ethan: *Get something manlier than peach. Maybe pineapple.*

I laugh again, head to the store to pick up the beer—no simple feat anymore now that people recognize me everywhere I go thanks to the success of our reality show—and I make the now very familiar drive from San Diego to Los Angeles...something I'd even be willing to do on a daily basis if I needed to. If it meant seeing the woman—and family—I love.

Speaking of my father, in the last ten weeks, Zoey and I have managed to find eight more women who are willing to testify against him. We found a few others who wanted to remain silent, and I respect their decision. I've been in constant contact with a lawyer who is putting together the lawsuit now, and every part of me feels total and complete relief that justice will be served to the man who took advantage of my Zoey.

Once I get to his house, Ethan answers the door before I even ring the bell. "Maci's just getting Eli down," he says.

He opens the door wider to let me in, and we head for his kitchen where we each crack open a can of pineapple beer.

"So what's new, man?" he asks.

I drain half my can then take a deep breath. I need to get this over with or I'll be nervous the entire time I'm here. "I need to talk to you about something."

His brows furrow. "What's going on?"

"You know how much I love your sister," I begin, and he nods encouragingly. "Well, I want to ask her to marry me, but I wanted to get the blessing of the one man she'd want it from before I ask her."

"And that's me?" he asks, and I laugh nervously.

"Yeah, that's you."

"Hm," he grunts, not making my sudden nerves any better. He studies me with something between a glare and a squint, and I try not to fidget like a child. I'm a man, dammit. I can do this. I'm about to open my mouth to break the silence when he speaks first. "You think this is something she wants?"

"I think we both know that this is it. We've talked a lot about how neither of us wants to be with anybody else."

He blows out a long breath, and then he drains his beer. He stands and grabs another, and holy fuck why isn't he just giving me a goddamn answer?

"Okay," he says when he sits back down.

"Okay?" I ask as both of my eyebrows shoot to the top of my forehead. "Okay?"

He nods. "Yeah." A smile finally forms across his face. "I think you'd do a good job taking care of my little sister the way she deserves." He stands again, and this time I stand, too. He slaps my back in a bro-hug, and I laugh.

"You had me going there," I say, relief coursing through my veins.

"I wasn't sure if I was gonna say yes." He moves back to sit again, and I mirror him. "After that shit you pulled, I wasn't sure if you deserved her. But you've really proven how much you love her over the last few months, and I can appreciate that. Who am I to stand in the way of a man and the woman he loves?"

"Stand in the way?" Maci asks, making her first appearance in the room. She points at Ethan with a scary finger. "You better not be getting in *anybody's* way, Ethan Fuller."

He laughs and holds up both hands. "Brody's gonna propose," he blurts, and I laugh as I shake my head.

"And apparently I better do it fast because this guy can't keep a secret," I say, jerking my thumb toward Ethan.

Maci giggles but comes over toward me, and I stand. She gives me a hug. "Congratulations, Brody. We couldn't be happier for you both." She claps her hands together. "Oh my God, have babies. Do it! Now! Eli needs a cousin."

My face blanches, and both Ethan and Maci laugh hysterically.

Maybe someday down the line...like *way* down the line...but I'm not ready to start producing cousins just yet. I haven't even popped the question yet.

But all that's about to change, and then, because of the road that got us here—or maybe in spite of it—we're going to spend the rest of our lives together.

EPILOGUE

BRODY

Mark arranged for us to get a private studio on Monday morning to refilm our final interviews...and this time, we're doing it *together*. The episode where we broke up aired just last night, and even though we're back together, it haunts me.

The look in her eyes on our front porch in San Diego after she'd seen Jessa kissing me...God. It was like some animal that had been attacked, mauled and mutilated beyond human comprehension. I can't get the look of fear combined with grief in her eyes out of my head. I hadn't even seen the cameras out there, and neither had she.

I was surprised so much of our season focused on our love story, but, then, that's what seems to sell to television viewers. Even though there was an entire second half to the tour, it's all going to be covered in the final episode.

But this next episode is going to end with a bang.

Jake, one of the producers Dax hired, is waiting for us when we enter the studio. "I heard you two were back together," he says when we walk in. "Congratulations."

I force a smile through my nerves. "Thanks, man."

Jake grins. Clearly Mark filled him in on my plan, and while I'm thrilled this is all about to be caught on camera, I'm nervous as fuck this guy's going to blow my cover or she's going to say no or any one of a million things is going to go wrong.

Jake fixes us up with our mic packs, tells us where to sit, and says, "I'm just going to ask you a few questions. Talk to me like you did in your individual interviews, but it's okay to talk to each other, too."

We both nod our understanding and head over toward our chairs.

"So tell me how you got back together," he says.

We glance at each other, and she nods at me to start. "It was a tough road. We were apart for the remainder of the tour, and it was when I got back that I first ran into her at our record label."

She cuts in. "I managed to score some time alone with him, which wasn't easy, by the way, and I told him everything I'd been needing to say since I left the tour."

"And, like a complete idiot, I walked away." I look at her as I say the words. "I'm sorry."

She gives me a tiny smile. "I know."

"But then something Dax said resonated with me. He asked me why I wasn't with her if I still loved her, so I called her up. We tried again, but there were still things holding me back."

"What things?" Jake asks.

"Personal things," I say, even though it'll all become public record once Zoey testifies in court against my father. We'll deal with the fallout then. "Once I sorted things out with the people involved, I found my way back to her. I had to fight some major demons, but every fight was worth it because of where I ended up."

She looks over at me with pure adoration in her eyes, and this is the moment that feels right.

"What's next for you two?" Jake asks.

Zoey looks at him while she starts answering, but the words are gibberish to my ears as I slide off my chair and to the floor.

"What are you doing?" she asks when she spots me on one knee in front of her.

I haven't taken the box out of my pocket, so she hasn't puzzled together what's going on just yet. "I love you, Zoey." My voice shakes on my first words, so I draw in a deep breath to try to steady my nerves.

We've talked about the future—about wanting this for ourselves someday, so I'm not sure why I'm so nervous. Maybe because I only plan to ask this question once, and I want it to be perfect.

"I love you. I love holding your hand through the hard times and laughing with you through the good. As tough as it's been, I love the bad decisions we made together that shaped our past, and I love that we didn't start over completely because it's part of our story, as messed up as it is."

Her brows draw down in confusion.

"But most of all I love our future. I love that every time I look at you, I see forever. I see the person I want by my side through this crazy life, and I see the mother of my future children I didn't even know I wanted until I met you. I see the woman I want to spend the rest of my life with, and I hope you feel the same way." I reach into my pocket and she gasps when I open the lid. "Will you marry me?"

Both her hands cover her mouth and her eyes stare widely at me. "Are you serious?" Her words come from behind her fingertips.

I ignore the racing of my heart as I gaze into her gorgeous blue eyes and nod. "I've never been more serious about anything in my life."

A small smile plays at her lips. "Knock knock."

I clear my throat. "Uh...who's there?"

"Yes."

A surge of relief washes over me, but I play along anyway. "Yes who?"

She giggles and smacks me in the arm. "Yes, I'll marry you."

I slide the ring onto her finger, and it's a perfect fit. I stand and pull her up with me, and then we're kissing, and this is the only woman I'll kiss for the rest of my life.

It only took a string of bad decisions to get here, but the benefits will last the rest of our lives.

ACKNOWLEDGMENTS

When my husband told me he had an awesome book title over a year ago, I fell in love with it. We talked plot a bit, but other projects took over first and I kept this title in my back pocket. Fast forward to writing Zoey's story, and I knew her line of bad decisions would be perfect for the title Matt suggested all that time ago. The original plot we talked about is pretty far away from what this book ended up to be, but one central theme is the same: the big forbidden twist that (hopefully) you didn't see coming. So thank you to my husband not only for the title, but for the plot chats, marketing discussions, business management, support, and just being an all around great guy, wonderful husband, and an awesome dad. And thanks, of course, to my sweet boy Mason and the bun in the oven scheduled to greet the world this August.

Thank you to my editor, T. I don't know how I did this before we met. I knew I had a great story and a decent first draft, but when I'm so close to the story I can't always see what's missing. Somehow you put words to my jumbled thoughts and help me figure out how to turn a great story into what I think is the best story I've written to date. Thank you for all you do.

To my fabulous beta team: Stephanie, Jen, Diane, and Kelly, thank you for the quick feedback, the honest chats, and the help you always give me.

To my amazing ARC readers: Thank you for continuing to read, review, and love my books. Some of you have been with me since the beginning—twenty-one books ago—and I love you whether you've been here for one book or all of them.

This cover. I think it might be my favorite cover ever. I searched for *months* for the perfect couple before finding them in Wander's files (even after I'd look at his stuff multiple times). They so perfectly represent Zoey and Brody to me. And it was just random bad planning on my part that I ended up working with someone new for the cover design, and Najla Qamber freaking *nailed it*. I'm in love.

Thank you to my proofreader, Katie. You always spot those extra/missing words or funny wording (he sat on his elbow? How does that even work?).

Thank you to Give Me Books for the cover reveal and the release blitz, and to my Bookstagram team for always posting gorgeous photos of my covers.

Thank you to Team LS and the Vail Tail Fangirls, my two Facebook reader groups. I love you and being with you is my favorite place on the web.

A big thank you to all the bloggers who work hard supporting authors like me.

As always, thank you to you. If you're reading this, I hope you enjoyed the book and I'd love if you'd leave a review on Amazon. Please keep in touch!

ABOUT THE AUTHOR

Lisa Suzanne is a romance author who resides in Arizona with her husband and baby boy. She's a former high school English teacher and college composition instructor. When she's not cuddling baby Mason, she can be found working on her latest book or watching reruns of *Friends*.

ALSO BY LISA SUZANNE

A LITTLE LIKE DESTINY
A Little Like Destiny Book One

#1 Bestselling
Rock Star Romance

TAKE MY HEART

#1 Bestselling
Rock Star Romance

Made in the USA
Middletown, DE
04 October 2022

11689941R00241